The Counting Tree

Jennifer Arrington

Dear Linda,
   I thought you would
      relate to part of
      the breast cancer story ♡
   Hope you have a
      beautiful Christmas,
         ♡ Jennifer

BEACH HOUSE BUSINESS

ISBN:979-8-9866213-1-9
Library of Congress: 2022920956
Cover design by Bronwyn Lowe

For my former students ~ may the world treat you well

ACKNOWLEDGMENTS

Albrey ~ I love our life together; thank you for gifting me
the opportunity to pursue this dream
Lauren ~ for that very first edit
Ashley ~ for understanding all the things
Domenica Giallombardo ~ for editing extraordinaire
Debbie Guerrant ~ for the final edit and discussions
Bronwyn Lowe ~ for creating a beautiful cover design from
my vague verbal description

And to my readers and critique crew: Tenika Bloemfield,
Karen Ledingham, Gillian Davies, Dona Lowe, Aly Carver,
and my dear mother, Dot Moorman

Thank you all for making this project possible.

FOREWARD

I spent most of my childhood in Johannesburg, South Africa. Apartheid was the cultural norm during that time, and I remember being horrified by it. As an American, I held to the hope that things would be different once I moved to the States. And, at first, as an idealistic college student in the US, everything felt dramatically better until, eventually, I realized it wasn't....

I understand that what I've witnessed of apartheid in South Africa and racism in the United States has always been from the outside looking in. Nobody can truly know the horror of a failed system until they have themselves lived on the wrong side of that system. My desire was to capture my observations on these pages and weave them into my fictional narrative with the goal of highlighting disparity. Any errors in memory and perspective are my own. My hope and prayer is that we challenge our personal circles of influence to give equal respect and opportunity to those around us.

Proverbs 3:27 Withhold not good from them to whom it is due, when it is in the power of thine hand to do it.

Part I

⌘

Northern Transvaal, South Africa

1987

CHAPTER 1

"Ladies and Gentlemen, this is your Captain speaking. We are about—"

Heidi jolted awake, an unopened bottle of water on her lap. She had barely slept an hour, but it was better than nothing. They would be landing soon, and then the adventure would really begin. She was scared to death.

She turned her face toward the window, her eyes not focused on the view below her. The problem with two days of travel was there had been too much time to think. What had she done? Up to this point, all the preparations and planning had propelled her forward. And now, reality crashed against her expectations. She was about to arrive and no longer felt anticipation or a sense of purpose. She was hungry, lonely, dirty, and tired, and she couldn't even remember how she was supposed to find the people meeting her.

The plane banked, and she focused on the scene beneath her. The skyline of Johannesburg lay before her, and she blinked in surprise.

Was this Africa? She saw a large sprawling city that could've been any major city in the US. Building after building stretched before her, windows reflecting sunlight. The grid of visible roads was congested, and radio towers blinked their red warnings. Beyond the buildings stretched a network of highways and then suburbia and low-lying hills.

The seatbelt sign came on, and she shifted to the window seat, her eyes scanning the changing landscape. She had read that Johannesburg was dry, but the houses below her were surrounded by green dotted with ovals of blue. There seemed to be as many swimming pools here as in her hometown of Jupiter, Florida. Farther out, the hills looked dry. Maybe the towns were simply well-watered, and her reading hadn't been entirely misleading.

Confusion clambered.

Africa could not be beneath her; Africa was supposed to be primitive and in need of American mission work. The city below didn't seem to need anything but more room. She felt the twinge of changing pressure and worked her mouth to pop her ears.

Everyone had said that traveling to Africa to do what she could have done in America didn't make sense. Maybe they had been right. Regardless, now she was about to land in Africa while America and everyone she loved was two days of flying and endless details behind her. She yawned again to relieve the ear pressure and swallowed. She needed to quit analyzing and start focusing on the present.

Heidi felt the plane bank once more, watched as the landscape rushed up to meet her, and felt the wheels jolt meeting the scorched asphalt.

Africa.

There was no turning back.

She unbuckled and stood with the other passengers, anxious to disembark. In a daze, she followed those in front of her onto the tarmac and to a waiting bus. She squinted against the harsh sunlight and dry heat as the bus maneuvered toward the terminal.

She followed the stream of people to passport control, where a stern-faced man greeted her.

"How long do you plan to stay?"

"One year... um, at least... maybe two?" Her voice felt foreign and brash in contrast to the clipped flat tones of the man standing behind the desk. She had initially planned to stay a year, but that was when she had hoped Chris would wait for her. Now, there would be no need to rush back.

Then, stamped passport in hand, she followed the signs to the luggage return and stood patiently waiting for her bow-adorned suitcases to parade by. She lugged the first one off the carousel and waited for its mate as the crowd around her thinned. She thought back to check-in in Miami nearly two days ago, remembering how the lady had told her that her bags would go straight through to Johannesburg despite her connection in Brussels. So where was the other one? She had packed so carefully, anticipating a scarcity of shopping – all her favorite clothes, pictures of the twins, her journal, shoes, extra toiletries, and make-up. Now half of it was probably sitting at a lost and found in Brussels or beyond. With a sinking feeling, she realized she couldn't remember which suitcase held what, but she certainly hoped the one with her had the most important things.

The carousel shuddered to a halt. Empty.

Heidi glanced around in dismay at the backs of retreating passengers – passengers with their luggage. The signs above her pointed toward customs, and she moved slowly, wondering what to do.

Heidi squared her shoulders. Maybe the people meeting her would know. She walked on towards long low tables where guards were singling out people to search. She cringed, picturing a stranger pawing through her belongings, and kept her face forward, avoiding eye contact with anyone. She breathed a sigh of relief as she walked past, undisturbed, through the customs gate and on towards the ropes cordoning off the greeting area.

She scanned the people, searching for a sign with her name. Nothing. Her heart sank further; nobody was waiting. She would have to report her missing luggage and find a phone and try to contact the camp to see who was coming for her. But that would mean first exchanging her dollars for what they called rands so she could use a phone. She took deep breaths; she could do this, yet her pounding heart had found the logical response. Every fiber of her being screamed to turn around and get back on the plane and fly home. Instead, she found a seat, placed her solitary suitcase under her feet, and clutched her carry-on against her chest. Willing herself to breathe deeply, she studied her surroundings.

Maybe she would see a place to change her money, and then she could find a phone and perhaps a snack shop. Yes. A plan. But the teeming monstrosity of humanity paralyzed her. She watched, a lump building in her throat, as people greeted their relatives and friends, rushed past her to their destinations, or, like her, sat waiting. She analyzed those around her. Could one of them be waiting for her? Wiping her sweaty palms on her jeans, she willed herself to focus on the detached people with signs and not on the joyous reunions mocking her aloneness.

There on the far wall, "Luggage Claim" caught her eye. Her suitcase!

Dragging her lone bag, she walked to the counter and filled out the required form. The lady behind the desk was brusque and unhelpful.

There was really no way of knowing when or even if Heidi's suitcase would be found.

She headed back to the waiting area. So far, nothing had gone as she had imagined, and she needed to find her ride. Maybe the time taken in customs and baggage claim had been longer than she thought. Maybe someone was sitting right there and had a sign with her name on it.

Heidi craned her neck, analyzing each person, until her eyes came to rest on a young man at the end of her row, slouched low and sound asleep in a chair much too small for his frame. Thick dark blond hair stuck out at strange angles, a rumpled shirt stretched over broad shoulders, and his crossed arms masked what appeared to be a logo. An upside-down sign lay on his lap. Maybe he would wake up and flip it over. She kept up her vigil, studying the waiting people, her eyes repeatedly returning to the sleeping man. Could he be from the camp? If only he'd move his arms so the logo was visible or, better yet, drop the sign so she could see if it sported her name.

She sat, debating. She had assumed the couple she had corresponded with would meet her. She knew they had a daughter close to her age who also worked at the camp full time. They had said a camp would be in session the day she arrived, so maybe they had been unable to get away and had sent Mr. Snooze over there. She grinned slightly at her corniness. Back in America, safe in her

4

own surroundings, who would meet her hadn't even occurred to her. Now, sitting here alone, worried about her luggage, surrounded by everything foreign, it was overwhelming.

Her stomach protested again, and she glanced back over at the young man. The sign had started to slip from his grasp.

She swiveled around to scan the arrivals area again, hoping to see if new people were standing there with signs. It seemed everyone had someone greeting them. Everyone but her. Her thumb went subconsciously to where her ring had once been, and the emptiness there magnified the desolation filling her chest. What had she been thinking? She had left her family and flown halfway around the world to sit on her own in a foreign airport. What had possessed her?

As soon as the self-pity took hold, frustration washed over her. She would not be helpless. She needed to act. In a surge of bravado, she stood and lugged her suitcase nearer where the man slept. She would start with him. He was the closest, and he had a sign. He was obviously there for someone, even if he wasn't there for her. She took a deep breath. Time for action. She leaned over and poked his arm with her finger.

"Excuse me," her voice seemed to squeak out of her. She cleared her throat, embarrassed.

The man didn't budge.

She leaned forward again and poked harder. A pair of startling green eyes flew open as he raised his arms in a defensive posture.

In any other situation, she would have laughed. But he was a stranger, after all, and he didn't exactly seem happy.

"What the...?" He stood abruptly, and the sign landed on the floor, name side up.

And there it was: "Heidi Richmond," scrawled in black marker.

It had been him all along.

***

Johann blinked furiously, looking around to see if anyone else had witnessed this rude invasion. But nobody paid them any attention, and the girl before him, with smudged mascara and wild hair, stood glaring at him, a mixture of anger and triumph in her wide brown eyes.

"It *is* you!"

He ran his hand through his hair. This was a first – being woken by an angry American who looked like she'd won a competition or something. Well, she had finally arrived, and she had found him. What a relief he didn't have to hunt her down. Mentally shaking the sleep from his brain, he stuck out his hand, "Johann."

She took his hand. "Yo-hahn?"

He shrugged. Close enough. "Is this all you have?" Most Americans came with enough luggage to open a small shop, and she only had one suitcase? Granted, it was large, but still, only one item.

"No, I...."

He watched in resignation as various emotions flitted across her face.

Then she took a deep breath. "They lost my other suitcase. They don't know when I'll get it."

"Did you fill out the forms at the luggage claim station?"

"Yes."

"Well, if they find it, they'll contact us. You did leave the camp contact information, didn't you?"

"Oh... no."

"What did you leave?"

She palmed her forehead, clearly embarrassed. "My... my home address."

"*Ai-ja-jai*, let's go back over there then." He stopped himself just short of griping at her. "We don't want them to send your luggage back to America." He hoped he'd tamped down his condescension sufficiently. Apparently, he hadn't.

The American girl stepped back and snapped her head up. "No need to mock me; I'm not the one who fell asleep on the job."

Amusement flickered in his eyes as he wrenched the suitcase free from her grasp. At least she had spunk. He'd give her that. And beautiful eyes. Normally he would apologize for falling asleep and scaring her. He would explain her plane had been late, and he was functioning on only a few hours of sleep. Normally he would be kinder and more patient. But being nice simply couldn't be part of the grand plan.

***

Heidi turned on her heel and strode back towards the lost luggage section, not even bothering to see if he had followed her. What a rookie mistake giving them her home address. But she was tired and confused and dirty and hungry, and she had spent frightening minutes believing she was stranded in a foreign country. Nobody would think clearly under those circumstances. Regardless, she needed to get a grip. Even though the camp worker had fallen asleep, she still wasn't making her best first impression, and the camp *had* picked her over other applicants.

Back at the lost and found counter, she hurriedly explained her error to the same lady who had first helped her. Quickly she located the camp's address and altered the form, doing her best to ignore Johann looking over her shoulder, reiterating her statements in a language she didn't recognize.

As soon as she'd finished, he took the suitcase from her. "We'd better go. We don't want to get to camp after dark." And with that, he took off walking so quickly she had to half run to catch him.

Anger at his rudeness surged, a welcome change to her earlier helplessness. "Fine! But listen, I really need a restroom, a money-changing place, and something to eat."

"Yes, Madam," he responded stiffly in mock condescension. "The *toilets* are right this way." And he waved his hand with a flourish towards a large sign that did, indeed, proclaim 'Toilets.'

Heidi sighed and marched towards the offensive sign, her carry-on in tow, her suitcase left with her unhappy chauffeur. Everything appeared clean. She went to one of the sinks and stood there for a moment, stunned by her appearance. Mortified, she turned on the faucet and began furiously splashing her face with cold water.

Then, she dug in her bag, located her face wash, and scrubbed until her skin squeaked. Finally, pausing to catch her breath, she turned to grab some paper towels only to realize the dispenser was cloth, and although it seemed you were supposed to be able to pull it down to get a fresh piece, it appeared stuck in one position. She wasn't touching a pre-used towel. So, she wiped at her wet face, shook her hands off, and attempted to contain her hair with a scrunchie.

With fresh determination, she walked out. She had read the judgment in Johann's eyes, but she would surprise him. She knew how to rise to a challenge. "OK, now I should change my money." She kept her voice matter of fact.

He raised his eyebrows but, instead of responding, started walking again. Heidi tried to stay even with his long strides as they rounded a corner, and once more, he gestured with a flourish, this time towards a miniature bank.

Heidi rolled her eyes and walked away, wondering why Camp Guy had clearly decided to dislike her. She dug in her purse and took out all her dollars, finding the exchange rate worked in her favor despite the fact she couldn't remember what she had studied about the currency they were counting out in her hands. Surely there would be enough to buy herself a decent meal and replace at least a few of the missing items. The vast city she had seen from the airplane must have plenty of places to shop.

Walking back over to Johann, she stopped before him to keep him from taking off again. "Now, I know we have time constraints, but is there any way we can get some food? I have money, and I'll gladly pay for it. I haven't eaten anything substantial since Brussels."

He glanced at his watch, "Well, we'll have to get something outside the airport. There's nothing like that here."

They navigated through the crowded airport and out to the parking garage, people pressing on them from all sides. Many were well dressed, confidently striding towards their destinations. But others looked beaten down, dressed raggedly, their demeanor of utter defeat. She wanted to ask Johann about the disparity but decided it would be best to remain aloof with her unwilling chauffeur.

As these thoughts clashed through her mind, she watched a man approach Johann. With his head downcast, he gestured towards her suitcase and said something.

"*Ja,* OK," Johann responded and handed over the suitcase.

"Wait!" Heidi gasped. Why was he giving her suitcase away? She grabbed his arm to protest and then realized the man was walking along with them.

Johann shrugged her off and continued walking, engaging the man in talk Heidi couldn't understand. The language sounded less guttural and more phonetic from what he had spoken to the woman at the counter. But what did she know? Maybe her brain was too befuddled to recognize any differences.

When they finally got to his small truck, Heidi watched in interest as Johann paid the man. It must have been more than he was accustomed to because the man clapped one hand on top of the other in what seemed to be a gesture of thanks. Then, Johann took a folded sheet of paper from the front of the vehicle and called him back. He handed the man the paper, gesturing and explaining, all in that same phonetic language.

Johann took her suitcase and slid it into the covered back of the truck, so she turned and opened the door only to stop abruptly.

"So, you are going to drive us back to camp?" He stood right behind her, his tone amused.

Another rookie mistake: she should have remembered their steering wheels were on the other side. Avoiding his gaze, she turned, pushed past him, and walked around to the passenger door.

But it was locked, so she had to wait. Pretending not to care, she glanced around at the other cars, noticing they also had steering wheels on the wrong side, and the majority were high-end.

Of course, she would be getting into the only beat-up truck.

Finally, she heard the lock click. She opened the door and got in, pulling the creaking door closed.

"You have to give it more effort than that!"

"What?"

"The door," he gestured. "Open it and close it much harder; otherwise, you will fall out when we turn a corner."

"Oh," she mumbled lamely and fumbled with the door, opening and shutting it again, this time a little harder.

"*Ai-ja-jai,*" he muttered, unceremoniously reaching over and opening and shutting the door with gusto. She scooted back as far as the seat would allow, holding her breath at the close contact, trying not to notice his fresh outdoorsy scent, and determined to keep her expression neutral.

He put the truck in gear and turned to back out of their parking spot. "Seatbelt's broken," he offered, glancing her way.

The door might swing open, and the truck had no seatbelt. She would die before ever seeing the camp.

　　　***

Johann squelched the niggling guilt at his actions, doing his best to feign indifference. He had wanted Marie to get the counselor job this Heidi girl had taken. It frustrated him beyond measure that the camp board had picked her. Hopefully, the faster Heidi realized South Africa wasn't for her, the faster she'd leave.

There weren't enough available funds to pay Marie, and Heidi had apparently agreed to stay at least a year, maybe even two, not requiring a salary. That was the problem with these Americans. They had too much money at their disposal. So, here he sat, driving the wrong girl to camp.

He shook his head in regret making a right turn onto the highway as Heidi gasped in fear, grabbing the dashboard in front of her.

What now? He glanced over questioningly.

Her eyes were wide and turned on him, "Sorry, I... um... I thought we were going to have a wreck."

He didn't know how to respond to that.

"You... you drive on the other side of the road here," she offered lamely. She gripped the dashboard as sweat began to bead over her skin.

"Are you going to be sick?" He didn't like how she looked; campers got that look right before they were sick all over everything.

She closed her eyes and shook her head. "No, but I think finding food will help everything."

"OK," he acquiesced, softening his voice. "Why don't you roll down your window."

He watched her wrestle the half-broken crank into compliance, lowering the window, and raised his eyebrows. Even Karl struggled with that crank. She had turned her head into the wind; her eyes were closed. It appeared the fresh air was helping. The last thing he needed was a sick passenger. The week at camp had been hard enough. That, coupled with almost zero sleep the night before and that he'd had to drive to Johannesburg to get Heidi, had left him in a terrible mood. He hated leaving camp before it actually ended. And to think, all the campers he had spent a week building a rapport with would be gone when he returned. But Karl had insisted, and Karl was his boss, so here he sat, sleep-deprived himself, playing taxi.

His conscience nagged him for falling asleep at the airport. But he had arrived so early, there was time to close his eyes. He simply hadn't expected to sleep so deeply or for so long. He couldn't imagine Amy or even Marie approaching a sleeping stranger in a foreign airport and poking them awake. Truth be told, Heidi had grit.

He glanced over again, surprised, albeit grudgingly, at how pretty she appeared. Her curly brown hair was escaping that huge hair thing she had donned at the airport; her profile serene, faced into the wind as if it could wash away all her discomfort. And those large brown eyes of hers. They were so expressive; even red-rimmed and angry, he had noticed her eyes. And her smile.

He shook his head, frustrated she was pretty and frustrated she was American and the most frustrated with himself for noticing. She was the opposite of Marie. Marie was slim and toned and perfect. Marie didn't need make-up or brightly colored hair things to tame her sleek blonde hair. She was his girlfriend, and he shouldn't be sitting here comparing her to this stranger.

***

Heidi felt the truck stop and cautiously opened her eyes, appreciating the drier heat than in South Florida, where an open window in the summertime wouldn't have helped a bit. It appeared they were in the center of a town, and she turned toward Johann, questioning.

"We can eat here," he gestured.

Heidi liked how his "here" sounded, more like "heah." The low timbre of his South African accent resonated with her love of all things foreign. Of course, she would like his voice; she liked all accents, so she dismissed the positive thought, gingerly opened the creaking door, and climbed onto the sidewalk. She grabbed the side of the truck to get her bearings as Johann came around to her side.

"Are you dizzy?"

She didn't respond but gratefully allowed him to take her by the arm and guide her toward the restaurant. Her safari-chauffeur was an enigma: equal parts abrupt and perceptive.

They walked into a restaurant called "Wimpy." Heidi hoped that wasn't a negative foreboding about the food but was pleasantly surprised when a few minutes later, a plate of French fries and a hamburger were placed in front of her. She hadn't even remembered ordering, but everything was perfect. She sipped the coke and finally glanced up at Johann, who was slowly and thoughtfully consuming his own plate of food.

Maybe they needed to start over. She stretched out her hand. "Hi, my name is Heidi."

He quirked an eyebrow, stared at her offered hand, and reached out to grasp it.

"And my name is Johann." And then he smiled.

She smiled back, appreciating how his smile brightened his face, making his eyes seem alive yet intense. Brianna would call him hot. She glanced down quickly, hoping to hide her thoughts. She hadn't come to South Africa looking for a cute guy, especially a cute, obnoxious guy. They finished their meal in silence.

When they got to the truck, she paused, deliberating. "Do you mind if I look in my suitcase?"

He looked at her quizzically.

"I, unfortunately, can't remember which one has all the important stuff, and I need to check." She felt her face flush with embarrassment. How could she explain to this no-nonsense guy that one of her suitcases contained items like Pop-Tarts, pictures, and books? She had packed those items to stave off any possible homesickness, but now she simply felt sick, knowing none of those items would do her any good if she didn't have clothes to wear.

He glanced at his watch in resignation and reached under the tarp to slide her suitcase towards her.

Gratefully Heidi quickly unzipped it, and with one glance, she knew she had the wrong one. She took a deep breath and turned towards him. "I'm sorry, but I have to stop at a store."

"You want to go shopping?" His voice was a mixture of incredulity and frustration. Any friendly gains made during their meal were gone.

She wanted to cower, but instead, she stood straighter and stared right into those green frustrated eyes. "I don't *want* to go shopping; I need to go shopping. Just for a few items. *All* my most important items are in the missing suitcase." Heat flooded her face as she stood her ground. Johann was clearly ready to hop in the truck and leave her on the sidewalk, but she needed to stand her ground.

"You mean, with all those things, you don't have enough to last two weeks?"

Her voice climbed a notch. "No, I don't!"

"Well, what's all that stuff in there good for then?"

"If I must spell it out to you," she retorted, "I need *personal* stuff."

He blanched but kept staring at her in bewilderment.

"You know," she forged ahead, "panties and bras and... and..."

He held up his hands to stop the flood of words, twin splotches of embarrassment on his lean cheeks.

"*Ja, ja,* OK, I will take you somewhere, just... just...." Then he

13

leaned across her awkwardly, zipping her suitcase closed and sliding it back under the tarp. Without another word, he got in the truck and started it, waiting for her to get back in.

They rode in uncomfortable silence as he jerked the truck from gear to gear, mumbling under his breath at the traffic.

Eventually, he parallel parked on another busy street, not saying a word until he had killed the engine. Then he pointed down the street. "See down on your right?" Not waiting for her to respond, he went on. "There's a Woolworths there, and they will have everything you... um... need. I will wait here."

Heidi, grateful to escape the confines of the small truck, grabbed her wallet from her carry-on and hopped out, slamming the door behind her as loudly as she could. But, out on the street, her bravado instantly vaporized. There were crowds everywhere, and she was completely disoriented. She heard the other truck door slam, and Johann was beside her.

"Come on!" He grabbed her arm, guiding her firmly down the street. She heard him mumbling about helpless people, but she didn't care. She was simply grateful for Johann's presence. She would have gotten lost in the mayhem and knew when to concede defeat. Besides, she would have plenty of time in the days ahead to prove to him that she was anything but helpless.

After walking into the store, she was amazed. How could this be Africa? It was as modern and pleasant as any store in the US. Still, with a grip on her arm, they took the escalator to the correct floor, and Johann released her. "Now, I am going to sit here and wait for you. You have to do this part by yourself." He spoke like he was talking to a 2nd grader, but she nodded in response. Now was not the time to be affronted.

Once in the right section, she hurriedly made her selections. The sizing was all in centimeters, and she hoped she was grabbing what looked like the correct sizes. Then she found a changing room and, with the salesperson's help, hurriedly narrowed her choices down. She could tell the salesperson wanted to engage her in conversation and that she was openly curious about the rugged man waiting on the periphery, but Heidi stuck to business. She didn't want to turn this into a pleasure trip and anger Johann further.

Eventually, she returned to him, bag in hand, hoping she had spent wisely and anxious to get back on the road. He appeared relieved to see her so quickly and stood to lead her back down to the store entrance, then down the even more crowded street back to the truck.

He kept glancing at his watch. "*Ai-ja-jai,* we are going to get stuck in a traffic jam now."

Heidi looked over at him, but there was nothing she could say. She had her personal items and one suitcase. She had a full stomach, and even though he was grumpy, she knew he would safely get them where they needed to go. Maybe once they got out of the congestion, he would relax a bit and talk to her, but if he didn't, she would be fine.

She watched in awe as they drove through the city, craning her neck to see the buildings, amazed this huge thriving city was Africa. She had so many questions but didn't attempt to ask them.

At length, the traffic began to thin as they headed north. The sun was starting to set, and the barrage of sights and constant fear every time they turned onto what seemed like the wrong side of the street made her close her eyes. She felt confused by her preconceptions of Africa and the reality surrounding her. She had known, in theory, she was coming to a modern place, but she hadn't expected it to be America-modern. She was full of questions and wished Johann would act more like a tour guide and less like he was trying to hate her, but she wouldn't force conversation.

Instead, she balled up her jacket and smashed it between herself and the side of the truck and, with the wind in her face, gave herself over to sleep. She opened her eyes once to glimpse Johann's profile, her reluctant rescuer.

At least he had gotten her food and found her a store, and she was safe from all the apparent danger her dad had warned her about before coming. With that thought, she succumbed to the overwhelming need to sleep.

***

Once her breathing was even, Johann allowed himself to look over at her. He wanted to dislike her but sleeping like that with her hair blowing around her face, her carry-on clutched on her lap, her new purchases at her feet, she looked utterly serene. The earlier anger and fear and disbelief at his rudeness she hadn't been able to contain was gone, replaced by a relaxed relief. His conscience assaulted him once more for being so impolite. He couldn't imagine Marie handling herself the way Heidi had, but Heidi was the interloper, and he needed to remember that.

He knew Marie was young for his 24 years. From the first day of camp, when he had seen her standing on top of the capture-the-flag hill, pumping her fist in victory, he had decided she was the girl for him.

And then, later that night, when she had picked up a guitar and strummed along while they sang choruses at campfire time, he was smitten. If he was honest with himself, he knew it also had to do with the way her hair fell in front of her face as she leaned over her guitar, the way her long tan legs were folded underneath her, and the way she caught his eye over the heads of the other campers.

He glanced over at Heidi once more, still sound asleep, her arms hugging her carry-on, legs crossed beneath her, bright pink toenails adding color to an already colorful outfit.

He supposed she would sleep the rest of the drive, knowing she had probably lost the majority of a night during her trip, and he felt his prior resentment begin to dissipate. She had flown halfway around the world to come to a strange place, lost her suitcase, and was then confronted by his animosity. No wonder she had responded so aggressively. Maybe she wasn't as pampered as he had surmised.

He felt a strange sense of protectiveness pervade his senses and then hit the steering wheel in frustration at his own disloyal thoughts.

CHAPTER 2

Heidi opened her eyes slowly. She had been dreaming about Chris, that he had told her he would wait for her. As her mind sought to grasp her surroundings and how she had gotten there, a warm feeling filled her heart. Maybe Chris truly loved her, maybe the dream was real, maybe he realized he had been mistaken, just maybe....

Her reverie was cut short as a door opened slightly, and bright light forced her to shut her eyes in protest. The warm feeling disappeared and was replaced with a sense of dread. How had she landed here in a bed when she last remembered driving in Johann's truck?

"Heidi?"

The visitor quickly entered and then shut the door returning the room to dimness.

Heidi tried to focus. "Yes?"

The person came closer.

"I'm Amy, and they sent me to wake you up." The voice was sweet and tentative.

Heidi raised to her elbows. Bunk beds were everywhere, stacked three high, lining three walls.

Her bed was on the fourth wall under a window and next to the door. There were dark curtains over the window, and bright light filled the room once more when she reached out to move them aside. She must have slept late.

"Um, when... how... did I get here?"

The girl perched on the edge of Heidi's bed. "Oh, it was the most romantic thing ever. You got here just after dark, and we couldn't wake you. So, my mom just told Johann to carry you from the *bakkie* to the cabin. He was so angry, and you were so pretty and

17

sound asleep. Even my mom thought it was funny!"

Heidi groaned. She was glad to meet her first friendly South African, but the picture she painted was beyond embarrassing. She had obviously gotten off on the wrong foot with "Yo-my-name-be-grumpy-Hahn," and now he would dislike her even more. She smiled as the unbidden play on his name came to mind wishing Brianna was here so they could have a good laugh.

"Now, do you want some breakfast, or actually, maybe lunch?" Amy was talking, and Heidi willed herself to concentrate on the girl in front of her.

"Uh... what... what time is it?" The fog in her brain felt thick enough to cut, and she desperately needed a bathroom.

"It's half past eleven," Amy smiled. "Mom said if we let you sleep anymore, you wouldn't be able to go to sleep tonight."

"Um... can you tell me where a bathroom is?"

"Well, we don't have bathrooms, but we do have toilets and sinks and an area with showers and more sinks," she laughed nervously. "It is a camp, after all."

"No, no – a *toilet* and shower and sink will be perfect," Heidi tried to reassure her as confusion mixed with the fog swirling her thoughts.

Amy nodded, looking relieved.

Slowly, Heidi swung her legs over the side of the bed, dismayed by her rumpled clothes. She must have slept in the same outfit she had been wearing since... she tried to think back, but the effort was too great. She squinted around the room trying to locate her things, relaxing slightly when she saw her suitcase, carry-on, *and* Woolworth's bag piled onto a nearby lower bunk.

She carefully crossed the room and began rummaging through her things while Amy stood off to the side. After grabbing what she hoped were the right items, she dug in the shopping bag to retrieve part of her purchases and glanced over at Amy. "Wouldn't you know they lost my suitcase with all the most important stuff?"

Amy laughed. "*Ja*, Johann said you had to make an emergency stop at Woolworths. At least he was clever enough to take you there.

Hopefully, they'll find your suitcase and telephone us, and then we can go back to fetch it."

Heidi's hand paused in midair, staring at Amy in interest, attempting to make sense of the English words that didn't seem quite English to her. She noticed Amy's hair wasn't unlike her own... long, brown, and curly, tamed by two girlish braids. The room was too dark to notice her eyes, but her cheery smile was a balm to Heidi's homesick soul.

"OK, I'm ready," she stood and squared her shoulders. "Lead on to those *toilets* and showers and sinks, please!"

Amy giggled in response and stepped out of the cabin.

The sunlight accosted her, and Heidi immediately covered her eyes. Amy giggled again and grabbed her arm. "This way."

Heidi kept her eyes trained downwards, feeling she was on show for whoever was out there, hoping nobody would want to meet her until after she had showered.

When they reached the bathrooms, which reminded her of those at the local public pool where she had spent most of her childhood training to become the Next Great Olympic Swimmer, Amy left her with a promise to come back in a few minutes and show her around. Heidi heard her stomach grumble in response, and Amy laughed again, promising food would be next on the schedule.

Then, she disappeared out the door, leaving Heidi in the dimly lit bathroom that smelled strongly of a mold problem.

She sighed loudly and warily set her stuff down on a wooden bench near the showers hoping it wouldn't get wet. She turned the handle, grateful the water came out warm, and turned her face into the stream, closing her eyes in relief. She would finally be clean.

Suddenly she heard men's voices, talking and carrying on as if they were right in the same room. She checked the edges of the shower curtain, pushing them against the concrete wall to prevent any gaps, and held her breath.

The voices continued as mortification filled her. They couldn't possibly be co-ed showers but, regardless, she went through the motions as quickly as possible, then grabbed her towel and dressed hurriedly, her skin still dripping but not caring.

Grabbing her stuff haphazardly, she stepped back outside, sighing with relief that nobody had seen her, only to be greeted by Johann coming around the corner of the building, damp and obviously fresh from a shower.

She stood there in shock, stock still, hoping he would just walk right by.

"Well, well," he stopped, "if it isn't Sleeping Beauty."

She didn't respond.

"Heidi!"

Heidi turned gratefully towards Amy, who was coming towards her eagerly.

"You were really quick."

She walked over and took her arm, glancing at Johann questioningly. "Here, let's put your things down, and then I'll show you the kitchen."

Heidi followed her, feeling helpless and inept.

As they walked, Amy pointed everything out. Heidi took in the cabin area that was the girls' side and then the open-air eating area that led to the indoor kitchen.

"You can see that everything is quite close together for us girls," Amy explained. "We don't have to go far to the showers or the kitchens. The boys' cabins are exactly opposite to ours. Actually, their back wall joins the wall of the girls' cabins, but they have to walk around to get to the showers and the kitchen. That way, at night with little girls, you don't have far to go in the dark."

Heidi willed herself to pay attention to Amy as they walked through the open-air eating area and into the kitchen. It was simple but with industrial-sized appliances and a large stainless-steel table in the center surrounded by wooden stools. Heidi assumed it served as both a prep area and a table. An African woman was at the stove stirring a pot of something bubbly. She turned and smiled as the girls walked in.

"*Dumela,* Mavis," Amy greeted the woman with a quick squeeze around the shoulders, "I want you to meet Heidi, the girl from America."

"Ooo, yes, the American girl," Mavis smiled even wider. "Welcome to our camp!"

"Thank you," Heidi murmured, liking Mavis instantly. She was about Heidi's height, dressed in a full skirt and blouse, an oversized apron tied around her ample waist. Her head was wrapped in cloth in a style Heidi had never seen before, and her brown eyes were bright and friendly.

"Are you hungry for some stew, Miss?" Mavis asked.

Heidi assumed she was talking to her and nodded anxiously. Yes, she wanted that stew. In fact, if she didn't get something in her stomach soon, she felt she would faint.

Before she knew it, Amy had sliced thick pieces of bread, set out butter and a plate, and Mavis had placed a bowl of the steaming stew on the stainless-steel table. Mavis then took a large iron kettle off the stove, poured what Heidi assumed was tea into a tin cup, and motioned for her to sit.

Heidi eyed the hot tea warily. She liked tea but also wanted water, so she glanced at the sink. "Can I drink the water from the faucet?" she asked carefully.

"You mean the tap?" Amy asked, her mouth quirking into a smile.

Mavis looked like she was about to laugh when Heidi saw the outline of what had to be Johann filling the door.

"And what does our American friend need to know?" he asked innocently.

"If she can drink from the tap," Amy responded merrily.

Heidi didn't know what they all thought was so funny, so she decided to take matters into her own hands. There were cups in the dish drainer, so she grabbed one, turned the faucet on, and filled it with water. If something was wrong with the water, hopefully someone would stop her before she drank it. Then she sat back at the table while the other three watched. She locked eyes with Johann, daring him to stop her, and put the cup to her lips, taking a large swig.

"Do you think all the parasites have been cleaned out of the tank yet?" Johann asked Mavis.

"Yeee, I don't know, Master Johann," Mavis laughed, shaking her head back and forth.

"I think my dad was planning on doing it tomorrow," Amy added, sending a quick wink Heidi's way.

Heidi seeing the wink, still felt her stomach turn. Surely, they were all, including Mavis, testing the *American girl*. Regardless, the alternative was too awful to contemplate. She swallowed a huge spoonful of the stew before barely tasting it.

"I suppose the parasites cook out of the stew and simply add to the protein content then?" Heidi asked, doing her best to look casually between the three of them. Mavis was now laughing, slapping her knees with glee, and Johann looked at Heidi in grudging admiration. Amy's look bordered on sheer pride that her prodigy hadn't fallen prey to the prank.

Johann was the first to answer her. "Yes, I suppose so. It helps us keep food costs down."

Heidi tilted her head and nodded in pretended understanding. "That makes sense." Then without skipping a beat, she turned to Mavis. "This stew is delicious, by the way. I thought I was going to starve to death."

Mavis bowed her head and clapped one hand over the other in the same gesture of thanks Heidi had seen the man do in the parking garage at the airport the day before.

Amy sat opposite Heidi, and Johann straddled a stool and did the same.

"So, you really didn't fall for it, did you?" Amy asked breathlessly.

"Amy!" Johann was clearly disappointed.

"Fall for what?" Heidi asked innocently. If Johann and his people planned to test her, they would find the more they did, the tougher she would be.

"So, Heidi, has Amy shown you around camp yet?" Johann seemed anxious to change the subject, not ready to concede that the

American girl had scored one over them.

"Just this general area and the... um... showers." Heidi tried not to grimace.

"I'm afraid they are not quite up to your standards, are they?"

Heidi measured her words carefully. She was thinking of moral standards, not practical ones. "Oh, they were more than functional, thank you." She would have to ask Amy about the male voices later.

Just then, another woman walked into the kitchen. Heidi looked toward her, having the odd sense of being part of a scene in some play, and she hadn't studied her character's role. Perhaps it was jet lag, or perhaps it was simply the lack of anything familiar.

Amy jumped off her stool instantly and put her arm around the woman, leading her towards Heidi. "This is my mom, Vera. Mom, this is Heidi!"

Heidi instantly saw the resemblance between Amy and Vera and stood to greet her, wondering if a hug or a handshake were the accepted norm. Vera took the lead and wrapped Heidi in a quick hug, welcoming her profusely and warming Heidi's heart. It seemed Heidi had two women on her side here. Maybe Johann was to be her only adversary.

"And how was your trip?" Vera had stepped back and was holding Heidi at arm's length.

"Very long," Heidi rolled her eyes for emphasis.

"Did you sleep much?"

"Hardly at all."

"But it seems like since she landed, she has been making up for that." Johann's dry voice was a stark contrast to the sing-song friendliness of Vera and Amy.

"Now, now, Johann," Vera admonished, "if you don't talk nice, I'll make you carry Heidi around for her tour!"

Heidi reddened, swiveling towards Johann, who appeared more angry than embarrassed. She could hear Amy and Mavis laughing in the background.

"I'm sure that won't be necessary," she tried. "But I am anxious to see the camp." Maybe she could change their thought direction.

"I'll walk you around, then," volunteered Johann.

Heidi glanced back at him in surprise, catching a glint of something in his eye. Surely, he wasn't planning to sabotage her. She would have to be wary.

"Well, let the poor girl finish her tea." Vera was bustling around now, opening drawers in the massive refrigerator and writing furiously on a notepad. As if on cue, Amy joined in, perusing what looked like a pantry and calling out items.

"Aunt Vera manages the cooking for camp."

Heidi, wondering briefly at his use of "Aunt," glanced back towards Johann, surprised at his first helpful comment since she had met him. He must have caught her staring in interest at the interplay between mother and daughter.

"We're going to the shops this afternoon, have to replenish supplies," Amy explained. "Do you want to come with us?"

"No, we don't need all three of you together shopping and forgetting to come home before dark."

Heidi turned, startled by the deep guttural voice.

"I'm Karl." He was shorter and solid. His cropped dark hair was combed over with way too much greasy product, and his black-rimmed glasses were slightly crooked over his stern face. He was wearing what she would eventually learn was called a safari suit; it reminded Heidi of a military outfit.

He came towards her with an outstretched hand which she shook briefly and then turned towards Vera. "It would be best if Heidi stayed here and got accustomed to camp."

Heidi shifted uncomfortably, feeling like she was a twelve-year-old trapped in an alternate family structure. Karl was the head of the camp and Vera's husband. They were the couple she had communicated with the most, but she had only referred to them as Mr. and Mrs. Voskamp.

"Well, I'm finished here and ready for the tour." She tried to sound natural, but her voice sounded foreign and decidedly unnatural.

"Good. Johann will take you." His voice left no room for

argument.

Heidi stood quickly and moved to clear her dishes.

"Mavis will get those; you two get started. The day is half over, and you have a lot to learn." Karl's voice begged an apology from her for sleeping half the day, but she mentally refused. She had traveled halfway around the world, across multiple time zones; if he didn't understand that, it wasn't her fault.

"You coming?" Johann was by the door, waiting impatiently.

"Wait!" That was Vera. "Do you need us to get you anything, Heidi? I heard you lost your suitcase."

Heidi turned gratefully. "No, I should be fine for now."

She would have loved to have gone off with the friendly ladies and left the men behind. But hopefully, her luggage would materialize soon, and she was anxious to see the camp, despite her sleepiness. Although fragrant and unique, the tea obviously contained zero caffeine, and she wished for something to clear the fog that permeated her thinking.

***

The tour started next door to the kitchen at a small snack shop they called the "Tuck Shop."

"We open the shop every afternoon for the campers during one of the break times." Johann was explaining the procedure, but Heidi was lost in her longing for a Coke from the small refrigerator.

"Do you mind if I have a soda?"

"Well, usually even counselors have to pay, but it's OK this time," he shrugged.

Gratefully, Heidi took a chilled bottle and looked around for an opener.

"Here." He grabbed it from her and used an opener stuck to the side of the counter, handing it back.

"Thanks," she mumbled, taking a grateful swig. It seemed he was actually a nice guy, but he definitely had something against her. It didn't make sense that someone as grumpy as he had acted around her could run a camp. The problem was clearly with her, and she would have to find out why.

They walked through the outdoor eating area under an archway covered by a magnificent bougainvillea providing the perfect frame for the view ahead. Heidi stopped. Before her lay a series of wide steps leading to a pool, playing fields, and beyond that, in the distance, a large lake bounded by mountains. It was a piece of heaven.

Tiny sailboats dotted the shimmering water and miniature speed boats whipped between them. She could feel Johann's assessment, but there were simply no words to describe the beauty before her. She felt she had seen it all before, like all those childhood pictures she had drawn of a lake and mountains with the sun peaking overhead were of this very scene. She would have to ask her mom to dig them out. Even now, when she drew with the twins, she always returned to that one scene. And here it was before her.

"Heidi?"

How to explain it to Safari Man? She simply couldn't. It was a miraculous confirmation that she was exactly in the spot God intended. He had placed this image in her heart for this reason, for this moment of assurance. Hope swelled. She knew in the days to come, she would pause here often.

"Heidi?"

She glanced briefly at him. "You need a painter to paint this scene," she attempted. "They can call it 'Beauty in Real Life.'"

He smiled briefly and motioned for her to follow him down the wide steps towards the pool area. Heidi tried to picture the area teeming with children and teens, splashing or laying out on the warm concrete. It made her want to grab her bathing suit and forget the tour.

A bench swing sat off to the side, facing the long end of the pool with the view of the lake and mountains to the left. They walked down more steps where an in-ground trampoline lay, hidden initially from their view. Off to the right was a fire pit surrounded by concrete benches built in a circle, using the natural relief of the hill to stagger upwards at least five or six rows.

"This is where we often have our evening meetings – around the fire." He gestured to the left and beyond. "From this vantage point, our campers can see the sports fields, tennis courts and all the activities that have kept them busy all day but, in the evening, they can watch the sky change and the mountains in the distance reflected off the dam. It provides a great place for them to think and contemplate their Creator."

Heidi nodded appreciatively, taking it all in. "Is the dam part of camp?"

"No, but if we have a small enough group, we sometimes walk there and swim in the marked-off swimming area."

Heidi made a complete circle, her chest filling with admiration at everything before her. "And what sports do you have?"

He shrugged, "All the usual stuff: rounders, touch rugby, soccer, capture the flag. Of course, there's tennis, and we usually have one tournament per camp where the winner's team gets a special treat. And, there are water sports, too."

At least she understood most of the games, but she would have to have Amy fill her in on 'rounders' and 'touch rugby.' She wasn't about to ask Johann, nor was she going to let him know tennis and swimming were her two fortes.

They headed down towards the fields and veered to the right towards a garden area centered by a majestic weeping willow. Heidi inhaled sharply, awestruck. The Tree, filled with what appeared to be chimes or placards, covered the size of at least half a tennis court. Heidi stepped through the hanging branches towards the center and noticed the benches around the center trunk. With the privacy of the branches, she felt like she was inside a ground-level tree house.

She walked closer to inspect one of the wooden placards and noticed it contained a word, scarcely legible. She moved to another and then another – they all included a word or two, along with the date. A few of the dates seemed to be as early as the 1970s, but these were the most difficult to read, so she wasn't sure.

She turned, looking for Johann, waiting for an explanation, but he had produced a small pair of garden sheers and was studiously clipping the lowest branches to about a foot above the ground. Sensing her watching him, he looked up. "We have to keep the branches off the ground; otherwise, they get a fungus."

But that didn't explain the placards with the words and dates. She moved to a bench closest to the trunk and sat, leaning back until she felt the bark against her spine and gazed up through the leaves to patches of blue sky.

The twins would love this tree; it would be an ideal playground, the sweeping branches a perfect canopy for childhood imaginations. She sighed at the ache of missing them and forced her thoughts to the present, wondering again at the placards.

"We call this the Counting Tree." He was standing only a few feet in front of her, the shears dangling from his left hand.

"Oh!" He had startled her, appearing as an apparition before her, if not for the garden shears. She wanted to laugh at the ridiculous combination, but he looked serious. She willed her voice to be neutral, "the placards?"

"Yes – we call them chimes. Originally they tried to make them out of metal, but it was hard for the children to write on metal, and plus, it got too heavy for the branches, so we use an engraving tool to burn the letters onto the wood. Then, we varnish the wood to make it weatherproof and come out here and hang them on the last day of camp."

He was rambling, and Heidi was trying to catch it all. "What are the words?"

"Blessings… we come here to record and count our blessings. The children have the choice to take their wood chime home or hang it here."

Tears pooled in her eyes as she scanned the hundreds of chimes hung throughout the branches. How beautiful and what a contrast… every placard proclaiming a child's blessing hung in a weeping willow. Words from the Psalms came unbidden, "*We hanged our harps upon the willows in the midst thereof…*" she quoted softly.

"*…For there they that carried us away captive required of us a song.*" He finished quietly.

28

The quoted words of Psalms resonated between them, filling the space; their eyes locked, his startled by the depth of her understanding, hers grateful for the connection.

"A lot of our children come from difficult backgrounds," Johann said. "They have sad secrets. We teach throughout the week that God is present in any situation, no matter how difficult. We only have them for a brief period, usually not long enough for them to trust us enough to fully help them. So, instead, our goal is to equip them with the knowledge that God is present, that God loves them more than they can comprehend, and that there is always something or someone to be thankful for.

"The weeping willow symbolizes not only the sadness many of them experience but also the blessings. And blessings can happen in the middle of difficulty; we only have to look for them.

"Sometimes, we have the privilege of fully helping a child. They learn to trust us enough to tell us of their situation, and then we move heaven and earth to try to help them. But, even then, sometimes it's not enough." His voice caught, and he took a shuddering breath. "But if we can teach them God is present and that He loves them more than they comprehend... then...." Johann stopped and stepped away, turning to clip a branch.

Heidi, frozen in place, wiped at the tear on her cheek and wondered if she was equipped to work here after all. Would the children placed in her care ever trust her enough? Did she have the depth it took to communicate the deep love of God?

It made her question if she could actually do this – could actually help.

"So, this tree symbolizes what we are about. More than anything you see today, we want our counselors to remember that."

She lifted her chin and looked him squarely in the eye. "I will."

He met her gaze, green eyes piercing, measuring. "Of course, many of our children don't have heartbreaking problems; they're just kids here to enjoy camp. But you just need to be prepared for the ones that do. But the Counting Tree is for everybody; everybody can count their blessings and see how God is present in their lives."

They left the Tree, walking on in silence as Heidi mulled over everything Johann had shared with her.

"Do you have any questions so far?"

She stopped. "Yes, I do." She paused, tentative, debating. "Couldn't it be wrong to tell a child in, for example, an abusive situation that they need to thank God, though?"

He almost seemed disappointed by her question. "Heidi, we are not telling them to be thankful for the awful situation they are in, but we are teaching them to find something, anything in their lives to be thankful for and to focus on that and thus experience the love of God."

She nodded briefly.

"We have had a couple children grow up and come back and tell us how the lessons of the Counting Tree gave them hope in their bad situation. They find the chime they made, and they hold it and cry and...." Emotion caught his voice, and he shrugged.

Heidi listened in admiration and kept silent, wondering at the depth of his feelings and worrying again if she had the insight to handle the job that lay ahead. She wondered, too, if he had a chime and, if so, what it said.

***

Heidi, she was deeper than he had thought. To quote the scripture, to ask the questions: there was more to her than he had assumed.

When he pointed down the hill where their workers lived, he expected the usual American horror, which, he had to admit, he understood. The disparity was too great. The camper cabins looked palatial next to where Mavis and Tom lived with their five-year-old daughter Fiona. The sad fact was Mavis and Tom's house, though, and even Beauty's little house beyond that, was, in turn, palatial compared to what many others lived in.

He had only ever been on the outskirts of Soweto, but even from a distance, he could tell thousands lived in abject poverty and deplorable conditions.

But Heidi was quiet, so quiet he couldn't resist asking her if she had even been aware of apartheid.

"Well, I did read that book. You know... um... *Cry the Beloved Country.*"

"Ah, standard school reading for everyone here," he responded.

"Really? Does that not make everyone want to fix things? I mean, if all the white schools are reading it, then surely it would make people want to change the system."

"The book was first published in 1948...."

"But it brought the problem to light around the world at least?"

"Yes, so we get boycotted by the Olympics and get sanctions, and South African Airways can't fly over the rest of Africa, but here, things are the same."

There was an uncomfortable silence. Heidi looked back down the hill, noting another woman talking with some children. "Does she also work for camp?"

His eyes followed her gaze. "Her name is Beauty. She helps in the kitchen, too."

"And the children?"

"Fiona is Mavis's daughter, and Samson is Beauty's son."

"Well?"

He sighed deeply. Heidi was too perceptive, and he didn't want this conversation today. "What about them?"

"Do they get to be part of camps?"

"No, Heidi, they don't."

He saw her eyes widen, and the disparity hit him in his gut afresh. African children were playing in the dirt only a few steps away from a camp equipped to give them the best of everything, yet it was decreed they had to be kept separate.

"Look," he turned her towards her, and he knew he sounded defensive. "I know it's a shock because you are American. But this is South Africa, and there's nothing you or I can do about it but pray for a solution. OK?"

Her eyes were wide, and she didn't respond.

"I don't like it either, Heidi, and I... um... do what I can when... others are not around. And you are not to say anything, do you understand?"

She nodded slightly, her mind apparently flashing back to her arrival. "The man who carried my suitcase? At the airport?"

He shrugged.

***

At least it seemed Johann's love for children didn't contain color barriers, and for that, she was grateful. But the camp workers' conditions appalled Heidi, and she had only seen their homes from a distance. And distance had a way of softening appearances.

Yes, she had read Alan Paton's book to prepare herself, but reading about something and seeing it firsthand was utterly different. For now, she wouldn't ask Johann any more questions about it, especially since he vacillated between tolerating her and trying to be rude to her. She would wait until she was on surer footing.

The mood of the tour lightened as they continued past the trampoline, where he warned her to shine her light underneath before jumping in case there were poisonous snakes, and the pool where she needed to check the filter for toxic frogs. At the swing, she needed to shake off the cushions to look for scorpions, the tennis courts where you had to check the ends of the net poles to look for wasp nests, and on and on it went. Heidi highly doubted there could possibly be that much danger here with new batches of kids coming every week, but she played along to the best of her ability.

For now, she would let Johann think she believed him.

The tennis courts were the last stop, and Heidi turned with Johann towards the main buildings.

"Um, I have to go down the hill now and check on some things. You know your way back?" He was looking at her intently.

Heidi nodded, her eyes skittering across his face, wondering. Was that a reluctant admiration she saw? Had she passed some hidden test?

As she walked back to her cabin, she took a deep cleansing breath, praying that Johann would accept her, praying for all she had just seen, and then allowing her eyes to sweep the entire camp from her vantage point at the top of the berm. The entire 360 degrees of space filled her with wonder. From the dam and mountains in the distance to the Tree, the whole area spoke of the wonders of God's Creation. There were no ringing phones, traffic jams, office typewriters, or word processors. But even amid beauty, there was darkness. And maybe, once she got to know Johann better, she could help him "do what he could when others weren't around."

CHAPTER 3

Heidi had planned to unpack her things once she got back to camp, but aside from the bunk beds, there wasn't any other furniture. So, she organized her suitcase in piles, realizing afresh how the wrong suitcase had been lost. There were scarcely any clothes in this one, and if they didn't find her other one soon, she would have to purchase many new clothes. She sighed and slid it under her bed with the top unzipped, hoping that would provide easier access. She took out the framed photo of Darrin and Darla with their twin grins and set it on the wide windowsill. Then, her finger running lightly over their sweet faces, she saw the children playing in the dirt at the Lower Camp and, in a moment of decision, took the picture and placed it tenderly back in her suitcase.

A pang of homesickness swept over her. She wondered what her mom was thinking, how her dad was. Were the twins asking for her? Heidi felt tears prick her eyes; she couldn't stand to think she had added to their sadness. You couldn't explain time or distance to three-year-olds; she knew they would simply think she had deserted them. She thought of Darrin grabbing her face between his chubby hands to assure himself of her undivided attention... "Aneidi?" She loved the unique name they had for their Aunt Heidi. Were they asking for her? Were her parents doing their best to explain her absence?

There was a knock at her door and Heidi, grateful for the distraction from her morose thoughts, jumped to open it.

"Heidi?" It was Amy, dressed in a black swimsuit and wrapped in a towel. "Do you want to go swimming?"

Heidi smiled, grateful for this apparent overture of friendship, and nodded eagerly. She pulled out her suitcase, thankful she had seen her bathing suit when she organized and pulled it out.

33

"Did you finish shopping already?"

Amy shrugged. "I decided to stay behind and work on the letters. My dad went with my mom instead."

"Oh," Heidi wondered what the letters were. There was so much to learn and so much to ask, but she still hadn't processed the Counting Tree nor the houses down the hill and couldn't find the energy to ask.

Amy, watching her with her suitcase, spoke up. "You should probably zip your suitcase. Scorpions, you know."

Heidi grimaced and pulled the suitcase back out. "I thought Johann was just making that up to scare me."

Amy giggled, "Probably, but zipping your suitcase is the clever thing to do." She paused, thinking, "What else did he tell you?"

Heidi shrugged, "To beat the wasps out of the tennis nets, scare off snakes from under the trampoline with a *torch*, um, check the pool filter for poisonous frogs before swimming...." Heidi stopped when she realized Amy was laughing. "I guess I started to fall for some of it, but then I thought he must be just trying to scare me, so I figured none of it was valid."

Amy smiled, nodding in understanding. "Well, there was a tiny bit of truth in each one; he just embellished it all." She patted Heidi on the arm, "not to worry, we'll find a way to get him back." Then, seeing Heidi standing awkwardly with her bathing suit in hand, she went on. "I'll just step outside so you can change, or you could go to the showers and change."

Heidi shook her head.

"Oh, Heidi," Amy giggled, "I should have warned you about the showers. Did you hear boys talking?"

Heidi gave a quick nod.

"Come, I will put your mind at rest; bring your costume with you so you can change there in privacy." She grinned at her addendum.

Heidi wanted to resist, wondering what she needed a *costume* for, and then, bathing suit clutched against her, followed after Amy.

"See that door," Amy explained, "that's the girls' entrance."

She glanced at Heidi to see if she was following her. Then they walked around to the back of the bathroom building. "Now see that door," Amy waited for Heidi to nod, "that's the boys' entrance." Then, walking through the girls' side, she pointed to the wall the showers and sinks backed up against. "And that wall divides the two places but see how there is a space at the top?"

Heidi nodded, heat flushing her cheeks. How much stupidity could she blame on jet lag? "So, you can hear them."

Amy clapped her hands. "Yes!"

"So, do boys ever try to peak over?" Heidi was eyeing the gap, wondering what had possessed the builders to leave it open.

"No," Amy laughed again, "It's too high and too small. My dad says it helps keep air flow and prevents mildew from forming as easily. I don't know if it really does, but I do know you can't come in here and tell your friends your deepest secrets because someone might hear you!"

Heidi felt relief at this latest explanation. Without Amy, she would have probably already thrown her suitcase back into Johann's truck and insisted he take her back to the airport. "You know," she said slowly, "don't tell Johann you explained anything to me. We can just pretend I believed everything he told me and let him think I believe the showers are co-ed, too!"

"*Ja*," Amy threw out her hands in excitement, "and we get him back even better than he tried to get you!"

Heidi smiled in anticipation as she changed. The rat would fall into his own trap, and it would serve him right!

After jumping in the pool and chatting with Amy for a bit, Heidi gratefully slipped into lap mode. She had swum competitively until her early high school years when tennis crowded out pool time, and she finally had to choose. But she still loved to swim laps. The repetitive motion and the feel of the power in her arms, pulling her through the water, never got old. She glanced over to make sure Amy didn't mind, but she was laid out on a towel soaking up the sun, so Heidi continued, grateful for the chance to exercise after all the travel.

She swam until her arms burned and then stopped, her back to the edge of the pool, drinking in the view. The similarity of her childhood drawings was uncanny. Maybe her mom could find and send them. It would be fun to show Amy how as a child, she had pictured a scene so like the one she was now living.

"Hey, Johann!"

Heidi turned towards Amy, her heart sinking, hating the intrusion. She really didn't want him to see her in her bathing suit. It shouldn't matter what he thought, but it irked her that after finishing college and working in an office, she had gained weight. Her entire life, she had been in the pool or on a tennis court, but her office job had wreaked havoc on her previously fit lifestyle. Plus, the stress of the wedding plans had all compounded into an uncharacteristic craving for junk food. Maybe it was because she had been dissatisfied with her job and, deep down, had known Chris wasn't right for her. She was sure someone, for a fee, would psychoanalyze her post-college 25-lb weight gain, but she mostly preferred to ignore it.

Johann had stopped next to Amy, his expression decidedly grumpy.

Heidi wanted to splash water at him but knew the gesture would be misconstrued, so she pointedly ignored him.

"Heidi is probably a faster swimmer than you, Johann." Amy wasn't afraid to tease him.

"Oh, *ja*?" He quirked his head towards Heidi, a challenge flashing through his eyes. "Does she need to race?"

Amy looked at Heidi expectantly.

"No thanks, I have used all my energy capturing poisonous frogs from out of the pool filter," she stated dryly.

Johann shot a glance at Amy, who shrugged in response. "She's not your regular fall-for-Johann's tricks American, Johann, so don't look at me like it's my fault she doesn't believe your lies."

Heidi grimaced inwardly. So much for keeping Johann in the dark.

He looked hot and irritated as he stood there in his swim trunks.

36

But then he turned on his heel and left.

Amy giggled and turned to Heidi. "I love it when Johann gets surprised by a girl, especially an American girl."

Heidi put both hands on the pool's sides and got out. Her arms felt like jelly from the unaccustomed exercise, and getting out of the pool wasn't the easy one-movement motion it used to be. She would have to come and swim laps as often as she could.

She grabbed her towel and sat down on the cement next to Amy, pulling her knees to her chest and staring out once more at the mountains. "I take it he isn't a big fan of Americans."

Amy made a face, "Not really, but he'll be fine."

Heidi wondered at that but decided to let it go. She wasn't here to figure out Johann; she was here to work. "So," she started, ready to change the subject, "do you usually have this much time off when there are no campers?"

"Well, when school is out, they usually leave on Saturdays, and then we spend the day cleaning up. But this last group was different; they were here from Friday to Tuesday and left before you arrived," Amy responded. "When school is in session, Wednesdays are usually our day off since weekends we are nearly always full of campers."

Heidi turned to her, interested.

"Right now, school has just started again, so we will have mostly weekend camps from now until the next school holidays in April. So, my dad decided that Wednesdays would be our Saturdays. Sometimes we go into the city on these days to do some shopping or, like I decided to do today, sometimes we just stay around here and relax. Since you had just arrived, we figured it was best for you to stay around camp today."

Heidi nodded but stayed silent, hoping she would keep explaining.

"Now, once the holidays get here, we run camp from Sunday to Friday or Monday to Saturday, always trying to keep at least 24 hours open between camps so that we can recover before the next group comes in." Amy flipped over onto her stomach and leaned on her elbows.

"During school, when we have days off, we do a number of things, but our main focus is the Stamp Club."

Heidi looked at her quizzically.

"We'll explain it all later this afternoon, but it's like a mail-in Bible study thing." She sat up and adjusted her towel. "We also go into schools and give talks. We take our guitars and sing choruses and then Johann talks to the students. He's very good at it."

"They are allowed to do that in all the schools?"

"Oh yes – every school has RI, Religious Instruction. You don't have that in America?"

"No, definitely not. Only private Christian schools allow that."

***

That evening, Heidi stared warily at the sausage and what resembled congealed grits on her plate. She wished the food would match what the outdoor eating area held in ambiance. She glanced at the roof over them and then over to the second floor, where she assumed Karl and Vera were eating. Their living quarters had not been part of the tour. Eating outside suited Heidi just fine, though. She could barely make out the colors of the bougainvillea that graced the entrance to the eating area and the outline of the mountains changing as the sky darkened. Pinpoints of stars became visible, creating enough light to illuminate the dam. She was captivated by the view, like staring at an artist's rendition of a landscape through a window. Only this wasn't a painting, and she wasn't looking out an imaginary window.

"Amy, I do believe our bug zapper is giving Heidi indigestion."

Heidi registered the challenge in Johann's tone and turned from her reverie. She had barely noticed the bug zapper. "Actually, I find it quite fascinating," she responded coolly.

Amy's eyes danced, clearly anticipating the upcoming interchange. "As fascinating as our showers, Heidi?"

"Not quite, but I have a solution for that," she patted Amy on the arm convincingly. Maybe Amy was going to play along after all.

"But the bug zapper." Johann had leaned forward, clearly intrigued. "Does it bother you?"

"Well," she thought quickly, wanting to play along but not appear obvious. "You see," she began, "here are these unsuspecting bugs, flying around the air doing what they do best, looking for some human blood to suck on." Her voice sounded clinical, detached.

"And?" Johann was watching her closely, unsure.

"They see a bunch of their friends, so they fly closer, clearly excited at the prospect of meeting up for the party when ZAP!" And Heidi stood and clapped her hands so loud Johann nearly fell off the bench, and Amy collapsed in a heap, her laughter filling the outdoor space.

Heidi sat, her eyes sparkling but willing her lips into a flat line, satisfied she had won this round. Then, without missing a beat, she launched into her bathroom speech. "The way I see it, we can avoid problems at the showers and toilets and sinks between boys and girls if we make up a schedule."

"Schedule," Johann corrected, only he pronounced it 'shhedule.'

Heidi shrugged, "SHHHEdule then. Anyway, I can make up a chart in the morning, and we can have boys' and girls' times alternating every hour. We can post it outside the door along with a clock—"

"The clock will have to be waterproof," Amy advised sagely.

"—a waterproof clock," Heidi nodded, "Then when they have to go, they can just check the SHHHEdule, and if it's their time, they can follow nature's call, and if it's not—"

"They wet their pants." Johann finished.

She shrugged, "So be it, that's better than the alternative."

"Which is?" Amy was confused now.

Johann and Heidi turned to her and stated almost simultaneously, "Boys and girls in the showers at the same time."

"Ahh," Amy was giggling now and moved to stand, stacking their plates as she did. "I'm going to find us some sweets and make coffee."

Heidi, taking her cue from Amy, stood to help only to be waved off.

"No, sit, Heidi," Amy admonished. "I'll be back with something yummy."

Heidi sat back down reluctantly, looking across at Johann. He leaned forward, his elbows spread on the table, tapping absently with his fingers. His expression was part bemused, part admiration, and part contempt. She was glad. She wanted to keep him guessing, wanted to make him realize she wasn't the typical American girl who had come to play cabin counselor.

They sat in silence, Heidi absently noticing a line of ants trailing along the yellow stucco. She had so many questions. When the next set of campers arrived, what was expected of her? How many girls would be in her cabin? What was the general schedule? The questions whirled as she smoothed her shorts on her legs, idly wondering where they did laundry since she was almost out of clean clothes. She hated awkward silences, but she wasn't going to cower beneath his stony silence.

"All we have are Marie Biscuits," Amy set the package of cookies and plates down with a huff. "Someone," and she rolled her eyes towards Johann, "must've finished all the milk tart. At least we have coffee… it's almost ready."

Without a word of acknowledgment, Johann opened the package and began eating the cookies. Heidi took one, glad for something to do, thankful Amy was back. She read her cookie out loud, "Marie Biscuit."

"That's MAH-ree not Muh-REE," Johann corrected.

Amy rolled her eyes, "He's just offended because you are butchering his girlfriend's name."

Heidi pretended ignorance. "You're dating a cookie?"

Amy started giggling again. "It's not a cookie; it's a biscuit."

Heidi looked at her, "So, he's dating a *biscuit*?"

"No, he's going out with a girl named MAHree," she explained between giggles and mouthfuls of cookie. She motioned for Johann to keep explaining.

He stood, twin spots of color showing on his cheeks despite the dim light. "I'll get the coffee." He stomped into the kitchen, slamming the door behind him.

Amy dissolved into another fit of giggles. "Oh, Heidi, I'm so glad you are here!"

"Why, thank you, Amy." She was glad someone was. She needed a few more Amys to counter Johann, but for now, she was simply thankful she had Amy. Vera had already been friendly, and Mavis too, but Karl would definitely be a challenge. She had sensed an undercurrent of distrust with him and couldn't imagine why. Maybe he hadn't wanted her to come either, perhaps the board had made the decision, and he hadn't had a choice in the matter.

"Johann's girlfriend's name is Marie, and they have been going out since last September." Amy sighed. "She's beautiful."

Well, that was that. Safari Man had a beautiful girlfriend and hated Americans. She nibbled on her second cookie. It still didn't explain his actions, but it was helpful information.

"How many spoons of sugar do you take, Heidi?" Johann stuck his head out the kitchen door.

"Wow, he's going to serve us?" Amy raised her eyes in surprise.

"Um, just one, thank you," Heidi answered weakly. She really didn't want coffee this late at night, but she wasn't going to tell him that.

A few moments later, he set a tray of three steaming mugs and a sugar bowl in front of them. "One spoon of sugar for Heidi, two spoons for Amy, and this one's mine," he said, placing each cup directly in front of them.

He sat back across from Heidi, a look of challenge in his eyes, and lifted his mug in the form of a salute. "Enjoy."

Heidi didn't like what she saw in his eyes; there was undoubtedly something in her coffee that shouldn't be there. She had been around enough guys to recognize the look when she saw it. So, with a deep breath, she locked her eyes on his and steeled herself as she took the first sip of coffee. She blanched inwardly as the liquid hit her taste buds but kept her expression neutral. It tasted like hot coffee-flavored ocean. He had undoubtedly added salt instead of sugar. "Delicious," she murmured, her eyes never leaving his. "Are you sure you have enough sugar, Johann?"

His face reddened again, "Oh, I'm fine."

"No, please, allow me," and she took a heaping spoon of the suspect seasoning and dumped it into his coffee. "You need to keep your energy up," she added sagely. Now they would see if he could drink with a straight face, too.

"Why, thank you for your kindness, Heidi," he muttered and locked his eyes back on hers, pushing the mug away from him.

"You don't want it after all?" Heidi asked innocently, steeling herself for another sip of hers. She swallowed carefully despite her screaming taste buds. "This is the best coffee I've ever had. Thanks so much."

Amy was looking between them and the sugar bowl, and then she took her finger and dipped it in, licking her finger carefully. "Johann, *jy is 'n idioot!*" Then she grabbed Heidi's mug and threw the contents into the bushes.

Heidi started chuckling, and Johann grudgingly joined in, shaking his head in disbelief.

"Johann, you go in there and make some more!"

He stood, holding his hands in surrender, "No, I'm going to my office. I have to get Friday's schedule together."

Amy sat back down. "Well, Johann has met his match in you; that's all I can say." She took the sugar bowl and dumped it out.

"Does he do this to every newcomer?"

"Well, not exactly."

Heidi could tell Amy was being evasive, so she tried a new line of questioning.

"I suppose he just wants to make sure that whoever comes to the camp will be the right person to make the camp run well."

Amy nodded and flung her hands wide. "Oh yes, he even has a bunch of counselor camp rules.'"

"Camp rules? Should I know these?"

Amy shrugged, "Not really, especially since he already failed at his first rule."

"Which is?"

Amy posed in her best Johann stance and pointed her finger at Heidi, lowering her voice in an attempt to match his. "*Rule 1: never go out with another counselor.*" Then she straddled the bench and rolled her eyes. "Marie helped him break that rule."

"Oh, Marie was a counselor?" Heidi asked casually.

"*Ja,* last September, she came with her church for just a weekend camp. I noticed her more than the other workers that came with the church because she was so pretty. And, I noticed her even more when Johann started acting downright weird around her."

Heidi smiled, encouraging Amy to keep going.

"Then she showed up at camp two weeks later with a Brownie group."

"So, groups don't have to be from a church?"

"Oh, *ja.* I mean, churches get the first spot, but if we have an opening, other groups are welcome, provided they will follow our general curriculum." She paused. "Anyway, Johann was beside himself with joy when she showed up again. It was comical." She stopped and smiled, leaning forward, her eyes filled with mirth, "I even made a sign of Rule 1 and hung it on his cabin door, but he didn't think it was very funny."

Heidi chuckled as she imagined him finding that sign. "So, ever since then they've been dating?"

"Dating?" Amy narrowed her eyes at the terminology, "if you mean going out, then yes. Ever since then." She played with her now-empty coffee cup in front of her, "In fact, he goes nearly every Wednesday to visit her. She's starting at Wits."

"Wits?" Even as she asked, the picture was becoming a little clearer. Tuesday, he had picked *her* up from the airport. Maybe the trip on Tuesday had prevented him from visiting his beloved on Wednesday, and maybe that's why he had been so disgruntled with Heidi.

"The University of the Witwatersrand," Amy explained wistfully. "I had my acceptance to go there, you know."

Heidi glanced up sharply; this was something new. "Why didn't you go?"

Amy looked down, "My father... well, it doesn't matter." Then she stood abruptly. "I'm here, and because I'm here, I've gotten to meet you, and we are going to have a fantastic year being camp counselors together!"

Heidi rose, too, trying to buoy Amy's forced exuberance. "Yes, we are, Amy. Yes, we are!"

CHAPTER 4

The following day, it rained, and Heidi wondered briefly how the outdoor eating area would hold up, but it turned out it was covered sufficiently to keep the tables dry.

She positioned herself facing the bougainvillea, noting the faint grey outline of the mountains, and set her bowl of porridge-looking stuff they called *mieliepap* in front of her. She wondered if she could slip inside and make herself toast, but Karl was talking.

"You know, this church was just here six months ago, so you'll have to do a different series of lessons from the last time they were here." Karl was looking at Johann over his glasses.

"Actually, Karl, Heidi gave me a great idea for a lesson based on our bug zapper."

Everyone looked up expectantly.

"Sin is attractive, so you get closer to see what it's like and then, ZAP!" And with that, he slammed his arm down on the table, causing everyone, including Karl, to jump.

"Johann!"

Amy started giggling uncontrollably. "So, Heidi, you can see why Johann is so effective with the teenagers. They—they—" she stopped as another fit of hilarity took over. "They leave here in fear of being zapped if they step one foot in the wrong direction."

Karl was standing shaking his head at their antics. "I'm too old for this." He turned to his wife. "Vera, let's finish our coffee inside."

He wasn't exactly the most personable man she had ever met, and Heidi wondered what he was doing running a camp. Maybe he simply remained behind the scenes while Johann, Vera, and Amy interacted with all the campers. She smiled at Vera as she dutifully followed her husband inside and then glanced back at Johann and Amy.

"So, what else do I need to know?" She asked dryly.

"I think we need to find you some food you will eat." Amy was looking knowingly down at Heidi's barely touched *mieliepap*.

"Oh no, this is fine!" She didn't want Johann to label her a picky American on top of everything else he probably thought of her.

"Just leave Mavis's fresh-made *melk tart* for me!"

"I'm sure it's not ready yet. I'll go check. Heidi needs to eat."

Heidi stared down at her partially eaten food. Maybe the mystery dessert would be better than what was in front of her and make a good alternate breakfast choice.

"I'll get it for you ladies." There was a gleam in his eye that Heidi didn't like.

"No!" Both pairs of eyes looked at her in surprise. "I mean, no thank you," she faltered. "I'll just come and get my own." Knowing Johann, he was planning on sprinkling hers with rat poison, and she didn't want to spend the first few days in a strange place sick as a dog or, rather, dead as a rat.

She followed Johann into the kitchen and watched as he removed what resembled a vanilla-looking pie sprinkled with cinnamon from the refrigerator. Amy wasn't far behind them, and she grabbed plates and forks, setting them down next to the tart.

"Has it set already?"

"Looks like it – Mavis must have made a bunch of these last night and hidden them from us."

"Here, let me," she slid the tart away from Johann. "I've seen you cut a milk tart before."

She cut three generous slices and, placing one piece on a plate, handed it to Heidi. "Do you like milk tart?"

"I've never had it."

"Most Americans hate it." That was Johann.

"Well, I'm not 'most Americans.'" And with defiance in her eyes, Heidi took a huge forkful of the dessert, hoping it would be good, and put it in her mouth, instantly appreciating the smooth texture and sweet taste.

"Looks like she was right, Johann."

Heidi savored her last bite. If she had this for breakfast every day, she would have zero trouble maintaining her post-college weight gain, but she suspected once camps started, there would be no time to stand around and eat desserts for breakfast.

After they had finished, they all entered a room down a hallway off the kitchen where Karl and Vera were already busy working.

Karl cleared his throat. "Heidi, this is what we call the Stamp Club room." He paused, waiting for Heidi to take it all in.

The room was large, with shelves lining one entire wall and filing cabinets on the two other walls. Heidi could see labels on everything. On the fourth wall was a narrow table lined with tape dispensers, glue, pens, stationery, and then three large bins labeled "In," "Out," and "Address." The "Out" bin was full of letters.

Karl turned to Johann, "You'll have to take that one in today because I won't be able to."

Johann nodded as Karl focused once more on Heidi, who was staring with interest at the large table that filled the center of the room. It looked like a conference table, similar to the ones she had sat at in her dad's office back home.

"The Stamp Club is a Bible correspondence course using the postal system," Karl explained. "Vera is in charge of all the organizing and filing, although we all help her. But, if there is a question, we go to Vera. We have five record books – one for each year that we have been doing this—that includes the name of every camper that has been to our camp over the past five years."

As he talked, Vera grabbed one of the books and handed it to Heidi. She paged through it, astounded at the meticulous detail and lists of names. "Um, how many campers do you usually see in a year?" She couldn't imagine keeping track of them and realized Vera had her work cut out for her.

Karl reached over and took the book from her. "Well, according to this book, we saw 1,253 campers in 1985."

Heidi's eyes widened. "How do you see that many kids with so few of us working?"

Johann pulled out a chair and sat, tipping it onto the two back legs, which earned him an instant disapproving glance from Vera. "Like *Oom* Karl said, we are just the skeleton crew. Every church that comes brings their own workers. When they preregister for a camp, they give us an estimate of the number of children that will be coming, and then we calculate how many workers they will need. *Oom* Karl does that." He looked over at Karl, who was also pulling out a chair right as Mavis entered the room with a tea tray.

Once more, Heidi had the weird sense that she was on the set of a play and was merely an actress playing a part. When the scene was over, she would go back to normalcy. This particular act included tea being served. At a camp. What strange collision of worlds had she entered? The vibe was of a British manor, but in reality, she was in an office that lacked air conditioning, getting ready to play pen pal on a scale she had never imagined.

"Do you want rooibos or black tea, Miss?" Mavis was right next to her.

Heidi darted a startled look at Johann, unsure how she should answer when she saw the challenge in his eyes. "Oh, I would love some of that delicious Roy-boss," she recovered quickly, cringing at her pronunciation, remembering the fragrant tea from the morning before. There were sugar cubes and plain-looking cookies on the tray, and Heidi decided if she added enough sugar and ate a few cookies, it would substitute for the Coke she was craving. Maybe she would survive camp on Mavis's stew and all the readily available baked goods.

The others grinned at each other except for Johann who was practically scowling, while Mavis poured her tea.

Heidi glanced back over at Johann, wondering what his problem was. She could play the game of the British Manor lady. His frown held a challenge, and she knew how to rise to any challenge. She calmly reached out and spooned a couple sugar cubes into her tea and stirred them daintily as if being served tea at 9am every morning was the most normal thing for her.

Karl cleared his throat and continued. "Once we determine how many workers the church needs to bring, we send out a packet of training materials that they must complete at least two weeks before the camp starts. If we don't get the materials back, I telephone the pastor of the church and talk with him about the importance of having all the information. Usually, they comply, but sometimes, well, sometimes they do not, and then those camps do not go as smoothly."

Karl stopped and took a sip of his tea, and Heidi had the urge to laugh. Here was a stocky, burly man with a guttural voice sipping tea as daintily as a lady from a Jane Austen novel. Determined to avoid Johann's glare, she shot a look at Amy, who grinned back at her. Heidi knew Amy didn't find anything comical in the scene but was merely eager to please, and the shared grin helped anchor Heidi, even if only slightly.

"If this happens," Karl went on, "I make a note of it, and the next time the church phones us to make a reservation, I remind them of last year and give them one more chance to comply. If they don't, then they are not welcome back."

Johann jumped in. "We have become so busy over the past few years that we actually can do this. The churches all over the Transvaal love our camp and want to come here, so they are eager to do as we ask."

Apparently sensing Heidi's surprise, Vera explained in a quiet voice, "We can't have workers coming who don't go through the training. We want to ensure all our workers are prepared in advance to share God's love. We also use it as a way to screen people."

Heidi nodded, surmising the training materials and information were in place of the background checks her church at home had recently started requiring of all Sunday School teachers.

Karl stood and turned to Johann, his tea half-finished. "I'll let you explain the rest; I have to get to my office."

Heidi shifted her attention towards Johann, doing her best to focus as he outlined the program.

On the first day of camp, campers were given the first lesson to complete as a class. Then the work would be graded, or *marked,* as Heidi noted was the matching South African term. The campers' names would be entered into the record book, and so it began. From then on, every completed lesson was duly recorded. That way, when a camper returned, even years later, they would be given the next lesson in the series. If it had been too long, they would often pull the camper's file and let them go over the completed lessons.

"It's quite sweet, actually," Amy explained with a catch in her throat. "Some of them start when they are young, maybe eleven years old. Then, they come back as teenagers, and we pull their file and go over their old lessons. Often, they get so emotional, seeing what they wrote as a child and knowing that the God they were close to at eleven is still the same God who wants to be close to them at fifteen or sixteen."

Vera smiled at her daughter, "It makes us all realize that what we do has a lasting impact."

Heidi glanced at Johann and back to the women, an excitement building within her. This is what she had left her preplanned cookie-cutter life in the States for, to come and be part of something that made a difference.

"So, when do they get their first lesson?" She wanted to know everything about how it worked. She couldn't imagine keeping track of all those campers, much less keeping them from quitting from one camp year until the next.

Johann's excitement was palpable as he continued the explanation. He went to a large shelving area, pulled a lesson from the lowest shelf, and handed it to Heidi. Each day of the camp, they would complete another lesson, and on the final day of camp, they would receive an already stamped and addressed take-home lesson. The stamp was included so there would be no reason not to mail it back, hence the name "Stamp Club." Initially, they had tried other names but finding the stamped return envelope became such a symbol of the course it had eventually morphed from "Bible Correspondence Course" to simply, "Stamp Club."

Campers were to complete the new lesson at home and mail it back to the camp. And that's what the "skeleton crew" did between camps. They read and graded and recorded the mailed-in lessons.

Then, they would mail out the next one along with a note of encouragement. The graded lesson would be filed in the camper's file. Vera oversaw the filing as well. If a church brought more workers than were needed for counselors, she would use them to help with filing and addressing, but nothing ever happened without her oversight. If they got behind, they would solicit help from volunteers at various churches until they were caught up. With the meal planning and the mailing, she was a busy woman, and Heidi looked at her with a new appreciation.

While Johann had been explaining, Amy and Vera had grabbed lessons from the incoming bin and were opening them and marking off names along with the completed lessons. As she watched them work, making notations in red and writing in the margins, she wondered what would happen if the camper got everything wrong.

Amy glanced up. "When you mark a lesson, you can use the answer key from our answer books on the shelves. But since we have marked so many of these first lessons, none of us need the answer key anymore. Once a camper gets past a certain number, I usually refer to the answer key, but people like Johann," and she rolled her eyes at him, "never need the answer key."

"But, Heidi, we want you to always use the answer key." The edge in his voice was unmistakable, causing Vera to look over in consternation.

"—just until you get used to the lessons, Heidi," she said gently, her eyes darting to Johann.

Johann looked down and then abruptly turned, grabbed the answer key off the shelf, and plunked it in front of Heidi before getting his own handful of lessons to work on.

Heidi, doing her best to ignore him, looked at Amy and Vera. "If I grade one, will you check and make sure I am doing it right?"

"Oh sure," they both chimed.

"In fact," Amy added, "why don't you look at these that I've just finished and compare them to Johann's *answer key*." She frowned at Johann, and Heidi watched as the same twin splotches of red appeared on his cheeks.

She would have to quit analyzing safari-man with his penchant for blushing. She turned her focus back to Amy. "What if a camper gets everything wrong?"

"That happens quite often," Vera smiled, clearly trying to be extra kind to counter Johann's abrupt behavior. "When it does, we enclose the same lesson with the marked one and send it back to them, encouraging them to try again."

Heidi nodded, eager to get started. She stood and, mimicking what the others had done, grabbed her own handful of lessons from the "In" box. Her mind filled with anticipation, and taking a sip of the tea, she started to scan her first lesson.

Eventually, Vera left the room and Johann stood to stretch. "I'm going to take these finished ones to the post," he said to no one in particular.

Amy jumped up eagerly. "And Heidi and I are coming with you!"

Heidi looked between Amy and Johann, expecting him to refuse, but he simply shrugged and started transferring the completed letters to a bag. Watching those letters go into the bag, she had the overwhelming urge to write home, even if it was only a short note.

"Wait!"

Johann paused without bothering to turn around.

"I mean, can I put a letter in there for my parents?"

Amy's look softened while Johann remained immobile.

"I just have to run to my room and grab it. Do I have time?" She didn't bother to tell them she hadn't actually even written the letter; she was sure she could get something down in a hurry. But the fact letters were leaving camp meant her parents could hear from her sooner than she thought.

"We go to the post office every day." Johann had resumed his task but was now jamming letters into the bag with a vengeance.

Amy shot him a warning look and then patted Heidi on the back. "We will wait for you, Heidi; take as long as you need. I... um... want to change my clothes anyway before we leave."

"You want to change your *clothes*?" Johann thundered. "Since when do you change your clothes before we go to the smallest *dorp* in the Northern Transvaal?"

Amy flipped her hair and winked at Heidi, "Since *today*." And she fluttered out of the room, leaving Heidi with Johann, muttering as he tied off the bag.

"Tell *Amy* that once she has on the right *clothes,* I will be waiting in my office." His voice reeked of disapproval, and he stomped out of the room, slamming the door behind him.

Heidi stood there a moment, stupefied by his continual rudeness. Yesterday on the tour, he had actually seemed nice, especially when explaining the Counting Tree. How did someone this moody lead children at a Christian camp? Then, remembering her chance to get word home, she turned to go to the bunk but remembered that her letter-writing materials were in the missing suitcase. So, she grabbed a piece of stationery from the shelf.

> *Dear Mom and Dad,*
>   *I arrived safely yesterday and was met at the airport by one of the camp workers.*

She paused. She couldn't and wouldn't expound on her chilly reception. Nor did they need to know the airlines had lost her luggage.

> *We drove past Johannesburg, which is a huge city, probably bigger than Miami, on the way to camp which is about a two-hour drive north of the city.*

Her Dad liked geography and would enjoy that tidbit.

> *We stopped to get something to eat at a restaurant called Wimpy. I was a bit worried because of the name, but the food was delicious. By the time we got to camp, it was dark.*

And she had stopped to buy bras, and, after falling asleep, Johann had carried her into her cabin. More information they didn't need to know.

Today we are answering letters that are part of the Bible correspondence course that the camp does. When I heard they were going into town to mail them, I decided to jot you a quick note and tell you I am fine and love you both very much. Because of the correspondence course, there are probably a lot of trips to the post office, so we should be able to stay in touch quite easily.

> *Please give the twins lots of hugs from me,*
> *Lots of love,*
> *Heidi*

As she was grabbing an envelope and addressing it, Amy came back in the room in the same outfit she had worn all day.

"Mr. Ants-in-his-pants is sitting in his *bakkie* ready to leave yesterday already." She raised her eyebrows.

"OK!" Heidi hurriedly sealed and addressed the letter.

Amy jumped into the truck, and Heidi followed, letter in hand. Johann glanced at Amy and then stared at the letter in Heidi's hand.

"You used camp stationery." It was a statement more than a question. Then he threw the truck into reverse, spinning tires on gravel as he maneuvered out of the parking area.

"She can use as much camp stationery as she wants, Johann." Amy would protect Heidi. "In fact, since Heidi isn't taking a salary, I would think that…."

Johann flung his free hand in the air, palm facing outward. "OK, OK, I get the picture." Then, in an apparent attempt to shift the subject from his attitude, he added, "and you look nice in your fresh clothes, Amy."

"Why, thank you, Johann." She was all sugar sweet now, glancing sidelong at Heidi and winking dramatically. "I wanted to look my best for the *smallest dorp in the Northern Transvaal.*"

Either the guy was oblivious, or he was playing Amy as much

as she had played him. The letter with the Camp Timothy logo felt weighty in her hand. She needed to go shopping. She didn't want to be accused of taking advantage of camp resources again, even if Amy said it was fine. Amy certainly wasn't in charge, even though she was doing her utmost to smooth Heidi's path.

For the umpteenth time since that morning, she was grateful for Amy. As clear as it was that Amy and Vera were glad to have her, it was equally clear Johann and Karl resented her presence.

"Did Johann tell you he and I are practically brother and sister?" Amy asked, breaking into her reverie.

"Uh... no?"

"Amy...." Johann's voice held a note of warning.

But Amy went on. "Yes, Johann came to live at camp when I was only ten."

Heidi could tell Johann was uncomfortable with Amy's reminiscing, but she hoped she would continue. Maybe it would explain why Johann was such a grump and hated Americans so much.

"I was so glad to finally not be the only child." She elbowed Johann playfully, ignoring his scowl. "Actually, he was only here for school holidays or when the school released him for a long weekend, but it was so much fun going to the bus station to fetch him each time."

Heidi was intrigued. What had happened to his parents? Was he truly related to the Voskamps?

"So, Heidi, do you have any camp questions so far?" Johann clearly wanted to change the topic of conversation.

"Yes!" She held out her hand, ticking off fingers as she spoke. "So, campers come tomorrow. What is the schedule? How many girls will I have? How does everyone hang their chimes every week and not destroy the Counting Tree?"

There was a stunned silence after she finished, and then Amy burst into laughter. "Sounds like she has some questions, Johann."

"*Ai-ja-jai,*" he rubbed his hand over his face. "Let's start with the easiest one. Remember, everyone is allowed to hang their chime on our tree, but we encourage them to take them home and hang them somewhere at home as a reminder. It really depends on the group we have. Some kids who come back year after year tell us of their own tree at home that has a chime from every year. Others like to hang it here. Anyway, it works out and keeps our tree from getting weighed down from all the blessings since that would kind of ruin the symbolism."

"Sorry, kids, the weeping willow is dead because we hung too many blessings on it," Amy intoned. "Please stop thanking God."

Laughter filled the truck, and Johann continued. "I'll answer the other questions later when I go over the schedule with you."

"You know, Ian is coming to work with us this weekend," Johann winked at Amy.

"He is? Since when?" Amy's eyes sparkled with something new. "How did you find out?"

"Well, there's this thing called a telephone...."

"No, you *domkop*," she elbowed him in the ribs, "how did it happen that he is coming with this week's group?"

Listening to their banter, Heidi sighed inwardly. It seemed Amy had someone named Ian, and Johann had his biscuit-girlfriend. She fingered the empty spot on her left hand and wondered if Chris was missing her. She turned her head, effectively blocking out their chatter, and watched the scenery pass by. She had been asleep for this part of the drive and watched with interest the long grasses blowing in the wind. The terrain was hilly in one direction and flattened out ahead of them. Few trees dotted the landscape, and the wide-open spaces warmed Heidi's heart. Everything was bright, including the dirt on the side of the road. Florida dirt was almost grey, but here it was a bright orange-brown swirling in miniature whirlwinds as the truck passed.

They drove into a small town and parked outside a post office and a convenience store. Heidi handed her letter to Amy and went in to find stationery. She had just settled for a stack of plain paper and envelopes when she heard hostile voices.

"Please, I wanted money back." A young African woman was

at the counter with a few purchases.

"Well, it's *Chappies* or nothing!"

Heidi watched in horror as the proprietor threw a handful of brightly covered little candy squares onto the counter. The woman bowed her head and collected the scattered candies, scooping them into her hand. Heidi bent to help her get them off the floor when the man bellowed behind the counter.

"What do we have here, a K—lover?"

Heidi stood. She could feel the color drain from her face as shock and confusion set in. She placed her stationery on the counter, making a beeline for the exit. She quickly walked into the post office searching for Johann and Amy, only to find a hush descending on the crowded room as everyone turned to stare at her.

"Madam, you need to go next door." It was the lady with the *Chappies*. She pointed through an opening, and Heidi realized, horrified, that there were two sides to the post office, and she was on the wrong side.

What was this place? How could she function in a place where segregation was normal? She turned quickly and went back to Johann's truck and climbed inside, tears slipping down her face. Hearing Amy and Johann, she hurriedly wiped her face. How could she not have prepared herself for living the reality before her? Had she really thought reading one novel was sufficient? She should have researched and talked to the South Africans that lived around the corner from her parents. She should have been prepared. There was no excuse for naivety.

"Scoot over, Heidi!" Amy was at the door, waiting to get in. Her smile faltered as she took in Heidi's expression. "You OK?"

Heidi nodded quickly and scooted in. Now she would be smashed between Johann and Amy, and there would be no hiding how upset she was.

Johann climbed in a slammed the door. "Ok, back to camp and the schedule and then—" He stopped, taking in Amy gesturing towards Heidi and Heidi's downcast face. "What happened?"

Amy shrugged.

Heidi sighed, "I'm sorry, I just didn't know—" Her voice caught, and she swallowed hard to counter the pressure of tears.

Amy put her arm around her gently. "What happened?"

She angled her head towards Amy and wished Johann was far away. "The man in the store. I was in line. And this lady asked for change, and then he just threw these candies at her instead, and they went all over the floor, and I helped her pick them up, and he—he well, he called me a name. And the poor woman! And what are '*Chappies*' even?"

Silence.

"They do that sometimes, Heidi." Amy's voice was gentle. "*Chappies* are little squares of gum that cost 1 cent each. We used to come and buy them as kids. They have cartoons inside. But sometimes the shop owner doesn't have change, so he just gives people *Chappies*."

"Has he done that to you or Johann before?"

"No." Johann's voice was rough.

She turned to him, trying to analyze his tone but was unsuccessful. "Then I came to find you in the post office, but I went on the wrong side and…." She stopped.

Amy rubbed her arm. "You will get used to the differences, Heidi. I'm sorry."

But Heidi didn't want to get used to the differences. She wanted to fix this. How could she live and work here and simply 'get used to' segregation? How could she function in this place?

The drive back was subdued, everyone lost in their own thoughts. As soon as they reached camp, she went directly to the bathroom to wash her face and gain composure. Staring into the mirror, she knew she needed to be stronger and less emotional. Johann and Amy shouldn't have to worry about her reactions; they needed a tough coworker they could rely on. She suspected there would be many more surprises coming her way. She needed to be ready.

CHAPTER 5

That evening after dinner, Johann sat opposite Amy and Heidi with a stack of papers. He was all business now, and Heidi was relieved. Nobody had mentioned the post office. Plus, it seemed she was finally going to get some information about what was expected of her.

Amy, seeing the stack of papers, stood. "I'll find us dessert and make coffee," she offered. "Don't worry, I'll sugar it myself." Her voice trailed off as she entered the kitchen.

"Just let me organize these, and then I'll be ready," Johann said.

She was happy to wait and focus on the scenery beyond him. Then, covertly, she shifted her gaze to the enigma working in front of her. She wondered where his own family was and why he called Karl and Vera Uncle and Aunt.

"So, what's the verdict?" He had caught her out.

"About what?"

"About your analysis of me."

"Don't be so egotistical." Her face was beet red as she took the first paper he held out.

"This is our basic schedule," he intoned. "Every counselor gets one to follow. You can stick it on the wall of your cabin with some *Prestik* or just keep it with you."

Heidi had no idea what *Prestik* was, but she nodded, taking the paper from him. She glanced over the schedule, relieved to see quite a bit of structure. She had worked at enough children's activities between church and volunteer work in high school to know that things quickly fell apart without enough structure, making the workers' jobs even more difficult.

"Here is the outline of the topics we will be discussing during the group meetings this weekend. We tailor the topics based on how often the church comes. Then we break into smaller groups. We come up with these groups according to where they are in the Stamp Club. Usually, the largest group is the newest group. It takes a while to divide the children accurately, but Vera is quite organized, and most of the time, we get it right. Of course, there's always the child who maintains they've completed five levels, and we have no record of them. Then, they're not too happy when we put them in the beginning group." He shrugged. "I'll put you, for this weekend, in the second group. The topics are still basic, but the group size is smaller."

She wanted to interject that she was perfectly capable of handling big groups and complex topics but decided to leave it alone. At least he would trust her with her own group at her first camp. She smiled and looked past him, noting the distant mountains tinged with pink as the sun lowered in the sky. Here, in this beautiful setting, she had the opportunity to make a difference.

He followed her line of sight and then handed her a stack of sample worksheets and an answer key. "These are what your group will work on. They complete it independently; you're just there to answer questions and expand when they ask. Don't give out answers, even when you're tempted to."

She wanted to roll her eyes but refrained. "How will I have enough of each one?"

His stern demeanor softened, and he smiled. "That's where Vera comes in. Not only will she know who gets what, but she will also have enough of each worksheet available. This system couldn't run without her organization."

Grateful for the genuine smile in her direction, she nodded again. He really had an attractive smile; it enhanced his eyes, and she could easily get lost in those eyes. Thankfully his rudeness towards her would keep her in check. She bet every camper fell in love with him the instant he smiled.

"Here are some issues you may encounter with your girls."

She snapped back to attention, inwardly berating herself for daydreaming. Quickly looking down at the paper he was handing her, she was surprised at the depth: anorexia, bulimia, sexual activity, bullying, inferiority complex... the list went on. This tied in with what he had been telling her at the Counting Tree the day before, and it was beyond important to get it right.

"Now," his face was earnest, "it is my experience that all of these issues have a common root: lack of thankfulness."

Heidi balked, opening her mouth to protest, thinking of how such an assessment would be laughed at by her peers.

"I know people might think that's an oversimplification," he hurried on, "but let's take the anorexic, for example. Every camper, no matter how often they return, is reminded that they're unique, created by the Creator of the universe, who loves them unconditionally and has created them for a unique purpose. Now enter a young girl who struggles with her body image. We go back to this fundamental truth of being created by a loving God for a unique purpose, and we try to get them to internalize this truth. Then, we hopefully lead them to thankfulness for this truth.

"So, we ask them what they love to do. Let's say the girl says she loves to paint. We talk to her about her painting, about her art. We try gently lead her to the realization that maybe her art is her unique gift. Or maybe she's naturally good with little kids. Regardless, we show her that this is a gift that makes her unique. It is hard to be self-destructive if you are focused on being thankful.

"Of course, there's always the kid who says they're not good at anything, so we bring up how good we've noticed they are at rounders or swimming or listening during the meetings or cleaning up after meals... you get the picture.

"But we try get them to be thankful for something that makes them unique. The beauty is that this concept works for many teenage issues that they deal with. And remember the three things I told you yesterday." He held up his fingers, enumerating as he spoke. "We want to communicate the knowledge that God is present, that God loves them more than they can comprehend, and that there is always something or someone to be thankful for."

Heidi still felt doubtful. If only it were that easy.

"You have to understand that we only see our campers for a finite time. We are not psychologists, although a psychology degree would be helpful. We don't have time to delve into their past, but this basic, simple principle works... trust me. Just make sure, when and if they tell you their problems, that you validate their experience." He paused, apparently noting the question in her eyes.

"OK, imagine you came to me and said you were being bullied."

Heidi tilted her head, ready to listen.

"And it was difficult for you to confide in me because you were scared the bully would find out."

Heidi nodded.

"And then, instead of validating your story, I said something dumb like, 'I'm sure they are just teasing you and don't mean it....'" He paused again. "Then, what would you think?"

"That I should never have confided in you."

"Yes, it trivializes their pain." He smiled in approval. "So, we always validate their experience, even if, at face value, it seems insignificant to us."

Once again, despite her doubt, Heidi felt a glimmer of excitement take hold that she had experienced earlier in the Stamp Club room. Here was a place intentionally doing something to grow the hearts and minds of children and teenagers, and she was now part of it. At the same time, she felt overwhelmed and unsure. Would she really have to deal with all these issues with every group of campers that were part of her cabin over the next year or two? Was she actually supposed to tell a struggling teen they simply needed to be thankful? Did that line of reasoning really help in all situations?

"Can you tell me again what you do about abuse?" She didn't want to be negative but couldn't fathom telling an abused child to be thankful.

Johann blanched and looked away. "Abuse," he sighed deeply, "there is no weekend solution for abuse or many of the issues we often face. For many kids, the solution may require lifelong work. Our hope and prayer is to start them on the path to healing."

She watched him carefully, her heart sinking. He hadn't seemed as bothered by the topic the previous day, only disappointed she wasn't getting it. This was obviously something he had great difficulty with, and she wondered why. She wished she could take the question back to save him from his obvious discomfort. But it had been born out of an earnest desire to be as prepared as possible.

He straightened and began again. "Like I said yesterday, we are not trying to teach a child to be thankful for a terrible situation; we are trying to teach them that God is present, He loves them more than they can comprehend, and to find something, anything, in their lives to be thankful for." He spoke slowly like she was a five-year-old.

Heidi nodded. She *had* heard him, all three times. "But surely we have to do more?"

"Well, like I told you yesterday, usually in the span of camp, we don't have the time to build up enough trust for campers to tell us the truth of their situations. However, we always stay on alert, looking for signs. And, if we suspect any ongoing abuse at all, we speak immediately with the church or group leader that the child is with. They then have the awful responsibility of researching the situation after they get home. We, as a short-term camp, simply don't have that ability. But we can, however, stay in touch with the child, encourage them in their growth in God through the Stamp Club, and pray that the adults in their lives are actually going to do something about the situation." He shook his head, disgust evident. "Many times, I fear after a situation comes to light, people simply look away, not wanting to deal with it, forgetting that a child's life is hanging off a cliff." He stopped again, staring past her.

Heidi waited, barely moving. Was this the reason Johann had come to live with the Voskamps?

Still avoiding her gaze, his eyes darting to the side, his voice flat, he continued. "If we find out abuse occurred in the past and are convinced it has stopped, then we spend our time reassuring the child that the guilt they feel is not from God. We help them memorize I Timothy 1:7, 'For God has not given us the spirit of fear,

62

but of power and of love and of a sound mind.' We go back to our theme – that they are unique and loved by God *unconditionally*. We focus on that: the unconditional love of God and the fact that the abuse is *never* their fault."

Heidi sat quietly, jotting notes on the handout he had given her, her thoughts racing. She imagined a different Johann, a scared, hurt, guilt-ridden little boy, and she wished she could hug that child and tell him she would protect him. She could feel tears pricking the back of her eyes, but forced them away to focus on what Johann was handing her.

"This is a sample notebook we want all our counselors to keep."

She opened it, looking at the list of names, dates, anecdotes, and prayer requests.

"This is my book, but if you want to see a better one—hold on." And then he turned towards the open kitchen door. "Amy!"

Out she came with the half-eaten milk tart from that morning and three mugs of coffee. "Yes, dear?" Her tone was mocking, and Heidi watched as Johann raised his eyebrows.

"What took you so long?"

She made a face at him.

"Never mind. Can you go get your perfect camper notebook and show it to Heidi?"

After she brought out the book, Heidi paged through it, feeling utterly overwhelmed. Between the campers coming tomorrow, the Stamp Club, and the conversation she had just had with Johann, she felt wholly inadequate.

After taking a few bites of dessert, Amy sighed, "Heidi, let's go lie on the trampoline and talk while Johann washes the dishes. She's learned enough for today, Johann."

Heidi watched as Johann once again gave Amy a surprised look and nodded.

"At night?" Heidi asked, wondering if Amy had sensed she needed a break.

"Sure, I do it all the time. We can watch for shooting stars; it's almost dark enough."

"Well, OK. But won't we need a flashlight?"

Johann glanced up instantly, "Don't worry, Heidi, I will get you a torch. I'll be right back."

Amy stared into the darkness after Johann's retreating back, "I'm going to run to my cabin and fetch my torch," she spoke over her shoulder, rushing out of the kitchen.

Heidi watched Amy's retreating figure. It seemed the last time Johann had been super helpful, she had gotten salt in her coffee. She knew one thing, her sense of unreality, as if she was on the set of a long play, was getting worse, not better. She still hadn't recovered from their trip into town, and her brain fog was confusing everything. At least the pie or tart had been just as good as that morning, and there was food in her stomach. If she got hungry later, she could look for some leftover stew from the day before. That had been infinitely better than the sausage they had served tonight. She stacked the dessert plates and put them in the sink with the other dirty dishes, and turned to leave. And there stood Johann, flaming torch in hand, just beyond the doorway, a teasing glint in his eyes.

Safari Man had returned. And he expected her to carry fire.

Well, she wasn't going to act scared in front of Johann, so she moved towards the open door. "So, this will scare the snakes away?" She tried to sound casual, like talking to a man holding a torch was the most natural thing in the world.

He quirked his head to the side, considering, "Most of the time."

Most of the time. Heidi wanted to grimace, but she merely stepped outside and moved to take the torch from him.

He pulled his arm back. "Make sure you carry it away from your head; we wouldn't want your hair to catch fire."

Heidi felt herself flush. Her hair wasn't that crazy. "I think I know how to carry a torch safely, Johann," she countered, her voice laced with sarcasm. Then, with as much confidence as she could muster, she took it from him and, without a backward glance, headed towards Amy's cabin. His warning fresh in her mind, she held it as far away from herself as possible and wished Amy would hurry.

Halfway to Amy's cabin, she froze, worried the wind would

blow a spark onto her clothes. With relief, she saw Amy exit her cabin, and her eyes widen in shock. At the same time, she heard Johann laughing uproariously from behind her. Obviously, she had fallen for something and wanted to turn and punch him, but she was too scared to move. The fire was now consuming most of the stick, and with the wind's aid, had gotten twice as large.

"Just drop it!" Amy cried. "You're standing on dirt; it won't hurt anything."

That was all Heidi needed, and she dropped the burning stick and jumped back, watching as it burned itself out on the ground. Johann had grabbed a hose, and in seconds he had doused the remaining embers with a stream of water while Amy yelled at him in a foreign language. Johann countered her tirade, his laughter punctuating the night.

Heidi didn't need to know what they were saying; she felt humiliated. Leaving them to play fireman, she retreated quietly, walking through the breezeway towards the steps that led to the pool. Once there, she sank gratefully onto the swing, inhaling the night air and trying to sort through her emotions.

She had expected to come here and work but hadn't expected opposition. She had been completely naïve. She had thought once she left Chris's disdain and her parent's sadness and Brianna's incredulity and was here working, she would be fine. But it seemed Johann would give her as much antagonism here as she had been handed before she left. She wondered at his dislike and why he obviously wanted to chase her away. She wondered why, if God had so clearly led her here, He couldn't make the transition a little bit easier. Tears slipped down her cheeks, and she wiped them away as quickly as she could. She didn't want anyone to see her crying and think she regretted coming.

It wasn't long before Amy found her. "Heidi?" Her voice was tentative. "Can I sit here?"

Heidi nodded in the darkness. She loved how they all said "here."

The swing creaked and moved as Amy joined her. "Heidi,"

Amy's voice was so quiet Heidi could barely hear her. She held out the flashlight towards her, and Heidi took it. "That's what we call a *torch* here in South Africa. I suppose you call it something else."

Heidi nodded mutely. She really had been duped. Score a major victory for Safari Man. She took a deep breath. "Yes, Amy, we would call this a flashlight. A torch is… well, you now know what we call a torch."

Amy giggled. "Yes, I now know, and I will never forget it either!"

Heidi turned to her and smiled. Amy's laughter sounded good. "I suppose I did look pretty frightening standing in front of your cabin holding fire like a cavewoman or something!"

Amy's giggles intensified, and then Heidi, picturing the scene from Amy's point of view, started to laugh too. The laughter, a stark contrast to the tears, was cleansing.

"You know," Amy exclaimed between laughs. "I think you had better check with me before you do anything Johann tells you to do, just for the first few days until he starts acting normal. Then when he figures out he can't get to you, he'll stop. Frankly, once the campers get here, though, I'll be surprised if he does anything subversive. Camp means everything to him."

Heidi seriously doubted Johann would ever act *normal* towards her, but she would take Amy's advice.

CHAPTER 6

Heidi woke the following day, excitement laced with fear buzzing through her. She was surprised and pleased with how much better she had slept and that most of the jet lag fog had lifted. And now, she was on her third morning, already waking with the sunrise. Jumping out of bed, she threw on her clothes and grabbed her Bible and journal. She would start her morning at the Counting Tree.

Slipping through the quiet camp in the early morning haze, the nagging sense of unreality returned. It still felt like she was part of a play, that at any minute, she would find herself back in the US. But she was indeed here, in Africa, getting ready to be part of the first camp. She breathed deeply of the dewy morning air, willing her mind to catch up with her new reality, picking her way along the stone steps and across the softball field to the Tree.

Ducking under its canopy, she settled on the wooden bench and gazed around in awe. The rising sun filtered through the hanging branches causing the dewdrops to reflect the light like thousands of diamonds. Stillness enveloped her, calming her trepidation. Truly God was here; she could sense His presence. Opening her Bible to Hebrews 2, she began reading,

13And again I will put my trust in Him, and again, behold I and the children which God hath given me.

That was her verse. The verse she had claimed for camp. The verse that would help her focus on each child she would have the opportunity to interact with. Every child would come with a need, would be placed in her cabin for a reason. Her God wasn't a God of happenstance, and she prayed she would be sensitive to the needs of all her campers, that she would have an impact on their lives, no matter how small.

She stood then, walking amongst the chimes, reading the dates

67

and the words the children had placed. Then she stopped at one in surprise. It had only one word on the front, "Karl," and the date was 1979. She turned it over in her hands, wondering, before gently releasing it, watching it oscillate until it was still.

Eventually, she gathered her Bible and notebook; she needed to find the others and some breakfast. She was sure Johann had a plan for them. Weaving through the branches and out into the full force of the morning sunlight, she came face to face with the man himself.

"Oh, good morning!"

He grunted a response, his gaze perplexed.

She lifted her chin. "Am I late for something?"

"Um, no."

She stood for a moment, waiting for an explanation but decided it was time to exit when none was forthcoming. Perhaps he came here every morning, or perhaps he had been looking for her but didn't want her to know. The fact was, it was Johann, and she needed to quit trying to understand him.

***

Johann stared at her retreating form with a tinge of admiration. Heidi had a way about her that was uniquely her own. It was only her third morning at camp, and, despite the time difference, she was already awake early enough to read her Bible at the Tree. He was slightly miffed she had taken his spot, but he had other places he could go. Maybe she really was genuine; maybe she was here to serve God and her campers.

He thought back to the day before and the *Chappies* incident. Clearly, she had a tender heart for others; and she wasn't judgmental about it. Others came and started loftily implying that if South Africans were smart enough, they could fix the situation. But Heidi, Heidi appeared to understand the depths of both the pain and the disparity. Then he thought how she had gamely taken the torch from him last night. Her eyes had said, "challenge accepted," even though he had read their fear.

He sighed. The last thing he wanted was to soften towards her this early. But he had to admit she was eager to learn and had been incredibly intuitive the previous night while he was explaining counseling her campers. Actually, her intuition had brought her too close to the truth. He shuddered at the thought of the American girl pitying him.

He kicked at the dirt. So, maybe Heidi was here for the right reasons, but it still didn't change the fact Marie should have been in her place. He needed to focus on that, yet, deep down, he wondered if he could. He was a camp director, after all. He loved God and knew he had a gift for getting to the heart of people. He shouldn't chase someone away who had the same goals as he did, regardless of his disappointment over Marie.

***

By four o'clock, Heidi was worn out. The entire day had been information overload. After breakfast, Johann had handed out typewritten schedules, copied with blue gel by a ditto machine she had never known existed. Then, they had gone into town to purchase last-minute supplies and driven to an even farther away town to shop for more groceries. The store was aptly called Makro and rivaled the Costco's and Sam's Club stores of home.

Upon their return, Mavis had immediately set to putting away the groceries and talking with Vera about the meals. Heidi sat in a daze at the steel table, nibbling on what they called a rusk, a hard, crusty piece of bread from a box titled "Ouma's." She had no idea what an *Ouma* was and was too tired to ask.

"You may want to go and rest for a little, my dear." Vera's voice was gentle.

"Oh!" Heidi flushed. Everyone else was still going full strength.

"Go on, now!" Vera could be quite commanding even behind all her sweetness. "You will need non-stop energy once the campers arrive."

Heidi didn't need any more convincing. Gratefully she slid off the stool and went to her cabin. She would lie down briefly. Falling onto her bed, she closed her eyes and then forced them open to take in the room. Everything was in order, her leaded eyelids closed, and she was asleep.

***

Johann was beyond irritated. The campers had arrived, and nobody had seen Heidi. He couldn't believe it. He glanced around, thinking rapidly. Maybe she had left a clue in her cabin. Motioning for Amy to keep everyone corralled at the eating area, he rushed over, knocked loudly, and barged in. And there she was, curled up in slumber, oblivious to the chaos that awaited her. He caught his breath, anger warring with the picture of serenity she created. His heart pounded loudly, and he swallowed hard before reaching out and gripping her shoulder.

"Heidi!" His voice came out in a croak.

She stirred and then settled back into what he assumed was a deeper sleep. No, no, no, she couldn't. Maybe her jet lag wasn't truly over after all.

"Heidi, wake up!" This time his voice was louder.

She stirred and briefly opened her eyes. "Yes?"

Oh, for goodness' sake, he wanted to throw her over his shoulder and dump her in the pool. "The campers are here. Wake up!"

Her eyes flew open and widened in a questioning shock. She sat up so fast he had to jump back to keep their heads from knocking together.

"What on earth...?"

"We need you at the tables. Now. Come on, Heidi!"

She groaned and rubbed her hand over her face. "I'm sorry, I... I...."

He backed towards the door, keeping a steady eye on her. "Are you awake? Can you be there in less than five minutes?"

"Ye... es." She stood shakily and then glanced up at him. "You can go. I'm... I'm awake."

With one last look to be sure, he left, slamming the door behind him for good measure. But it wasn't from anger; it was from fresh annoyance at how the picture of Heidi's sleeping form had already etched itself into his mind. He had a camp to run. He had campers waiting for him and church leaders needing instructions, and his traitorous mind had utterly derailed.

***

Heidi couldn't believe how awful she felt. She stumbled out to the bathrooms in a daze, not looking toward the tables. Inside, she splashed water over her face and scrunched her hair into a bun. It was a pity that a group of high-octane junior high strangers blocked access to serious caffeine. She should never have fallen asleep. What a way to start her camp counseling career.

She lifted her chin and squared her shoulders. She would fake some energy until the real thing hit. Then, with a deep breath, she stepped out into the sunshine and strode purposefully towards the campers, her insides quaking with every step.

She joined the outer edges of the group and shot a look over towards Amy, who was leaning into a young man. So, Amy's man had arrived. Heidi was glad for her. She wondered briefly if Johann's Marie ever assisted at camp. She returned smiles and nodded at the inquisitive glances thrown her way. These campers must be returnees and were obviously curious about who she was. But Johann was calling out boys' names and directing them to their counselor. There was a fringe of adults nearby, and Heidi assumed they were the counselors the church had sent. She looked forward to meeting them, but while Johann continued to read names, she slipped quickly into the kitchen.

"Oh, Miss Heidi, Master Johann is looking for you!"

"I know…. Um, is there any coffee?" She wondered once more at the form of address.

Mavis had seemingly assessed the situation quickly and poured tea into a tin mug. She thrust the hot cup into her hand. "You must go outside there with the campers now because Master Johann…" and then she shook her head and made what Heidi assumed was supposed to be a threatening sound.

Obediently, the tin cup burning her hands, she stepped back outside. She hoped this tea contained caffeine. *Master* Johann was reading girls' names now and sending the campers off with their counselors.

Johann looked over at her, his relief evident. "And, campers, fresh from the United States of America, we have Aunt Heidi."

Aunt? Heidi stared back, surprised. Why aunt? Was it a ploy to stave off homesickness? Share a cabin with your aunt and feel right at home? She took a sip of the scalding liquid, grateful it was black tea and hopefully contained enough caffeine to shock her senses into understanding. Why had nobody mentioned this? Only two people on earth had ever called her aunt, and she would give anything to feel their little arms hugging her neck.

Johann was reading a list and giggling preteen girls were heading her way, so she corralled her thoughts and tried to paste an enthusiastic smile on her face. Her *nieces* were heading her way. She had eight nieces, and they were all about ten years old. A giggle of her own escaped at the thought. Wait 'til she told Brianna.

The girls clustered around her as they told her their names. Anya, Tracy, Susan, Jane, Gillian, Amanda, Elaine, and Heather. She felt dizzy as she tried to keep them all straight. She glanced towards Amy for guidance and noticed Amy was heading her group of girls toward her cabin, so Heidi did the same. She would survive this first weekend by copying everything Amy did.

Once inside the cabin, a hushed shyness seemed to fall over the group. Heidi cleared her throat. Now was the time to make a good second impression. She felt sure her first impression had been a failure. "Well, girls, it's lovely to have you in my cabin. Let's go over your names slowly now, and I'll write them down here in my notebook."

The girls just stared back.

"Um," Heidi cleared her throat again, "who wants to go first?" When no volunteer was forthcoming, she tried again. "I'll tell you what, why don't you pick where you want to sleep first, and we'll get you settled and cozy, and then we can get to know each other.

OK?"

The girls shuffled around looking at each other and then began whispering about who would sleep where. Heidi was dumbfounded. Her memories of Junior high camp were far different from these girls. She could hear raucous laughter through the adjoining walls on all sides. Maybe they were simply stymied by her foreignness. She would have to put them at ease as quickly as possible; otherwise, it would be a long awkward weekend.

She purposefully moved around and inserted herself into the mix, trying her best to talk with them, to help unroll sleeping bags, and to make them feel comfortable. Eventually, she was able to eke out their names, and then the outside gong clanged, signaling game time.

Once Johann had everyone participating, Heidi sidled over to Amy. She wanted her advice, but Amy was distracted by her Ian. And Johann, the Superman, was too busy. She would have to pray for wisdom and wait for the right opportunities to help the girls relax around her. She knew enough about kids to understand that forcing yourself on them never worked.

CHAPTER 7

Her first opportunity came the next morning. The ongoing game tally sheet for girls' versus boys' cabins was even, and according to Games Director Johann, the way to break the tie would be a tennis match. Heidi perked up immediately. She knew tennis.

"Now," he said in his self-assured manner, "the girls pick a representative and the boys pick one, and then they play the best of seven games. Even counselors can participate if the campers wish!"

Immediately the girls began to talk amongst themselves, searching for who might be the best player. Glancing over at Johann, Heidi noticed the satisfied gleam in his eye. He was probably going to have the boys choose him. So, she would simply have all the girls choose her. Her competitive college years were about to pay off handily.

"Girls," she stepped into the middle of the cluster, "do any of you play for school?" Everyone shrugged.

"We play," one girl offered, "but just for fun at each other's houses."

Heidi tried not to look surprised. These girls had their own tennis courts? "OK," she said. "Well, if you don't mind letting me play, I have a good plan."

Instantly the circle tightened around her, and Amy gave her an approving nod. "I played tennis on a team in college, and I play quite well. But let's pretend you picked me, but that I don't really play well. Then, whoever they pick over there will let his guard down, and as soon as they do.... Whap!" The girls jumped and giggled. "Do you get what I mean?"

"*Ja,* that would be awesome!" The other girls were nudging each other and nodding.

"OK, listen up." Heidi lowered her voice, glancing toward the boys to ensure they weren't listening. Johann was already standing to the side, tennis racquet in hand, awaiting his victim. Heidi whispered the details to the girls, and then they all clapped and ran to the sidelines.

"Um," Heidi needed to make herself sound extremely unsure. "Um, where can I get a good bat?"

"A bat?" Johann practically guffawed. "Boys," he turned towards them in mock horror, "the girls need a tennis *bat*."

All the boys fell over themselves, laughing and mimicking Johann, but Heidi stood there, feigning confusion. She really *was* in a play, and she was warming to her role.

"You know," she insisted, swinging her arm for emphasis, "something to hit the ball with."

Johann, still chuckling, motioned towards a pile of racquets. "Take your pick; we have all sorts of *bats*." And the boys collapsed into hysterics once more.

Heidi walked over to the pile and frowned at the dismal options. "Is it better to play with a wood or a metal one?"

"At this point, I don't think it matters, does it, boys?"

On cue, all the boys began high-fiving and elbowing each other, nodding towards Johann in agreement.

Heidi leaned over and tested the feel of a few of the racquets, finally settling on an aluminum one that had all its strings. Hitting the strings against her hand, she grimaced but knew she would have to make do. Turning towards the girls, Heidi held up the racquet of her choice and winked. They giggled in response. She really should've brought her tennis gear, but then, the last thing she expected the camp to have was a tennis court. She had underestimated South Africa in so many ways.

"OK, I'm ready."

She watched Johann pump a victory fist towards the boys as she went to stand on her side in the area her earliest coaches had always called 'no man's land.' "Are you going to hit first?" She hoped her false confusion sounded genuine.

Johann grinned. "Sure, I'll *serve* first."

She shrugged in response, forcing herself to not get into the ready stance that was second nature.

He executed a perfect serve and just missed her feet. She jumped out of the way, trying to give a convincing yelp. The boys chortled, and the girls called encouraging words. She looked to Johann for direction as to where to go next and obediently moved to the other side of the court so he could aim for her feet once more.

The first game was over in less than a minute. "Now, do I hit it first?" It was getting harder to play dumb, especially since the taunting had escalated.

"Yes, stand behind the line and try to hit it into this square over here." He was standing relaxed, close enough for the inevitable killer return.

She lofted the ball and hit it at the right angle to bounce high in the correct quadrant. The return was as she had expected, hard and way out of reach. The boys were now in a frenzy.

"We can stop, you know." Johann almost sounded sorry for her.

"Why would we stop?" She countered loudly. "Girls," she turned towards them in mock confusion, "why do you think he wants us to stop?"

"Keep playing, Aunt Heidi! You can still win!" came the responses.

The farce had gone on long enough. She went to her spot on the other side and eyed Johann standing inside the service box, ready for another easy return. She lofted the ball again, but this time served fast and directly at *his* feet.

The ball hit its target easily, careening off his tennis shoes at a crazy angle. Johann merely stood frozen. Now it was the girls' turn to holler.

"I believe it's 15-all," Heidi smiled sweetly, moving with purpose back to the other side. She watched as Johann moved, uncertain now. She lofted the ball once more; this one was going deep out of his reach. She hit the ball with a solid thwack sending it immediately to his left.

He swatted uselessly, and a little girl yelled, "Ace!"

"30-15," she called. She was going to have to move fast before Johann really started playing.

At 2 games to 1, her favor, he stopped her as they switched sides. "I'm still going to win, you know." His look was both irritation and admiration.

She patted his arm and merely smiled. She wasn't even playing at her best, not that she was sure she could with her current racquet, but he wouldn't win; she was certain.

By the end of the 4th game, which Heidi won after two deuces, they actually had a competitive match going. The children were cheering, and the tension was high. But Johann was flustered and fumbled his service game, bringing the score 1 game to 4.

"We can stop, you know," she did her best to mimic his earlier comment.

"Oh no," he countered. "A man never gives up, right boys?" The boys nodded in response; their earlier exuberance gone.

Her service game got them to deuce multiple times, and Heidi could sense the children were losing interest. She wished Johann would call the game; she was the clear winner.

And then the lunch gong sounded. Johann froze, his eyes wide like a deer in the headlights. He sighed deeply and then walked to the nets. "Gentlemen," he bowed gravely, "it appears I have failed you in our quest for victory. The gong is calling, and we must stop."

"So that means the girls win?" A high thin voice called from the stands.

Johann turned towards the girls. "As much as it pains me to say so," he sighed again dramatically, "the girls have won."

The girls began cheering ecstatically while the boys looked on in envy. How quickly the tables had turned. Her campers ran down and surrounded Heidi, hugging her and clapping, slapping her on the back with glee.

She stared past them towards Johann, who was standing stock still. Their eyes met, and he dipped his head in grudging acknowledgment before turning to retrieve the rackets and balls. Her heart flooded with warmth, knowing it took a good man to admit defeat.

They walked back towards the dining area clustered in groups, the girls still replaying their victory, the boys silent. When they were close to the pool, Johann sidled over to Heidi.

"You know," his voice sounded theatrical, "we never got to shake on your victory." He extended his hand.

"Why, Johann," she smiled sweetly, "what a good sport you are." She gripped his outstretched hand in return.

"And you know, I've never been beaten by an American." He pumped her hand dramatically.

"Well, you must not have played many Americans then," she couldn't resist the jibe.

"Oh, I haven't, have I?" He was still pumping her hand, edging her toward the pool as they talked.

"Don't you dare," she lowered her voice, trying in vain to withdraw her hand.

"What's the matter, Heidi? You don't want to go swimming?"

"If you dunk me in this pool, Johann, and ruin the only good pair of shoes I have here, I swear, I will come in your cabin every night and dump ice water on you until you beg for mercy."

Johann's mouth dropped open, letting out a roar of laughter, releasing her hand.

Turning, he hollered for the boys to hurry and wash their hands so they could be first in line for once.

The girls turned to Heidi, "What did you even say to him?" Their eyes shone with admiration.

"It doesn't matter; we won!" She stepped away from the edge of the pool. "High fives for everyone." She raised her hand to slap theirs as they hugged and congratulated each other again. It seemed a tennis match had broken the ice with her campers, and she hoped the rest of the weekend would be just as successful.

***

As campers clambered for their spaces in the lunch line, Johann stood off to the side, keeping an eye on things and trying not to let his grudging admiration of Heidi show. She was in line with her girls, and their happy chatter filled the outdoor space. Once and then twice, he caught her eye and watched a small smile play on her lips. She had accepted his challenge earlier and won – in more ways than one. That's what continued to perplex his preconceptions: other challenges that people would avoid, she accepted. There was a barely perceptible straightening of the shoulders and a small telltale smile that said she was game. Game for whatever he threw her way – even when he handed her a flaming stick or salt-infused coffee. She did not back down.

He needed to fully accept that Heidi was different. And above all else, she was good for camp. And anyone good for camp, by necessity, should have his approval.

***

That first weekend of camp finished without a hitch. As they stood waving off the campers Sunday afternoon, Amy linked arms with Heidi.

"You were a big success, you know."

Heidi smiled, "Thank you, Amy. I was so nervous – especially the first night when none of them wanted to talk to me. And then we were so busy, I never got to know any of the church counselors, and I feel like I was just getting to know my cabin girls, and then it was over."

"*Ja,* I suppose you have to live through the brand-new thing."

Heidi glanced over quizzically.

"I mean, think about it. The rest of us have been here for ages, so usually, someone who comes knows us. And, even if one camper knows us, it breaks the ice for all the other campers."

"And it helps that all your girls know Ian and Ian likes—"

"Stop!" Amy nudged Heidi playfully. "You can't let my father hear you talking like that."

"Why not?"

Amy shrugged. "He's just funny… I don't know." She glanced down and scuffed the toe of her shoe through the dirt. "You want to go swimming?"

The change in direction took Heidi off guard. "Um, sure... do I have to wear clothes, or can I put on a bathing suit?"

Amy laughed. "You Americans. We call them *costumes* or *cozzies* here. A suit is something you wear to church!"

She opened the door to her cabin and then looked back to smile at Amy. "Well, a *costume* is what you wear to play dress-up." Turning to shut the door, she noticed a letter on her bed.

It was from Chris. She tore it open and read it hurriedly first and then slowly the second time. He missed her. He wanted her to come home. He was sorry how things had ended. Would she please call him collect? He needed to hear her voice.

Heidi sat on the edge of the bed, conflicted. If she called him, the wound would reopen. The sick feeling that had filled the days since their breakup had waned. She was gaining her footing here at camp and didn't want to ruin her progress. Instead, she would write him back, after her swim with Amy, of course. She would tell him she missed him, too, but that she was going to fulfill the year. Her heart swelled. Then she would tell him all about camp and the incredible opportunities here for service, for pouring into the lives of others. Maybe then he would see how important this was for her; maybe then he would understand.

CHAPTER 8

Heidi stood over her suitcase and sighed. She had phoned the airlines repeatedly, but there was still no sign of her other bag. She asked them at what point the airline would pay for losing it, but she had made zero progress.

The bottom line was she needed clothes and more than just the couple pairs of shorts and T-shirts she was alternating between. She stared down at the paraphernalia filling her existing bag and dug around until she produced a box of Pop-Tarts. What she wouldn't give to trade these for another outfit…. Maybe she could bribe Johann into taking her shopping with a few cherry-filled Pop-Tarts? She had cinnamon sugar ones, too; maybe those would do the trick.

Grabbing both boxes, she knocked on Amy's cabin door, showed her the snacks with a grin on her face, and then walked over to the kitchen where Mavis was finishing their dinner dishes.

"Mavis, do you mind if I use the toaster?" She was still unsure of herself in the kitchen.

"Oooo, Madam, this is not mine. You use all of it!" Mavis was shaking her head and laughing softly to herself.

Heidi stood in consternation. "Mavis," she tried carefully, "in my country, we just call each other by our names. Please, will you just call me Heidi?"

"Oooo, no, Madam, I…." She had gotten serious.

"But Mavis, in my country, 'madam' is for very old people, and I want to just be young Heidi. You don't call Amy 'madam.' I'm only a little bit older than Amy."

Mavis shook her head, plugging in the toaster.

"Here, do you want to try some American Pop-Tarts?" There suddenly seemed to be a lot riding on those Pop-Tarts. Any minute Heidi expected Amy to show up and Johann to follow. Where there was food, he was always present.

The first two popped up, and she put them on two plates and perched on a stool. "Here, come sit with me and try my favorite American treat."

"Oh no, Ma… Heidi, I'll stand here!" There was something akin to fear in her eyes.

Heidi jumped up as understanding dawned and placed both plates on the counter. "Well, let's stand and eat them then!" She slid a plate over in front of Mavis and then took a bite from her own plate. Heaven. This made up for whatever dinner had been. She felt permanently hungry.

Mavis took a bite, and her eyes widened with appreciation. "Very good… Heidi… very, very good."

"See, I knew you would like them," Heidi nudged her playfully. "You'll have to bring one to Fiona."

Mavis laughed harder and lifted the tart to take another bite before turning instantly serious, her eyes on the doorway.

"You may be finished for the evening, Mavis. Thank you." It was Karl, and his voice bore no trace of friendliness.

Heidi turned to Mavis, her heart sinking. "Take the rest for Fiona, Mavis, please. Tell her it's a treat all the way from America."

"Thank you, Madam, but I will leave it," she answered softly, clapping one hand over the other and then slipping out.

Heidi watched her go, wishing she could call her back and regain their camaraderie before Karl ruined it. She could feel his eyes boring into her back, but she didn't turn to acknowledge him; she simply stood there eating her Pop-Tart. It tasted like sandpaper now.

"Heidi, sit here." It was a command, not a request.

She turned and met his gaze; she wasn't going to shrink beneath him while he stood. She lifted her chin and tried to speak evenly. "Is something wrong?"

He placed his hands on the metal table and took a breath. "There are unspoken rules here that you will have to learn."

She quirked her head at an angle but did not respond, holding his gaze, willing herself not to cower. Let him explain it to her then; she wouldn't make it easy on him.

"You need to keep a certain... um... distance between the... um... help we have here."

"What do you mean?" She knew exactly what he meant but maybe, maybe if she made him say it out loud, he would realize how ludicrous it sounded. Did they not all believe the same Bible, that God created and loved everyone equally? How could he live such a double standard and...?

"Is everything alright?" Johann stepped into the room, looking between Heidi and Karl.

She wanted to turn to Johann and ask him why Vera, Amy, and Johann could be friendly with Mavis, but when Heidi was friendly, she crossed an invisible barrier. She wanted to ask why Karl seemed determined to keep the status quo at a Christian camp. But she stood quietly. Let Karl explain the tension. She was simply Heidi, who had been trying to share a snack with Mavis.

"Johann, come with me." Karl jerked his chin towards the door connecting the kitchen to the hallway and walked through it, clearly expecting Johann to follow.

Johann looked towards her, worry filling his eyes. Without thinking, Heidi fled from the kitchen, through the outdoor eating area, and down the steps towards the pool.

She walked to the swing and sat, banding her arms around her bent knees, willing the tears away. She wished Brianna was there, somebody safe. She and Brianna had been sharing secrets since they had discovered each other in detention as middle schoolers. Heidi couldn't remember why she had been in detention, but it hadn't mattered once she had met Brianna. They became inseparable and remained close all through high school and college. Now the ache of missing her friend and confidant was overwhelming.

It wasn't long before Johann's form showed against the purplish glow of the bug zapper. She watched him pause, clearly trying to make out where she had gone. Her heart beat faster, and her nausea intensified. She wished she could simply disappear into the swing, petrified he was going to come and finish the *explanation* Karl had started.

He moved towards her, his silhouette growing as he got closer and stopped within a few feet of the swing, his features scarcely visible. "Heidi?"

"Yes."

He sat on the swing, as far from her as he could be, and leaned forward, his elbows on his knees. "Do you mind telling me what happened back in the kitchen?"

She turned her head away, afraid he would see her tears. "I... um... was sharing some American food with Mavis, and we were talking and laughing, and then Karl came in. He told Mavis to leave and... had started to tell me that I had to keep my *distance* from Mavis, and then you came in."

Johann sighed and rubbed a hand over his face. "Remember what I told you about the Lower Camp on your first day here?"

"Yes." Her voice came out barely in a whisper.

"Remember what I said? That this is South Africa and that I... do what I can when I can?" He waited a while before continuing. "But you have to be careful, Heidi. You can't bulldoze your way in here and change an institution that has been in place for years."

"So, I can't help a lady pick her *Chappies* off the ground?"

Johann sighed. "No, I mean, but—"

"But why can you and Amy talk and laugh with Mavis, but I can't? Why does it make Karl so mad?"

"He was *mad*?"

"You saw him!" There was another disconnect here, and Heidi couldn't figure it out.

"Can you describe his madness?"

"His *madness*?"

"What on earth, Johann? He was *angry* with me." Once again, she heard English words but knew they were not communicating.

"So, he was angry, not mad."

Was *mad* the word they used for *crazy* in this crazy mixed-up place? "Yes, Johann, he was angry with me, and I don't understand."

"Look," he reached out and touched her arm. "You are not the first American to come and be shocked by this... this culture that's currently in place. But the best you or I can do is pray that the leadership will change and quietly go about distributing kindness to those who are treated this way. But you must be careful. People don't take well to Americans trying to come in and fix what they deep down know is wrong. It makes them angry and," he managed a half smile, "maybe a little *mad* too."

She glanced at him, relieved.

"So, be friendly as you can be, Heidi, but don't do it in front of certain people, and don't invite Mavis to do things with you that break the rules that are in place."

"But what are the rules?"

He shrugged. "Don't ask her to sit at the table with you, for starters."

Heidi widened her eyes. Had Karl been eavesdropping on them the whole time?

"Don't have the children come play in your cabin or go in the toilets we use. And, only let them swim in the pool if everyone is away from camp, except for us."

She reached up and kneaded the back of her neck. "I just don't know how to wrap my brain around all of this."

"What do you mean?"

"I read about apartheid before I came, but clearly not enough. I just assumed that at a Christian camp, the politics of it all wouldn't matter. I mean, we teach the kids they are unique and created by God, right?"

"Yes...?"

"But that only applies to the white kids in this country?"

"Well, no, of course not. It's just that apartheid is so deeply seated in our culture that—"

"But why can't we have camps for the black children? Why can't we teach them they are unique and loved and created for a purpose by a loving Creator? That we are all equal in the sight of God no matter what crazy mandates government comes up with? And why can't we have Karl attend those lessons, too?"

Johann glanced around quickly. "Talk softer, Heidi, if Karl heard you...."

"OK," she softened her voice, "but why can't we?"

Johann stared out into the darkness, and Heidi could tell she had struck home. "You've made me think, Heidi."

She smiled softly in acknowledgment. "What about Amy?"

"Unfortunately, Amy probably doesn't know what she thinks because she's under her father's thumb." He stood then, "I'm headed back to the kitchen." He hesitated but then continued, "Do you want me to rescue your treats?"

"No, it's OK. I'll go and get them in a little while… thanks."

"Good night, Heidi."

"'Night," she whispered to his retreating back. Her thoughts whirled and dipped but, overall, found an underlying sense of relief that Johann lived his Biblical values despite his country's mandates. She would watch him and do the same, being wary of Karl's presence and her foreigner status.

At least she had an ally in Johann. It felt good they had connected in one area.

***

Johann didn't go back to the kitchen after all. Heidi's words had struck home, and he needed to think. This country he loved so much was deeply flawed, and what was he doing about it? Secretly helping out people less fortunate when nobody was watching? Maybe he should be braver. Maybe he should do as Heidi had suggested: ask Karl to allow them to run a camp for black children and teach them that God loved them despite how their country mistreated them.

He took his notebook, Bible, and flashlight and went to the Tree. He would jot down a few thoughts and pray God would show him what he, just a young man working at one small camp, could do. He wrote across the top of the page, 2 Chronicles 7:14,

If my people, which are called by my name, shall humble themselves, and pray, and seek my face, and turn from their wicked ways; then will I hear from heaven, and will forgive their sin, and will heal their land.

He wasn't sure what he could do, but he knew he could do what the verse commanded: *humble himself, pray, and seek God's face. And God would heal this land*

.

CHAPTER 9

On Wednesday, Heidi found herself squished into the front of the *bakkie* between Johann and Amy, headed for a shopping mall somewhere. Amy maintained she had to sit by the window because the middle made her sick. This gave Heidi the uncomfortable position of having her knees smashed between the gear shift and Johann's elbow and hand. Every time he shifted, she would pull her knees as far over as possible, but there was simply no room. She could tell he was annoyed, whether it was having to play taxi to two girls or just by her proximity.

Finally, in exasperation, she spoke out. "I can't chop my knees off, you know!"

"What?"

"My knees – I know they're in your way, but there's nowhere else for them to go!"

Amy glanced over, seemingly oblivious to everyone's angst, and giggled. Heidi wanted to ask her why she was so happy until she remembered that there had been talk of Amy meeting Ian at the shopping mall. She sighed; here she was, stuck between two lovelorn people.

She angled her head at Johann, noticing the trademark twin spots of red on his cheeks, angry he wouldn't respond. "How about I control the gear shift?"

"What?"

"I'll shift. You pedal or clutch or whatever it's called, and I'll shift."

"Fine then."

"Well, fine then yourself. Take your hand off the shifter *then*!" If bumping her knee by accident made him aggravated, she definitely wasn't going to place her hand over his on the shifter. His nearness was already doing strange things to her heart rate.

He lifted his hand and held it open-palmed in resignation. "Don't kill my *bakkie*."

"Trust me," she retorted, "it's the last thing I'd do."

"Now, now," Amy admonished, "let's all be friends."

Heidi looked at her and winked, her hand poised on the shifter and her knees blessedly free. This should be fun, considering she had never operated a gear shift before. She stared back down at the knob and read the gear pattern. "So, are we in four or two?"

"What?"

"You have quite the vocabulary today, Johann. I asked if we are in four or two?"

Amy clapped her hand to her mouth in mirth, "Heidi...?"

"Have you ever even driven a car that isn't automatic?" Johann's voice was close to a roar.

"What's the big deal, Johann? Just answer my question – once I know what gear we're in, I'll be fine."

"Of all the stupid, idiotic things...." He flung his hands up, "just give me the gear shift back."

"No," she responded as seriously as she could, despite her overwhelming desire to laugh hysterically. "Let's try this. I'm tired of you hitting my knees."

"We're obviously in four, and I swear, if you kill my engine..." he warned.

"I won't kill your engine, Johann, so relax and drive. Just tell me when to shift, OK?"

"*Ai-ja-jai*, and this is my day off," he muttered.

Heidi stared at him; the twin splotches of red had spread to his whole face. Maybe they needed a change in conversation. "So, Amy," she fastened her eyes on the gear shift, "what do you and Ian plan to buy today?"

Now it was Amy's turn to redden as she leaned forward to see Johann's reaction.

"Don't look at me, Amy. I don't know anything about who you're meeting today." His voice held a warning.

An uncomfortable silence settled over them, and Heidi glanced worriedly at Amy and winked. "Don't worry, Johann, I am a wonderful chaperone."

His eyes were on the road, and he ignored her statement. "OK, Heidi, a robot is coming up. When I say, you need to put it in third and then second."

"OK." She looked around, wondering at the terminology, only to see a traffic light. She would have fun with that new word another time, but right now, she needed to focus on the job at hand.

"Now!"

She pushed the lever up and over, and he lifted his foot off the clutch as the gears ground, and the truck hopped and jerked forward.

"Not first, *domkop*!" He pushed the clutch back in and grabbed the gear shift, popping it into neutral and then applying the brakes. They came to a skidding stop yards from the traffic light. Nobody moved.

Keeping her head straight forward, Heidi tried to see Johann from her peripheral vision. "That went well, don't you think?" she tried.

Amy doubled over in hysterics, "Oh, Heidi, this is the best ride anywhere!"

Heidi smiled cautiously, still trying to see Johann's face without turning her head.

"Johann," Amy reached around and punched him on the arm, "come on, you have to admit." Amy was now gasping for breath. "Johann?"

"Well, I must say, Amy, I've never heard you laugh so hard…." He sounded almost grateful.

"On second thought, Johann, I think you should shift." That was Heidi.

"You think, hey? I think I'm going to have to…" and he reached over and caught her in a headlock and mussed her hair, "*klap* you well and good. Tickle her, Amy!"

"Noooo!" Heidi was gasping for air, and they were all laughing. "Amy, don't you dare!"

A car from behind started honking, and Johann released her. Johann turned to apologize to the irate driver who had now pulled up next to them and yelled a few choice things before roaring off.

They sat in stunned silence for a few beats.

"Sometimes it's good I don't know all your languages here," Heidi said.

That was all it took – they collapsed with laughter as Johann got the truck back in gear and took off.

***

They were back to square one, and Johann was once more in the uncomfortable position of driving in close proximity to Heidi, but her antics had lightened his mood. You never knew what the American girl would come out with next. He supposed it wouldn't bother him so much if he didn't feel an overwhelming attraction whenever he came near her. He knew he was overreacting, but he was going to visit Marie. He felt like an idiot for the zings of attraction that shot up his arm every time his hand grazed her knees. He was hopeless. It was one thing to accept her as a fellow worker but entirely another thing to be attracted to her. Regardless, he couldn't stay angry with Heidi; it was his own disloyal heart he should be angry with.

He had to admit, despite his conflict over Heidi, that she was good for Amy. Amy was always so sweet and compliant. He had never heard her laugh so hard, and it made him happy to see her so happy. She had been much less inhibited lately, which was a refreshing change. Heidi was clearly good for her. He worried about her now being older and still under Karl's thumb, worried she would never reach her potential. Karl, the one good father figure in his life, was way too hard on Amy.

He shoved a cassette into the tape player, hoping to distract all of them, and rotated his shoulders. They were almost to Eastgate, and then he would be free of both Heidi and Amy and, hopefully, all his disturbing thoughts. Then he could enjoy the rest of the day with Marie.

***

The Eastgate shopping mall surprised Heidi: it was bigger than her favorite mall at home, and she was glad Amy was there to help her get her bearings. Amy used a map to point out all the best clothing stores and then, glancing at her watch, said she was going to find Ian. After arranging a place to meet, they parted ways. Suddenly Heidi was aware of how completely alone she was. At camp, she was always surrounded by people. She shoved her thoughts aside and did her best to focus. She needed at least three more complete outfits, and she needed to get busy.

But the first shop that caught her eye was a camera store, and she was instantly sidetracked. Her prize camera was cushioned amongst her favorite clothes in the suitcase that had never made it. So much for planning to document every week at camp, to make a pictorial diary of her time in South Africa. But, after examining the cheaper cameras, she decided to wait a while longer. There was still the outside chance the airport would recover her lost items. Besides, once you took pictures with a good camera, using a cheap one was unacceptable. A written diary would have to do. Maybe it was for the best. The first group of campers hadn't had a single camera between them, and, in this way, they were different from American teens. Maybe her camera would make them uncomfortable... she didn't know, but she would wait.

She headed towards the clothing stores, overwhelmed by the choices. Shopping alone was no fun. There was nobody to model the clothes for, nobody to run and get another size, nobody to laugh with. It had always been an event meant to be shared with either her mom or Brianna or Jenna.

Jenna.

Jenna had been her idol growing up. Only three years her senior, Jenna had known clothes and always had a flair for fashion and an understanding of building a great outfit. She had shown Heidi how to put on mascara the first time, how to blouse her oversized shirts, bought her matching scrunchies for her colorful earrings, told her if her skirt was too long or too short....

She purchased a milkshake, found a place to sit, her few purchases at her feet, and watched the people going by. Aside from the clipped accents passing by, this could be any upscale mall in America.

She would never forget the weekend Jenna had gone over to the Bahamas on a boat with friends. Her parents had been against it, but by then, Jenna was 21 and doing pretty much what she wanted, when she wanted. She had come back pregnant and shut herself off emotionally. None of them had handled it well, especially when Jenna admitted she didn't know how to contact the father. Heidi thought back, wondering if she had missed vital information. Had Jenna known more than she let on?

"So, you're sure he didn't tell you his full name?" Heidi had pestered her for information more than once.

"No, Heidi," and she had tossed her head. "He was so good-looking; we didn't get to particulars like full names."

Heidi suspected Jenna enjoyed the shock value of her statements. The girls were brought up conservatively, but Jenna had increasingly enjoyed thwarting the Richmond status quo. In fact, throughout her pregnancy, she kept up what Heidi now believed was a façade of bravado.

Her parents had tried multiple times. "Those babies carry half his DNA, Jenna. We have to try and find him."

But Jenna had been adamant there was no way to find him.

"Was he Bahamian?"

"He sounded American, like me. You know," and she rolled her eyes, "Americans do visit other countries." Then she'd raised her eyes. "Who knows, maybe he's from South Florida, too!"

The twins' birth had been a shock. Jenna had struggled from the trauma of two difficult births, the fact that multiple forms the hospital gave her to fill out wanted her to list a father, and the immediate sleepless nights. The bravado spiraled into postpartum depression.

Before the birth, her parents wanted Jenna to give the twins up for adoption so Jenna could return to college, but she refused. After their birth, nobody made that suggestion. From the first time any of them laid eyes on Darla and Darrin, there was no question they would grow up in the Richmond household. But still, it was difficult, and Jenna refused any kind of outside emotional support, even though her parents offered it over and over.

The family did their best to pull together. With Heidi and her mom doing night feedings, her dad continually ran to the store for more diapers, formula, or a different kind of diaper rash ointment. Despite their best efforts, chaos reigned.

One day Jenna asked Heidi to watch the twins for her. Heidi remembered how Jenna seemed happier. She said she was going to the beach to watch the storm.

Lost in her thoughts, Heidi pushed the barely touched milkshake away and rested her head in her hands. Why hadn't she noticed the signs? Why hadn't she questioned her more? But Jenna had smiled and hugged her and thanked her, and Heidi had simply been glad. The twins were barely three months old. They were ready for another bottle when Heidi called her parents at the office.

Jenna washed up 24 hours and 32 minutes later. You don't forget the minute details of a tragedy. It all stood out, shouting each detail with importance, making you analyze and overanalyze and question every action and inaction, every nuance of every moment.

Her parents had been so strong. Between her dad's quiet confidence and calming presence and the fact that sweet Darla and Darrin gave each day purpose, they soldiered through the unrelenting grief. And the twins had given Heidi's mom a reason to bury her heartache in busyness. They had built a routine, and Heidi had finished college and started working for her dad. She had gotten engaged and been Aunt Heidi to the twins, filling in as often as possible to give her mom necessary breaks.

Suddenly, Heidi felt selfish for leaving. Her parents had lost one daughter and been let down by the other. Her mom's desire to help her plan her wedding and have her live close by had been thwarted by Heidi's desire to *go*.

Loneliness and recrimination engulfed her. Her longing to experience something different had cost them all. She threw away the warmed milkshake and went in search of a stationery store. After purchasing a pretty set, Heidi found a secluded table and wrote a long letter to her parents. She included a section for the twins – she needed to stay in their memories if that was possible with three-year-olds. The writing soothed her, and she made a pact to write regularly. Maybe that would heal her mom's disappointment and keep her in the twins' minds.

Camp life would be complete if they were nearby... but bringing them to South Africa was improbable, so she'd have to comfort herself with letters to them and the hope that her mom would continually explain her absence and remind them "Aneidi" loved them.

CHAPTER 10

Heidi woke slowly from a deep sleep and yawned. Another camp was arriving, and Johann and Amy both agreed the group coming was a favorite. According to Johann, they were from the Alberton area—not that it meant much to Heidi. She was most excited about the fact that an American missionary pastored the church, and even though the pastor and his wife weren't coming, two of their children were. She couldn't wait to chat with another American, someone who didn't speak of robots and *domkops*.

Finding her flip-flops and toiletries, she shuffled out to the bathrooms, her toes cold, wishing the cabins had ensuite bathrooms. Walking from cabin to toilet in her morning fog left her fearful of running into someone before she was ready to be seen. But she had developed a plan to prevent such a thing. She would peek out through the curtain and, if nobody were visible, would crack the door open. Then, if the coast still seemed clear, she would run for it.

This morning, halfway across the space, she saw Johann coming toward her. Of course, he was freshly showered and looked way too good. Her heart sank.

"*Goeie môre,* Heidi." Amusement punctuated his words as he planted himself directly in front of her.

"Morning," she mumbled, trying to maneuver around him, focusing her eyes on the surrounding dirt. She wondered vaguely why they hadn't ever grassed in the area.

"Looks like you slept well."

Yes, you idiot, she wanted to say, my hair is always like this in the mornings. Cautiously she reached into her toiletry kit and felt for her spray bottle. "What did you say?" She was all innocence.

"I was saying I can tell you slept well." His laughter was barely contained.

In one swift movement, she withdrew the spray bottle and started spraying him full in the face. Stunned at first, he simply stood there. But when he made a move to grab it from her, she ducked under his arm and ran the last few steps into the safety of the girl's bathroom.

Chuckling to herself, she glanced in the mirrors, and her mirth evaporated. Her hair proclaimed gravity didn't actually exist. She grimaced and walked straight to the showers.

   ***

At breakfast, Karl went over the numbers with them, and Vera gave out the groups based on her Stamp Club data. Johann reviewed the itinerary, reiterating that most campers were returnees, so the schedule differed from the previous weekend. The talks would be more in-depth, and there would only be one beginner Stamp Club group; the rest had advanced to at least the fourth level. In addition, the activities were different. They would be having a nighttime capture-the-flag plus something they called the "long hike." Time at the Tree would still be on Sunday morning, but they would have a bonfire both nights.

Looking over the "*shhhe*-dule," Heidi felt the now familiar bubbles of anticipation. This was why she had left everything: to interact with young people and strengthen their walk with God; to help them see that a life in line with Him was a life of purpose and fulfillment; to make a difference. She wondered where the "long hike" took them and how they controlled a capture-the-flag at night... she would need her flashlight, for sure.

"Any questions?" Johann stared at Heidi.

"Yes, are Amy and I the only girl counselors?"

He glanced at his roster before nodding the affirmative and added, "Ian will be working this weekend again... there's only a total of 33 campers, but when you consider it's only one church, it's quite impressive."

Heidi nodded, not wanting to contradict him, thinking about the big churches back home that had dozens in their youth groups. This church, though, must be about the same size as her home church, and she hoped she'd connect easily with them.

They parted after breakfast, each to their assigned tasks. Heidi would lead a level three group, so she went to the Stamp Club room to study the materials. Reading over the questions and answers, ideas for lesson improvement flooded her mind. Hurriedly, she started jotting down notes and ideas.

"Do you have any questions?" Johann filled the door, shattering her peace.

She slipped her notes under the lesson. Johann might not appreciate her desire to *help.*

"What are you doing?" He had caught her motion and stepped into the narrow room.

"Taking notes."

"You have questions about the lesson?" He was right above her now, so she shifted to put more distance between them.

"No, just thinking," then she took a breath. Why not say what she thought? He didn't like her most days anyway, so it wasn't like she had anything to lose. "I… uh… I actually have ideas for this lesson."

He angled his head, his expression unreadable.

"Does the Stamp Club ever allow people to modify their curriculum or take suggestions?" She said it all softly in one breath, wishing now she'd kept her mouth shut.

He pulled out a chair and sat next to her. "Like what?" He didn't sound intrigued, but he didn't sound angry.

She took a deep breath, uncovered her notes, and pointed to a portion of the text. "I mean, look here. They need to make it more personal. It's just, you know, a bit sterile."

He was quiet as he read over the section and then analyzed her notes. "Hmm," he finally said, "I think you have a point."

Heidi was astonished. She had expected backlash, not support.

Johann glanced at his watch, "After the camp leaves, I'll talk to Vera about this. She would know the protocol since this is her area." He slammed his hands onto the table abruptly. "But we have to get moving!"

Heidi sat there stunned. Who was this guy who was equally supportive and antagonizing, kind but then distrustful, friendly but then irritated?

"You coming?" He was back in the doorway.

She stood slowly. She was the same person every day. But he was ever changing. Fickle. But only with her. Nobody else. She wanted to say all those things, but instead, she smiled, gathering her materials.

At least now, she could present her ideas to Vera.

"Heidi, we can't be late!" Back to dislike and distrust, that's where they were again. She lifted her chin in challenge and stared at him, purposefully not responding. Let him hear his words echo in the quiet room and realize how rude they sounded.

***

Johann stared back at her, wishing for the thousandth time it was Marie sitting at the table, studying the lesson. He could've sat with her, explaining the lessons, expounding on what worked and what didn't. Although he had to admit, Heidi's ideas were good. He and Vera had talked multiple times about seeing if they could revamp a few lessons, but there was never time to put thought into action.

But this was Heidi, and he didn't trust himself to be near her. He had already made a fool of himself in the car the other day. Plus, she was American, and didn't Americans come to South Africa and act like they knew better? Well, he conceded, *most* Americans. He had a deep respect for Pastor Anderson of the Alberton church. But Pastor Anderson wasn't here on a short-term mission endeavor; he had been in South Africa for years. Maybe that was the difference. But Heidi... Heidi was clearly in the short-term camp. She wanted to come and serve, take her photographs, and return home with evidence of how she had helped the poor Africans.

He felt himself grow warm at her relentless stare, his conscience bothering him. Come to think of it; he hadn't even seen her take a single photograph. Once again, he was wrong about Heidi; yet her presence still meant Marie could not be here. He turned to leave. He would go and organize what he needed from game storage. Stamp Club preparation could wait.

***

The camp weekend went well, but Heidi was surprised that the missionaries' kids were fully South African. They had South African accents, went to South African schools, and even spoke Afrikaans. The younger of the two had even been born in South Africa. They said their family was returning to America to visit their supporting churches in the upcoming year, but they were dreading it.

"When we get there, Americans always ask us if we're glad to be 'home.'" The girl, Amanda, rolled her eyes. "South Africa is my home, and I usually spend the whole time in America feeling homesick for here."

Well, so much for commiserating with fellow Americans. Regardless, Heidi thoroughly enjoyed having Amanda and her friends in her cabin that week. The kids were impressively mature in their Bible knowledge, and Heidi found it fun to work on deeper lessons with them.

Many of them had also brought guitars. At night during the bonfires, the teens sat around and sang and played, led by Johann. Ian was trying to teach Amy to play, and Heidi watched them protectively, ensuring Karl didn't materialize and ruin their camaraderie.

These moments were poignant. Heidi liked to sit up and away from everyone, listening and letting the beauty of the moment fill her heart. The fire, the music, the happy teens, the mountains in the distance, and the faint chimes from the Tree filled her soul. To be part of this; it was a gift.

She wished Chris could sit here and experience these moments. Then he would understand. He had written her back, reiterating how much he missed her, and she had answered him again. She longed to stay for two years, not one, but she didn't mention it. She was simply thrilled he was writing her. If, by the end of the year, he was still writing her and wanting her to come home, she would gladly compromise.

CHAPTER 11

By March, Heidi found herself in a comfortable routine; she rarely had that odd sense that she was playacting. She suspected it was because camp life had become her new normal, and as the strangeness had dissipated, so had the feeling she was living in a play. The weather had started to cool a bit which was opposite to Heidi's Northern Hemisphere upbringing, and it made her forget what month she was in. According to her thermostat, it might be November in Florida, but it was March in South Africa. Their coldest month was July.

They found themselves in three full weeks of camps by the end of March and the beginning of April. The South African schools had a significant term break, so they shifted from weekend to weekday camps. The longer camps were exhausting but allowed time to connect with the campers. Heidi loved it.

***

It was mail time at camp, and Heidi watched, hopeful, as Postman Johann handed out letters to campers. She hadn't had a response from Chris in a long time. In the beginning, when she was accepting of his initial silence, he had abruptly started writing and given her hope. But after her second response, there had been nothing. Now she wished he had never written her at all. Those two letters had merely prolonged the pain of missing him and given her false hope. She tried to brace herself, to tell herself it didn't matter, that she didn't need or even want a letter.

Campers were getting postcards, and Johann made a big show of calling their names. Heidi felt her feckless heart beat hopefully. Finally, his stack almost depleted, he came to sit by her, elbows on the table, holding a letter between his hands. She tried to act as if she didn't care, but she was itching to grab it out of his hands.

"I'm not sure if this letter is for you or not." Johann squinted at the address.

"Do you need Fiona to come and help you read the envelope?" Her voice was saccharin sweet.

"Excellent idea," Johann bit back. He swung his legs back over the bench, placing his back against the picnic table, his shoulder almost touching hers, and called to the little girl playing near the kitchen. "Fiona," he waved her over, "Heidi needs help with some reading. Can you come here?"

Fiona looked at Johann and then back at her mom, scrubbing pots at the kitchen sink, before scrambling from her spot and running over to Johann.

Heidi rolled her eyes. Of course, he would take her attempt to gall him and turn it to his advantage. And, of course, both Fiona and Samson would do anything Johann asked. She continued to eat, feigning nonchalance. The food tasted terrible. She failed to understand how Mavis could make a great stew and a scrumptious *melktart* but nothing else. She suspected the bland food had more to do with the camp budget than Mavis's skills. Besides, this *mieliepap* they put with multiple meals was getting old. And, any piece of meat called *Boerewors* – they had told her it meant 'farmer sausage' as if that was supposed to make it more attractive – had already failed to impress her taste buds before her first bite. If she kept losing weight, she would have to find a way to go clothes shopping again.

Johann was pointing to the letter and helping Fiona sound out the words. Heidi rolled her eyes.

Amy looked at her, giggling. "You should just *klap* him with your plate," Amy suggested merrily.

Meanwhile, Fiona stood inside the circle of Johann's arms, clearly enjoying her important role helping her hero.

Finally, after continuing the charade a while longer, Johann whispered in Fiona's ear, and she nodded and tapped Heidi on the shoulder.

"Auntie Heidi, Uncle Johann says this is for you." Heidi would never get used to unrelated children calling her "Aunt," but she was grateful to finally have the letter coming her way.

"Why, thank you, Fiona," she smiled at the little girl, leaning forward and giving her a hug as she took the letter. "Please tell *Uncle* Johann 'thank you' for his kindness."

Fiona immediately turned to Johann and whispered loudly in his ear. "She says thank you!"

"She does?" Johann sat back, his shoulder touching Heidi's as he folded his arms across his chest, seemingly unperturbed as Heidi shifted away from him. "Even Americans must have manners then." He paused, waiting, and then went on. "It's such a shame Heidi can't read her letter right now because it's her cabin's turn to do the dishes."

Heidi had had enough; the letter was from Chris, and she suspected Johann knew it wasn't her usual letter from home. She looked at Amy imploringly. "Well, Amy's cabin and my cabin switched jobs, and *you, Uncle* Johann, deserve this." And without further warning, she picked up her congealed *mieliepap* and smashed it in his face.

Then she stalked off without looking behind her. She could hear the campers laughing at Johann, asking him how it felt to be a *mieliepap-kop* and why wasn't he going to throw Heidi in the pool?

"Don't worry, my friends," he called loudly to remain in her hearing range, "*paybacks* are always much, much worse."

Heidi ran to the grassy area below the tennis courts. At this time of day, she knew nobody would be there and could read her letter out of sight. The letter felt extra thick; her heart beat with anticipation. Chris had never been wordy, so the fact this letter seemed to have substance filled her with hope. Maybe he realized waiting a year for her wasn't so bad. Or, at the very least, perhaps he missed her friendship so much that he wanted to keep things alive until she returned.

She took a deep breath, savoring the moment, and then tore the letter open, surprised when two separate folded sheets and a smaller envelope fell into her hands. She crooked her eyebrows in surprise, opening first one sheet and seeing Chris's scrawl and then the other with Brianna's distinctive curly cue letters. What was this? Chris and Brianna were now holding letter-writing parties?

A feeling of foreboding washed away the hope from a moment ago as she scanned Chris's letter. The words blurred before her as she caught the snatches: he was sorry, he was in love with Brianna, he never meant to hurt her, but Brianna had been there for him, and she, Heidi, had not.

She released the letter and picked up Brianna's. This one had more detail, and she scanned the contents in disbelief, realizing before her lay an account of how and when Brianna and Chris had fallen in love. Dropping the letter as if it were on fire, she picked up the smaller envelope.

It was a *wedding invitation* requesting the honor of her presence at the wedding of Brianna Weld and Chris Mandison. This had to be a joke. She had scarcely been gone four months. Nobody had even warned her they were dating. Brianna had mentioned Chris a few times in her letters, but nothing had hinted at this. Maybe if she went back and reread Brianna's letters, she would find a clue.

Her mind swarmed with thoughts and questions, and she couldn't bring herself to read either letter fully. Humiliation warred with shock, and she burst into deep sobs. Why hadn't her parents said something to her? Shouldn't they have known? What about her other friends? Did nobody really care about her? Never in all her life had she felt so betrayed. Here she was, in *Africa*, and in four short months, she'd been so easily replaced by her *best friend*? And who could she turn to? Her mother had been so disappointed by her broken engagement that she probably wouldn't be very sympathetic. Her best friend had deceived her. And, she supposed, all her other friends might not want to get involved.

In the background, she was dimly aware of the afternoon gong sounding for game time. She had to get back and find her girls before anyone noticed her missing. She certainly didn't want anyone asking her what was wrong. How would she explain that in only two weeks, her best friend was marrying her former fiancé? If she hadn't come to South Africa, she and Chris would've already been married for three months. Yet here he was, getting married – to her best friend. So much for true and lasting love.

Somehow, she made it through the afternoon game time. She kept her hat and sunglasses in place and pasted what she hoped was a smile on her face. The girls were so giddy with the games they never noticed, although she caught Amy and even Johann shooting her concerned looks throughout the afternoon. She would've found Johann's concern almost comical if she hadn't been so upset. Maybe he had a soul, after all. Or, maybe he was still shocked about his *mieliepap*-face and realized there was more fight to her than he had imagined. Well, she would keep surprising him and all of them. Because nobody was going to find out how deeply she was hurt, nobody would ever know how difficult adjusting to life in a different country had been.

Amy walked with her back from the playing fields. "Are you OK?"

Heidi simply nodded. The news was too fresh and too raw to share with anyone just yet, although it dawned on her that if she wanted to talk, Amy would be a sympathetic listener.

She could feel Johann's eyes on her. Let him wonder. She kept up her charade throughout the afternoon and into the evening activities. As they were filing out to head to the cabins for the evening, he stopped her, gripping her arm, "Are you OK?"

Her eyes skittered across his face and met his gaze briefly. "Just fine, thanks." She turned abruptly, hoping he hadn't seen her reddened eyes. Thankfully, the ever-popular Johann was instantly surrounded by campers clambering for his attention. She glanced back once, though, and saw him looking after her, his head straining to look past the chaos. Their eyes met, and she felt a jolt of surprise at his now obvious concern. It hadn't been her imagination, after all.

That night, Heidi tossed and turned, silent tears pouring down her cheeks. She needed to get out of the cabin but had to be sure all her girls were asleep. She didn't know what would constitute firing a counselor, but it seemed obvious that leaving campers alone in the cabin at night would be a serious enough offense. The bolt was in place on the door, and she knew its squeakiness would wake the entire block of cabins. She would have to climb out of the window.

Heidi sat slowly, sliding the envelope and its dreadful contents out from beneath her pillow, her feet touching the cold concrete floor. She had left the window ajar, with the curtain closed. Scanning the bunks, she padded across the room and slipped behind the curtain. She sat on the wide sill, waiting to ensure she hadn't woken anyone. Then she swung her legs over the ledge and stepped out into the breezeway. The windows were practically a second door. There were no screens, and the way they swung outward made for a simple getaway. It made no sense that they would have counselors bolt the door but allow an open window for airflow. But, for tonight, she was grateful.

She stood awhile, letting her eyes adjust, making sure no one else was out visiting the bathrooms. Campers were to wake up their counselors if they needed the bathroom. But she found this rarely happened. Her girls were usually exhausted and slept through.

She carefully made her way along the breezeway, through the outdoor cafeteria, and then to the stone steps that lead to the pool. She caught her breath, the view arresting her progress. Beyond the pool and the fields, the water in the distant dam reflected the crescent moon still low in the sky, illuminating the shadows of the mountains beyond. Ethereal. What a contradiction to be heartbroken and yet encounter such beauty. Maybe God did care about her sorrow. Maybe He had orchestrated this moonrise. For her. It couldn't be a coincidence that she had stood at this spot at precisely the right moment, could it? For the first time since letter-time, she felt God's presence and comfort. He knew what she was going through. He cared.

Slowly she walked around the pool to the swing. From there, she could take in the view while hidden in the shadows. She removed the letters from the envelope and, cupping her flashlight in her hand to block most of the light, turned it on so she could read.

The letters told the same story. Chris and Brianna had started "hanging out" because they missed her so much, and then, one day, they realized they were in love, so they were getting married. She fingered the invitation; it was simple and nothing like the ornate invitations her mom had helped her pick out. *Two weeks...* there was only one reason Brianna would rush a wedding...

Brianna was pregnant.

As tears of disbelief flowed down her face, she remembered an argument she and Brianna had had right after Heidi and Chris had gotten engaged. "You're going to make him wait until the wedding?" Brianna had said with scorn.

"Of course, Brianna! Remember when we were younger, how we always said we would?"

"But we were kids. We didn't know what we were talking about."

"What do you mean? I knew and still know what I'm talking about!"

Brianna had simply shrugged, her eyes full of superiority as she shook her head at Heidi. "It's really not fair to Chris, you know. He's a guy."

"Brianna?" She had been incredulous. Why was her friend vilifying her for doing what they had once both believed in?

"Oh, come on Heidi, grow up!" Brianna snapped. "You need to get your head out of a Disney movie and realize that we live in real life and guys have real needs."

Heidi didn't respond; she just stared wide-eyed until realization dawned. "So, you're saying that you and Tim...?"

"Duh, Heidi. Of course. No guy is going to wait around forever, and it would be a good thing if you figured that out before you lose the best guy around."

Brianna had stalked out of her house and driven away, leaving Heidi gaping.

The memory faded as she hugged her knees to herself, fresh sobs taking her breath away. Brianna and Chris were pregnant, and they were getting married. That's why nobody had warned her they were dating. They had probably scarcely even dated, just "hung out." And Brianna had taken it upon herself to take care of Chris's "needs."

She felt sick. Chris had pressured her plenty of times, but she had always promised him the wait would be worth it. No wonder he had broken up with her when she asked if they could postpone the wedding. She wasn't worth *his* wait.

Heidi gazed back at the moonlit view, now blurred through her tears. The comfort from a few minutes ago had vaporized. She wiped at her eyes, trying to bring the scene into focus when she saw a figure coming down the steps toward her. She tried to switch off her flashlight but dropped it in her clumsiness. There it lay, illuminating a path straight to her. So much for escaping unnoticed. She tensed, wondering who it was and if she would be in trouble.

When the person got within a few feet of her, they stopped.

"Heidi?"

It was Johann, holding a flashlight and a package of toilet paper. She relaxed a bit. He might tease her and berate her and give her a hard time, but he wouldn't rat her out.

He leaned over and picked up the flashlight, shining it briefly towards her. "Are you OK?"

There was no way to answer him without sobbing uncontrollably, so she glanced away.

He stared at the letters now crumpled in her hands, turned off the flashlight, and sat next to her. "You can talk to me, you know."

She glanced toward him, wanting to believe him. Moments ticked as she debated. What if he made fun of her? Or worse, what if he used her sorrow as a camp joke story? Maybe he would take the hint and leave her alone if she didn't say anything. But surprisingly, she almost wanted him to stay – she had seen his wisdom and kindness with others plenty of times. Maybe if she told him, he would forget she was the American girl he disliked and provide advice.

She shuffled through the pages on her lap and, in a moment of decision, pulled out the invitation and handed it to him. "That," her voice quavered, "is a wedding invitation for my best friend, Brianna, and ex-fiancé, Chris. He broke up with me after I decided to come here for a year." She brought her hand to her mouth, trying to block another wave of crying.

He took it from her, not bothering to try and read it in the darkness. Then, slowly, he reached around and pulled her against him, pressing her head against his chest. One hand rubbed her back, and one gripped her head, gently moving his fingers against her scalp. "Oh, Heidi, no wonder you have been so upset all day." His voice rumbled against her ear pressed against him, his kindness causing her to cry even harder.

They stayed that way while she cried, and he continued to rub her back and shoulders and hold her, telling her she could cry for as long as she needed to. Never, in all the times she and Chris had spent together, had he made her feel this validated, this cared for. And this was Johann—mean, teasing, aggravating Johann.

Eventually, she pulled away, palming her cheeks, wishing she had tissues. Johann leaned down and picked up a roll of toilet paper. "Need some?"

She laughed shakily. "You patrol camp at night with rolls of toilet paper?"

He gave her his lopsided grin. "Let's just say there was a need, and I was setting out to fulfill it when I came to investigate the glow at the pool swing."

"So, someone has been sitting on the throne of thought all this time waiting for you?"

"They'll be fine." He shrugged and then pulled her back against him. "Are you going to write them back?" He indicated the letters with his chin.

"There's nothing to say… I mean, what *would* I say?"

Johann gazed at the view, absently rubbing his free hand along her arm.

"Or, I could just say nothing."

"Exactly." Johann nodded. "That's what I would do. No word from you makes them wonder a million scenarios – are you mad, happy, glad, relieved, miserable, etc." He picked up the invitation and shone the flashlight back on it, squinting to read the words at the bottom. "See here where it says, 'The favor of your reply is requested'? Well, you *ain't* doing them any favors, honey!"

Heidi laughed despite herself. "You need help with that American accent, Johann."

"*Ja*, we probably shouldn't talk about accents Miss-I-can't-roll-an-r-to-save-my-life." And he pulled her head back against his chest and mussed her hair, making her laugh in protest.

She leaned away and tried to fix her hair, feeling suddenly embarrassed. "Thanks, Johann," she felt her cheeks flush, "I never knew I'd be rescued tonight by a usually *mean* toilet-paper toting patrolman."

He reached out and gripped her shoulder, facing her head on. "I haven't been exactly nice to you, have I?" When she didn't reply, he stood, helping her to her feet, and hugged her hard, squeezing the breath out of her. "Oh, Heidi, you've been such a good sport. I think I need to tell you I'm sorry."

Heidi didn't say anything; she couldn't. Standing in his embrace, surrounded by the moonlit view, aware of his lean, solid body pressed against her, words wouldn't come.

"You know, we get American visitors on and off all the time. They come for their 'short-term' mission trips, as they call them. They stay for a week or two and take lots of photos so they can go back home and show everyone how they sacrificed two weeks of their lives helping us helpless Africans. I thought you were another one of *those,* but I was very, very wrong." He loosened his hold slightly and turned her head towards him, gazing into her eyes. "Your love for your girls each camp session, your hard work, your obvious love for God.... You're different from them, Heidi. Will you ever forgive me for being so terrible to you?"

"So, you based your dislike on me because you dislike all Americans?"

"No, no, no, I really don't dislike *all* Americans." He stepped back and sighed. "Here, sit for a minute longer, and I'll tell you the real reason...."

110

They sat once more, and he angled his body towards her. "When you applied to work at camp, so did Marie."

Ah, suddenly everything made sense. "And I took her spot?"

"Yes."

"I'm sorry, Johann, I never knew. I just saw the opening at a mission conference and felt this need to do something above and beyond what was set out for me, something different. It's like this camp called to me. Once I saw it, I couldn't get it out of my mind. Everyone was angry with me – Chris, Brianna, and even my mom; everyone but my dad. They thought I was throwing away my job, my fiancé, and the future I'd worked so hard for. But what they didn't understand... I wasn't ready to start my future before I found my purpose. And plus, there were signs with Chris that maybe we weren't exactly meant for each other, signs I had tried to ignore. And here, here I have purpose, and I feel so fulfilled. And even though I took Marie's place, and I'm sorry, I never knew, I just feel like God is here... I don't know... it's hard to explain because I know He's everywhere, but...."

He reached out and put his arm around her shoulders again. "I understand. And, you have been incredible, and I can see now that you are just what your cabin girls need. And you've already been good for the Stamp Club. And Marie is very happy at Wits. So, it all worked out. I'm just very sorry for being a jerk from the beginning."

Heidi turned to him, her eyes shimmering with relief. It wasn't lost on her that her relief at his apology felt bigger than her heartache over Chris's betrayal. She would need to analyze that at some point, but for now, she would let it be.

"Will you forgive me for judging you so wrong... for judging you at all?" The depth in his eyes caused her to take a quick breath and hold it.

"Yeah," she managed softly.

"Yes, you'll forgive me, or 'yes,' I've been mean and judgmental."

She gave him a lopsided smile. "Both."

He laughed and hugged her to him.

She shut her eyes, enjoying the feel of his arms around her, the fresh soapy smell of his shampoo filling her senses.

He stepped back. "Now, before I report you for leaving your sleeping cabin unattended, I suggest you get back to your room...." Then he stepped over and lofted the toilet roll package high in the air. "And I shall finish the task that I set out to do!" And with an exaggerated bow, he left, leaving Heidi to pick her way back up the steps towards her cabin.

He was a miracle man. No wonder everyone loved him so much. Here she sat, holding those offensive letters, the despair and betrayal that had consumed her earlier, a great deal tempered by *Johann*. As she slipped back through her cabin window and onto her bunk, she fell asleep with the memory of his embrace. Somebody *had* cared, and of all the people in the world, it had been Johann.

CHAPTER 12

Heidi awoke slowly to a sea of little-girl faces surrounding her in consternation.

"*Oom* Johann said we were to let her keep sleeping."

"But what if she's hungry?"

"She already missed breakfast."

"Maybe she's sick."

"Who will sit with us in chapel?"

"We can sit by ourselves!"

"But I always sit by Aunt Heidi...."

"Don't be such a crybaby."

Heidi rubbed her eyes and tried to choke out a "good morning" to her girls.

"You're awake!"

"She's awake!"

"Now we don't have to sit alone."

Heidi groaned inwardly, trying to smile at the anxious ten-year-olds. She needed a bathroom and a shower and a hot cup of tea, but she could already hear the gong for morning chapel. She swung her legs over the side of the bunk, automatically counting her girls. Yes, there were eight of them, all scrambling to find their Bibles and notebooks. And there sat Janelle, curled into the corner of her bunk.

"Janelle, honey, are you ready for chapel?"

"I'm... I'm going to wait for you," she whispered.

Just then, Amy popped her cheery head through the cabin door. "Morning, Heidi's Cabin! You are coming with me." She winked at Heidi as she carefully walked over to Janelle and took her hand. "And you, my lovely girly, are going to sit by me!"

Heidi watched gratefully as Janelle scooted off her bunk, taking Amy's hand.

"Thanks, Amy," she managed. Amy responded with a half wave and a worried smile before shutting the door behind her. Heidi knew Amy must be dying of curiosity. She needed to talk with her, but at the same time, talking would bring back the tears. And her head pounded from crying so much the night before. She wondered if Johann had said something to Amy. How else had he let her sleep in without alerting at least some of the staff?

Heidi grabbed her clothes for the day and then carefully slipped out to the bathrooms. She hoped a shower and caffeine would get her going. As the memory of the contents of yesterday's letter rose, she tried to squelch it. She needed to remain present for her girls, focus on them, and not wallow in the self-pity that threatened to drown her.

Her curly hair dripping down her back, she slipped into the kitchen, hoping for solitude. But Vera stood at the stove, and Heidi's heart sank.

Vera glanced up and smiled, her eyes full of questions. "Are you alright?"

Heidi nodded briefly. "Yes, just some upsetting news from home. But I'm sure a cup of tea can fix it," she said, lamely trying to copy Mrs. Voskamp's oft-repeated sentiment.

Vera nodded, turning back to the stove. "Johann said we were to save you some breakfast, so I left the pot of oatmeal on the stove. Would you like for me to heat it back up?"

"Oh, um, yes, please." Heidi grabbed a glass, filling it with water and then picked out an orange. They never bought orange juice at camp, but the oranges were the best. She sliced the orange with shaking fingers.

Vera came over, gently taking the knife from her. "How about you sit and let me take care of breakfast for you?"

Heidi moved away wordlessly, fighting the threatening tears. Sympathy would make her cry, and she did not want to spend the day crying; she wanted to jump back into camp life and forget the letters. If she stayed busy, then maybe she could shove the wave of betrayal that kept washing over her. She owed everyone an

114

explanation but wanted to make it simple and keep from becoming the target of pitying looks.

Vera placed the oatmeal, orange, and tea in front of Heidi and sat opposite her.

"I'm sorry for causing all this trouble," Heidi kept her gaze on her oatmeal, thankful it wasn't *mieliepap* or the stuff they all called *maltabella.*

"My dear, you are not causing trouble, in fact..." she laughed briefly, "you have been the best counselor we have had in a long time. Most girls who come here are so worried about themselves and their own comfort, they don't last at all."

Heidi raised her eyebrows. She had never thought about the girls before her.

"Oh *Ja*, they come, and they flirt with all the boys, and can't peel the first potato, and want to treat this place like a holiday. You are an excellent worker, and, by the way, it seems a writer, too, and we are lucky to have you."

Heidi stared at her directly now. Maybe this explained why Karl remained unwelcoming. He expected her to be a *prima donna.* The knowledge filled her with resolve. Not even her latest news would make her cave and become a liability. She would offer them a simple explanation and then get out there and do what she had come to do – make a difference in the lives of her campers.

"So, you liked my ideas?" Heidi felt a sliver of hope burst through the darkness.

"Why, yes, I love your ideas. Johann and I have been talking, you know. And I've already contacted the Stamp Club. They actually have specific lessons *they* want us to revamp now that we have someone willing to do so."

Heidi smiled softly. What wonderful news! Another purpose for being here. Something she could do that would last beyond her tenure at camp.

She took a small bite of oatmeal. The cereal stuck in her throat, and she tried to help it down with a sip of tea.

Heidi took a deep breath, ""That's... that's very exciting news, and it's nice to hear today." She looked up at Vera, who seemed to be waiting for Heidi to expand her thoughts. "I… I don't know what Johann told you, but I just found out yesterday…" she paused. She could hear the waver in her voice and took a breath, hoping to be in control of her emotions.

Vera sat patiently, reaching out and squeezing Heidi's hand.

"Anyway," Heidi continued, wishing they could grab Amy so she wouldn't have to repeat this later in the day. "I was engaged before I came, but he broke it off when I decided to come here to work."

Vera nodded and then turned her head to the sound of the door opening. It was Amy, appearing as if Heidi had wished her there.

"They're working on skits, and Janelle seemed happy, so I slipped out for a minute," she said, sliding onto the bench next to Heidi. "Are you feeling better?"

Heidi nodded and took another slow breath. "I just started telling your mom, but now I can tell you, too."

"I got a letter yesterday from Chris," she looked at Amy, "you know, my ex-fiancé?" When Amy nodded, she went on. "But actually, it was two letters – one from Chris and one also from Brianna, my closest friend at home." She glanced at Amy, curious to see if she remembered their talks about the two.

Amy nodded, encouraging her to go on.

"Well, yesterday's letter was from both of them, and they are getting married in two weeks." There! She had said it, and she hadn't started crying again. Vera thought she was strong and appreciated her hard work. At least the women liked her, and plus, Johann had been so wonderful the night before. Maybe he would be nice to her from now on.

She stared at her oatmeal, waiting for their reaction, not wanting to see the pity in their eyes.

Amy spoke first. "That's just horrible. What kind of friend would possibly do that?"

Heidi shrugged. She had wondered the same thing.

Mrs. Voskamp squeezed her hand again. "It sounds like God

saved you from marrying the wrong man."

Heidi narrowed her eyes, unsure.

"Any boy who was about to pledge his lifetime love to you and who would then marry somebody else a few months later would not have had the strength to last in marriage."

The quiet settled around her as the truth of her words took hold.

"That's a good way to put it, Mom," Amy whispered, tears in her eyes.

Heidi smiled wanly, comforted by the solidarity of Amy's tears. She had wished Chris would change his mind. It *was* a good way to think about it. Chris hadn't wanted to wait a year for her, so they had broken up. And Chris hadn't had the character to wait for marriage. So, Chris *had* been the wrong person for her. "Yes, it is," Heidi whispered back.

The sounds of the children tromping down from the meeting hall floated towards them, and Amy jumped up. "Here they come; time to get ready for a hike." She reached over and hugged Heidi. "Are you going to be able to come?"

Heidi took another deep breath. "Yes, yes, I am."

"Not until you eat all your oatmeal, skinny girl," Vera reprimanded.

Heidi grinned, finding it funny someone had called her skinny. She hadn't been this thin since high school and was amazed every day how different it felt without extra pounds stuck to her. She obediently swallowed more oatmeal and, after giving Vera a grateful hug, slipped out the door to find her campers.

They congregated at the top of the pool steps, clustering around Johann as he gave constant instructions. "Does your bush kit have a water bottle? Do you have socks on with your *takkies*?" Kids were milling and checking and running back to their cabins to get forgotten items as Heidi walked up. Johann, seeing her, cocked his head to the side. "Well, now Aunt Heidi has actually woken up from her extra-long sleep, maybe we are ready!"

The children turned and clapped, looking at her in anticipation of another possible joke from Johann.

"Aunt Heidi?"

"Yes, *Oom* Johann." She resigned herself to play along. His voice and smile were playful, but his eyes were solemn.

"We are going on a looonnnnng hike today."

"Oh, we are?"

"Those flip-flops of yours are the wrong shoes for such a long hike."

"Well then, if you will all wait for me, I'll go put on my... my...." What was the word they used for tennis shoes in this country?

"Your *takkies*?"

"Yes, I would like to look tacky in my *takkies*."

The laughter stopped as every pair of under-twelve eyes focused on her in confusion. Obviously, these English speakers didn't know her English. That's what she got for trying to be as funny as Johann. She mumbled she'd be quick and hurried to her cabin; thankful Johann had provided a segue for her to get back into the day. Plus, she loved this hike, and a morning of walking would be therapeutic.

After Johann had each counselor account for their kids, they took off, trudging along the dirt road towards the trail that would take them to the top of the closest *koppie*. It was the perfect length hike for the children, and the dilapidated brick walls of a long-forgotten structure at the top made for improvised stories while the children rested before the hike back down. The April breeze was refreshingly cool and an ideal counterpart to the bright sunlight. Heidi tilted her head towards the sky, smiling at the cobalt depths. She assumed the reduced humidity here made this African sky much bluer than the Florida sky she had grown up with. Her heart swelled; she loved this country. Breathing deeply, she felt her head begin to clear. Today was not the typical day for this hike. She didn't know why Johann had changed the days, but it had provided a splendid antidote to the sadness that had filled her since yesterday's letters.

Turning around, she found Janelle, trudging along next to two other girls in the cabin, and fell into step beside her.

Janelle smiled shyly and took Heidi's hand. "It's pretty here."

"It sure is," Heidi squeezed the small hand in hers. "Wait until we get to the top!"

Janelle looked up, swinging her free arm with gusto like she had found a way to escape whatever plagued her throughout the day. Heidi wished she had more than a week to help Janelle, but such was the nature of camp – you barely got to know your group of kids, and then they left. She would have to ensure Janelle signed up for the Stamp Club and they stayed in contact.

At the top of the *koppie*, when all the children were settled on a portion of the broken wall, Johann began his story. Heidi was squeezed between Janelle and the rest of her cabin, all mesmerized by Johann's tale. They were always different: Johann's prolific imagination never lacked novelty. Heidi watched him in fresh amazement. He was made for this job and clearly in his element.

After the story's dramatic conclusion, Johann instructed the children to explore around before they needed to leave. The kids jumped down from their respective perches, and Heidi glanced around for Amy. Spotting her, she saw Amy and Ian standing face to face, Amy's hand in Ian's, seemingly discussing something on the top of Amy's hand.

"*Ag*, young love." Johann's voice in her ear startled her as he jumped onto her section of wall, squeezing next to her.

She turned to him and half-smiled. "Amy's father isn't going to be very happy about that."

"Amy knows it. Why do you think they are only acting so friendly at the top of the *koppie*? You ever see Karl hike before?"

Heidi raised her eyebrows. She had never heard him assign negativity to Karl.

"Mr. Voskamp is a good man, but he is a bit too strict on Amy." He paused, clearly debating whether or not to continue.

"In what ways?" She had her own observations but had never dared to say anything. She'd assumed the difference in culture accounted for some of Karl's protectiveness and had thus refrained from broaching the subject with Amy.

Johann shrugged. "He wouldn't let her go to university after her *matric*. I mean, why doesn't he want his daughter to have some more education? Amy is so clever, but she is too nice of a girl to go against her father. He told her she had enough education to serve God at the camp.

Heidi looked back over at Amy, literally glowing in Ian's company. She felt secretly relieved to see her flirting with Ian because she had wondered if Karl's ultimate plan was to have Johann and Amy marry. And, for reasons she had yet to analyze, this made her extremely uncomfortable.

"So, how are you this morning?" Johann bumped against her shoulder.

"Sitting up here under your bright blue South African sky, watching the children run around, I'm feeling lots better." She turned and bumped his shoulder right back. Right now, her bad news felt far away.

He slipped his arm around her shoulders and squeezed, "one weekend when there are no children in camp, we will have to take you hiking to God's Window where the—"

"Snake!!!" A shrill scream punctured the moment. Johann jumped off the wall and ran to the voice.

"Everybody, freeze!" he yelled, his knife in his hand, eyes scanning anxiously. "Where is it?"

"Here," a quavering voice answered back. It was Dean, pointing a shaking finger at what only could be a cobra poised to strike.

"Please God," Heidi murmured softly.

Johann approached stealthily. In one swift movement, he flung his knife at the snake. The snake writhed, pinned in place. The campers gasped as Johann threw Dean to safety. "Heidi, grab that spade right behind where you are sitting."

Fear pounded through her veins as she looked behind her. A *spade*? Sure enough, she saw the handle of a shovel and grabbed it, jumping off the wall and coming towards him. She could hear the children whimpering. They stood frozen in place, eyes darting from the snake to Johann.

He grabbed the shovel from her and, in a series of decisive movements, chopped the snake into pieces. When he was finished, he removed his knife and turned back to the children. "Very good, you are now all snake experts." A few children giggled nervously; others remained still, their admiration for Johann's skill palpable.

Johann walked over to Dean and helped him up from where he had landed. "Dean, I declare you the number one hero today!" He lifted Dean's trembling arm high above his head as the children clapped.

CHAPTER 13

July came, and June's crisp weather turned into full-fledged winter – at least to a Floridian. Heidi, who had never owned a coat before, had to buy one. Waking up to frost was yet another surprise Africa held for her. Amy had insisted Heidi buy some slip-on boots for walking to and from the bathroom in the morning. Showering in the freezing bathrooms was another story. She learned to get it down to a science: run there in her boots with the coat over her pajamas, turn on the shower as hot as she could, disrobe, jump in, scrub fast, jump out, and then dress quickly before hypothermia set in. More than once, she wished the cabins had attached bathrooms. What had been a minor inconvenience during warm weather was now a different story.

With less outdoor activity, Heidi found more time for writing. Revamping the lessons filled the non-camp days in a way she found invigorating. When working for her dad, sitting at a desk all day had felt endless. But here, she found she could write all day, barely noticing the passage of time. It was a complete surprise.

The month of July included a nearly four-week school holiday, which Amy explained was the end of the second school term. And Camp Timothy ran full camps all four weeks. The current week was for the younger campers, the nine to twelve age bracket, and Heidi found them more manageable than the older campers. They were less complicated, she never had to guess at their emotions, and they warmed to her quickly. They had boundless energy but would settle down at night if she told them made-up stories. And, they mainly were unconcerned about their appearance, so she never found herself waiting around for someone to fix their hair or change their clothes for the nth time.

She had let these girls into the secret that she had multiple names for Johann, and they helped her add to the list every night. It was all fun until one of them decided to tell him, and then, in typical fashion, it was payback time.

They had just finished game time and were walking in clusters up the pool steps when Johann called to her.

She turned, wondering. "Yes?"

He was now beside her, a bucket of water in one hand. "Somebody," and he looked around dramatically, "and I won't say who—"

All the campers laughed and pushed closer.

"—told me you have many names for me," he roared.

Campers clapped and jostled and oohed and ahhed, ready for what was coming next.

"So, how many names do you have for me, *Aunt* Heidi?" He held her by the shoulder with one hand and the bucket of water with the other, poised, ready to dump it all on her head. They were near the pool steps, and the campers were clustered around, enjoying the show—her girls included. It would have been nice if they defended her, but they were way too smitten with Johann to ever do such a thing.

Heidi shrugged nonchalantly. "Oh, just a few, don't I, girls?"

They responded with more giggles, nodding their heads, winking, and nudging each other with glee.

"Girls?" Johann swept a teasingly stern glance across the group. "Does anyone care to share one of these names with me?"

"Girls!" Heidi warned, hoping they wouldn't cave. Let him dump the whole bucket on her head; she didn't care.

"African King." That was from little Beth.

"Yo-Yo-how-does-it-go?" That was from Cindy.

Three girls simultaneously finished for her. "Yo-I'm-too-Pretty-for-my-Safari-Suit."

Everyone laughed. The crowd had gotten larger.

"*Uncle* Johann," one little girl advised as the laughter abated, "she has a name for every situation!"

"Well then, let's hear some more!"

Heidi craned her neck, trying to see around Johann, looking for Amy. Right then, she caught a glimpse of her friend, almost directly behind him, lugging a similar bucket of ice water. Heidi glanced down, not wanting to draw attention towards her assistance, and shouted above the uproar, "I'll tell you the latest name if you promise not to dump that."

"The *latest* name?"

There was a chorus of cries from all the campers. "She has *another* one!"

Johann dropped his jaw, looking between the girls and their leader. He allowed the bucket to tip slightly, sending a stream of ice water over her face, but she barely flinched.

"Quite refreshing, Mr. Yo—" She stopped, making sure Amy had her cue, "-I-NEED-A-SHOWER!" And, right when she shouted the name, Amy, who had maneuvered herself onto a step behind Johann, dumped her entire bucket over his head.

He yelled what sounded like a war cry and then, in one swift motion, swung Heidi over his shoulders like a sack of potatoes and began walking toward the pool. "Come on, girls," he directed, "I think this name-maker needs to go for a swim!"

They followed in a chorus of part laughter, part disbelief.

"It's too cold!"

"She'll catch cold!"

"Aunt Heidi, we'll save you!"

But none of them attempted to thwart Johann. They were too enthralled by the scene to ruin it.

Heidi knew he would throw her in the pool, knew she was no match for his strength. So, she struggled halfheartedly until they got to the pool's edge.

"What should I do, girls?" He was the Pied Piper, and they were his followers.

"Throw her in!" They yelled back.

Little traitors, Heidi thought, poised and ready to grab onto Johann the minute he tried to release her. If she got a good enough grip on him, he would come in with her.

"Help me count!" he yelled as he began swinging her towards the edge.

"*Een!*"

She assumed that meant "one."

"*Twee!*"

That was definitely "two."

Before he had hollered the word for three, she plastered her upside-down face against him and roped her arms around his torso, gripping her hands with all the strength she could muster.

And it worked. As she began to fall, he had no choice but to fall with her. She could feel him struggling to release her hands, but her grip was too good. They hit the water simultaneously like a large awkward tree being felled, the freezing water a shock to all her senses. She released him and came to the surface as quickly as she could, gasping from the shock of the temperature, spluttering from the water clogging every available crevice.

They stood there, freezing, laughing at each other, Johann in clear disbelief that she had managed to make him fall in, too, while the campers around them cheered and yelled with delight.

***

Heidi was cold—probably too cold—and Johann's camp director mode kicked in as he reached out to steady her, ensuring she was OK. He knew he needed to concede defeat. These things could go on and on, and what started as a prank wouldn't stop, so in an act of good sportsmanship, he grabbed her arm and pumped her fist into the air.

"Ladies and gentle... um... ladies." This was an all-girls camp. "May I present to you the one and only Aunt Heidi-of-the-Arctic-Waters!"

The girls cheered louder.

He was freezing and knew she was too. Her lips were already turning blue. "And would someone please get us some towels?"

"I'll get them," called Amy.

Johann waded out of the pool, his hand clamped on Heidi's arm, pulling her onto the steps. He wished they would hurry with the towels; stepping into the cold wind would be brutal. He turned towards Heidi and drew her shivering frame against him. "Stand here out of the wind until the towels come," he instructed, turning to see Amy directly in front of him, with no towels, a strange expression on her face.

However, a few of the little girls had run back and grabbed their towels, and he accepted them gratefully while looking quizzically over at Amy. What had gotten into her? She was never this inept. He quickly opened the first towel and wrapped it around Heidi. "There, you crazy American, now go and take a hot shower before you get sick!"

"OK, Mr. Yo-I-Really-am-a-Nice-Guy," she mumbled softly but loud enough for him to hear.

He threw his head back and laughed uproariously. "Girls, I got my first good name!" he hollered towards the crowd, then he wrapped his arms around her, picked her up, towel and all, and deposited her on the poolside, steadying before he released her.

The campers clapped louder as Heidi and Johann stood eye to eye.

"Heidi," his voice was gentle, "you need to go and take a shower."

Johann grabbed the remaining towels, wrapping one around his shivering shoulders and one around his waist, and then leaned over to grab the remaining towels still on the ground, only to realize someone had moved to stand directly in front of him. Confused, he snatched his eyes up to the face of none other than Marie.

"Well, well," her hands were on her hips, her voice laced with ice. "It looks like I came at the perfect time to see you *in action*, Johann."

"Marie!" He furrowed his eyebrows, "You're visiting camp?"

"Surprise, surprise," her sarcasm was palpable.

He moved to hug her, but she stepped back with a scowl. "You're wet."

He glanced down at his drenched, towel-covered shivering self.

"Yes, I am. I'll go and get a hot shower and be back *chop-chop*," he promised lamely. "If you can find Amy or Mavis, they can make you some tea while you wait for me to change," he added as an afterthought, hoping she wouldn't simply stand there alone and angry the whole time he got dressed. Then, scarcely with a backward glance, he headed to the showers, his heart sinking in disbelief. Of all the times for Marie to surprise him at camp, it had to be then. *Ai-ja-jai*, he didn't know what she had seen, but he knew he had been way too tender with Heidi on the steps. He knew he had some explaining to do if only he could explain his scrambled feelings to himself....

CHAPTER 14

Johann was in a quandary. Marie's entire visit had been a disaster. Coming while a camp was in session hadn't been appropriate in the first place. Consequently, they had little time together. Instead of jumping in and helping, she grumbled that visiting on her July break was a waste of her holiday. Plus, she had had to sleep in the cabin with Amy and her girls, which led to more complaining.

Now, after four weeks of non-stop camps, they all had an entire weekend off. Karl and Vera were headed out to see family. Johann intended to see Marie, hoping he could fix whatever had gone wrong, and Heidi and Amy had planned a big shopping day. Then, Johann would pick them up and drive to Alberton, where they would stay with the Andersons and go to their church on Sunday. The church in Alberton had asked him to do a three-lesson course with the church youth.

At the last minute, Amy's parents decided Amy must come with them. She was devastated. Johann suspected her despondency had less to do with shopping and more to do with planned time with Ian. He felt bad for Amy, and he knew Heidi was disappointed. But Heidi took it in stride, probably because she knew she would've spent most of their "shopping Saturday" alone anyway.

***

Leaving early that chilly Saturday morning, despite feeling bad for Amy, Heidi couldn't contain her excitement. She was going to go shopping, get her hair cut, and sleep in a house with other Americans. Then, on Sunday, they would be at a real church, complete with what sounded like the South African version of a potluck afterward. But, if she were honest, the best part would be spending time with Johann. She tried to ignore the feelings, but they surfaced at the most inopportune times, and she was simply too excited about a weekend away for self-recrimination.

As they drove along the dirt and gravel road away from camp, she wanted to whoop for joy. But she could sense how pensive Johann was about his day with Marie. So, instead, once they hit the paved road, she rolled the window down, stuck her head out into the cold air, and let the wind rush over her, clearing her head and enhancing her senses. She was ecstatic.

"Shut the window, you crazy girl!"

But she ignored him, laughing with pleasure. Nobody was going to end her moment one second too soon. He was obviously in a grumpy mood, but his Marie problems were his, and she wasn't going to allow them to touch the joy bubbling from inside. In fact, maybe she could convince him to be a little happier. It would be fun to try.

"Heidi," he roared, "shut the window!"

She laughed harder; she was freezing, but it was worth seeing Mr. Calm-and-in-Control in a bit of a frenzy.

"I swear, I'm gonna *klap* you."

She glanced over, happily noting the smile playing on his lips. "This is what air conditioning feels like, Johann," she hollered over the noise. "We have it in America and…."

"You want air conditioning; I'll give you air conditioning!" And with that, he rolled his window down, too. "Now, we'll just see who's the toughest. How about that?"

Challenge accepted.

She moved to grab her jacket, but he was too fast for her. "Oh no you don't!" He took it and stuffed it between him and the door.

"Johann, you… you… *paw-paw*!"

He laughed uproariously.

"What?" Her teeth were chattering now despite her merriment.

"Who taught you that?"

"What?"

"*Paw-paw.*"

"Oh, Amy is giving me Afrikaans lessons," she tried to sound nonchalant above the roar of the wind.

"What other words is she teaching you?"

Heidi shrugged. "I dunno, things like *chommie, cozzie,* and my brain is too frozen to remember the rest."

"You're the one who rolled down your window first."

"And you copied me... you... you... *cozzie.*"

Now they both dissolved into laughter.

"Um, Heidi, what does *cozzie* mean?"

"Who knows? My brain is frozen!"

He leaned sideways and patted her head. "You just called me a swimming costume."

Heidi slapped her hands over her eyes and then split her fingers, peaking back at him. "First time for everything?"

He laughed, squeezing her shoulder. "Just roll up your window, *chop-chop!*"

"I can't. My hand is numb!"

"What?"

"See?" And she tried to wiggle her fingers at him, but they refused to cooperate.

"*Ai-ja-jai*, woman," he shook his head, slowing down and pulling off the road. "I really should *klap* you for this one."

"Yes, applause would be welcome anytime," she stuttered.

"What?" Confusion flitted across his face until realization dawned. "Not 'clap,' '*klap,*' surely Amy taught you that one by now." And he reached across her and began rolling up the window. "You really need to learn to operate my windows, you know. I know it's stiff, but if you can roll it down, you should be able to roll it up!"

Heidi didn't respond. She could smell his shampoo and had to resist the crazy urge to bury her face in his hair and breathe deeply. Suddenly she wasn't cold anymore, and the thought of wrapping her arms around his shoulders while he continued to crank the handle made her breathless. Her frozen brain had reverted to junior high giddiness.

Next, he cranked his window and then turned the heater full

blast. Rubbing his hands together, he glanced over at her. "Heidi?"

Still breathless and trying to get her traitorous mind under control, she gave him a weak smile. "Yes?"

"Put your jacket on, crazy girl." He spoke softly, and she wondered if he had been having similar thoughts.

She took the jacket from him and allowed him to help her into it. Then he rubbed his hands along her arms and gripped her shoulders, his face inches from her. "You OK?"

She gazed into those gorgeous green eyes. She couldn't respond, so she sat there, enjoying his hands on her shoulders and his eyes boring into hers.

He took her face in his hands, and her breath hitched a notch. "Your cheeks are freezing, One-Who-Misses-Air-Conditioning." His voice was even softer, and she wondered if he could hear her thundering heart. He leaned closer, his eyes on her lips, and she stopped breathing.

A car rushed by, honking loudly, causing them both to jump and laugh self-consciously.

Johann dropped his hands and looked momentarily confused, shaking his head. "Better start driving."

Heidi felt equally guilty and bad for him. He had just about kissed her on the way to visit his girlfriend. "Yes, Mr. Yo-I-Helped-Save-the-American, because I have lots of shopping to do." And she gave him the brightest smile she could muster.

"OK, then," he smiled back. "Windows gonna stay up?"

She gave him a mock salute and another smile as he put the truck back in gear and edged onto the road.

"So, tell me about the training sessions you're doing tomorrow." Heidi willed her voice to sound natural. She needed to distract him because she suspected he was inwardly berating himself for almost kissing her.

He let out a long breath before launching into his explanation.

***

What was it about Heidi? He glanced at her working studiously on her shopping list and resisted the urge to tease her. Truth be told, he would much rather spend the day helping her shop than trying to figure out Marie. A girlfriend shouldn't be so complicated, yet lately, Marie made everything complicated. And after being around Heidi, who found joy in everything, it was difficult not to make comparisons. He tried to focus on Marie and their plans for the day, but it was impossible with Heidi sitting right next to him, her crazy curls falling across her face as she studied her list.

To think he had almost kissed her! What had gotten into him? The car going by had been providential, and he needed to be grateful for it. But all he felt was disappointment and then confusion over his disappointment. Hopefully, after a day with Marie, his feelings would be back on track.

***

"Now, see where we are? Second floor, east parking lot, outside of the food area."

Heidi nodded meekly. She wanted to laugh but knew he wouldn't let her out of the car if he thought she wasn't paying attention. "What time did you say?"

"Half past five, Heidi." His exasperation was evident.

Didn't he remember she had flown halfway around the world alone, and he was the one who had failed to meet her?

"Five-thirty?"

"*Ja,* my American girl, five-*thirty.*"

The sudden tenderness in his voice warmed her heart, and she wished for the umpteenth time he would forget Marie and spend the day with her. Instead, she smiled brightly and saluted. "See you then!"

Stepping into the mall literally overloaded her senses. After months at camp and only a couple of visits here, the masses of people, labyrinth of stores, and sounds of commerce made her forget she was in South Africa. What a country of contradictions. Out at camp, it felt like Africa, but here, she could've been in any major US shopping mall and not known the difference. Taking note of her surroundings, she ventured toward a mall map to locate a salon. Her hair was first on her list. Then, she needed to buy clothes—lots of them. She'd hardly spent any money in six months, and the clothes she had arrived in and the few outfits she had purchased were now too big and no match for the South African winter. She had had zero preparation for how cold it would get, and the morning frost was a constant unwelcome surprise. Her heart lifted in anticipation as she headed with purpose toward a salon.

HEIDI RECHECKED HER watch and groaned. She had three hours left. She stopped near a Wimpy and smiled to herself, remembering. It had only been six months, but so much had changed. She fingered her freshly cut hair and glanced down appreciatively at her new stretch jeans. They said they were a size 10, which made her want to roll her eyes. These were much smaller than the American-sized 10 jeans she had packed in her permanently missing suitcase. One sales lady had explained the sizing was based on centimeters and not a random number decided on by the manufacturer. Sizing aside, changing into the new jeans and chunky sweater had been a good call. She had the satisfying feeling that came from knowing she looked good.

Even if she was alone.

She meandered over to the Wimpy counter and ordered a hamburger and a milkshake. Her bags weighed heavy as she maneuvered into a table, sitting gratefully and setting the bags between her feet. Johann had warned her about purse grabbers, and she wasn't about to lose her hard-sought purchases. Taking an appreciative bite of burger, she glanced toward the movie theatres. It seemed their movie offerings were way behind. She had Chris to thank for her movie knowledge; he loved movies. But she had gone only to spend time with him. She knew it was a weakness, constantly caving to what he wanted, but it had been easier than sticking up for herself. And, in the grand scheme of things, how important was taking a stand against going to another movie? Yet, now she wondered why she hadn't been more insistent on finding things they both enjoyed. With Johann and Amy, things were always fun, whether they were working or hiking or troubleshooting during what Johann called their "*boer maak 'n plan*" meetings. Self-retribution settled over her as she wondered about her prior relationship.

Heidi shifted in the seat and took another sip of the milkshake. Brianna would have loved this – the enormous mall, the foreignness of the people around them, the eclectic stores. But Brianna would be shopping for baby clothes or sitting in the movies with Chris....

She needed to redirect her thoughts. Immediately. Scanning the tables clustered in geometric sections, she couldn't help but notice a group of young people in the far corner. They were laughing and focusing on one blonde girl, who kept making statements and tossing her hair. Well, everyone except one young man on the fringes of the group.

Heidi squinted to get a better look. The girl bore a strong resemblance to Marie, and a shock jolted through her body when the bored young man looked up. Johann!

She glanced down in confusion, wondering if he had seen her. He was supposed to spend the day with Marie, not hang out with Marie's friends at the mall. She looked again, right in time to see him lean over and say something to the Marie-looking girl and then head towards her table. She stared at her food and fidgeted, unsure, until she could sense him right in front of her.

"Heidi?"

"Hey." She meant to sound casual, but her voice sounded more like a squeak. The quick beating of her heart told her she was way too happy to see him earlier than expected.

He straddled the seat across from her and turned sideways, Marie still in his sight. "Marie, well... uh, she wanted me to meet all her friends."

"Makes sense." It didn't make any sense. If Johann was her boyfriend and she hadn't seen him for days, she wouldn't share him with anyone. She lifted her eyes, worried he could read her thoughts, and felt herself redden.

"Nice haircut."

His eyes were appreciative, and Heidi's blush deepened. Since when was she at a loss of words around Johann? "Thanks." She ducked her head and shifted the packages at her feet.

"Looks like you found a lot today."

"Yeah." She tilted her head. "I threw my old clothes away."

"They were too big anyway," he acknowledged sagely.

"Too much *mieliepap*," she agreed.

He nodded and opened his mouth but then glanced back towards Marie. "You want to join us?"

"Oh, uh, no, that's OK...." She cleared her throat. "I don't want to cramp your style."

"Um, well, my style has been cramped, and it would be a lot better if you joined us. At least I'd have one person in my camp." The unintentional pun made them both smile.

Marie must have really pulled a fast one on him today. "Well, in that case," she rose and started grabbing packages, "help me with my stuff."

Walking over to the other side of the food court with Johann, she willed herself to be calm. She could already sense Marie's hostile stare and the interested looks of the others. She longed to turn and run.

She peeked over at Johann, and he winked. *"Most* of them don't bite, you know."

"Good to know," she countered. His implication was clear; she would sit as far from Marie as possible.

Arriving at the table, Johann made the introductions, and Heidi marveled at his ease. He had more than admitted to her his day wasn't going well, but instead, he casually introduced her like everything was normal.

Someone jumped up and made a space for her. She sat quickly, glad to be across from Johann.

"We were just trying to decide what movie to see," said one of them.

"You interested in going with us?" said another.

"Um, no, I've actually seen them all."

Marie narrowed her eyes. "How is *that* possible? They have the movies out at camp now?"

"No, I saw them before I left the States," Heidi responded evenly, wishing her accent didn't sound so pronounced. She could feel the interest of the table and cringed inwardly. Accents did that – made you stand out even when you didn't want to.

Marie rolled her eyes. "And how is *that* possible?" Her emphasis was more forceful this time.

"They come out there first."

"Ja, Marie," the guy next to her nudged Heidi playfully, *"Ons land, Suid Afrika,* is a little slow in getting movies."

Heidi caught Johann's eye, wishing she were anywhere but here, and he winked in encouragement.

"Well, I've had enough of this talking," Marie stood in a huff, "let's just pick one and go, *chop-chop.*"

Some of the others agreed.

"You sure you don't want to come?" It was the same guy.

"No thanks." She smiled and shrugged. "I need to take advantage of this chance to shop."

"Ah, stuck in the *bushveld,* aren't you?"

Heidi glanced at Johann again, who now looked as miserable as she felt. "Well, there are no shops there."

The guy laughed like she was hilarious and then took her hand and shook it. "Nice to meet you then, Heidi-from-America."

"Nice to meet you too," she mumbled and then turned back, grateful he was gone. She could tell Johann and Marie were now in a heated discussion, so she leaned over and pretended to search through her bags.

"…this was supposed to be *our* day." Johann's face was red.

"Well, it's quite ironic that Heidi is here then," Marie bit back.

There was a lot of Afrikaans then, but Heidi heard her name repeatedly, and her heart sank.

"…didn't drive all this way to sit in a movie." They were back to English again. She found it crazy how many South Africans she'd met flipped between English and Afrikaans.

"Well, then go shopping with *her*."

His voice changed then, softer and deeper. Heidi's felt her heart sink. How could he be so nice to Marie when she treated him so rottenly?

For lack of anything better to do, Heidi gathered her leftover food and went in search of a trash can. Surely Johann would keep half an eye on her packages for her, but she wouldn't be privy to their argument a moment longer. After dumping her items, she got in line at a kiosk that sold tea and coffee. She wasn't in the mood for something hot to drink, but staying away from their argument was a priority.

The line moved slowly. She wanted to shake Marie for being so ugly. And how could Johann not see Marie's true colors? If only he would….

"Can I join you?"

Heidi turned, startled. There stood Johann, her packages in hand, a sheepish look on his face.

"But...?"

"Gone."

Heidi stared at him, waiting for more.

"Finished, done, *kaput*." He made a chopping motion with his hand. "I should've known." He glanced down the line. "You're ordering tea?"

"No, just was killing time until…."

"Ah, are you finished shopping?"

"Yes."

"You want to see Joburg?" His voice was hopeful.

"Would love to."

"Then, let's go."

Heidi smiled and stepped out of line, grabbing at a package.

"No, I've got these." He held the packages away from her, grinning. "First, we are going to go to the top of the Carlton Center, and then, well then, we can just decide after that."

Heidi's heart lifted as she fell into step next to him. The day had turned sunny, and she would soak in every ounce. They walked in step towards the exit.

Eventually, he spoke. "You know, I knew things weren't right. Wits changed her."

Heidi stayed silent. He had listened when she needed to talk; she could do the same.

"I had a feeling today might go bad – just not that bad." He rolled his eyes. "But I think a tourist trip to Joburg can fix the day just fine."

They drove out from the top of the parking lot and eventually merged onto the highway, the skyline of Johannesburg quickly coming into view. In all her months here, this would be her first trip all the way downtown. Once they entered the city, Heidi didn't know where to look first. Cars honked, crowds pushed through intersections and, carried on the wind of exhaust fumes, multiple languages drifted through the open window. Once more, Heidi struggled to reconcile this city with her preconceptions of Africa.

"Watch these robots," Johann pointed at the next intersection, "they're perfectly timed. If we catch this one green… wanna bet we catch them all?"

Heidi squinted ahead to at least ten more intersections, all with red traffic lights, before following the throngs of people crossing. "No way."

Johann grinned. "Watch me." And then, like magic, each one turned green right before they got to it.

Her Dad would never believe her. This city made her hometown look positively backward.

They found a parking spot near the Carlton Center, and Heidi watched as Johann easily parallel parked in the mayhem. She craned her neck, trying to see to the top of the building, reading the signs.

"It's the tallest building in Africa, my lady." Johann put the truck in park and turned to grin at Heidi.

"And there's an ice rink here?" She scrunched her eyebrows in disbelief.

"Let's go to the top first, and then, if there's time, we can ice skate."

"You ice skate?"

"Heidi, I do anything... once."

She laughed, "Touché." And to think only an hour before she had been lonely and wishful and now....

"Heidi?"

"Huh?"

"You were off somewhere there...?"

"Oh, um, just thinking."

"Thinking about something happy?"

"Sure..."

"Want to tell me about these happy thoughts?"

"Nope." She really wanted to throw her arms around him and tell him how thrilled she felt to be with him, to tell him he was the most amazing guy she had ever been around. Besides, she was triply ecstatic because, as of an hour ago, he was nobody's boyfriend.

They rode an elevator to the top, reminding her of her childhood trips to the Empire State Building. There she had looked out at New York City; here, Johannesburg lay before her from all vantage points.

"I can't believe it," she whispered.

"What can't you believe?"

"This city. It's... it's incredible."

Johann pointed out various landmarks, including the layout of the gold mines from east to west and views of the skylines of Hillbrow and Sandton. "No mud huts and cows in the road here, hey?" He nudged her playfully. "Come on," he grabbed her arm, "I'll show you my favorite view."

She listened to him talk and was captivated by his voice, animation, and enthusiasm. She was truly smitten and turned from him, afraid of what he would see on her face.

"Heidi?"

"Mmm?"

"Have you been listening to me?"

"Why?"

"You just seem... um... distracted?"

Yes, she was distracted, distracted by the realization her former nemesis now caused her heart to pound uncontrollably merely by his proximity. How she had managed to keep her thoughts and feelings at bay at camp left her baffled. Maybe it was being away from camp, from Karl's watchful eye, and the need to be an example to every camper, but whatever the reason, a floodgate of feelings had opened. She couldn't dam them back up if she tried.

He took her arm and turned her back towards him. "You know what I was thinking?"

"No-o."

"I was thinking that maybe kissing someone else on the same day that I broke up with my girlfriend wouldn't be right."

"Oh?" She gazed up at him, her eyes wide, willing him to close the gap between them.

"But then, I very nearly kissed that someone this morning even before I broke up...."

"Yes, you nearly did." She remained frozen, unsure, desperate for his kiss, but afraid to take the lead.

"And I can't stop wishing I had." His face was closer.

"Me either." She saw joy flash through his eyes right before he leaned down and touched his lips to hers. The sensation swallowed her, and she closed her eyes as she felt his hands cup her face and the kiss deepen.

He stepped back slightly, his gaze soft. "Wow." He pulled her in towards him, and she breathed in his scent, felt the coolness of his jacket and the warmth of his chest, her heart pounding and her mind reeling.

Never once had Chris made her feel this way. Never once had their many kisses come close to this, and in that moment, gratitude filled her soul for her decision to leave everything and pursue this life halfway around the world from everything she had known.

"Oh, Heidi, my American girl, what am I going to do with you?" His voice was rough with emotion.

"Take me ice skating?" She didn't want to kill the moment, but she didn't know how to process all the feelings crashing through her.

140

He pushed back only enough so he could see her face. "Take you ice skating, hey?" He smiled as he fingered her freshly cut hair. "As a celebration of...." He glanced down at her and then back at her face. "You look beautiful."

"Thanks." Her voice was choked; nobody had ever looked at her with such frank admiration. It felt so good, especially coming from Johann.

"Well then," and he hugged her to him once more, "let's go then."

They ice skated and laughed and laughed and ice skated. Johann fell more times than Heidi could count, and the whole time she basked in the glow of his eyes and the memory of his kiss. She knew things would probably be different once they got to their destination later that evening, so she determined to enjoy every minute while it lasted.

IT WAS DARK when Johann delivered her to the Anderson's house before heading to stay with friends of his. Heidi was glad to see Amanda again and enjoyed sharing her room, sleeping in a comfortable bed, and taking a real bath. It felt wonderful to be warm indoors, and Amanda's parents were completely welcoming. To her, the funniest thing was listening to their American accents but noting their own children had South African accents. They were originally from somewhere in the Midwest, nowhere near Florida, but America was America, and it felt good to connect and to be in a real home again.

That night she fell asleep reliving Johann's kiss.

CHAPTER 15

After a full day at church, a potluck, and being introduced to dozens of people, Johann and Heidi were finally headed back to camp. The meetings had run smoothly, but not once had Johann given any indication of what had transpired the day before. There was no subtle acknowledgment, nothing. Well, two could play that game, so Heidi had, in turn, acted like they were barely acquaintances.

They left for camp around 4pm in the hopes of making it back before dark.

"How was your time at the Anderson's house?"

"Fine." Johann couldn't kiss her one day, act like she was a nobody in front of everyone the next day, and then act friendly once they were alone again.

She saw him glance over at her from her periphery. "Is everything OK?"

She shrugged. If he was going to kiss her, he had better treat her like a girlfriend in front of people; otherwise, she wanted nothing to do with whatever had transpired between them.

The drive went on in awkward silence. Heidi wanted to berate herself, but she had done nothing wrong other than misreading his attentions. Eventually, when they were only about 30 minutes from camp, he pulled over.

"You know," he said, putting the truck in park and looking over at her, "us being... um... you know... boyfriend and girlfriend is probably not going to work. Especially at camp. I don't think Karl would like it."

Unbelievable.

None of it made sense to her, but she wouldn't argue with him. She wasn't sure why Marie had somehow been workable, but she couldn't be.

"Of course," she tried to sound as unphased as possible but, inwardly, felt sick. "Then, please, don't kiss me again. Kisses mean something to me." Her voice had a harder edge to it than she intended.

"They mean something to me, too!"

"Well, good, then don't kiss me. Because I don't kiss just anyone."

"You sure kissed me back yesterday."

"Yeah, when I thought that was the start of something. But," she threw her hands up, "obviously not."

He looked at her steadily, and she willed herself to remain detached.

"Can we still be friends, though?"

"Friends? We've barely been friends since the day you picked me up at the airport!"

"But we've had friendly moments?"

"Fine, we've had friendly moments. But I don't randomly kiss those types of people." She knew she sounded sarcastic.

He reached out to take her hand, but she pulled it away.

"Do friendly moments mean we can ever hug each other?" He sounded despondent, but she steeled her heart. No matter her attraction for him, she wasn't playing a halfway game with Johann.

"Never." Her voice was as firm as she could muster. If he couldn't stand up for her because of Karl and camp and their different backgrounds or whatever his reasoning, then she wasn't going to play the part of the secret girlfriend. She wasn't going to be the pushover she had been with Chris.

He stared out over the *veld*, and she watched him, anger, hurt, and disappointment warring with attraction, wishing she knew his thoughts. Then, his gaze softened as he glanced back at her with apparent resolve of his own. "OK, Heidi, my friendly moments friend. I had the best weekend ever. Thank you."

She couldn't answer him. It had been amazing, until today.

"We better go," his voice was tinged with regret.

She didn't respond, merely turned and stared out the window. She could do this, work alongside him and pretend there was no attraction. She had been foolish to let her feelings show, and she would make sure it wouldn't happen again.

CHAPTER 16

The vibe back at camp felt different after their weekend away. Heidi and Johann were stilted in their interactions, the memory of the kiss radiating between them. Besides, Karl seemed in a perpetual sour mood, and Amy was heartbroken over the roadblocks she and Ian faced. Heidi suspected there was only one major roadblock: Karl. But she kept these thoughts to herself.

Despite everything, camp life went on, and Heidi busied herself in preparation, writing curriculum, and pouring herself into her campers. The work was fulfilling and gave her great joy. And as July rolled into August and finally September, the mornings no longer began with frost, and the weather turned pleasant. Once more, she could sneak out at sunrise and sit under the Tree to read her Bible. Every day, she thanked God for the opportunities camp provided.

Heidi and Johann eventually slipped into a cautious friendship, although Heidi kept a guard on her heart and their conversations. When camps were not in session, they would often meet at the Tree in the morning or at the pool swing in the evenings, but she never allowed their talks to be personal. Instead, they discussed campers or the curriculum or the day-to-day operation of camp.

She missed home and wrote frequently, regaling her parents with stories of her campers and life in this beautiful country. She found herself praying often for South Africa, for solutions, and followed Johann's example by slipping kindnesses to Mavis and Beauty or even little Fiona and Samson when the opportunities presented themselves.

Her parents wanted her to come home for Christmas, but she was scared that the opportunity to return would somehow evaporate if she left camp. Besides, her funding would last two years, provided she didn't use any on a plane ticket home. Now that Chris was obviously not waiting for her, the desire to stay away was stronger, despite the fact she missed her parents and the twins terribly. Brianna was due to have the baby in November, and she didn't want to return and face that. Plus, the counselors only took off from right before Christmas to right after New Year's. That short of a trip did not justify the cost. At some point, she needed to talk with Johann and see what could be arranged for a Christmas in South Africa.

October warmed into November, which faded into December. By then, she was back in her element, swimming laps daily, wearing flip-flops, the cold months all but forgotten. Christmas loomed closer, and the urgency to make a plan intensified. But she was afraid to broach the issue with Karl and Vera in case they insisted she spend the holiday with them. It defied logic how Vera and Amy could be reasonably happy under Karl's thumb.

"I assume you are planning on going to the States for Christmas?" Karl asked one day at dinner, his gaze directed at Heidi. Vera had gone inside, and Heidi could hear the cadence of conversation between Vera and Mavis. Now she wished she had followed Vera indoors, too.

She needed to reply but wasn't sure where to begin, so she waited. She had definitely decided not to go home until her two years were complete. The cost of a ticket alone could support her for nearly five months at camp.

"—if we are already gone and you need to get a ride to the airport, just arrange it with Tom. They stay here for Christmas," Karl concluded, seemingly satisfied he had settled the matter so easily.

Heidi glanced around in surprise. Had she just missed an entire discussion? Was that it? Everyone assumed she was heading home for Christmas, yet she hadn't even said a word. It was almost comical how Karl tried to manipulate everyone's lives, including hers.

"So, Johann, you will be heading to the South Coast again?" Karl had moved on.

Heidi watched as Johann nodded, refusing to look her way. She wondered who he visited, not that she even knew where the South

Coast was. If Karl thought she was going to the US, it would at least buy her time to make alternate plans.

"—so just wait until the 19th before you leave, OK?" The question at the end was useless, Karl was making a statement, and Johann would obviously comply. And for the second time in minutes, Heidi had missed out on vital information. It sounded like Johann would be the last to leave. That would give her a chance to explain why she couldn't go home and to see if he had other suggestions for her at such a late date. It was evident from his current refusal to meet her gaze that he must not want her along with him. But, she had met many families through the entire year of camps who had extended invitations for her to visit them, especially the Andersons in Alberton. They probably hadn't intended for Christmas, but she wouldn't know if she didn't ask. The urgency of her situation didn't escape her; if only she could find the right time to talk with Johann. She assumed he could drop her off before he headed to his South Coast. She needed to get her address book and get to work.

The following two weeks of camp were the fullest and busiest they had had all year. Amy and Johann had warned her it would be busy, but she hadn't counted on it being quite so chaotic and hectic. For one of the weeks, she had two girls sleeping on the floor of her cabin. And what made it worse was that the two camps were back to back. It seemed they had barely seen the exhaust pipes of the one group's vehicles disappearing down the long dirt road before the next group pulled in.

Heidi felt drained, and all thoughts about making Christmas plans slipped into the background until the 18th, and she found herself telling Amy goodbye. She had meant to let Amy know she wasn't going to the US, but the opportunity for private talk had never presented itself. Besides, Heidi held onto the fear that Amy would insist Heidi spend it with the Voskamps. Plus, sweet, love-struck Amy was so excited about her upcoming opportunity to spend part of Christmas with Ian that Heidi hadn't wanted to put a damper on her excitement.

146

Heidi worked well into the evening of the 18th, cleaning her cabin, organizing the Stamp Club files, and crossing off Karl's to-do list with vigor. She was relieved she would have Johann to herself, even if only for a few hours, yet increasingly anxious to tell him that she had zero plans for Christmas. They hadn't talked privately since this last run of camps, and she was beginning to wonder if she had imagined the bond between them, despite the kissing hiccup back in July. She worried about where he had gone but suspected he had taken one of the workers to their bus stop.

Heidi paged through her address book with a heavy heart and circled a few names. Exhaustion warred with her need to find a solution. There were options, but she had probably waited too late.

That night, she slept fitfully. Her dreams were a mix of Amy's giggling, Karl's reproving glances, and a to-do list that somehow morphed into Santa's wish list. Every time she crossed off a gift item and wrapped it to put into Santa's bag, another item would appear below it. Eventually, the list turned into one wish: "Johann." It was written repeatedly, in identical lettering, and Santa kept yelling because his sleigh had to leave. She could hear the beating of the reindeer hooves on the ground when she woke with a start and realized the beating sound was the rumbling of a truck.

Johann's truck.

Heidi snapped her eyes open, her heart pounding, her mind trying to clear the dream and recognize reality. She jumped out of bed and pulled back the curtain. The grey mist of dawn shed enough light to tell her one thing: Johann's truck was gone.

She fell back onto the bed in disbelief. This couldn't be happening. Johann had just left without saying goodbye, and she was utterly alone. Fear blanketed her as she tried to think clearly. All rational thoughts were clouded out by an overwhelming sense of rejection. Johann hadn't even bothered to tell her goodbye or to find out her plans. Why had she let them assume she had a ride to the airport? Would she be safe here on her own? Was there enough food for her? How long until they returned? She would have to go into Karl's office and look at the master calendar. How had she allowed this to happen? Why had she thought Johann would check in with her before he left? Why had she put so much stock in confiding in him once everyone else was gone? Her overriding desire to avoid Karl's micromanagement had led her into this situation, and now she was stuck, filled with equal parts self-retribution and fear.

Sliding her feet into her flip-flops, she headed out to the bathrooms. Maybe she should move into Amy's old room in the Voskamp's upstairs apartment for more safety. A single girl alone at a camp wandering out at night to visit the bathroom or the kitchen wasn't safe. Frightening stories she had heard her campers whispering of came unbidden. The bars on the windows in the towns, the homes hidden behind 6-foot walls and 8-foot gates guarded by snarling dogs, and the staying-home-at-night rules that many lived by were an increasing necessity. And her campers said they never went anywhere alone. Come to think of it, Heidi and Amy never even went into town alone. That was just how it was here. And now, she was stupidly alone. And it was her own fault.

If she moved to Karl and Vera's place, she would have a telephone, and all her needs could be met under one roof. She knew Karl would disapprove, but Amy and Vera would understand. Of course, they'd probably locked the house, but Tom and Mavis would hopefully have a spare set of keys.

Her mind continued to whirl with possibilities and questions as she dressed and headed to the kitchen to eat. The morning air was still cool, and the dew stuck to her toes in her flip-flops. She had her address book with all the phone numbers of people who had invited her to visit them. Was she brave enough to call these people and ask them to come and get her for Christmas? Or would it be better to wait out Christmas alone here at camp? Should she walk down to Mavis's house and tell them she was here? But she couldn't stay with them. Shoot, Karl wouldn't even be happy about her visiting them. He seemed to be content with the arrangement that the ugliness of apartheid afforded.

She leaned into the kitchen door, scraping her hip through the thin material of her rumpled shorts, wondering why it wouldn't budge. It was always a difficult door to open, so she wiped her sweating palms on her T-shirt, stepped back, and tried to remember Amy's instructions. She pushed the latch down again, pressed her shoulder into the door with more gusto, and felt it give only to catch again. Was she locked out of the kitchen? Tears blurred her vision as she walked around the outside eating area and climbed the stairs to the main house. If the kitchen was locked, the Voskamp's house would also be locked, but she had to at least try. She went door to door – testing each entry point – the house, Karl's office, the door to the meeting room... everything was locked.

Tears were flowing freely now as she wiped her eyes and walked around the main buildings to look down the hill towards Mavis's house. Although there was no sign of movement yet, she felt a measure of relief when she saw the vehicle they used. They were probably grateful to sleep in, and she would wait before she went and asked for help. Besides, she needed to gain composure before heading down there; she didn't want them telling Karl or Johann how upset she had been.

She turned her back to the wall and slid slowly to the concrete, sitting on the stone pavers, resting her forehead on her bent knees. Sobs came in great gulps; she had been deserted, and the last person to leave – Johann – hadn't even bothered to make sure she had a way to fend for herself. After a whole year of working with them, nobody had even tried to check on her before they left. And Johann? She had thought Johann cared for her, maybe not as a boyfriend, but as a friend. Obviously, she had been horribly wrong – about Johann, about Jenna, about Chris, about Brianna. Everyone she had counted as a friend had deserted her, and the blackness of isolation overwhelmed her. It was Christmastime, and she was completely abandoned, and nobody even knew. She couldn't even call her parents without access to a phone.

As the tears continued, her mind turned to anger – anger at herself. She needed to quit feeling sorry for herself since her current situation was wholly her own fault. She should have spoken up when Karl asked about her Christmas plans and let them all know she didn't have any. Instead, she had stupidly kept quiet, thinking it would afford her some time with Johann and away from Karl. Her entire logic had been thoroughly idiotic, and now she was paying for it. Had she seriously thought she could make Christmas plans in the brief time between the Voskamp's leaving and Johann's departure?

She wiped at her tears and took a breath. She needed to get a grip and figure out a way to find food.

What about Johann's cabin? If it wasn't locked, surely, she would find his set of keys? She doubted he would take all his keys with him. Shakily, she stood, leaving her wet shoes behind, and turned towards the cabins. At Johann's door, she took a deep breath, pushing the latch down with vigor as she leaned into the door, almost falling into the room as the door opened easily. She stood for a moment in the semi-darkness, waiting for her blurring eyes to adjust as she glanced around.

Johann was such a boy scout – everything was neat as a pin. Maybe his two mandatory years of military service continued to influence him. She needed to look for a hidden hook, maybe towards the back of one of the beds or under the bottom bunk of each set of beds. When she came to what was obviously his bed, she slid all the way underneath, looking at each corner, and sure enough, there hung a set of keys! She scooted a little further and stretched for them, just able to catch the ring with the tip of her fingers.

Careful to keep her head low and her hair out of the springs, she scooted backward. But, halfway out, she heard a loud, decidedly male exclamation.

She raised her head in shock, hitting the frame, yelping from the pain. Her heart beat wildly, and she lowered her now-throbbing head to the floor, fully aware of her vulnerable position and praying it was only Tom checking on things.

In one swift movement, a pair of hands grabbed her calves and slid her out from under the bed.

"Heidi!" It was Johann, and he was angry.

She didn't even bother to look up at him as a double dose of relief coursed through her. For one, she wasn't going to die; for two,

Johann hadn't left yet! She closed her eyes and felt the coolness of the floor against her cheek.

"Heidi!" His voice was now more alarmed than angry.

Maybe she should open her eyes, but she wanted to savor the moment. She had gone from entirely hopeless, fearful, and alone to finding Johann's keys and then being found by Johann himself! She didn't care she was on the floor, disheveled and tear stained. All she knew was relief.

His face was now next to hers, his fingers pressed to the pulse on her neck, his other hand running lightly over her head, feeling for the inevitable knot. She needed to open her eyes and let him know she was fine, but this present care and concern felt far better than the earlier anger she had heard in his voice. He *had* abandoned her for Christmas; maybe he deserved a few moments of fear. In the same breath, Heidi knew this was all her own fault, so she opened her eyes.

"Heidi!" This time there was relief. "Can you sit up?"

She nodded as he carefully helped her roll over and into a sitting position. He placed his pillow behind her as she leaned against the edge of his bunk. She glanced briefly at him, aware of his scrutiny, taking in her tear stained face, bare feet, rumpled clothing, and the keys still clutched in her hand.

"What were you *doing*?" His voice was incredulous.

She didn't know where to start, so she held up the keys. "The kitchen was locked, and I was hungry."

"But I thought you left last night with the Voskamps?"

Heidi gawked at him in disbelief.

"When Tom said he wasn't taking you to the airport, I assumed Karl was. I mean, you didn't ask me, and you were gone last night, so I thought you had left with them."

"I was here the whole evening, wondering where you were." This didn't make any sense.

Johann sat back on his haunches; confusion etched on his face. "I saw you at the car with Amy, and you had a bag in your hand right before they left. The phone was ringing so I went to answer it, and when I came back, you were gone. But, to make sure, I went down to Tom's and asked him if he was taking you to the airport, and he told me nobody asked him to take you anywhere, so I assumed the Voskamps took you."

Now it was Heidi's turn to be confused. "No, Amy left, and I couldn't find you; so I went to sit under the Counting Tree for a while, but you never came back, and this morning, when I woke up, your truck was gone, and they locked everything, and I had no way to get any food." She knew her words were running together as tears began to slip down her face. She wished she could gain some composure. Johann must think she was a complete idiot. She glanced away from his steady gaze and wiped at her face.

"But what about your ticket?"

"Huh?" She couldn't look at him.

"Your ticket to America?" He spoke slowly.

Here came the truth: "I don't have a ticket...."

Frustration flashed in his eyes. "What do you mean you don't have a ticket; did you lose it?"

She ducked her head, her voice barely audible, "I'm not going."

"Did you miss your flight?"

"No...."

"Then...?"

"I'm *not* going."

He gripped her shoulder, "What do you mean you're not leaving?" When she didn't respond, he grabbed her arm and shook it slightly. "Answer me, Heidi!"

She took a shuddering breath, "I... I, um, I never bought a ticket."

He removed his hand from her shoulder and rocked back. "You mean you never even meant to go?"

When she nodded the affirmative, he stood, pacing in the small space. "And when did you plan on telling *anyone*? Did you think you could just stay here *alone*? Are you *mad*?"

Something in her snapped, and she lifted her head. "Don't call *me* crazy, Johann. You... you... you people never let me answer after Karl asked me what I was going to do. How *mad* is that? And...." She held up her hand to stop him from interrupting and continued. "And... I was going to tell you, but... but... you haven't exactly tried to talk to me lately...." She paused, wondering if he would counter that, but he just looked away. So, he *had* been avoiding her. Again. She hadn't imagined it. "And," she straightened her back to give herself some height, tilting her head so she could match her angry eyes with his, "I looked all over for you last night to explain to you and never found you and then this morning you just... just drove off and left me here alone."

He sat back and softened his tone. "I didn't leave yet, Heidi; I've been driving around finishing all the things that Karl never did so camp is safe while we're gone." He touched her arm, "I thought you had left without telling *me* goodbye, and I was rushing and trying to finish so that I could get out of here by lunchtime."

"But... you... you locked me out of everywhere."

"Heidi," his voice was gentle. "I told you, I thought you were already gone. Besides, I didn't lock anything. Karl must have locked everything up before they left last night." He reached out and placed his other hand on her shoulder and then slid both hands so he could grip her upper arms and gently pull her nearer to him. "You know, I didn't want to be here with you gone... knowing you hadn't wanted to say goodbye to me."

"Oh." She was mesmerized by the look in his eyes.

"Come here," his voice was a comfort as he pulled her against him, holding her head with one hand, gripping her tightly to him. "Seems like you and me got ourselves all mixed up."

"Yes," she whispered.

They sat like that, not moving, wrapped up in each other and in the knowledge they were together, with nobody around to interrupt them, until Heidi's stomach protested loudly.

"Do we need to unlock the kitchen for you?" He laughed softly, the sound a low rumble in her ear.

"Yes, please," she murmured as she reluctantly pulled away. She smoothed her hair shyly, aware she looked terrible. "I need to change my clothes, and then I'll meet you in the kitchen." She glanced at him quickly, warmed by the look of care and humor on his face, and stood and gave a half wave as she stumbled before quickly exiting his cabin.

Once in the bathrooms, she realized she wasn't being careful again. She had kept Johann at arm's length, or, rather, they had kept each other at arm's length for months, and now Karl was gone, and things were already different. But the relief over not being left behind was so huge she simply didn't care. And it was Christmas, after all. And Christmas break was longer than the short weekends they sometimes had without Karl, so maybe they would have time to sort it all out.

CHAPTER 17

"So, do you want to spend Christmas with me?" Thick slices of Heidi's favorite bread had just popped up from the toaster, and Johann started buttering them for her.

"But you didn't invite me way back when Karl was interrogating us all."

Johann paused. "You really don't like him, do you?"

Heidi looked away. "I'm sorry, I know he means a lot to you, but he just seems so... so controlling of everyone. To tell you the truth, the fact he didn't even wait for my answer when he asked me what I was doing but just assumed I was going home really irritated me. And the way he locked everything last night while he knew I was still here... I mean, was he trying to starve me?"

Johann smiled wryly. "No, I think the camp has done its best to starve you without any help from Karl. If you get any thinner, your parents aren't going to recognize you when you do go home."

"Well then, make me some eggs to go with my toast, kind sir."

Johann was already digging in the monstrous refrigerator, looking for anything to cook. "As far as Karl trying to starve you," came his muffled voice, "I highly doubt it. Look how easily you and I got mixed up. I'm sure he thought Tom was taking you first thing today, and he knew I had a key, so, out of habit, he just locked up."

Heidi shrugged and then realized Johann's head was still in the fridge. She didn't want to argue Karl's merits with Johann, who revered him. She had already said too much.

"*Kyk hier!*" He turned triumphantly, kicking the door shut with his foot. "I found some of your 'farmer sausage,' which you've apparently decided to like now, and some eggs, and there's even more bread in the freezer we can try thaw."

Heidi felt herself salivating; she was so hungry it all sounded perfect. Which was comical—six months ago, farmer sausage was the last thing that would've gotten her salivary glands working.

She walked over to the fruit bin and began digging around, finding a couple of decent-looking oranges, and raised them in her own stance of triumph.

They worked together in companionable silence. Heidi was dying to ask where he was going for Christmas, but for now, she would enjoy the fact she hadn't been abandoned. Evidently, in the space of the last hour, with Karl gone and camp empty, they had become the best of friends again.

"So, why didn't you go home?"

"Honestly?"

"No, lie to me." He widened his eyes in exasperation. "Of course, honestly, Heidi!"

She shifted uncomfortably. "Lots of reasons, but mainly Chris and Brianna's baby was born last month, and I...."

"Ahh." His eyes were serious.

"Being alone at camp sounded better?" She attempted, trying to make light of the situation.

They turned over a couple of stools that had been stacked along the table and set out their hastily assembled feast. Heidi took a bite of toast, closing her eyes as she chewed. South Africa had the best bread. Feeling silly, she opened her eyes to Johann watching her intently. She lifted her eyebrow, waiting.

"So, my stowaway, what made you realize Chris just didn't love you enough – you know, back before you left?"

"Uhhh, duh," she rolled her eyes dramatically, caught off guard by the sudden question. "How about when he said he couldn't wait a year for me?"

"*Ja, ja,* I know that part. But I remember you saying there were clues along the way that let you know he might not love you enough."

Heidi took a sip of her rooibos, delaying her response. She glanced away, watching the dripping faucet, thinking how to answer. She must have been on Johann's mind, which meant he thought much more about her than she'd realized. She blew at the surface of the tea and then quietly spoke. "He never thought I was amazing," she said.

The words hung in the air, and her eyes skittered over his face hoping he understood.

"So, you think a person needs to think someone is amazing in order to love them?"

She shook her head in the negative and smiled sadly. "No, you can think someone is amazing and not love them. I think lots of people are amazing, and I don't necessarily love them. Like...."

"Me, for instance?"

She quirked a half smile, embarrassed. This was too hard to explain, but now she was committed. "OK, we can use you as an example. Maybe I think you are amazing because you can peg a snake with a knife from eight feet away, but it doesn't mean I love you." She could feel the heat spreading to her neck.

Johann had cocked his head sideways and was looking at her intently, waiting for her to go on.

"But...." She sighed. Why couldn't she have thought of a less awkward example? "*If* I loved you, I should, by the nature of what love entails, think you are amazing." She pressed on. "If I loved you but didn't think you were amazing, my love would not be sufficient. It would mean I would want to change you, to make you into someone who could be better or *amazing*... But then, I wouldn't really love *you* because I would be trying to change you." She tilted her head, wishing she had never tried to explain. "Does that make sense?"

"*Ja.*" His voice was low and kind. "You know, Miss Heidi," and he gently placed his hand over hers, "I think you are amazing."

"You do?" she choked out.

"And, you know what that means?"

She shook her head.

"One day, if I tell you I love you, then you will have to know it's the real thing." His eyes were boring into her, willing her to meet his gaze.

157

She wanted to respond but didn't want to break the spell. So, she sat there, bathed in the admiration in his eyes, secure in the warmth of his touch, and savored the moment.

"You know what else?" He cut another piece of sausage and speared it with his fork.

She raised her eyes inquisitively, still unable to talk, her hand missing his touch.

"I think it would be nice if you hopped in my little blue *bakkie* and visited the South Coast for Christmas with me." And he popped the bite of sausage in his mouth, grinning at her through pursed lips.

"Really?" Her voice was a squeak.

"*Ja, really.*" He tried to mimic her squeak, and they both laughed self-consciously.

"But, what about your... where will I... do you need to call someone and check?"

He laughed again. "No, my aunt Gillian will love having a real American for Christmas."

"But shouldn't you at least call them and warn them?"

"Oh," he nodded sagely, "so they can prepare themselves?"

"Johann!" She protested and reached over and punched his arm. "*Eina!*"

"Who's she?"

"Who's who?"

"Anna?"

He sat puzzled for a while and then started laughing so hard he doubled over on the bench.

"What?"

"You still... you still... after all this time...." He took a breath to stem his hilarity. "How long have you been here?"

"A *year*, smart aleck, and long enough to know I should call you a *dummkopf* for making fun of me!" She stood and placed her hands on her hips. "Now, are you going to call your Aunt Gillian or not because... well, because I'd much rather go with you than stay here and starve alone."

He stood, too, still laughing. "Absolutely, and *dummkopf* is

German, and we speak Afrikaans in this country, just in case you wanted to know." He started to stack their dishes and then glanced at the clock. "I tell you what, I'll clean up and call my aunt and maybe even *Anna*," he winked, "while you go and pack some clothes so we can leave *chop-chop*."

"Should we tell Karl and Vera, though?"

Johann raised his eyebrows. "Why would we do that?"

"Shouldn't they know?"

"No, they think you are in America. They can just keep thinking that, and maybe I can, maybe I can just—Oh, Heidi, it's just so complicated, but I need to figure things out so we can have," and he moved his hand back and forth between them, "*this* all the time, no matter who is around."

She stood before him, a thrill coursing through her. *She* had somewhere to go for Christmas, and it was with Johann! Only an hour ago, she had been in despair, wondering how she would survive Christmas, and now—

He gripped her shoulders and bent his knees until they were eye level. "Heidi?"

That snapped her out of her reverie, and she nodded quickly. "OK, I'm off to pack." She jogged towards the door, looking back once over her shoulder to send him a smile of anticipation.

"Wait! Heidi?"

She stopped and turned.

"You probably should know by now that '*Eina*' means ouch...."

CHAPTER 18

They left in under an hour, the truck kicking up dirt and stones on the road that led towards civilization. Heidi was so excited. She wanted a map to follow exactly where they were going, but Johann maintained he didn't need a map. Once they were southeast of Johannesburg, there was only one road to the coast.

"So, do you miss having snow at Christmas?" He looked over at her, a smile tugging at the corners of his mouth, watching her hand play in the wind outside the open window.

She tried to grab at tendrils of wind-tossed hair as she turned to him in amusement. "I'm from *Florida,* Johann. Do you not know the geography of the United States at all?"

He shrugged, waiting for an explanation.

"You know, for someone who laughs at all my confusion over South African things, you sure are kind of clueless about America."

"OK, ask me some questions," he challenged.

"AHSK you some questions," she retorted, attempting to mimic his accent.

He smiled at her attempt and nodded.

"OK, does it ever snow in Florida?"

"I'm guessing no."

"Well, that was a giveaway. Let's try something else. Hmm, there are so many differences, I don't even know where to begin...."

"Sounds like you just can't think of anything to catch me out."

"No, no... here we go," she snickered. "Question 1: name one of the most common poisonous snakes, Mr. Bushman."

"Easy as can be, that would be a rattlesnake."

"OK," she nodded grudgingly. "Question 2: why aren't there places to go to the *toilet* on any of your roads?"

"Hey!" He leaned over and punched her playfully. "This is

supposed to be questions about America, and, for your information, there are many places to go toilet in South Africa. If you cast your eyes to the left," he gave a dramatic sweep with his hand, "you can pick any number of privacy bushes."

She rolled her eyes in distaste. "Well, please pull over and let me find my bush."

"Seriously?"

She nodded. "And, I want you to find the bush for me, beat any snakes out of it, and then walk back to the truck so I can have some privacy."

"It's not a truck; it's a *bakkie*. We've been over this before. Trucks are big like lorries that carry lots of things. This little vehicle," and he patted the steering wheel fondly, "is a *bakkie*."

"OK, I'll call it a *bockie* or whatever it is, but please, let's find me a snake-free bush right now!"

Johann chuckled as he slowed the vehicle and pulled onto the dirt on the side of the road. He made quite a show of stomping the ground and beating a bush, yelling like a warrior while Heidi looked on.

"Hurry up, Johann; I really have to go."

"Well, it takes a while to scare all the snakes away."

"I don't have a while, and besides, you're not playing fair by making me laugh at such a critical time."

"You know, I thought this was a good bush, but I think this one could be dangerous...." He paused in deep concentration.

"Johann!" She marched towards him, trying to be angry but unable to keep from laughing. "I deem this bush acceptable, so you'd better get back to the truck and give me some privacy before you regret it!"

"Heidi," he was laughing now, trying to hold her back, "I wouldn't use this one; it's not the place for you."

"Well, I don't believe you!" She shoved him away and turned only to see a snake slithering away from them. Her scream was enough to make anyone cringe, and he bent over, laughing at her.

"Now..." he could hardly get a word out from laughing so hard.

"Now that all the animals in the entire *bushveld* have been frightened, it's safe to go."

"Turn around, Johann," she managed to say with enough anger to get him to acquiesce. She watched as he turned and walked towards the truck, his shoulders still shaking, and then she crouched down with relief, only to realize she had brushed against something prickly. Muttering to herself, she completed the task and then turned in surprise: little black stickers were attached to her clothing.

"Johann!"

"What?" He started to turn around.

"Stop!" she yelled back desperately.

"Well then, what do you want?"

"There are black things stuck everywhere."

"You mean, *everywhere?*" He angled his face but kept his eyes averted. "Do you need any help?"

"I'm going to *klap* you. What should I do?"

"Pick them out," he called back, "but hurry. We need to start driving again."

Grumbling, she gingerly began picking the offending black thorns from her clothing. Finally, she tromped back to the truck, embarrassed and decidedly uncomfortable.

He came to the passenger side and opened the door for her, gallantly waving her into the truck while laughter escaped his lips.

"Now is not the time to pretend you are a gentleman!" she retorted and scooted into the truck, protesting as an errant thorn pierced the back of her thighs. She leaned forward, pulled it from her shorts, and then held it out for him to see. "What are these evil things?"

"Oh, just some blackjack seeds," he gave her a devilish smile. "Are you sure you don't want me to check to see if any are left?"

"We need to start driving again," she mimicked, torn between giggling at her predicament and covering her face in embarrassment.

"I think this will be Episode One of my diary entry tonight: 'Heidi spreads blackjack seeds from the highveld to the South Coast.'" He winked at her as he slid into the driver's seat.

"I'm sure you don't even keep a diary," she muttered.

"Yes, but I can already tell that this will be a Christmas to remember, so tonight might be a good time to start one...."

She allowed herself to crack a smile which was all he needed to break into hysterics.

"Oh Heidi," he managed between breaths, "if... if you could only have...." And he broke into more laughter. "You know, you could have used '*Eina*' back there – it would've worked.

"Still sounds like I'm calling for a woman, no thanks," she said. A smile tugged at the corner of her mouth. This was going to be a fun drive.

They continued south, skirting around Johannesburg, and Heidi watched in awe as the city's skyline stayed in their periphery.

Once they were away from the mountains and *koppies* that surrounded camp, the land flattened out, the Johannesburg skyline behind them. Now, flat, empty land stretched in all directions. Just one single-lane road would take them all the way to the coast. Grasses blew in the wind, dotted by random rocky outcrops, and then the terrain changed as they approached a place called Van Reenen's Pass. It was beautiful.

"Johannesburg is on a plateau," Johann explained, "and now we're leaving it. Van Reenen's Pass is only about 36 kilometers, but our elevation will change by over 650 meters."

Sure enough, they drove through beautiful country dotted with random Cape Dutch houses. At times, the road carved into the mountain, a high embankment blocking their view, but then, just as swiftly, the landscape would open, causing Heidi to catch her breath. Other times, the embankment would only be on her left, with a valley out to the right and mountains outlining the blue sky far along the horizon. Long grasses, or *veld* as Johann called it, carpeted the land. A few trees dotted the vistas. And always, the blue sky capped the scenery; never had Heidi seen skies this blue. She wanted to jump out of the truck and spin in delight or lie in the grass to watch little white clouds scudding across the endless blue.

Road signs warned of rockslides and sharp turns and steep

163

grades, the implied danger adding to the sheer excitement of the landscape. Where the road lay more exposed, windsocks blew, heralding the wind's direction. The sun was slightly behind them now, bringing out the yellows and greens of the grasses, the shades shifting constantly.

Brown signs pointed to places to stay, and sometimes she could see thatched roofs capping stone cottages in the distance. *Rondavels,* Johann called them. She imagined stopping to stay at one, sitting on the *stoep,* drinking in the views, Johann by her side.

He called the flat-topped trees acacia tees. They sprinkled along the roadside; she imagined a giant coming along and hedging them, keeping their crowns flattened at a slight angle. The angle gave her pause, but a sign caught her eye before she could frame a question. "Goats?" She swiveled in her seat to hopefully get a better look. "They have a sign for goats?"

Johann shrugged. "So many accidents on this pass," he explained as a car zipped past them. "People go too fast and ride their brakes, and then their brakes fail. I think it's the deadliest road in all of South Africa. My little *bakkie,* though," and he patted the dashboard, "always gets me there safely."

They drove a little farther, and then Johann pulled off onto a dirt road. Putting the truck in park, he shut off the engine and turned to her. "Welcome to Windy Corner," he grinned.

They got out of the truck, and Heidi stood in awe of the views surrounding them. Rolling green hills and mountains stretched to the horizon in all directions. She felt like she was on the set of *The Sound of Music and* wanted to break into song. "I wish I had my camera," she whispered.

"This is all part of the Drakensberg Range," Johann explained. "It's so green now, but if we drove down here during the dry season, it would be tall, dry grass, all different shades of yellow, depending on the sun." She tried to imagine the mountains as he described but failed. She stood silent, absorbing the view, breathing a prayer of thanks for this unexpected journey.

THEIR DRIVE TOOK them through Ladysmith and then Pietermaritzburg and, finally, to Durban and the ocean. Humidity filled the truck, and the air reminded her of Florida.

"Now my hair is really going to be curly, just like at home. This is the kind of air we have," and she breathed deeply. "I never thought I'd be happy to greet humidity," she smiled. "You had better prepare yourself for some wild hair!"

He reached over and mussed her hair even more. "It's happy hair; let it be!"

He drove her along the beach in Durban, slowing so she could ogle the Maharani hotel with its glass elevator outside the building, the high rises reminding her of Miami. They passed a crowded amusement park—umbrellas and chairs across the street from it, filling every available space of beach sand.

Then they hugged the coast passing through towns with musical names: Amanzimtoti, Ifafa, Hibberdene, and then, Port Shepstone.

"Only 20 minutes left!" Johann was clearly excited.

"Don't let me fall asleep, Johann," she breathed, "I want to put my toes in the ocean tonight!"

"Heidi," he smiled, "I don't think it's possible for you to stay awake in a car, especially after dark."

She threw her hands wide. "Watch me!"

They drove on through a tiny beach town called Shelly Beach, and then he finally stopped at a parking lot overlooking the most breathtaking beach Heidi had ever seen. The sun was setting, and the colors and salt spray and rocky outcroppings were almost too much to take in at once.

"Welcome to Uvongo Beach, Heidi." He smiled happily. "Let's get out before it's completely dark."

Heidi fiddled with the door, finally flinging it wide, and jumped out.

"Slow down, crazy girl!" he muttered, shutting the door behind him and running to catch her.

The wind rushed around them, and the crash of the ocean filled the air. "It's wild out here, Johann!" And she spread her arms like sails, lifting her head and closing her eyes, joy radiating from every part of her.

***

Johann's fatigue from his early morning and the long drive melted away as he absorbed her exuberance. He had never met a girl who demonstrated such uninhibited joy. Happiness unfurled. It was contagious. He felt her awe and wonder and, suddenly, wanted to share in every part of it. "Come on, I'll show you the cliffs!" he cried, grabbing her arm and pulling her along with him.

They climbed over the stone wall that separated the parking lot from the beach and, after kicking off their sandals, ran through the soft sand parallel to the beach.

"Wait!" She called, pulling away from his grip, "I have to at least get my toes wet!" And she ran towards the water, filled with the sight of the white foam catching the ambient light from the waning sun.

"Heidi!" She was up to her knees in swirling water by the time Johann caught up with her. He pulled on her arm once more, willing her to get back. "You can't swim here at dusk!"

She looked at him in surprise. "I'm not swimming!" And then she turned back towards the waves just in time to see a huge one barreling towards them.

"Run!" He roared above the noise, pulling her along as he took giant steps through the rushing water.

She screamed with glee and grabbed Johann for support as the wave caught them, tossing her against him, who, by sheer determination, had his feet planted firmly enough to stay upright. His arms came around her, and as the water began to pull back, he half carried, half dragged her back to the shore, plunking her unceremoniously on the dry sand and then throwing himself next to her.

"You can't swim here at night," he said again, breathing heavily from the exertion.

She widened her eyes, "Oh Johann, are you mad with me?"

"No." His voice was gruff as he stood, hesitated, and turned towards her. In one swift motion, he grabbed her hands, pulled her against him, and brought his lips to hers, kissing her with a desperation that took her breath away. And then, just as quickly, he set her away from him and placed a trembling hand on her cheek. "No, I'm not mad with you, Heidi-my-Heidi," his voice was so low she could barely hear him, "I just don't want you to get eaten by sharks."

***

Heidi's mind whirled with the suddenness of his actions, the feeling of his kiss, and the sweetness of his tone. She wanted to step back into his embrace but felt unsure, so, instead, she took his hand, "Will you still show me the cliffs?"

He nodded briefly and turned; they walked side by side, hand in hand.

Heidi's shorts were wet and stuck with sand, but she hardly noticed it as she watched their feet in sync, parallel footprints along the sand. Her heart still beat wildly, and if it wasn't for the reassuring grip of his hand, she would wonder if she had only imagined his kiss. The moment had been incredible, one she wished they would repeat, but their first kiss had been five long months ago, and it hadn't served to advance their relationship at all. In fact, it had done the opposite. She touched her lips briefly with her free hand; she would treasure the moment, nonetheless.

They stopped, and he looked at her with concern. "Are you OK?" His voice was tinged with regret. "I know what you said about kissing and Heidi; I'm—"

She put her fingers over his mouth. Oh, she didn't want him to apologize—the moment had been too special, the day too incredible. She had stuck to her resolution for five long months. Maybe things would work out this time. They would have days together to see where it could go. She would be cautious. "Don't say anything," she whispered. She did not want to hear a repeat of his words after their last kiss, "you are an *amazing*" – they both smiled briefly – "guy, and today has been one of the most wonderful days of my whole life."

His stance relaxed, and he reached out and touched her face briefly, "And you, Heidi-my-Heidi, are the most amazing American girl that has ever crossed my path."

His voice held a hint of teasing, but despite the back-handed compliment, calling her *his* Heidi was all she needed to hear.

"And," he added with a wicked glint in his eye, "now that we both think each other is amazing, if we ever fall in love, it will be the real thing."

Heidi smiled, a lump in her throat. Johann, even when he teased, understood. He listened and took to heart the things she said. Maybe that lump was her heart in her throat. She couldn't tell and needed a diversion; otherwise, she would throw herself at him, willing him to kiss her again. She looked around, "So, where are your cliffs?"

"Huh?"

"The cliffs!"

He laughed, "Oh, the cliffs. Well, they are right there." And he gestured into the darkness.

Heidi squinted. "Are they imaginary cliffs?"

"No," he laughed again, "We'll just have to come back in the morning when it's not so dangerous and dark out here." And he bumped against her playfully. "If the moon would come out, you could probably see what I meant. See how the water comes in here?" He pointed towards the waves and then where the water got calm.

She nodded.

"That's a lagoon, and the cliffs surround the lagoon on two sides, forming an angle at the back. And that's where the waterfall is." He put his hands in a V-shape to demonstrate and then pointed back to the cliffs. "See how you can just make out the lagoon water, and then it's black?"

She nodded again, her heart hammering from his closeness.

"Now, follow the blackness up until you see stars... do you see?"

Her breath caught in her throat. She did indeed see – the faint stars appeared to be a lid to a vast black bowl.

"If we're here during a full moon and you promise not to swim with the sharks, we'll come back. The effect is fantastic." He turned and slipped his arm around her shoulders. "And now, we need to get to my aunt's house, so she doesn't worry about us."

They walked together, Heidi enjoying the feel of his arm on her shoulders, the smell of the ocean spray in the air, and the joy of walking in step with him. After squelching her feelings for him for months, her chest expanded with relief. Their closeness and camaraderie had flowered in one uninhibited day. To think he had called her *his Heidi*; she would play those words repeatedly in her head. Nobody, not even Chris when they were first in love, had made her feel this special, this incredible, this cared for.

As they got back in the truck, she leaned her head against the seat, closing her eyes in gratitude. She had gone from facing a Christmas entirely alone to this wonderful day, all because of Johann. A niggling fear grasped at the edges of her happiness, reminding her of the last time she had spent an equally amazing day. And yes, he had kissed her then, too, only to set her away from him once they returned to camp. Maybe this time would be different. Maybe after ten days of being together, away from the confines of camp, they would have a chance to be themselves. Maybe something solid would come from it, something substantial, and Johann would be willing to be her boyfriend despite any opposition. She needed to be careful, though, to guard her heart.

CHAPTER 19

She awoke in a cozy room, still wearing her damp clothes. She could hear people talking and laughing – a female voice and then the rumble of Johann's voice. *Heidi-my-Heidi*, she played the words repeatedly, hugging herself, running through the events of the night before.

Slowly swinging her legs over the side of the bed, she frowned at her wrinkled shorts. Digging in her suitcase someone had placed in the room, she found fresh clothes. And then she nearly whooped with joy when she realized the room had an adjoining bathroom. Grabbing her toiletries, she showered hurriedly, changing into clean clothes and combing her wet hair. After folding the blanket someone had covered her with, she walked into a hallway toward the voices.

"Well, here's the one who can NEVER stay awake until the destination. I think you just like to make people carry you everywhere," said Johann.

"You had to carry me in?"

"My dear," an older woman looked up and winked, "you walked in on your own; Johann just had to guide you. And you must be Heidi!"

"And you must be the famous Aunt Gillian." Heidi took her offered hand and then was pulled into a hug.

"I am. And Johann says camp is starving you. So, I'm making crumpets, and we can have fresh butter and jam on them, and there will be no more going hungry."

"It smells heavenly." She glanced towards Johann, her cheeks heating at the memory of their oceanside kiss. Twin spots were evident on his cheeks, and he grinned.

"Come sit by me," he said, "I'll pour you some tea, and we can tell Aunt Gillian how you tried to get eaten by sharks last night." He pulled a chair out for her and, when she sat, hugged her sideways. "You smell so good."

"There's a shower, Johann, and a bath. In my room!" And she spread her hands wide and laughed.

Heidi took a sip of the tea and sighed. "Thank you so much for letting me come at such short notice. I nearly messed up Christmas for myself, but you and Johann rescued me from my own—"

"It's our pleasure," Aunt Gillian said, setting the crumpets down on a hot pad on the table. "Now, eat up because we've got some sightseeing to do today. I've been making plans ever since Johann told me he was coming!"

"Should I not call Pastor Voorden first, though?" Johann asked.

"No, Johann. You're not calling anyone. You're going to have a real holiday. And nobody is going to put you to work for at least the first few days you are here. I suspect you haven't had a day off in weeks."

Heidi watched Aunt Gillian's expression in interest, curious at the undercurrent. Maybe she thought Karl worked Johann too hard. Maybe she shared Heidi's distrust of the man, too. And it also appeared Johann had no problem acting like Heidi was someone special in front of Aunt Gillian. Her heart sang with relief and in anticipation of the upcoming days.

CHAPTER 20

They spent their first day at Uvongo Beach, renting kayaks and paddling up the lagoon towards the waterfall. Heidi had never imagined a beach this beautiful – the cliffs, the waterfall, the waves, the narrow stretch of sand. She also couldn't get over the size of the waves barreling in. People had to swim in a guarded area bounded by shark nets, and as the waves rolled in, they would scream before trying to duck under or dive over them. It reminded her of a rollercoaster, everyone screaming before a giant drop.

"You know, if you came to Jupiter to swim, you could walk in and swim anywhere you wanted; for miles, the beach just goes on and on." She flung her right arm out for emphasis.

"What about shark nets?" said Aunt Gillian.

"We don't have them."

"You don't have sharks?" Johann frowned in disbelief.

"No, silly, we don't have shark nets."

"So, what about the sharks, then?" said Johann

"I—I guess they don't bother us."

Aunt Gillian and Johann laughed.

"Must be very nice sharks," Johann said, nudging his aunt.

"Maybe they are just not," Heidi held up both hands like claws, "*killer* sharks."

Everyone laughed.

Later, they went into town to do some Christmas shopping.

"Heidi, you must keep a firm grip on your handbag around here." Aunt Gillian's look was pointed. "For some, your handbag is more valuable than your life."

Heidi nodded. Here it was again, this warning, the dangerous undercurrent she sensed almost everywhere, even amongst her campers.

***

That night, as Aunt Gillian explained the plans for their second day, Johann came in with a carefully wrapped box for Heidi. "Merry Christmas," he blushed, pushing it into her hands.

"But Johann, it's not Christmas yet!" Heidi hadn't even wrapped his gift.

"Just open it!" Aunt Gillian was clearly in on the surprise.

Heidi tore into the package only to see a brand-new camera nestled in its packaging. She couldn't believe it. She had missed her camera all year, and here he was, giving her a beautiful new one.

"It even has the new autofocus technology! How did you know?"

"I'm brilliant, that's all; you can hug me for my brilliance."

"Oh Johann," and she reached forward and hugged him. "This is incredible. Wow. It's way nicer than the one from my missing suitcase, too. But how did you...?"

He shrugged. "Aunt Gillian manages the little bit of money the camp pays me. She's smart that way. And, I have no true expenses so.... Plus, she says you'll need this tomorrow."

Heidi looked up and saw Aunt Gillian's eyebrows rise in confirmation. Then Heidi ran her hands over the contours of the camera. She would cherish it always.

***

Not surprisingly, Aunt Gillian was right. As they drove to a place called Oribi Gorge, about an hour away, Aunt Gillian filled her in. "It's actually a canyon. Like your Grand Canyon is cut by the Colorado river, this is cut by the Umzimkulwana River."

"Umzimkulwana," Heidi tried, liking how it flowed off her tongue.

"I think your Grand Canyon is about 1800 meters at its deepest point. The gorge we'll hike into today is about 400 meters – which is why we can go down and up in one afternoon."

Johann nudged Heidi, "I don't think Americans speak in meters, Aunt Gillian."

Heidi rolled her eyes, "Oh, give me a break, Johann. I went to school. Sounds like you should've warned me to bring hiking boots, though." Then she paused. "Will we see any wild animals?"

"Snakes!" Johann nudged her.

"I hope you brought your knife; you know Johann can peg a snake like nobody's business, right?"

Aunt Gillian laughed. "I suspect we'll be too noisy to see snakes and much else, but we might see a monkey or a leguaan."

"Like a big lizard," Johann clarified.

They turned onto a dirt road that led to a parking area. Climbing out of the car, Heidi was struck by the beauty surrounding them. Her heart jumped in anticipation, "I can hear water."

"That's the waterfall," said Aunt Gillian. "We can even swim at the bottom if we want."

They followed the signs to the first rock ledge, where Aunt Gillian had Heidi and Johann walk out for a photograph.

"Don't get too close to the edge, Johann! No teasing on that ledge – I don't want to hike alone…." She laughed at the look on Heidi's face and snapped some pictures.

There was so much to take in: rocky outcroppings, trees and brush hugging the cliffs, and the waterfall rushing over the side of a rock and plummeting below. Heidi leaned out as far as she could but barely saw the bottom.

Next, Aunt Gillian led them along the trail to the bottom. At some points, the rocks lent themselves to steps, other areas weren't as convenient, and Heidi's tennis shoes sank into the mossy ground. Bees clung to flowers, and colorful moths flitted around them. And at every turn, the spray of the water guided them downward.

"Why Oribi?" Heidi asked.

"It's a small antelope that lives here," said Johann.

"Have you seen one?"

"Nope, I always come with noisy hikers."

Heidi slapped the back of her hand on his arm. "I can be quiet if I have to, but it's better to scare the snakes away. You have your knife, right?"

He gave her a thumbs up.

When she thought her knees were ready to give in, they arrived at the bottom. She tilted her head back, the perspective of looking up at the falling water incredible.

With a war cry, Johann stripped off his shirt and shoes and jumped into the water. "Come on in, ladies!"

"Not me." Aunt Gillian sat down on a large flat rock, looking like she'd arrived home.

Heidi peeled off her clothes down to her bathing suit and tiptoed to the edge.

"Jump!" Johann was floating on his back.

"Is it cold?"

"Not as cold as being thrown in the pool in July," he countered sagely.

Heidi laughed and jumped, coming up spluttering.

"Lie on your back like this," Johann demonstrated.

She copied him, taking in the falling water and sheer cliffs capped off by the South Africa-blue sky.

He found her hand and squeezed it. "Pretty cool, huh?"

She squeezed back. Sometimes words were not enough.

CHAPTER 21

Far too soon, the ten days were over, and they needed to head back to camp. Heidi was sad; she had connected with Aunt Gillian and would miss her. "This has been the best Christmas I could have ever wished for," she said, hugging the older woman. "And I'm really going to miss your bathroom."

They all laughed, and Johann hugged his aunt fiercely. "I love you, Aunt Gillian. Thanks for everything and for... well, everything."

On their way out of town, Heidi stopped to pick up the pictures she'd sent to get developed. There was one of the three of them she would frame and send to Aunt Gillian as a thank you. But the one with her and Johann at Oribi Gorge was splendid, and she knew she would treasure it for the rest of her life.

A smile played across her lips as she absorbed the image. Johann reached over and took her hand. "Heidi?"

"Yes?"

"Will you be my girlfriend?"

"What about Karl?"

"He already knows."

"How?"

"He phoned, wanting me to go back early, and Aunt Gillian told him off."

"What? When?"

"You were having one of your baths," he rolled his eyes, "and she answered the phone. It was Karl. He asked for me, but she told him I wasn't around and asked if she could take a message.

"I was kind of surprised; I was standing right there, you know? Anyhow, he must've told her I needed to come back early, and she told him no, that wasn't possible: she was enjoying having her nephew and his *girlfriend* visiting, and there was still plenty to do before she could let us come back.

"So, I can hear Karl yell, 'his *girlfriend?*' and then Aunt Gillian just says all calmly, 'you know, the American girl, Heidi.' So, then I hear Karl say something about you being in America and Aunt Gillian telling him that you didn't catch your flight and were going to have to stay at camp alone, so she had you come there and what a wonderful girl you are and how nice to see Johann so happy. Now, I'm just standing there the whole time with my mouth wide open, and Aunt Gillian gets off the phone and says to me, 'Now, don't you dare mess things up. That girl is a win, and you know it and I know it and now Karl knows it, too.'"

"Wow." It was inconceivable. Aunt Gillian understood, and Heidi wondered why Johann hadn't come to live with his aunt when he needed a family. Perhaps camp life had given him purpose like it had Heidi. If that was the case, she understood why he had stayed.

"So, will you?"

"Will I what?" She was lost and trying to comprehend Aunt Gillian standing up to Karl… for them. They wouldn't have to arrive at camp and explain the last ten days.

"Be my girlfriend?"

"Hmm," she joked, a sparkle in her eyes, "let me see…."

"Heidi!"

"Drive straight, Johann; we're going to wreck!"

"Heidi?"

And she reached out and took his hand. "Yes, Yo-Man-of-the-Bushveld, I would love to be your girlfriend."

CHAPTER 22

They celebrated Heidi's first year at camp with *melktart* and candles. Heidi blew out the candles with gusto and then hugged Amy and Johann. The evening sparkled with happiness, and they laughed over shared memories. The year ahead felt vaguely uncertain, but she dared hope it would include plans for a lifetime with Johann.

And that begged the question: what was it about improbable plans? She knew she wanted a life with Johann by her side, so why did it feel impossible? Why did her thoughts hit a wall? Was this a gentle warning from God or mere pessimism?

A few of her favorite campers returned, and she was especially thrilled to see the progress Janelle had made. The timid, nervous little girl from the year before had blossomed. In addition, having her former campers greet her with such affection made her heart ache a little. She could see how the longer she stayed, the harder it would be to leave.

Letters from home were shorter but more frequent. Her mom had been having health problems and was waiting on various tests. Heidi offered to come home, but her mom called it all a blip on the radar and told her to stay. These letters gave her twinges of guilt, and she wondered if she were sacrificing her own family for service to others. She missed home less and less but, at the same time, felt increasingly sad that the twins would no longer know her when she returned. She supposed missionaries had this continual conflict – how to balance caring for their own and the people they felt called to serve

Camps continued to run and keep them all busy. Heidi had almost the first three courses of the Stamp Club rewritten and often sat up late writing, trying to get her thoughts down before she went to sleep.

Amy continued to date Ian, and Karl, it seemed, had softened towards Heidi. Occasionally, she would get her camera out and take pictures of the view from the eating area at sunset, trying to capture its beauty. She had also taken pictures of Amy and Ian and framed her favorite for Amy as a birthday gift. But there wasn't much time for the level of photography the surroundings begged for.

Above all, Heidi enjoyed the sweet feeling of working alongside Johann. During camp, they kept their feelings for each other mostly hidden. Neither wanted their relationship to become a barrier to running a smooth camp. Instead, they would trade a brief conversation between activities or a shared look across tables during a meal. What they avoided during camp sessions, they made up for on breaks by taking hikes, sitting at the swing talking, or spending time after dinner scrounging around for dessert and talking late into the night. Often Amy would join them, and it seemed Ian was present more and more. Heidi wondered if he had deferred going to Wits, but since he never offered an explanation, she never asked. The foursome would play games until Karl would come out and say they were keeping him awake.

Heidi's favorite times were spent on the swing, snuggled against Johann, her hand in his. Johann often talked about his dreams for the camp, how he would love to expand it; Heidi was always in these plans, and the knowledge comforted her.

"You know, if we got married, we would have to build ourselves a cabin. Maybe a *rondavel*, right over there." He pointed towards the fields.

"Oh, so a softball can crash through our window?" Heidi had lifted her head and was watching his face. He had started to interject the 'get married' narrative more and more into their conversations.

He ignored the question. "But when campers came, we would sadly have to split up temporarily."

"That would be strange."

"Or fun... after, like a very good reunion every week." He wagged his eyebrows at her, and Heidi was glad he couldn't see the blush stealing up her cheeks.

They rarely kissed. The feelings were too powerful. One night, falling asleep in her cabin, Heidi realized those moments involved only a handful of times. Heidi remembered the last time so clearly.

"You know I just want to kiss you all the time, Heidi-my-Heidi?" They had been out beneath the Counting Tree, trimming the branches back.

She had stopped and turned, shears held open and in the air.

"All the time." And then he gently took the shears from her, setting them on the ground and kissing her before sighing and stepping back. "So, if you are ever wondering why this boyfriend of yours hardly kisses you...."

Heidi rolled over in bed and remembered each one – Carlton Center, Uvongo Beach, Windy Corner on the way back from Aunt Gillian's, once at the swing, and now once under the Counting Tree. That was it. They also hadn't seriously talked about getting married, and she supposed that was wise – the obstacles made her head hurt. So, she needed to be grateful for what they had and for Johann's care.

The next six months flew by, and before their July camp season hit, Karl declared they would all have a holiday. He and Vera had their own plans; Heidi, Johann, Amy, and Ian decided they would go to the Eastern Transvaal together so Heidi could see places like Blyde River Canyon and God's Window. Karl and Vera were reluctant to let Amy go until they found out the group would be staying at one of Aunt Gillian's timeshares, and she would be with them.

Until the day they left, Heidi worried Karl would change his mind and make Amy go with her parents instead. Miraculously, he didn't, and the four young people set off together in Ian's car, the confines brimming with exuberance.

Five hours later, Aunt Gillian opened the door to their rental chalet and pulled the young people into hugs.

Heidi couldn't wrap her mind around the beauty of the scenery. The surroundings were all part of what was aptly named the Panorama Route and Paradise Country. On the first day, they took a hike that led along a trail filled with lush vegetation, following the signs posted for "God's Window." The climb was steep, but everyone, including Aunt Gillian, was up for the task. Heidi wanted to take picture after picture at every viewpoint, but Johann kept cautioning her that the best was yet to come. He was right.

Standing at the final overlook felt like standing on the edge of the earth. Johann pointed out Blyde River Canyon and the Lowveld and even Kruger Park. He said they could've even seen part of Mozambique's coastline if it had been clearer. While he was talking, she stared into the incredible vista, wholly mesmerized, unaware the rest of their group had stepped away. She turned, wondering, only to see Johann down on one knee, a ring box open in front of her, and his dear green eyes looking up at her, brimming with hope and love.

"Will you marry me, Heidi?" His voice was low and shaky.

She brought her hands to her face in utter surprise and stepped backward, almost falling.

He reached out and grabbed her hand. "Don't fall off the edge! You can say 'no' if you need to!"

She started laughing then. "Of course, I wouldn't say no, Johann! My answer is yes, yes, yes!"

"Well, that's a relief," he whispered, slipping the ring onto her finger and then standing and hugging her to himself.

"Oh, my goodness, how... when... where is everyone?" Heidi was overcome. There had been zero clues. The ring was beautiful, a single small stone set in platinum, exactly her style.

"Surprised?" His face was inches from her.

"Beyond surprised!" And she closed her eyes as he kissed her deeply.

And then she heard clapping and turned to see Amy, Ian, and Aunt Gillian cheering on the side. Amy snapped pictures with her little camera, and Heidi took her own camera and gave it to Aunt Gillian to get a few posed photos.

By the end of the hike, Heidi's face hurt from smiling so much. The setting, the bubbling happiness, the companionship, the surprise—it was all-encompassing.

That evening they sat outside, taking in the views and talking while Ian and Johann grilled dinner. They called it a *braai*, and Heidi, sitting with Amy and Aunt Gillian, wondered what the next few months would bring. Surely, they wouldn't wait long to get married. Would they build their own place on the campgrounds? Would she be able to go home first and see her family? Did Johann have the funds to visit with her? Her family needed to meet him. Could they get married at camp, or should they get married in America so her family could participate? They wouldn't be able to come here, and she needed to tell Johann why, but not now, not today.

Her mind spun until she caught herself. She needed to enjoy the moment: the setting sun, the people around her, and the love of one incredible man.

They spent the next two days exploring Berlin Falls, Horse Shoe Falls, and Bridal Veil and even discussed trying to raft Blyde River Canyon. But in the end, there was just too much glorious hiking to do. The rock formations, spectacular views, and lush fauna inspired awe. Here, anything felt possible, like God had touched this corner of the world with something extra special. Heidi thought back to Uvongo, the incredible beaches, Camp Timothy, and its people; she knew South Africa had become part of her. The news that the current prime minister, P.W. Botha, was working on reforms for this beautiful land was encouraging, and Heidi prayed he, or a future politician, would work to end apartheid. Then, the opportunities in South Africa would open for millions of people and allow them to expand the camp's outreach.

"You're looking awfully serious for a newly engaged lady." Johann had come up next to her, taking her hand.

She turned to him, stopping and taking his other hand as the others walked ahead. She needed to talk with him but didn't want to mar any part of this perfect trip. Not that he wouldn't accept what she had to say, but her delay would hurt him. So, she would wait, just a little longer.

"Heidi?" He looked worried.

She stepped forward and kissed him. "How are we going to run camps when all I want to do is this?"

He hugged her to him, and she could sense his relief; her dishonesty made her feel guilty.

"That's what's bothering you? I think this will be easier than walking around and pretending that I don't care about you, which I probably did all last year."

She stepped back. "Seriously?"

"Ah, Heidi, you made me crazy from the beginning; it just took me a while to realize why. And then I was scared of Karl. And then we went to Uvongo, and Aunt Gillian took matters into her own hands. And then I was still trying to downplay my feelings from everyone at camp, just not as much. But now," and he flung his hands wide, "now the whole world can know how much I love you!"

She hugged him and promised herself as soon as they got back to camp, she would really talk to him. About everything. And they would plan the rest of their lives.

Together.

CHAPTER 23

July camp season turned out to be busier than Heidi remembered from the previous year. Adding to the stress were the frightening letters from home. She wasn't sure why it had taken so long, but her mom had a diagnosis: breast cancer. Her mammogram and biopsy had been a few weeks ago. They didn't know if this was the reason for her fatigue and general malaise, but they were working quickly to get her a surgery date. As far as they knew, if the cancer was contained, there should be no systemic effects, so her symptoms were a huge red flag.

To make matters worse, Child Protective Services (CPS) had come by and questioned her parents – apparently, her mom had fallen asleep at home one day, and a neighbor had seen the twins outside playing alone. Instead of taking the situation at face value, she called CPS. Now, her parents had the added stress of home visits, trying to prove they were adequate caregivers.

After the last letter, Heidi called them. Her mom told her about the lumpectomy scheduled for the following week, reassuring her it would all be routine.

But a week later, Vera came in and got her attention in the middle of a camp meeting. Heidi looked over at Amy to ensure she knew she was leaving her campers, then slipped out the side door.

"Your Dad just phoned," Vera said. "I told him I would find you, so he could phone again in ten minutes."

Her heart pounding with fear, Heidi took the stairs two at a time to the upstairs apartment, hoping Karl was elsewhere. The only phone was in their main living area, and Karl would often sit there, oblivious to her need for privacy. While she stared at the phone, her mind imagined various scenarios. None of them were good.

The shrill ring made her jump, and she grabbed the receiver with a sweaty hand, pushing it against her ear. "Dad?"

"Heidi." And then silence. Had they been disconnected?

"Dad?"

"I'm – I'm here." And then he lurched into an explanation.

Nothing about her mom's surgery had been routine. She had had a mastectomy. There was lymph node involvement. And CPS had stopped by for another visit while her mom was still in the hospital. They had decreed the twins' care inadequate, even though a babysitter had been present, and Heidi's parents had a limited time to meet all their requirements. Otherwise, the twins would be moved to foster care. Heidi needed to be home well before then. Once her mom was managing and CPS's demands had been satisfied, they could talk about Heidi returning to camp. But the doctors said her mom would need chemo, and it would be a long road.

Heidi struggled to set the phone back onto its cradle. She had suspected she would eventually need to return and help her parents, but she hadn't expected this suddenness. She had imagined she would only be needed for a few months to help get her mom through chemo and help parent the twins. Then, once her mother was managing, she could return. But this was her mom's second bout with cancer, the first one had been uterine cancer years before, and she could hear the resignation and fear in her dad's voice. Nobody expected her to get better this time. Nobody.

She heard the lunch gong, and the thought of eating roiled her stomach. Vaguely, she hoped Amy would keep an eye on her campers as she slipped down the back stairs and ran towards the far side of the tennis courts. She would sit there out of sight until she had regained her composure, and then sometime that day, she would have to tell Johann she was leaving.

Her tears came in heaving sobs; she could scarcely catch her breath. Her mom was dying, and the twins were undoubtedly confused and afraid without the presence of their beloved Momee. Layered on top of everything was the heartbreak of leaving Johann. There would be no wedding plans; their future together was on hold. Indefinitely.

She sat there until she was convinced lunch had ended, and they were in their afternoon meeting, and then slipped back up to camp and into the restrooms. Now that she knew she had to leave, everything looked different. Once more, the bathrooms seemed strange to her, with the opening at the top allowing her to hear the boys' loud chatter on the other side of the adjoining wall. The mustiness seemed stronger, the sun when she stepped outside harsher, and the dry air colder.

After scrubbing her face to remove signs of crying, she slipped her sunglasses over her reddened eyes and went to her cabin to change into something less rumpled. She didn't know when she would find time to talk to Johann, but thankfully this camp session ended the following day, and then it would be the weekend.

Meeting up with her campers at game time, Johann pulled her aside.

"Where have you been? Amy's been pulling double duty."

"I... I had a phone call from home." She turned her head, her eyes blurred, noting absently how the campers seemed to be impressionist figures milling about. She wanted to lash out at him. She never disappeared.

"*Ja?*"

So, he needed an explanation now to warrant her disappearance? Sudden anger struck at his insensitivity. They were all tired, it had been a long three weeks of non-stop campers, but surely, he had to know if she received an emergency phone call from home, something wasn't right. Oddly, she felt almost grateful for this anger; it would keep her from falling apart in front of the campers. "I have to go home. My mom's cancer is worse than they thought, and there is nobody to care for the twins." Her voice was flat.

She watched his anger evaporate, and he reached out to grip her shoulder, but she took a step back.

"When?"

"As soon as possible."

The children were clamoring around him, pulling on him, teasing him about talking to his girlfriend instead of starting their game, and he swatted at them absently while staring at her in dismay. Then, he blew his whistle and explained the game, handing the clipboard and whistle over to Ian, telling him and Amy to take over. Motioning towards the road that led to the dam, he headed that way, indicating Heidi should follow him.

They walked in silence until they were out of sight, and then he turned to her.

"What happened? I thought everything was fine?"

She shrugged helplessly. "Somehow, between our last phone call and the surgery, they decided on a mastectomy, and there was lymph node involvement, and they couldn't get clean margins... maybe?" Heidi paused, "I don't know if I'm getting it straight and, to be honest, it doesn't make sense to me. But now she will have to have chemo. And she's still in the hospital. But my neighbors called CPS because they thought the children weren't being cared for adequately, and now, they are threatening foster care if," Heidi air quoted, "a 'fit and able family member' doesn't step in and care for them."

"And CPS is an organization that can do this?"

She forced a laugh. "Oh yes, they can. After Jenna first had them…." Then she stopped; there was no need to get into that now. She needed to focus on the pressing need. "I have to go home, and I have to go *now*."

"For how long?"

"For… until… Johann, I can tell my dad thinks mom is dying."

She expected him to take her in his arms, to comfort her like he had in times past, but he merely stood there dumbly. She wished he would say something – anything – but instead, he stood, silent. Surely, he didn't need further justification for her leaving?

Eventually, he spoke. "And why can't this CPS accept that your father is there for the twins?"

"Because my father is still living at the hospital with my mom!"

"Who's caring for them now?"

"I don't know, Johann! Friends? Nosy neighbors, who think the friends are inadequate?" How could he not see she had zero option but to go back and care for them? How could he not comprehend if she only had a few days left with her mother, that every second mattered? But it seemed he needed justification, and it cut her to her core.

"Do you think that after you had been there for a few months, your father would be able to be their full-time caregiver?"

"No!" She rolled her eyes in disdain. "My father runs a company; he works sixty or seventy hours a week. The children need a parent who is *present*."

Johann turned then and began walking slowly again. She watched him, dumbstruck.

He spun toward her, a glimmer of hope in his eyes. "Could you go back with the intent of eventually returning with the twins?"

"No," she said slowly, "that would be too complicated."

"Why is it complicated?"

"How can I be a camp counselor and have children to care for? I would be their mother, not just their babysitter."

"But Heidi, if you were staying, we would have had children."

Heidi blushed, thinking for a moment how idyllic that sounded. But she had to reign in her dreams and focus on the pressing need of getting home as fast as possible.

"But I am not married to you."

"Of course not; we would get married – that's why you are wearing my ring!" His frustration was palpable.

"It's just more complicated than that. I… I can't bring the twins here."

"Well, why not?"

She looked dully away, afraid to tell him the whole truth, not wanting to see the shock in his eyes, not wanting to hear anything negative said about her twins. She tried a new tactic. "What if… if eventually, you came to America? We have camps there."

"I'm not moving to America," he responded stiffly.

"But why not?"

"My life and work are here; this is where I belong."

"Well, the twins' life is in America with their grandfather – that's where they belong."

He turned angrily. "I don't understand! They are children. Children can adapt and change. For them, it would all be a big adventure."

"No, for them, it would be a big mistake!"

"Why?"

"Because, Johann, it just would be, OK?"

"Heidi," he lowered his voice, "children can get used to any situation. Trust me, I know."

"But you… you just don't understand." Her voice was resigned. She would have to tell him the truth.

"What? How can't I understand? It's a good solution."

"No, it's not!"

"Well then, why?"

"Because, Johann, because here in this country of yours, they would be called… I think you would probably refer to them as *colored*." There she had said it. Let him think what he wanted.

"What?" He grabbed her arm and faced her. "How is that possible?"

"Because the man who fathered them was black." Shock registered on his face as she waited for her words to sink in. "And you want me to bring them *here*?"

They stood there facing each other, their anger and his disbelief

187

pulsating between them.

"And where will they go to school? To the colored school down the road? Oh wait, that won't work; Darla has *blue eyes*. Can't send them there." She was yelling and shaking violently. She never knew she had the capacity for such anger, yet she couldn't make it stop. "OK, then, they can go to the white school." She slammed her palm against her face. "Oh, wait! That won't work; they have dark curly hair and beautiful skin that's too dark to be considered *white*." She spat out the word in distaste.

She watched as a thousand emotions flitted across Johann's face. She wanted him to say he understood that he would try and come to the US to work so they could be together. But he simply stood there, watching her.

"You see, *you* don't even know what to say. And you're the one who always knows what to say." Her voice was mocking now, and she knew she should quit, but it hurt, hurt so deeply that he wouldn't even consider coming to the US for her.

"And you never thought to tell me this?"

Heidi didn't respond. She didn't know how.

He held out his hands in helplessness. "They could still come here, Heidi. Here at the camp, it wouldn't matter. I'm sure they couldn't possibly be that different."

"Oh, maybe to you and me and Amy and probably Vera, it wouldn't matter. But it would matter to *Herr Karl*."

Johann flinched at her implication. "Heidi, don't—"

"No, don't tell me what I can say. They are my family, my flesh and blood, and I will not bring them to a country that's going to ostracize them, refuse them opportunities, make them ride a different bus, won't let them stand in the same line in the post office, throw *Chappies* at them, won't—"

"Stop!" His chest was heaving as if the effort to contain his anger was too much.

They stood facing each other, and then Heidi turned and walked away. Tears blurred her eyes; she stumbled but caught herself and kept going. She would walk until she couldn't walk any further. She didn't care camp was in its final evening. They would have to run things without her in a few short days anyway. Her mother was dying, and she had to go home as soon as possible. Each part of their conversation had been like a knife plunging into her gut. He hadn't even addressed the fact that she might lose her mom. And that, coupled with the hurt over his immediate refusal to even consider coming to America, made her wonder at his love. His flat and instantaneous refusal spoke volumes.

She walked until she reached the dam and then sat along the water's edge until her body was stiff and sore in the cold. Now Johann knew the truth, but she couldn't bring the twins here, despite what he said to the contrary. She knew things were changing in South Africa, but it wouldn't be fast enough for her twins. She knew many white South Africans disagreed with apartheid but still lacked a path forward. She saw plenty of people doing what Johann had taught her, quietly making a difference in small ways until the country could really change. She hoped and prayed that day would come soon.

Clouds gathered on the darkening horizon, and the wind picked up; she could smell rain in the air. She trudged back to camp as the sun slipped behind the camp buildings, casting her mountains in a shroud, and hid at the Counting Tree, hoping the rain would hold off. Tomorrow morning, she would have to figure out how to get to a travel agency and book her ticket, but today, she couldn't; she had stupidly wasted the afternoon on her sorrow. Now she would have to wait at least twelve more hours before she could do anything. What had she been thinking? Her self-condemnation was swift and brutal. What if the agency didn't open on a Saturday? Everything shut down here on the weekend, but maybe the agency was like the grocery stores and stayed open at least until noon. How could she have been so pathetic? She was just as wrapped up in herself as Johann seemed to be with himself. Instead of action, she had run off to nurse her wounds and garner sympathy from Johann, and now she had lost a whole day. What if her mom died before she could get back? What if the twins were taken away to foster care because of her absence? She would never forgive herself.

Amy found her there, shivering in the cold. "Here, Heidi, I brought you some tea and food. You're freezing. Take my jacket."

"Thank you, Amy." She struggled into the jacket, her arms refusing to cooperate.

"Johann told us about your mom. What are you going to do?"

"I'm going to go home – I need someone to take me into Pretoria to the travel agency first thing tomorrow to see what they can book me." She took a shuddering breath. "It has to be soon, my mom... my mom...." She couldn't finish.

Amy hugged her hard. "Oh, Heidi, I am so sorry. We are all so sorry. I have to get back, but I've got your campers. I should have enough beds."

Heidi turned to her gratefully. She couldn't face her campers. "Could you tell them I'm sorry, that I love them but that...."

"Don't worry, I'll tell them."

"Oh, Amy, thank you." She squeezed her gratefully, and then Amy was gone, back to the normal Heidi had been part of only a few hours ago. She snuggled into Amy's jacket and took a sip of the lukewarm tea. The weeping willow branches moved softly in the evening chill, and she watched them mesmerized. Beyond those branches, the stars were pinpoints in the cold night air, and the realization of God's presence came swiftly. The God of the Universe who had placed each star knew about her heartache and cared for her. She had no solution, but she would hold to that truth.

***

"I knew I would find you here." His voice was hoarse. It must have been late for Johann to be free to come to her.

She nodded into the darkness, hugging her knees to her chest, wishing he had a remedy but knowing there was none.

He sat next to her, wrapping his arms around her, tilting her against him.

She remained balled up, protecting herself from the onslaught of what was coming, yet he held her. "I'm sorry, Heidi, I never knew."

"How could you?"

"Why didn't you tell me?"

"What would've been the point?"

"And I'm very sorry that your mom is... is... so sick."

Heidi's eyes welled with fresh tears.

"I never told you the whole story about me, Heidi. I... I just don't talk about it." He gripped her tighter. "But I think if I tell you, it will help us know what the right thing is."

He shifted slightly, tucking her head under his chin, and began.

"Over there hangs my chime. I wrote Karl's name on it. Because Karl saved me, first from the mental anguish of living with an alcoholic father and then from an abusive stepfather. I was just a scared kid when I started coming here to camp. I thought my dad's drinking, and later my stepfather's abuse was somehow my fault.

190

But here, here I was taught I was unique, created for a purpose, and that I had a heavenly Father who loved me. I came here every year from age ten. When I was fifteen, my mom and stepdad decided they were moving to Australia. I was at boarding school by then, so Karl and Vera agreed that I could stay with them on short breaks. On longer holidays, I would go and live with Aunt Gillian. Then, when I went to Wits, I split my time between Wits, camp, and Aunt Gillian's. After Wits, I did my two-year military service, and after that, it just made sense to stay here where I had work that I loved. I was conflicted because Aunt Gillian and I are so close, but I felt that I could do for others what the camp had done for me by staying at camp. And, well," he shrugged, "you know the rest."

"And your mom?" There were tears in Heidi's eyes, imagining a younger Johann, wishing she could go back in time and somehow comfort that little boy.

"I barely hear from her. You know, I think she feels guilty, and I think I remind her about the worst parts of her life. I don't know. I don't hold it against her. But don't you see, if it hadn't been for Karl and Vera stepping in...." He paused again. "So, my chime is still here; I put the name Karl on it because he was the first man who acted like a real dad towards me. Here was a Christian man who treated me like I had value and truly cared about me... If it hadn't been for them.... " His voice cracked, and he stopped.

Heidi waited.

"I... I, more than anyone, understand how you obviously need to go to your mother, but even more how you need to go and be a Karl and Vera for those children. If you don't...."

That was it, what she had needed to hear. She knew in her heart if she didn't go, Darla and Darrin might be lost to her. She owed it to her suffering parents, but, most of all, she owed it to the twins. She would go home and be their mom no matter how long it took. But, somehow, despite what she knew, she had needed Johann to support her, to understand, fully and completely. Her verse from Hebrews came unbidden,

And again I will put my trust in Him, and again, behold I and the children which God hath given me.

God had given her 18 months of camp life and dozens of children to love and to let go. Now, He was giving her two lonely confused children who called Grandma "Momee" and had no concept of who their actual mother had been. Well, one thing wouldn't change. She would still be Aunt Heidi, but instead of Aunt Heidi to dozens, she would be Aunt Heidi to two. Now, the choice was evident, and choosing her family was her new calling.

"Heidi?"

She realized she hadn't acknowledged his statement. She had never seen him cry before, and the tears in his eyes made her own flow faster.

"I know," she choked out.

Johann stood abruptly and roughly pulled her to her feet, clasping her against him. "Oh, Heidi-my-Heidi...." They stood there, crying and holding on to each other, willing tomorrow to be different but knowing there were no other options.

Heidi must go home.

She wished he would promise he would come and visit her, that they would find a way to be together, but empty promises were pointless. Johann was right; his life was here at camp.

She glanced down at her ring. What was the point? Unless her mother made a miraculous recovery, Heidi was not hopeful of coming back. She couldn't imagine Johann leaving everything and moving to a land filled with Americans. She would've smiled at the thought if her heart hadn't been breaking. He was watching her play with her ring.

She lifted her eyes, wondering.

"Keep my ring, Heidi," his gaze softer. "Maybe a miracle will happen for us."

"But what if it doesn't?" She turned her head to the side so she wouldn't see the sorrow mirrored in his eyes.

He gently turned her face back to him. "Do you want to stay engaged?" His voice was laced with fear.

"Engaged? I want to marry you tomorrow so that we *have* to stay together!" And she flung her arms around him, sobbing uncontrollably.

"I know, Heidi-my-Heidi, I know." He tangled his hand in her hair, gripping her as if afraid to let go, holding her until her sobs quieted.

"You know," she said, her face against his chest, "I always go to the swing when I'm sad. The Counting Tree is supposed to be a place of blessing and thanksgiving. But I thought if I came here, I would find a way to be thankful in spite of...." She broke off.

He set her away from him, gripping her shoulders and looking into her eyes. "I'm thankful for you, Heidi. For what you taught me about love and laughing and... and Americans."

She smiled then, "And I'm thankful for you, Johann. You taught me so much, even, even that a man can love a woman and... and wait for her."

He shook his head then, as if in physical pain. It would be so easy to give in, especially now. They were alone, and in only a day or two, she would be gone. She watched as the emotions flitted across his face, his mind and heart warring with his body, and then he took a slight step back. "And for that reason, Heidi-my-Heidi, I need to go back." He touched her cheek briefly with the tips of his fingers and turned and walked away.

She wanted to shout at his retreating back, to tell him it didn't matter, but the words stuck in her throat. She watched as the darkness swallowed him; foreboding filled her. One minute he had been here, holding her, and now he was gone. And she knew the image of his silhouette melting into the darkness symbolized finality. She willed the ominous feeling away, yet it persisted, even as she walked slowly back to her too-quiet cabin and slipped into bed.

She dreamed of their wedding day. She was standing in the church waiting for him, yet, somehow, they were on two separate continents. Every time she thought she caught a glimpse of him, he retreated, and she could never quite catch him. Her wedding dress kept tangling around her feet, slowing her down, and no matter how hard she tried, he remained beyond her reach.

Finally, at the first glimmer of dawn, she got up and went to the showers. She needed to shake the dream's images and hold onto what they had: a deep love, friendship, a desire to serve God, and a ring, a symbol of it all.

***

The next morning as soon as the campers left, Johann took her to a travel agent in Pretoria, where she booked the first available flight for Monday morning. The ticket was exorbitantly priced, but her parents wired the money immediately.

"I wish you could come with me," she whispered softly, knowing it was unfair to place such a burden on him, knowing it was impossible.

He hit the steering wheel, his anger evident.

193

Heidi watched the emotions parade across his face, and her heart pounded with fear. She didn't want to return home with an engagement ring when she was afraid she would never see Johann again. It would invite too many painful questions and knowing looks. She would become the girl who got engaged but never got married.

In a moment of decision, she wrenched the ring from her finger and held it out. "I can't go home wearing this if we don't have a plan."

He drew his eyebrows together. "I thought we sorted this last night. You don't *want* to be engaged anymore?"

She had to make him understand. "Johann, I told you last night: I want to be married *today*."

"Then why won't you wear my ring?"

She could hear his anger and hurt, but she had to make him understand.

"It's going to be hard enough to go home and face everything that I have to face. And if I wear this ring, everyone will want me to explain *us,* and the questions will make it harder rather than easier."

"Fine." He took the ring, his face stony.

"Johann," she shook his arm in frustration and fear. "I love you with all my heart, but my family and friends are going to...."

"If you don't want people to know about me, then I understand." He was sullen, his stance stiff.

He put the truck into gear and merged into traffic.

They barely spoke on the way home.

Once they got back, the first person they saw was Karl.

"So, you have to leave?"

She saw him looking at her hand, but surely, she imagined his glimmer of speculation. Amy and Vera, however, were more circumspect. Amy helped her pack, and Vera kept popping in the cabin to check on her, asking if she had enough cash to get home, asking if she wanted to pack snacks, reminding her that they loved her, that Heidi was the best American ever to come work at their little camp.

That night she went to the swing, and Amy came to sit with her and asked about the ring. Heidi tried to explain but got upset, so Amy told her she understood.

"After I'm gone, will you try help Johann understand?"

"Yes, Heidi. Of course, I will." And Amy hugged her and left with a whispered promise that she'd be praying.

Heidi waited until 2am, but Johann never came. Finally, exhausted and defeated, she went to bed, knowing she would have to be packed and ready to leave after breakfast the following day. She would ask Amy to give her boots and coat for Mavis to use or pass along.

Her flight wasn't until Monday morning, the day they would be starting their fourth and final camp week of the July camp season. But this next church was bringing their children on Sunday evening. So, Karl decided Johann would take her to the Anderson's house to spend Sunday night, and then the Andersons would take her to the airport on Monday. She wished Johann could take her, but she knew neither of them could handle it.

As she hugged Amy goodbye, the foreboding threatened to swallow her.

"I'll send you lots of letters, Heidi," Amy promised, hugging her fiercely.

Heidi couldn't speak. She would write Amy as soon as possible to tell her everything, to thank her for being the reason she had made it through those first weeks in South Africa, to tell her she thought of her as the kind of sister she had always wished for. Amy truly was her South African twin.

She clung next to Vera and then Mavis and then shook Karl's hand. He seemed almost happy telling her goodbye, but Heidi chalked that up to her own raw emotions and lack of sleep.

Johann slung her single suitcase into the back of the *bakkie* and told everyone he would see them later that day in time for the new campers' arrival. After he dropped Heidi, he would bring back the missionary's daughter to help with the week-long camp. Amanda was old enough to work with the youngest girls. Eventually, they would need a permanent replacement for Heidi.

Heidi watched through tear-filled eyes as camp disappeared from the side-view mirror. Dust kicked up from the road, blocking her final view of the Tree and the mountains and the dam and the blooming bougainvillea.

They drove on, the silence breaking Heidi's heart. About thirty minutes from camp, Johann pulled the *bakkie* over. He got out and took her hand, walking her along a faint trail until they got to a weeping willow tree.

"I always notice this from the road but have never pulled over.

It looks just like our Counting Tree, doesn't it?" He paused, looking at her, anguish in his eyes. "I won't be able to say goodbye to you properly after this, Heidi."

She wanted to cry and beg him to come and visit her, to move to America. But she knew she couldn't ask such a thing of him. His life and work were here. Her life and new work were now back home. They would be living necessary lives on two separate continents. There was no immediate hope. They would have their letters and pray for a miracle.

He took her hand, reached into his pocket, and held out the ring. "Keep my ring, Heidi," he said gently. "You don't have to wear it, but it's yours. It can be our private symbol of the miracle we are praying for."

Tears blurred her eyes as she tried to focus on the ring in his hand. "You... you understand?"

He crooked a slight smile. "After I finished being so angry at you and everything else, I thought about you going back home to Chris and Brianna's baby and your sick mother and heartbroken Dad and the twins and then...."

He watched as she took the ring from him. "I wouldn't want to answer all their questions either, you know." He paused again and then, reaching out and wiping her tears, quirked another half-smile. "You know how I hate it when Americans ask too many questions."

She smiled wanly. "I will cherish our ring, Johann. Thank you." She wanted to say more but couldn't. There were just too many emotions and not enough words.

He took her in his arms and kissed her deeply. When he lifted his head with enough space to speak, he whispered. "Someday, somehow Heidi-my-Heidi, I am going to make you my wife. And, when that happens, I will never let you out of my sight." And he lifted her, hugging her tightly, refusing to let go. "And that's a promise."

She felt a crack of light pierce the dark foreboding and lighten the weight of her sadness.

When they got to the Anderson's house, he made a big scene about rushing, giving her last-minute instructions, and hugging her between each one. Did she have her passport? Did she have their pictures? Make sure she didn't lose her suitcase. Don't talk to strangers. Don't let cute American boys flirt with her. Hug the twins for him. Did she have some snake repellant for the plane?

This was her Johann, acting strong and silly for both of them. At the last minute, he handed her a flat, square, brown package.

"Open it on the aeroplane," he said.

She looked at him quizzically.

"I had it made for an early wedding present…."

Then with one last bear hug, he was gone.

Mrs. Anderson, sensing her sorrow, offered her lunch and a quick trip to the shops to get anything she might need. Mostly, though, she left Heidi to herself, understanding her need for quiet. So, Heidi sat in Amanda's empty room and wrote Johann her first letter.

She analyzed the brown paper packaging Johann had handed her, debating. Then, in a moment of decision, she opened it.

Inside lay a painting with the title *Beauty in Real Life*, a painting of her view, the bougainvillea framing the window to the pool and mountains beyond.

He had remembered. All that time ago, when he had seemingly grudgingly been showing her the camp, he had remembered her reaction. She shouldn't be surprised. He was Johann, after all.

Tears dampened the paper as she wrapped it carefully and slid it between the clothes in her suitcase.

THE PLANE TOOK off and banked over the city. Here was her Africa, the Africa that had stolen her heart, the Africa that she did not want to leave. Right now, campers would be just starting their day. Mavis would be dishing up *mieliepap,* and Johann and Amy and Ian and Amanda would be corralling the kids at the eating area, explaining the schedule. Vera would be in the office already, putting out the stacks of Stamp Club materials for later, and kids would be laughing and talking and nudging each other, excited for their first full day at camp.

Heidi watched Johannesburg's skyline get smaller and smaller as a tear slipped down her cheek, splashing onto the armrest. Here, in this country, she had learned the value of thankfulness, the necessity of counting her blessings. And although the heartsickness that permeated her entire being felt crushing in its weight, she knew she would find the strength to face what lay ahead. Because God was on her side. And one day, somehow, she would return, return to Johann and camp life, return to serving the children God sent her way. But, for now, on another continent, two precious children were waiting for her, needing their Aneidi, and she would be their Karl and Vera, just as Johann had said. She would pour her heart into them, love them, and cherish them because now, *they* were indeed the children God had given her.

Interlude

⌘

Jupiter, Florida

2001

CHAPTER 24

Nobody had warned her it would feel this way.

Heidi had an aisle seat plus an entire row saved close to the stage. Her camera had fresh film and batteries. The twins were in line, bursting with energy and promise. But she felt completely off kilter; her children were graduating. And in a few weeks, both would be gone, carried on the wave of finished exams, their senior trip, and this night. Neither seemed to realize the finality of it all, but for Heidi, the upcoming changes attacked from all angles. She fiddled with her camera; she had one chance to get these photos. This, she realized afresh, was the downside of twins: they left home... together. She would go from parenting two to an empty nest; dread filled every crevice and weighed her down.

The day had passed in a flurry of preparations – ironing their regalia, running to Walmart for a hot glue gun to decorate graduation caps, picking up food and the cake for the party, helping Darla with her hair, convincing Darrin he needed to shine his shoes. But the entire day felt surreal. Darla was leaving for summer session at the University of Florida in only two weeks, and, in ten days, Darrin was leaving to work at Camp Makarios near Maggie Valley, North Carolina. Heidi found herself struggling to process the sudden life change.

When they were five, thirty minutes to herself had been a gift. When they started school, the hours they were gone had given Heidi time to handle the endless stream of necessity that accompanied parenting lively twins. There had also been more time to work for her dad, managing contracts, fielding phone calls, maintaining records, and keeping customers aware of job delivery.

As the twins had grown, their camaraderie had created enjoyable moments that were no longer work. To keep an eye on them, she had opened the house to a stream of kids and then teenagers. It had made for busy, chaotic days but had kept her own kids close. Plus, it had helped fill the void of her dad's passing only eleven months before. And now, abruptly, everything would change. There would be no gradual tapering with one child and then the other. They were twins, and they were both leaving.

Gone.

Her job was done.

An empty summer stared her in the face, and she was acutely aware she would be utterly alone. After the busyness of the last fifteen years, she couldn't fathom what that meant.

The orchestra was warming up, and the sounds of tuning instruments jolted her back to her surroundings. She looked over and counted out the seats again. Two for the McManns, the twins' youth leaders at church, six for Sierra and her crew, and one for Gladys, her dad's longtime girlfriend.

Sadly, there was no spot for her dad and the ever-present ache intensified. Her dad had eventually become her rock and the twins' superhero. Prior to his passing, they had worked together to sell his company. As a result, Heidi had a tidy nest egg, along with the house and a few investments. So many blessings, yet they were wrapped in grief.

The house felt foreign without her dad's calm, reassuring presence. He and Gladys had been friends for so long that Gladys had become a surrogate Grandma to the twins. Heidi wondered why they never married, but she supposed it had made life easier in the long run, albeit lonelier. There was no property to share or complications with the will. She and Gladys had remained close, and Heidi found herself grateful for her presence in the twins' lives. They had lost so much; any positive influence was an advantage not to be taken lightly.

The twins had missed their grandma, their "Momee," so much during those early days when Heidi returned from camp. Her mom was still there, but the illness had so far progressed that Heidi had to become an instantaneous mom. It was a miracle Heidi had survived it. Sitting there waiting, surrounded by the hum of voices in the rapidly filling auditorium, her mind went back, all the way back, to those first days—days when the sorrow of watching her mom waste away had been almost too much to bear; days when the twins couldn't process why "Aneidi" responded in place of her own mom.

"I want Momee." The calls had come nightly after her mom's death.

"Want Momee."

The duet would be a cacophony in no time if she didn't think fast. Heidi lugged herself from bed and slipped into the twins' room, catching them both to her and whispering soothing words, smothering them with kisses and telling them she loved them. They were sleeping together again, their insecurity manifesting nightly with bedwetting and the continual fear of being alone. She carefully felt their night pull-ups she had resorted to, relieved they seemed dry.

"Roll on your tummies, and I'll rub your backs."

"Don' leave us, Aneidi."

"Don' leave us." Darla always mimicked Darrin.

Heidi sighed and inserted herself between them, drawing their heads onto her chest. "I won't leave you, sweeties; just close your little eyes, and soon it will be morning time." She waited, tensed for their protest, but having won her presence, it seemed they would go back to sleep. She relaxed slightly, relieved. Camp life had been a walk in the park compared to mothering two grieving four-year-olds.

"Want Momee," Darla whispered, her eyes still closed.

"I know, sweetie." She wanted her mother, too. It had all happened way too fast. Two months. Two measly months was all she'd had with her mother. Maybe if she'd been home, she would have noticed the increasing fatigue and insisted her mom get herself checked out. Maybe if her dad hadn't been working so much, he would have noticed. But they had waited too long. There had been too little warning and not enough time.

What if she had swallowed her pride at seeing Chris and

Brianna and had come home for Christmas? Would it have made a difference? Could they have caught it in time? She thought back to her decision to stay in South Africa over Christmas and her subsequent perfect Christmas with Johann as guilt assayed her. Could her presence here have made a difference, or would her mom have hidden her fatigue from Heidi as well?

Heidi would never know. It was too late to play what-if because nothing could erase the harsh reality of her mother's death. Now she was mothering the twins almost solo. Her dad's grief had placed an impenetrable barrier between them. After always being close, she found this emotional distance hard to bear. He had moved out to the mother-in-law suite by the pool and told Heidi she could have the master suite. But Heidi had stayed in her room, unable to disturb her mother's things. It was too soon.

She remembered the twins falling asleep against her like this, night after night, while tears slipped down her face. She had lost everything and everyone – her sister, Chris, Brianna, Amy, Johann, her dear sweet mom, and, it seemed, her dad. There was nobody left. Nobody.

And again I will put my trust in Him and again, behold the children which thou hast given me.

The verse came spontaneously, halting and redirecting her thoughts so effectively it could have been audible. She stilled, listened, and heard the words again...

I will put my trust in Him... children... given me...

Darla and Darrin, that's who God had given her; they were the reason she had come home. They were her purpose, her sole reason for being here. She would pour her life and energy into them.

Heidi's phone pinged, bringing her back to the present and the graduation. Sierra.

Running late.

Heidi fumbled with the phone keys and typed back a clumsy 'OK.' The teens loved texting, anything to keep from talking on a phone, but Heidi found it awkward. Maybe if they came out with phones with an actual keyboard, she would adapt.

Sierra and "late" went together. Running late was easy when you had to corral so many. Heidi smiled softly. The day God had placed Sierra in Heidi's path was a miracle.

The twins had only been six. They had stopped to play at a park after school and had inadvertently inserted themselves into a three-year-old's party. Heidi could tell a few of the party parents weren't happy.

"Excuse me." A woman had planted herself in front of Heidi, and her stance fit the part; Heidi knew what was coming. "Do those kids belong to you?"

"What kids?" Heidi kept her voice even.

"Those kids." She released one hand from her crossed arms to point at Darla and Darrin.

"Why does it matter? They're just playing." Heidi kept her tone low and calm in complete opposition to the anger building.

"Well, we're trying to have a party here." The woman's arms were crossed again.

"I didn't realize you could rent out the entire park."

"Um, we didn't, but maybe—"

"Maybe what?" Heidi stood eye to eye with the offended mom in her perfectly fitted shorts and matching top. Things were going to get heated because Heidi and her twins were staying put.

The woman staccato-tapped her pedicured sandaled foot. "Kids like that play rough, and we have three-year-olds here."

"I don't understand – kids like 'that'?" Heidi used air quotes.

"Well, you know, most... uh...," she grimaced, "you know, these types of kids play rough, and plus, they're older."

Heidi stepped towards her, about to unleash all the fury of every misrepresented innocent child, when a cheery voice interrupted from behind. "Cindy, everyone is waiting for you!"

Heidi turned to see a brightly dressed woman carrying a baby and holding a toddler by the hand. "Hi, I'd shake your hand, but no free hands. I'm Sierra."

Heidi didn't respond. Was this woman coming to defend her or coming to support 'Cindy?'

"Cindy," Sierra gave the woman a pointed stare, "I said everyone is waiting for you."

Cindy rolled her eyes at Heidi and marched off.

"I'm surprised you know her, being that your kids are 'these types' and all." Heidi couldn't keep the bitterness out of her voice as she looked at Sierra.

"Girl, I'm Jamaican. I deal with Cindys all the time. But I want to apologize on behalf of my group for whatever just went down here. You OK?"

Heidi nodded briefly. She wanted to grab the twins and run to her car, but that would be giving in and wouldn't help her kids in the long run. Instead, she shakily sat on a bench.

Sierra moved over, tilting her head for permission, and then sat on the other side of the bench, the baby now on her lap and the toddler pulled up against her legs.

"I never realized America was like this, you know." Heidi heard herself speak and couldn't believe she had said the words out loud.

Sierra nodded, and the baby and toddler looked at Heidi with big, beautiful, serious eyes.

Heidi took in Sierra's open, friendly face and decided to continue. "I grew up here. I had friends of all colors. How did I not realize how much harder it was for some of them? Was I stupid?"

"No, honey, you were just a kid living your life."

And that had been her introduction to Sierra Barnes, and eventually, to all her children and to Big Tony, the best husband of multiple kids she had ever watched in action.

Today, "Little" Tony, their second oldest, was graduating. He was now over six feet, yet the moniker had stuck. The oldest daughter was a sophomore in college, and the youngest a sixth grader. Sierra had had a child every other year, and when they were little, they stair-stepped in the cutest way and had provided her twins an example of a traditional family.

Heidi heard their arrival before she saw them and snapped back to the present. They were her surrogate Jamaican family that embodied all things wonderful. "We're here!" That was Tyson, the youngest. "And so is everybody else!" And before Heidi could barely say hellos and hug Gladys and the McManns, the strains of "Pomp and Circumstance" filled the space, silencing the auditorium and bringing everyone to their feet. She watched them walk in through a blur of tears, Darla smiling like a million bucks and Darrin suddenly serious.

The audience settled as the first speaker came to the podium. It would be a long evening, but one to be savored if Heidi could only fully comprehend her twins were actually graduating.

After returning from South Africa, the days had been a blur with her mom's illness and the twins' needs. It had been hard to play catch-up, and watching her mom suffer from one treatment to the next was heartbreaking. Often at night, after the twins were in bed, Heidi would go into her mom's room, sit by her in the stillness, and hold her hand. Sometimes her mom wanted to talk, but many times they simply sat in the quiet. Once when her mom was more lucid, she had asked about Johann.

"We're just friends now." Heidi managed the lie with difficulty.

Her mom turned her head slowly and gave her a quizzical look.

"We write to each other, but, for now, we aren't going to make plans." She altered the lie since her mom clearly did not buy the first one.

"But you were engaged?" Her mom's face mirrored confusion and the effort of speaking.

"Yes, we were." Heidi rubbed her mom's arm softly. "But not now. His life is there, and I want to be here."

"I'm so sorry, sweetheart." Her eyes were closed, but her words were strong.

Tears filled Heidi's eyes, and she turned her head away. Why did Johann hardly write? Why had Amy only written twice? Why nearly complete silence? There was simply no way to keep up with them without letters and phone calls. But nobody had called her. She had tried once, but the phone rang and rang. Answering machines had not made their way to Northern Transvaal. She had debated contacting Aunt Gillian but didn't have her phone number or address. She just didn't understand this great silence, like the 18 months in South Africa had never happened, and the people she had come to know as family had ceased to exist. Her days were exhausting enough; she simply didn't have the energy to devote to solving this mystery. Everyone needed her here. With her mom's time so short, she couldn't spend precious minutes chasing Johann and Amy. But that didn't alter the fact the silence cut deeply.

People were clapping in the auditorium, so Heidi followed suit, jolted back to the present by the noise. Heidi caught Sierra's eye and smiled, hoping her mental absence hadn't been noted. Sierra was quick to analyze and understand a situation, and Heidi didn't want her to worry. Sierra needed to celebrate her Tony without worrying about Heidi.

A new speaker came to the podium, and her mind drifted again, cataloging the years. After her mom's death, she had gratefully watched as the twins chiseled away at her dad's wall of grief. They, in effect, brought their "Gwamps" back to the father Heidi recognized. Her twins were little miracle workers and, within a few months, had traded "Aneidi" for "Mommy." At first, she had wanted to correct them but then decided against it. What children had had three mothers by the time they were five? So, if they wanted to call her "Mommy," she would lovingly respond.

Towards the end of the twins' first-grade year, she received the earth-shattering news that Johann and Amy had married. It was a *deja vu* of the worst kind. Another letter in the mail. Another incomplete explanation. But this time, no cute camp guy to comfort her and hold her while she cried; no explanation as to what had happened to Ian. Just a drought of communication capped off by a wedding announcement. Heidi had carried around a knot of bitterness for days until one evening, Darrin looked up at her and said simply, "Mommy, if you are sad, you are supposed to tell God so He can fix it." His sweet words hit their target and softened her heart.

She had never understood the profound silence that had accompanied her return to the US. Somewhere in a drawer, her ring lay hidden in an envelope; below that, she had stashed their few pictures and the painting, but it had been years since she had pulled anything out. The children knew nothing of their engagement and very little of her time in South Africa. They had been too young when she returned, and so carefully had she dealt with any remaining feelings regarding her time there, even thinking about it became a personal taboo.

During the twins' second grade year, she had tried dating but had temporarily given it up when the well-meaning man tried to parent her twins. Her children didn't need adult figures marching in and out of their lives while she tested the waters. When they were eleven, she almost got engaged again but figured two broken engagements were enough for her. So, she had said no when he popped the question. Besides, she knew deep in her heart the maybe-love for her suitor could not compare to the consuming love she had once had for Johann. For her, that love had been a once-in-a-lifetime love, and nothing she'd experienced before or since held a candle to it. Her friends were shocked by her rejection, but they wouldn't understand. And trying to explain would bring those beautiful but bottled-up memories back to the forefront. Besides, between the kids, her dad's business, and her dad, she couldn't see her life meshing with anyone easily, and she hadn't had the energy to try. As she joked to Sierra, losing two fiancés to best friends was enough to put her off for life. And she definitely didn't want to lose Sierra.

Sierra had laughed uproariously. "That would be kinda hard to explain to Big Tony, don't you think?"

After that almost-engagement, she had boxed up any desires of the romantic kind and relegated them to the vault that housed her South Africa memories. She had a clear job description, and a sufficiently full and rewarding life, even if it was deemed non-traditional by some. They were involved in church, and she assisted with the youth group and became the go-to hang-out house for the kids' friends. She forged close friendships with a few of the parents, and she was grateful for her church, her circle of support.

Heidi shifted in her seat, clapping quietly with the audience at the end of the second speech, and remembered finding her dad in the kitchen late one evening.

"I want to adopt Darla and Darrin." Her voice broke the stillness, and her dad turned, clearly struggling to process her statement. Heidi waited, hoping he would stay and talk with her. She needed his advice desperately.

"You… ah… how?"

Heidi exhaled, "That's what I think we need to figure out."

He came slowly to the table, coffee cup in hand, and sat. "We had… uh… started that process before… you know."

"Do you have the papers?"

"Um, I think so… I'll go look in her desk."

He made to stand, but Heidi reached out, laying her hand on his arm. "Wait, Dad, I need to know… I need to be able to show… you know money and stability and…."

"Well, yes, we… find the papers first. Maybe if I put you on payroll… like a work-from-home position?"

Heidi nodded briefly, her throat hurting from the effort not to cry.

The adoption had been messy – they had to prove there was no knowledge of the father. Also, she was young, but her dad had hired a good family lawyer who helped them through the endless red tape and welfare checks until the day Darla and Darrin were legally hers. They had always called her dad "Gramps" or "Gwamps" in the younger years, so she eventually became "Mommy" in both name and legality. These were the children God had given her, and she immersed herself into parenting them with all the energy and gusto it took, which served a double purpose: her life had meaning once more, and the busyness quelled the memories of what could have been. Throughout the adoption and helping her dad with the business on the side, their relationship strengthened, and their household took shape. Whenever a nagging feeling of discontent would creep in, she would use the lessons of the Counting Tree and count her blessings. Her life was whole; she would not feel cheated.

Heidi had run into Chris and Brianna a few times. The first time had been incredibly uncomfortable. Chris was in the grocery line holding the fussy little guy looking overwhelmed, and she had felt sorry for him.

Chris and Brianna had left her church for another, which made things easier. Seeing them every week would have been too painful. She had lost two of her closest friends, to be replaced by Johann and Amy, only to inexplicably lose them, too. Next, she lost her dear mom, and then life had seemingly stabilized in losses. Now, the loss was overwhelming again, crushing her because her two primary purposes for life were getting ready to fly the coop. Without a goal or purpose, she found herself weighted by an ever-increasing blanket of loneliness.

"Here comes your girl." Sierra had leaned over to whisper in her ear. Maybe Sierra realized Heidi was far away reliving the last years and needed to bring her back. The school choir was singing their opening notes, and there was Darla, front and center, glowing with youth and joy and promise. Darla had had a much easier time than Darrin. She was a diligent student, and academics came easier for her. Her outgoing, bubbly personality made her a magnet for the right friends, and she was loved by students and teachers alike.

Heidi vividly remembered the night Darla had woken her up crying, her little body curled into Heidi's from outside the covers.

Heidi quickly sat up, hugging Darla and pulling the blankets around her shaking frame. "Sweetie, what's the matter?"

But the little girl sobbed, inconsolable.

Heidi reached out to grab tissues and knocked her water glass over instead, her spirits plummeting further as she heard the water spill down over her nightstand. The mess would have to wait. "Can you tell me what's wrong?"

"I—" she hiccupped again, "everybody has a Daddy but not me and Darrin – we don't."

"Oh, sweetie," Heidi pulled her little body against hers as tightly as she could. "You, sweet girl, you have me and Gramps. We are your family. And we love you," she squeezed even more tightly, "this much."

"But it's not a Daddy like Kara and Susie. All of them have a Daddy. They told me," and Darla backed up from Heidi, mimicking, wagging her little index finger, "'we have Daddies, and you don't!'"

"What did you say?"

"I push – pushed them, and Miss Sher'dan told me I was bad."

Suddenly, it all became clear. Mrs. Sheridan had spoken with Heidi that afternoon about the incident, and Heidi had forgotten to ask Darla about it. Her heart sank. A good mom would've remembered and tried to figure out why a typically compliant sweet little girl would shove her friends.

Heidi sighed and reached for the lamp switch. "OK, Missy. Now that makes me understand everything!"

Darla was instantly calm. "How come?"

"Well, maybe if my friends were mean to me, I would feel like pushing them over, too!"

"Mommy!" Darla giggled reproachfully. "You're a grown-up!"

"Grown-ups get mad, too, silly." And she reached out and took Darla's little hands in hers. "But listen, getting mad doesn't help us much." Heidi sighed, her mind searching, her heart praying. "Do you remember I told you that you do have a Father, you just can't see Him, but He's always there for you?"

"You mean God?"

"Yes, sweetie. We can't see God, but if I'm sad and pray to Him, I can feel Him right here." And Heidi touched her heart. "He makes me not feel lonely or scared or sad. And you know what I think next?"

Darla shook her head solemnly, "No?"

"I say, 'Heidi, God is your Father, and you are His daughter, and He loves you super-duper much!'"

"And then you feel better?"

Heidi had kept talking with Darla, she was so young, but she explained to her about God's love, how Jesus had died for her, that she could ask Him to come into her heart, to forgive her for pushing her friends, to be her Father forever.

"I can pray and ask Him right now?"

"Yes, sweetie, right now."

"And He'll be my Father?"

"Sure will!"

And the prayer Darla had prayed that night was music to Heidi's ears. She remembered Darla waking up the next day telling Darrin all about it, telling him he better hurry up and pray, too.

But Darrin hadn't understood or grasped the love of God so young. Darrin had struggled, especially as he got older. That was it in a nutshell. Where was his father? How could they not know who his dad even was? Was he Bahamian or American? Could he go to Nassau and try search for him?

"I'm sorry, Darrin," she had tried carefully multiple times. She didn't have an answer and was way out of her depth. She had relied heavily on Big Tony to help with Darrin. And Tony had done his best to fill the void for Darrin, taking him on fishing trips and including him in family time. Tony had been Darrin's "Dad" at father-son activities and had helped guide him and turn his discontentment into something productive.

And then there was Gramps. Gramps who was quiet and solid and always ready to listen. Heidi remembered the night Darrin had come in sweaty and frustrated from basketball practice, slamming the door to make his presence known.

"I have to do a history presentation, and all the topics are during the time when there were slaves."

"Well, son, that's a sad part of our nation's history. We aren't proud of it, but...."

She had heard his steady voice explaining how we were to learn from history and not repeat past mistakes; how learning about slavery and the holocaust was necessary, so humanity knew what it was capable of.

Gramps had continued to talk in his calm, steady voice. Then, he had asked Darrin if he could talk about people from the revolutionary war.

"I dunno," Darrin shrugged.

"Because I happen to know Paul Revere wasn't the only person who did a midnight ride to warn the people about the British."

Darrin looked up, trying to hide his interest. "Oh yeah?"

"Yeah, there was this man named Wentworth Cheswell, and he rode north while Paul Revere rode west to warn the colonists. Cheswell also became the first African American in the United States elected to public office.

"Maybe you should do your talk on him? Teach your friends and maybe even your teacher a few things. There are many people the history books have ignored, but if we can tell their stories, you can realize all kinds of people helped build our great country."

The image of her dad with his hand on Darrin's shoulder, sitting at their kitchen table talking in his quiet, strong voice, was burned in her memory. And that's what Gramps did. Somehow, he got it. Somehow, he understood what Darrin was going through and knew what he needed. Only after his passing had Heidi found out her dad had spent countless hours getting advice from a former army buddy. But that was her dad. He never talked about what he was doing; he just *did*.

And then Gramps died. With her mom, there had been warning and some time – albeit too little – to adjust. They'd had zero inkling of what was to come with her dad. One heart attack and then gone, barely a year ago, the end of the twins' junior year. Darrin had taken his death the hardest.

The twins were seventeen by then, and Darrin had come in livid one Friday night. He and his friends were driving home after a basketball game when they had been pulled over for speeding. Darrin and Little Tony were made to get out of the car, but the other boys were not.

"I'm not even gonna repeat what he said," Darrin spat out.

Fear and shame filled Heidi as she listened to Darrin, and she wondered anew how she could not have known what her black friends were experiencing. Years before, she had lectured Johann and judged everyone in South Africa for their awful apartheid, and here, not only had she done nothing, *she hadn't even noticed*.

That event, so close on the heels of her father's death, brought all Darrin's frustration back to the surface. The following year was a struggle. Heidi tried everything, read everything, sought advice both near and far, and, finally, at the end of herself, she had stopped trying and just prayed. She would fall asleep praying and wake up on the floor where she had been kneeling. She would wake up at 3 am, go into Darrin's room, and pray for him quietly so as not to wake him.

And then, a friend told her about Camp Makarios in North Carolina. Their website was abysmal, but the camp got rave reviews from a friend of a friend. They had fishing and took campers white water rafting and mountain climbing, and Heidi hoped the outdoor physical activity and change of scenery would be what Darrin needed. Heidi was desperate, so she signed Darrin up to go with another church during his spring break. Darrin was livid. He refused to go. So, she took his car keys and grounded him. He would give this camp one week of his life. If he hated it, it would be over in a week. She threatened to drive him there herself.

Thankfully Darrin found out that he knew a few of the kids who would be going, and his opposition decreased. Heidi suspected it mainly had to do with one exceedingly cute camper, but, for whatever reason, Darrin got on that bus and came back a week later a changed young man. In fact, he was so transformed that he applied to work at the camp full time starting at the beginning of the summer. He would defer college for a year, but Heidi, so relieved by the change, agreed immediately. College was important, but it might not be the right path for her son.

Heidi shifted again, mentally trying to shake herself free from the weight of sadness tonight meant for her. She would get the kids off and then brainstorm. Who else did she know could say they were unencumbered and financially stable at 37? The possibilities were endless, right? But the thought only depressed her, and the loneliness felt bottomless. It wasn't like she could complain to anybody. Being free to do whatever she wanted would be a dream for most people. Obviously, she was thankful; she simply didn't know what to do with herself. She needed a purpose. Camp Timothy had given her a purpose. Darla and Darrin had given her a purpose. Now she needed a new purpose.

She tried to adjust her focus to the positives. Darrin had found his place at the camp in North Carolina. The camp owner, John, was apparently from Australia and structured Camp Makarios in ways that reminded Heidi of Camp Timothy. The irony wasn't lost on Heidi that she had yet to visit the camp or meet any of its leaders, but the change in Darrin after spring break had been palpable – no more simmering anger and frustration but direction and enthusiasm. If Darrin could spend a year under such positive influences, maybe it would help him find his place in the world. She had, in effect, done the same thing after college – taken a break from her planned life and gone off to South Africa to serve. And her parents had not vetted the place at all. So, she, of all people, could understand Darrin's need to go.

Before she knew it, caps were in the air. Everyone was whooping and hollering and hugging and crying. Heidi stood dazed. She had missed the whole thing and somehow relived fifteen years in ninety short minutes.

CHAPTER 25

Stillness pervaded, and the day stretched endlessly. The house felt dark even with all the lights on. Heidi had tried to talk herself into a productive, enjoyable day, but she missed the noise. No doors banged, no muffled arguing over the bathroom... just silence. Projects she had decided to tackle popped into her head but were summarily discarded. Her opportunities were endless, but somehow that didn't give her any joy or motivation. Instead, it depressed her.

Life had been a series of busy events punctuated by crises for the past fifteen years. Now, it was all oppressive silence. She needed a plan, something to get her out of the funk the time alone was doing to her. But she didn't want to seek advice – everyone always had great advice for what they thought you should be doing, and if she wasn't careful, her days would get filled with someone else's plan. To that end, many well-meaning people had already solved her problem. The local Christian school had asked if she would consider housing international students for the upcoming school year; her church had offered her more volunteer opportunities with the student ministry; a lawyer in her church had told her she should apply to law school – family law intrigued her; the window company that had bought out her dad's business had offered her a position; but nothing fit. Her life was a holding pattern, and any thoughts about the future were blank.

A deepening realization had settled in over the past few days. Until now, when she had lost someone, no matter who, she had replaced the void they had created with someone new. Johann had replaced Chris; Amy, Brianna; the twins had filled the void after her mom and, later, her dad.

But the void was never satisfied, merely shoved aside or ignored by the busyness of life. Now there was nobody or nothing to fill it, and she wasn't quite sure what to do. In the days before the twins' departures, she felt like she had a 10,000-word paper due and needed to turn it in but was afraid she had missed something.

When Darrin drove away, she shed tears but was kept busy by preparing Darla. But once she left Gainesville after helping Darla move into her dorm, there was nobody to provide distraction. Heidi drove about 30 minutes and then pulled over at a rest stop and sobbed until her tissue box was empty. Gut-wrenching heart-broken sobs would start afresh every time another memory flooded her mind. Her babies were gone. Her job was done. How would she survive?

She went into the restroom to wash her face, and someone called "Mom!" Heidi turned, expectant, and then her new reality hit.

Eventually, she got back on the road and drove while tears leaked from scratchy eyes. Her head hurt, the pit in her stomach leaden with sadness and nostalgia. Her empty arms ached to hold their toddler-selves once more, feel them melt against her in sleep. She longed for the oomph of a running hug in the school pick-up line. Her ears missed the vibrating music wars that would accompany their drives to anywhere and the banter and teenage gossip and arguments. She fiddled with the car radio hoping for some noise... anything. Frustrated, she turned the dial back to "off" and started to pray out loud. She poured out her heart and told God how bereft she felt.

Deserted.

Stranded.

Adrift.

Her mind heard her words, and her heart knew God was listening. And somehow, as in times past, she knew He would carry her through. But while she waited for relief, she needed to bury herself in activity even though, once home, she wanted to curl up on one of the twins' beds and cry.

The following morning, Heidi paused in the hallway by their bedrooms, stopping in the open doorways. The rooms vibrated with memories, two separate time capsules, every item an echo of years gone by. She turned away, unable to process the ache of missing them, and meandered to the garage, staring despondently at the menagerie of bikes stacked in a corner. Dusting off her seat, she tested the tires and rummaged for a bike pump. She loaded the bike into the back of her van and drove to Jupiter Island. The island was over ten miles long. She would ride until her legs burned, and she would ignore the nagging feelings that had been plaguing her.

She found her rhythm quickly and, enjoying the uncharacteristically cool breeze, set a steady pace northward. As she rode, she allowed herself permission to think through all the significant people she had lost over the years, starting with her sister. As she mentally addressed each person, she relived the sadness of the loss and then gave it to God: Jenna, Chris, Brianna, Amy, Johann, her mom, her dad, and now, even Darrin and Darla.

It was time to stop replacing people with more people but let God fill the void. Fully. Not just until the next person or quest or responsibility presented itself but because, regardless, God would do as His Word promised: *He would never leave nor forsake her.*

That evening on the phone with Darla, peace filled her heart. Darla noticed, teasing her that having an empty nest at age 37 must be suiting her just fine. Heidi knew her legs would be in agony the following day after the unexpected exercise, but tonight, she reveled in the knowledge that God would soon give her direction. She would be open to learning from Him, allowing Him to fill this temporary holding pattern with His wisdom, peace, and grace.

With this newfound sense of calm, she began filling her days productively – addressing the difficult task of cleaning out her dad's room and donating most of it to charity. Gladys had called her; Sierra had texted; the McManns had asked for help with the youth, but she had put them all off, telling them she was on a mission to get her house orderly while she had the enthusiasm for it. She would take long bike rides or swim laps at the county pool in between working.

She ignored most phone calls, only picking up when caller ID indicated Darla or Darrin. She was buried deep in a pile of the kids' school projects when Darrin's name popped up.

"Mom, why don't you come up here for 4th of July?"

She paused. Why not? Darla had been invited to a friend's house in St. Augustine, and she would be alone.

"I suppose I could come, but won't I be in the way?"

"Nope. John says there are no camps over that weekend because families usually have other plans then."

"So, just you and John will be at camp?" That sounded a bit awkward.

"Nope – other people live here and work, but you can stay in the guest cabin. John says it's free."

"Free as in available or free of charge?" Heidi joked, warming to the idea.

"I'm sure he means both...."

"Should I talk to him first and make sure?" She didn't want to show up, looking like she expected a handout.

"Nope. He said it was cool. Plus, apparently, they climb the mountain and watch all the fireworks from there."

She would need hiking boots and to prep her flat-trained legs for the mountains. And, before she left, she would trade in her van for a car, provided she got a rooftop carrier for her paddleboard.

Darrin had gone on to expound on all the reasons she should come, but Heidi had already decided. A trip to North Carolina to escape the Florida heat sounded heavenly.

Part II

⌘

Maggie Valley, North Carolina

2001

CHAPTER 26

Heidi stood under a Counting Tree, memories and emotions crashing over her. The chimes echoed in the wind, the branches swaying in cadence. In a single moment, she had seemingly been transported from North Carolina to the Northern Transvaal, South Africa. Tears rose and threatened to overwhelm her, and she took a deep breath, willing herself to remain composed. Darrin would be there any moment, and she didn't want to have to explain herself or open the door to what she had kept in the most private places of her heart for fifteen long years.

From the corner of her eye, she saw a figure outlined against the afternoon sunlight. Her heart pounded in her chest as the man spoke.

"Heidi?"

She turned to him, a roaring in her ears and a swelling in her chest, her eyes questioning, her mind confused. Was she in North Carolina, or was she back in South Africa? What was happening? Was this Johann standing before her? She opened her mouth to speak, but no sound came. It couldn't be him; he hadn't wanted to come to America; South Africa was his home. This transplanted Counting Tree was playing tricks on her mind. She needed to leave, to get back to her car and collect herself. Where was Darrin?

The man spoke again as he moved closer. "Heidi?"

She spoke one word. "Yes."

He stood now only three paces from her, the same Johann she had last seen in South Africa all those years ago. The same eyes boring into her soul, questioning, simmering with emotion and confusion.

"Johann." It was a fact – an acknowledgment. By some trick of fate, they were in the same time and place, standing under the same tree that had brought them together. But it couldn't be. South Africa was a memory, and, from all reports, Camp Timothy had closed. She wanted to collapse, to cover her eyes, to shake herself from this dream, but those green eyes held her captive. She couldn't move, couldn't process.

He took another step closer.

"How... why are you here?" Confusion flashed in his eyes, and his voice was strained, but it was the same deep accented voice she had fallen in love with as an idealistic college graduate.

Why was she here? What was she doing, standing under the Tree, staring at the only man she had ever truly loved?

Darrin. She was here for Darrin. She had to communicate this; she must clear the confusion before Darrin showed up and wanted an explanation.

She opened her mouth and closed it. Opened it and tried once more to speak.

"I came to see my son."

"Who?"

"Darrin."

"Darrin is your *son*?" He turned his head as if looking for Darrin to appear, clearly trying to process and understand how this present fit their past. He turned back to her. "You're... so, you are Darrin's mom?"

She nodded slightly. Twice.

He stood there gaping at her. She felt lightheaded and disoriented. Time and place had seemingly converged. It was as if she were 22 and 37 at the same time, that Camp Timothy had superimposed itself on this place. None of it seemed real.

"Darrin was one of the twins?"

"Yes."

"But..." He paused and paced backward as if to put space between himself and this new reality.

She waited and knew what was next.

"But Darrin is very...."

A long awkward silence filled the space, but Heidi was ready for these next words. She had heard it over and over the last fifteen years. This was something she knew how to respond to.

"Darrin is nearly nineteen? Darrin is a fabulous young man?" Her voice seemed to echo in defiance. "What *exactly* is it you want to say?" She was livid. The shock of seeing Johann without warning after a lifetime of mothering her twins was shoved aside for this fight. She was well practiced in it and ready for anyone who dared question how her children could actually be hers. And she was confident of one thing, she would not make it easy on anyone, especially on this man. She watched his face as he took another step backward and finished quietly. "Darrin is my son."

"Is his sister also…?" Once more, he couldn't finish his question.

"What?" Her quiet, controlled anger shocked even her. "Is she what?" She had told him all those years ago; had he not believed her, had he forgotten? How could he forget something so significant?

He paced, ran his hand through his hair, looked at her in disbelief, and paced again. "But how are you here?"

"How are *you* here?" She knew he was delaying the inevitable questions, trying an easier tack.

"I live here – three years now." His voice was so quiet, his eyes filled with questions.

She shook her head in disbelief. He had been in the country for three years and never tried to contact her. But, she supposed, she had stopped trying to find out news about him and Amy after discovering they were married. Johann and the associated memories had remained locked away since then.

She wanted Darrin. To hug her son and tell him she couldn't stay. She couldn't unlock the vault and handle the memories of love and friendship and excruciating loss again. A wave of anxiety crashed over her, and she shaded her eyes and looked toward the buildings. "Where is Darrin?"

"Oh, um, probably… I can go find him." He made to turn and looked back at her questioningly, his eyes searching her face.

She couldn't stay there, surrounded by this Counting Tree and its blessings hanging from the branches. "I'll just, maybe, I'll just go to my car. Tell Darrin I'm at my car." She gestured vaguely, and he didn't respond, so she set off back the way she had come.

Her periphery blurred as she walked toward her car. She wanted to collapse, to cry, to scream at the absurdity of what was happening but instead willed herself to place one foot in front of the other. The roaring in her ears contradicted the serene surroundings, and she knew if she didn't sit soon, she would fall over.

Back at her car, she managed to open the door and slid in gratefully. She cranked the engine and turned the AC to maximum, leaning her head back against the seat. Taking deep breaths, she wiped her perspiring palms on her jeans. Looking out the passenger side, she saw Darrin approaching, with Johann a few steps behind.

Darrin threw the passenger door open and hopped in. "Mom!" He gathered her in an exuberant sideways hug and laughed. "What're you doing in your car? Wait! Is this the new car?"

Heidi clung to him, unwilling to open her eyes and face Johann and the questions Darrin would inevitably ask.

"Mom?" Darrin pushed her away and looked at her. "Are you car sick?"

"Must be." She tried to smile.

"I knew it! When John said you were sitting here, I knew it! All those hills and twisty roads." He jumped out of the van and rushed to the other side, opening her door. "Here, I'll help you out and get you to your cabin and bring you ginger ale."

John? Johann was John here? She allowed Darrin to pull her out and stood unsure, glancing at Johann, her mind attempting to compute this new reality.

Johann was *John.* John the guitar player, John the mentor, John the man she had meant to email and thank for being such an influence on her son. Darrin had said John was from somewhere in Australia, *the south part*; she could hear his explanation even now. Not once had she ever imagined that John was Johann. Her legs trembled, and she turned and leaned into Darrin. She needed to concentrate on breathing – one breath in and one out. Nothing else. The confusion was too great.

"Man, you got it bad," Darrin quipped. "John," he whipped around, "help us out here."

Johann took a step closer, and Darrin stared at him. "Are you sick, too?"

"I can walk, Darrin," Heidi managed.

"John?" Darrin gave him a confused look as Johann mumbled unintelligibly and reached in to grab Heidi's bags.

"John, this is my mom." Darrin straightened to look at John more fully.

John nodded mutely, and Darrin shrugged. "Here, man, take her bag." He handed off the bag and linked his arm protectively through Heidi's.

They set off towards the cabins in an awkward formation, with Darrin talking and gesturing a mile a minute. Heidi was grateful for his chatter and tried to respond in kind. The longer she could delay the inevitable, the better prepared she might be.

At the cabin, Darrin glanced hurriedly at his watch and told her he'd be back with ginger ale and that John could show her everything.

"You don't need to stay," Heidi spoke stiffly, her eyes taking in John's scuffed hiking boots.

"Ah, *ja,* OK, I'll talk to you later." And he turned with a long backward look, as if staring at her would explain her presence.

She lowered her trembling body to the bed and waited. It wasn't long before Darrin returned with the promised drink and crackers. "Alice is the main cook," he explained, "she said these would help, too."

Heidi nibbled at the crackers while Darrin ran through the remainder of the afternoon. It was the last full day of camp, and Heidi was not surprised to learn the schedule ran similarly to Camp Timothy's.

"You can stay here and rest or walk around camp. I can't show you around proper until after the campers leave tomorrow, but then we get July 4, and we'll do lots of stuff." He stood, propelled by an outside gong, hugging her briefly before leaving.

She rubbed her clammy hands along her jeans and took a few shaky deep breaths. Johann then Darrin, it was like emotional whiplash – shock and then joy. She went to the sink and turned on the faucet, splashing water over her face. She couldn't cry until tonight – once she started, she wouldn't be able to stop. Her mind refused to process everything, and she sat back down and tried to breathe.

She wanted to leave but didn't have the heart to put that on Darrin. Based on the schedule he had just told her, she hoped she could avoid Johann for at least the next 24 hours. That would buy her time to collect her thoughts.

Standing slowly, she changed her sweaty shirt and redid her ponytail. She opened the cabin door, glancing left and right, and stepped out into the breezy shade.

It appeared her room was in a row of buildings that faced a stream. Signs pointed everywhere: the cafeteria was to the right, next to an office, and the meeting hall was to the left of this same main row. She assumed her cabin was for their guest speakers since she didn't see any of the kids' cabins nearby. If she headed out over the little bridge, she would be back at the Counting Tree, so, instead, she turned left, following a sign that indicated "Soldier Mountain." She could see another path leading to what she assumed were cabins and bathrooms and open fields. She studiously avoided that area where she thought Johann or anyone else might be and took the pathway that led upwards, away from camp. The views were breathtaking, and she paused at what seemed to be a designated lookout spot to catch her breath.

And there sat Johann on a nearby boulder as if waiting for her. She turned, hoping he wouldn't see her, but he was already standing. He looked like he was having as much trouble processing her presence as she was his.

He cleared his throat. "The view, um, here is outstanding." He gestured for her to join him.

She perched on the edge of the rock, inwardly berating herself for running into him.

They sat in awkward silence. She was determined not to be the one to break it, either. There was no logical starting place, so she waited.

He cleared his throat again. "It's a shock, right?" He looked at her, willing her to agree on this one thing.

She nodded and glanced away as the silence stretched between them again. He looked conflicted, clearly debating his next words. Questions swirled, but she kept her mouth clamped shut. She wasn't going to guide this conversation.

"So, I ah, um…." He shifted uncomfortably as if deciding. "So, Darrin is your son." He blurted the words quickly.

She tilted her head in acknowledgment but kept her gaze forward.

"Why didn't you explain properly?" The question came out fast and forced.

"Explain what?" She kept her voice even, knowing what was coming.

"About their, um, heritage?"

She stood defiant. "What do you mean? I told you! How could you have forgotten?"

He shook his head, "I guess I just never thought – I'm ashamed to admit I thought you must've been exaggerating. Your leaving was so sudden and so… so horrible. I wish you had been clearer, though. I still think you could have brought them to the camp; we could have—"

"Could have what?! We already had this fight, Johann! Fifteen years ago, we had this fight! Remember what I said?" She paused, drawing in a shaky breath. "Where would they have lived? Lived in Karl's house or in the whites-only cabins? Or lived down the hill with the workers? Gone to a segregated school with no hope of higher education? Been ostracized for the color of their skin and their parentage? I would never, ever, ever have done that to my children. Besides, I told you this, I told you back then it was the reason I was leaving, and you obviously didn't believe me then. Just shows that you would not have had the strength or ability to stand up for them." She was in his face now, punctuating each word with her finger inches from his face, angry with him and every other person who professed everyone was equal but didn't mean it.

He narrowed his eyes and stood quickly. "That's not fair." He took a step back. "You didn't play fair. You should have been clearer. You just said we wouldn't accept them, and then you left." He paused. "I always figured that they were your excuse, that you were so overwhelmed with your mom's sudden illness that you just used them as a reason not to try come back."

"Oh, my goodness! Are you not listening? Did you not listen to me? And besides, I asked you to come to America, and you said you never would, that Africa was your home." She was yelling. "And now you've been here for three years and never thought to let me know?" The rage was so deep she was afraid of it.

He backed up and held his hands up as if in surrender. "Yes, you know back then I couldn't have come." He held out his hands, grasping at words. "I mean, you never tried to come back to us. I would have done everything to make it work for you and the twins."

Silence. She wanted him to hear his words, to let them echo, so he would realize the absurdity of what had come from his mouth.

"What can I say? I held onto hope for a long time...."

"Not that long," she responded with venom.

"Besides, apartheid was abolished in 1989, and then everything changed."

"Oh, was that when you married Amy?" Her voice held a challenge.

"No, Heidi. I married Amy in '91, a long time *after* I was told about your wedding."

"My wedding?" She was incredulous. "I'm sorry, but did you just say my *wedding?*" She made a sound that even to her ears sounded crazy.

They faced each other, their anger and confusion palpable.

227

Heidi clenched and unclenched her fists.

Eventually, he spoke softly, "Will you walk with me?" He indicated a pathway over his left shoulder.

She wanted to refuse, but campers were ahead, scrambling to get back from what she assumed was a hike. She shrugged and followed.

They fell into a tense silence as they walked back down the pathway towards the stream and over the bridge until they were back at this camp's Counting Tree, another Weeping Willow filled with its own placards proclaiming God's blessings. The campers were now out of sight, but she could hear the distinct sounds of game time ramping up.

"I'm sorry for my anger, Heidi." Johann had stopped under the Tree; his hands were in his pockets, and he was staring at the ground. "I guess because of the silence, I created my own narrative, and I was completely wrong."

She looked over at him mutely. What silence? There were too many questions, too many years gone by. She grasped at the first question that came to mind.

"You've been here three years?" Heidi was desperately trying to piece it all together. "In the United States?"

"Yes. Three years."

"Oh." And why did you leave South Africa? Where was Amy? How did he come to be running a camp here? The questions flooded her mind, but she couldn't seem to get past the fact Johann was in front of her.

"Heidi?"

"What?" He had been talking, and she hadn't heard him.

"I asked where Darrin's stepdad is. He has never mentioned him."

"Darrin's stepdad?"

"Your husband?" His tone was accusatory.

The roaring intensified. There it was again. The man she had *married?* Her emotions were like a powder keg, civility impossible with all the unanswered questions and accusations. An ache expanded through her chest, and a wave of anger filled all the hurt spaces, an anger so strong that it threatened to burst. Her entire body shook with the effort of standing there.

"And the *woman* YOU married." Hers wasn't a question; hers was a statement filled with all the bitterness she thought she had

228

long ago relinquished. A flash of sorrow cut through his eyes before a hardness covered them.

They couldn't talk for more than two minutes without animosity rearing its head again.

He mumbled something unintelligible and looked away.

Dread filled her, instantly and overwhelmingly. Was she going to have to face Amy *and* Johann together? Were they both here to mock her aloneness all these years later? "Is she here?"

"Who?" His voice was quiet yet harsh.

"Amy!" Why was she yelling?

"No!" He responded in kind.

She turned away, putting her hand out as if to stop him from saying anything else. "I don't understand," she managed.

He looked off toward the mountains. "She was murdered." His voice was flat.

The statement echoed off the trees, the mountains, the nearby stream, snatching her back around to face him.

Murdered.

Shock coursed through her body. What trick was this? Why had no one told her? She had to get away, to leave this place. She needed to get back to the cabin, pack her things, to call Darrin and tell him that she could not be there, that something had gone terribly wrong.

But even as she turned once more to go, she saw Darrin coming up the path.

"I got game time running! Man, I'm so happy you're here! Standing talking to John." And he laughed and hugged her and then stepped back to look at her before confusion and concern stopped his celebration. "Mom?"

She stepped back into his youthful arms and hugged him tightly. "And I'm so happy to see you, Darrin."

But he set her away from him, looked at her, then looked at Johann and back at her. "What's going on?" His eyes were filled with disbelief, questioning why he had to keep running interference between his mom and John.

"I just got some bad news," she managed. "I'll be fine, don't you worry." And she hugged him again, wanting to cover her anxiety. "I'm here now, and my – ah – car sickness is over, and I'm ready to see your camp." The fakeness of her enthusiasm made her grimace.

"John?" Darrin had turned towards him.

If her mind were whirling with questions before, now it was a carousel running at Mach speed, a single word spinning round and round... murdered. Right now, she needed to concentrate on breathing – one breath in and one out. Nothing else. The confusion was too great, and the crushing reality of what had happened to Amy too much to take in. She kept her eyes on Johann; she didn't want his answer to Darrin's question to tell the whole truth. Not yet.

As she stared at him, the warning clearly in her eyes, she heard Johann offering an explanation as vague as hers. He and Heidi had realized they knew a few of the same people from South Africa, and she had just discovered an old friend had died. He watched her the whole time, looking to see if she approved of his explanation.

The action felt as ironic as his betrayal.

That was her fate in life, over and over again. Her brain stalled, cataloging events, one after another, relentlessly mocking her in a vicious cycle: death, love, betrayal, recover, death, love, betrayal, recover.

Amy had been her friend, and, yes, Amy had stolen her fiancé. And now Amy was dead? Questions swirled and crashed; she was caught in a rip tide, helpless against it. She felt she must be drowning.

Now Darrin was in front of her, his earnest youthful eyes full of love and compassion. "Mom?"

"It will be fine, Darrin. I've just had a shock, that's all. Maybe get me something cold to drink one more time, and I'll just wait here." Thankful to have something to do, he charged off, calling over his shoulder that John was to watch her, to take care of his mom.

Johann took a step toward her, and she raised her hand in defense. She wanted to lash out at him in bitterness, but the echo of his words provided the drum beat against the cacophony in her head. She wouldn't spew anger at a man who had lost his wife, even if that wife had been her South African confidant and friend. But that didn't stop the bitterness and irony of the situation from filling her with something she had never experienced before... was this hatred? Her pitiful love life: betrayed by two best friends and two fiancés. She had worked for years, taken care of her family, endured nights of loneliness and regret, and finally rekindled her peace and closeness with God, allowing Him to fill her void. Only to run into

Johann and face feelings and memories she had relegated to the past. Johann needed to stay away; she didn't want anyone to see the bitterness she thought she'd conquered long ago. She needed solitude.

"Please... go away," she managed. He flinched as if he had been slapped and narrowed his eyes. She looked into them, saw the anger mirrored in his eyes, and felt a twinge of misplaced triumph. She was glad he was angry, glad that she wasn't the only one struggling, but he must simply leave her alone. He looked at her for a moment longer and then abruptly turned away. She watched his retreating back, blurred by the tears filling her eyes and spilling over, and in a moment, she was transported back, watching him walk away from her standing underneath the other Counting Tree.

She wanted to sob, rant, and collapse into a heap all at the same time. Yet, Darrin was on his way back, so she did what she had always done. She straightened her shoulders, wiped her eyes, and took a deep breath. She looked towards the set of buildings she had recently come from and saw Darrin headed towards her in all his youthful eagerness, the worry evident in his stride.

"Oh God, help me," was all she could manage. As she prayed, the wind shifted, and the chimes responded. And she heard the whisper of the old hymn, "*Oh God our help in ages past....*" She allowed the imagined melody to wash over her and breathed the words over and over. She felt her pounding heart begin to slow and turned with what she hoped was a smile towards Darrin as he sat.

"Mom?" He was holding a bottle of water out to her, which she accepted gratefully. She didn't respond, just opened it and drank, willing the action to buy her enough time to come up with an explanation for her son. She sat the bottle down and looked at Darrin, one of the two reasons her life had changed irrevocably, the reason she had now watched Johann's retreating back twice in her life, but the reason she knew that God had placed her on the earth. The verse that had guided her back to America all those years ago once more filled her mind,

...I will put my trust in him. And again, Behold I and the children which God hath given me.

God had given her Darrin and Darla; there was no question, and here was Darrin, a testimony to her personal sacrifice and God's guidance and grace.

She reached out and hugged him to her, then sat back and

looked into his worried eyes. "I'm sorry for scaring you, honey. I've had a shock and...."

"But who? How did you know the same people as John? When did...?"

She held up her hand to stop the flood of questions. Darrin wasn't going to settle for vague half-truths. How could she answer him without exposing the depth of her sorrow over leaving Johann all those years ago? She knew Darrin, knew that he would feel guilty, that as a four-year-old child, it was somehow his fault that she hadn't stayed with the man she loved. She wouldn't allow it; he needn't know the depth of her sacrifice, only that she loved him completely. She searched in her mind for a valid explanation and came upon the one thing that would possibly make sense to him. She took a wavering breath and began.

"Do you remember when you were little when I first started caring for you and Darla?"

Darrin shrugged – how much could a four-year-old remember after all? But trauma had a way of marking memories like other events could not.

"I had just come back from working at a camp in South Africa." She looked at the surrounding landscaping and the buildings in the distance. "You know, it was a lot like this camp. That's one of the reasons I wanted to come and see you here." She smiled at him sadly. "Your descriptions and stories made me remember a very happy time when I was young." She paused and took another shaky breath. "You know that camp even had one of those trees."

"A Counting Tree?"

"Yes, one just like this." She smiled and looked around. "I couldn't believe this was here – you never mentioned it in our talks."

Darrin shrugged, "I think I thought it was a little weird, but I knew when you saw it, you would like it...."

She squeezed his hand and continued. "Anyway, when I got here, the memories of my time in South Africa just washed over me. And then, while I was thinking and remembering everything, Johann walked up."

"Yo – Hahn?"

"Well, John, I guess. We called him Johann back then."

"You knew *John*?" Darrin jumped up, his incredulity evident in the crack in his voice. He laughed self-consciously. "Didn't know that could still happen...." He cleared his throat and tried again,

"Seriously? You *know* John? But he said you just knew the same people, not that he *knew* you!"

Heidi looked away, afraid that he would read the whole truth if he saw her eyes. "Well, I guess he is shocked to see me too, but I knew *John*, as you call him." She could hear Darrin suck in his breath, ready to barrage her with questions, so she hurried on. "I knew Johann; I mean John, and many other wonderful people too. I had a friend, Amy. She was my dearest friend – I thought of her as my South African twin." Tears began to slide down Heidi's face as she pictured Amy, the second girl who had seemingly betrayed her, but she would not focus on that right now. Darrin didn't need to know his mom was battling a resurrected bitterness and that she was crying not only from the shock of hearing Amy was dead but from the realization of the betrayal all over again. She paused, knowing she needed to choose her words even more carefully. "Anyway, when Johann walked up, we started to talk, and I found out that Amy," she took a deep shuddering breath, "Amy was killed and...." Heidi couldn't go on. Sobs gripped her so hard it took her breath away.

"Oh, Mom," Darrin hugged her, "no wonder... wait!"

He set her away from him and looked at her in horror. "Was Amy John's wife?"

"Yes," she managed.

He hugged her while she fought to gain composure, while she wondered if the explanation had been enough for him, wondered if it was a lie to let him think that the tears were only for the news of Amy's death.

"But you knew John?" He was back on that. Couldn't seem to grasp it. "Were you friends?"

"Yes, we were friends," she took a shuddering breath, "and it was a surprise to see him." *That* was an understatement.

"Well, why did he walk off after telling you such terrible news? That doesn't seem like him – I'm going to go and find him and...."

Heidi laid a cautioning hand on his arm. "No, dear, you are not going to go and barrage Joha... *John* with a bunch of questions. I think," she paused; how would she say this and not feel like she was stabbing herself in the back? "I think," she tried again, "I think he must've loved Amy very much, and seeing me brought back... brought back... um... the reality that she is gone."

"Well, should I say something to him, like I'm sorry about

Amy?"

"No, I wouldn't."

"Well, it's pretty cool you two knew each other. I mean, you are both my favorite people—of course, you're my favorite because you're my mom, and we love each other. And John, John is the most awesome Christian man ever. He loves God so much, Mom, and he is making me see how God has a plan and a purpose for all of us."

And what was her purpose – to be everyone's savior with nothing left over for herself at the end? Bile rose in her throat, and she did her best to smile at his enthusiasm, all while trying to squelch the ugly head of bitterness.

"Can I tell him I think it's cool that you both knew each other?" He looked at her questioningly. "I won't mention Amy or anything sad. I'll just tell him that you told me you knew him from before, at his camp in South Africa." He paused then, squinting his eyes, "Wait a second... I thought he was from Australia?"

Heidi shrugged. "Geography was never your strong suit, Darrin, and yes, it's fine if you tell him you know we knew each other." Now, she needed to return to her room, recover her stability, shake the anger and confusion that filled her... and start pretending. For four days, she would have to pretend and smile, and she had no idea how she would achieve that.

CHAPTER 27

Johann scarcely remembered getting to the top of Soldier Mountain; he had started walking and landed at his favorite spot. Despite the coolness of the late afternoon, sweat stung his eyes. He sat on his rock and surveyed the view before him, thoughts colliding with questions, uncertainty, sorrow, and anger. Why had Heidi shown up after all these years? How could she be Darrin's mother? Where was her husband? Why hadn't Darrin mentioned his father – surely the man would have adopted Darrin? Perhaps he had remained simply a stepfather, present but not really there, not enough to register on Darrin's radar when he talked about his family. And had Darrin said he had a twin? Darrin had talked about his sister, but Johann was sure he had never mentioned that she was his twin. There had not been any signs that Darrin was Heidi's son; if there had, he had completely missed them.

Heidi's inflection of anger and bitterness over him marrying Amy was surprising. Why did his marriage matter if Heidi was married herself? And how could Heidi not have known of Amy's death? Had she not stayed in contact with *anyone*? Maybe Heidi had done what he had done, made a conscious effort never to find out any more information. Maybe after she had married, she had boxed up his memory and stashed it in the attic of her mind, never again to be opened. Maybe, like him, the anger came from the shock of seeing each other and was a stark reminder of what they had both lost.

Johann heard the camp gong ring, the warning signal for the next set of games. He should be down there, but he couldn't move; someone else would have to substitute. He couldn't face a group of eager rambunctious teens with his emotions vacillating between sorrow and bitterness, confusion and anger. He squinted his eyes towards camp, trying to make out the figures, it would take too long to rush back anyway, but he hated to let them down. He felt for his walkie-talkie to call the office and tell them he had been held up when he saw Darrin striding purposefully over the last rise. Johann stood to meet him, willing his face into what he hoped was a neutral expression.

"John!" Darrin was out of breath – he leaned over, his hands resting on his bent knees, sucking in deep breaths. "Man, ran... still so unfit... need to run uphill more often."

Johann waited, letting him recover, not knowing what he would say to him once he stood back up.

Darrin looked up from his stance, worry and questions written all over his face. "John," he paused, clearly looking for a way to phrase his question. He straightened back up, his hands resting on his lower back as if ready to stretch, and then started again. "My mom said she knew you, that you used to be friends?"

Johann nodded.

"But ever since she got here, both of you... well, everything has been strange. She said a friend of hers had died, and I know she should feel sad, but she's been in her cabin a long time. That's just not like her to hide from people. I mean, I couldn't wait for her to get here because she's always been so much fun around other kids and my friends."

"Maybe she just needs time to get used to what she found out today." Johann knew his voice sounded strange.

"Nah," Darrin looked away back toward the camp as if he could make out his mom from this distance. "My mom is the toughest lady I know. Every time something really bad happened – like when my grandma died and even when my grandpa just died – she was sad, but she never hid away."

"Maybe she needed to call her husband." The words came out tight and strained.

"What husband?" Darrin snorted, "My mom never had a husband!"

Darrin's words hit him like a kick in the gut, "What do you

mean she never had a husband?"

"My mom never ever got married," Darrin said. "She always told us we were her family and didn't need a strange man to come in and ruin things for us."

Johann bent over and sat, his head between his knees, his hands covering his face.

"Um, John?"

Johann knew he needed to respond, but he was struggling to breathe.

"John?"

Johann willed himself to look up. "Darrin, I'm sorry," he began carefully. "I... I need to stay here and sort some things out." He smiled wryly. "I need you to help me out and run back down the mountain and cover for me. I'll be back before tonight's meeting."

"OK," Darrin was already turning away, apparently grateful for direction. "Uh," he looked back, "what should I tell everyone when they ask where you are?" The evening meeting was hours away.

Johann rubbed his hand over his face. "Tell them I needed extra time to prep for tonight's closing session." He looked at Darrin, the worry visible across his youthful features and his heart clenched. "And Darrin?"

"Yes?"

"Don't worry, OK?"

"But what should I do about my mom?"

"Just do nothing for now. I'll see if she'll talk to me after the meeting tonight, alright?"

Darrin nodded, lifted his hand in a half wave, and started back down the mountain.

As Darrin disappeared, Johann could feel a wave of sorrow and horror building within him. He covered his mouth to muffle the wrenching sobs he could not stop, not wanting Darrin to come rushing back.

Heidi had never married?

Heidi had never married.

What trick was this? Who had lied to him? How had he believed them?

Someone had lied and changed the course of his adult life.

Had he been that weak and gullible to fall for such a lie? Had he been so ready to give up on his love for Heidi that he had been an easy target? But *who?* Who had started the lie?

He remembered, clear as day, sitting in the office listening to the man he had thought of as his mentor and father.

Karl showing him the letter.

Had someone made that up? What horrible trick was this?

Had Amy known?

Waves of anger and bitterness filled him, the depth scaring him. He needed to deal with it because he couldn't stand in front of a room full of teens and talk about God while filled with bitterness.

He sat there until sunset, wrestling with his thoughts like Jacob in the book of Genesis had wrestled with God. He cried out to God, begged and pleaded with Him for release from this sudden anger and bitterness.

And then, with the last ray of light, peace flooded his soul. And he knew what he would talk about tonight. Someone had wronged him and Amy and Heidi deeply. Yet, God was still sovereign, despite how other people messed things up. He picked his way down the mountain in the gathering darkness, grateful he knew the path.

***

Heidi needed to get up, she knew Darrin was worried, but she couldn't seem to mobilize herself into action. Fifteen years later and Johann was here. And he happened to be the same man Darrin idolized and worked with every day. She couldn't quite grasp the reality of the situation nor understand why he had asked about her so-called *husband.* Did he really think she had been married all this time? And then to hear that Amy had been murdered! Was that the reason he had left South Africa? Was it to escape the memories?

She rolled over. That *must* be why; he certainly hadn't wanted to leave South Africa fifteen years before.

She tried to take a mental step back from her emotions, to view the situation objectively. Johann was here, in America. He lived and worked here now. He had suffered immeasurable loss, so he had come to America to build a new life. That was it in a nutshell. He also hadn't aged much and had the same strong, deep accented voice she had loved so much.

Realization dawned. "Loved" was past tense. So, she needed to get up, make herself presentable, and go out there and make Darrin glad his mom had come to visit.

Grabbing her sunglasses to hide her red eyes, she stepped out into the crisp early evening air, walking from her cabin toward what she assumed was game time. The playing fields lay beyond a row of cabins near the parking area, placed there, she supposed, to maximize the flat space. As she approached the open fields, the sight lifted her spirits. She wasn't sure if what she was watching was a game of four-way soccer or not, but all the campers seemed to be having a great time. The opposing teams were engaged in a back and forth yelling match of "We've got spirit..." and there in the middle of the fray was Darrin, whistle in his mouth, arms waving like a madman. Four balls were in play, and confusion was rampant. She remembered the frenzy of game times and, for a split second, forgot her sorrow and smiled at the mayhem.

Heidi settled on the grass, close enough to watch Darrin in action but hopefully far enough away to avoid a wayward projectile. Darrin, seeing her, waved vigorously before returning to his directing. She waved back, hoping he could see her smile.

The game continued, and Heidi watched in amusement as the team with the green armbands managed to corner the blue ball and score in their opposing team's goal. It was such a cleverly executed plan that ordinarily, she would've clapped and cheered. Instead, she smiled.

The green team erupted in victory yells, and she heard Darrin's whistle blow loudly, calling them all to the center where he stood. His back was to her, and she watched as he instructed the campers to clean up and prepare for dinner and then sent them on their way.

The campers scattered in small groups, chattering and taunting each other. A few looked at her quizzically, and a few smiled a friendly greeting, but many walked by in typical teenager fashion, purposefully pretending that they hadn't seen her.

She smiled at Darrin as he approached her, sweating and full of energy. He plunked himself next to her and rested his elbows on his knees. "Whew, that was quite a game!"

"Great job, Mr. Games Director!" Heidi hoped she sounded upbeat.

"Thanks... that was what you might call a last-minute scramble." He looked over at her, concern evident in his eyes. "Um, you feeling OK now, Mom?"

She didn't want to answer, so she side-hugged him and focused on his first statement. "That didn't look like a last-minute scramble to me. You had everyone under control."

"Yeah, but it was supposed to be our Grand Finale games – thankfully, the kids didn't know any better."

"Why didn't you do them then?"

Darrin shrugged, "John... uh, he couldn't run them like usual. Said he was working on something and kind of left me to figure this out last minute, which has never happened." He looked at his mom questioningly.

So, Johann hadn't wanted to run the game time. Heidi wondered where he was and what he was thinking. Seeing her must have been a shock to him, too. Maybe it had brought back everything about Amy that he had tried to forget. She could feel Darrin's eyes on her, and she knew she should say something, something that had nothing to do with Johann. "What time is dinner around here?"

"You hungry?" Darrin seemed relieved to talk about something easy like food.

"Sure am," she smiled and elbowed him.

"Well, you've got at least another half hour...." He jumped up and grabbed her hand to pull her up. "Why don't I show you around, and we'll end up at the food? Where did John take you so far?"

"Um, well, the mountain, the Tree, and of course the row of

buildings where I'm staying."

"OK, then, I'll show you the camper cabins and the bathrooms because if you are way over here, you wouldn't want to go back to your room." He paused and looked around, pointing. "And down that road is where Alice and Bill live; I'll introduce you later. Their house has been here forever and is so cool, and there's like two other buildings that way but just boring storage or something. Johann's house is on the other end of camp on the other side of the stream but closer to the cafeteria – if there was another bridge, that is. Sometimes I see him just wade through the stream if he doesn't want to take the time to walk to the bridge, which is funny."

"How many campers can you have here?" The camp was beautiful, and the distraction of discussing it was a welcome relief.

"Well, we don't like to put more than eight to a cabin, and there are four cabins on each side of this building. If it's a mixed camp, we put the girls on the side facing the mountain and the boys facing the game fields. But if it's not a mixed camp, then it doesn't matter. So maximum 64 campers, but we like to keep it around 50 since we don't have a very big permanent crew."

"But don't churches bring their own workers?"

"Wow, Mom, you did work at a camp, didn't you? Yip. And sometimes they bring so many that our job is very easy and other times, well, not so much."

They ended their tour at the dining room that looked as typical as any school cafeteria with a bunch of loud kids. Girls kept stopping by to flirt with Darrin in the guise of meeting Heidi.

"I think they're using me as an excuse to talk to you, Darrin," Heidi winked, thrilled to be with her son again. The weeks of separation already felt surreal.

Darrin rolled his eyes.

After dinner, Darrin explained that since the weather was good, they would have their meeting outdoors at a fire pit near the Counting Tree instead of in the meeting hall. She walked with Darrin over the bridge again, and this time, they took a left down a path she hadn't been on yet. The path opened to a clearing with a fire pit as the center, and benches staggered against the hill in a semicircular fashion. The kids hopped over one another, finding their places, and Heidi set off to the side to observe. A fire was already burning, and a church worker was feeding the flames, keeping watch that no camper stepped too close.

The scene was mesmerizing – both serene yet filled with the energy of youth. She was glad for her spot high and off to the side where she could observe and not be observed until a little boy, she guessed about seven or eight, came to stand in front of her.

"Hi, I'm Jacob. Are you Darrin's Mom?"

"Why, yes, I am!" Heidi was instantly drawn to his mischievous face and adorable smile. He was camp-dirty and the picture of boyhood. His green eyes were familiar, but Heidi dismissed her thoughts as fatigue from an emotionally taxing day.

"Cool." And with that, he scrambled off towards some teen girls begging him to sit by them.

Heidi smiled, remembering Fiona and Samson, and wondered what had happened to them. They would be in their mid-twenties by now. Heidi looked again towards Jacob, captivated by his smile and mannerisms.

The campfire was in full swing now. Heidi watched as older boys helped stoke the fire and fed the logs at the appropriate time. She proudly watched as Darrin, guitar slung over his shoulder, came to the front to lead the teens in choruses, and her heart lodged in her throat as they sang a few from her days as a camp counselor.

Her eye caught movement. Off to the side, she saw Johann slip into place on the far end of the first row. He turned, scanning the crowd until he saw her, and nodded in acknowledgment. She felt her heart lodge in her throat. With the distance and campfire light, he looked like the same Johann from 1987.

Time contracted, and she was once again 22 and in love with Johann, sitting next to Amy, watching over her own row of campers. She closed her eyes, willing her mind back to the present, but the similarities were overwhelming, and she struggled to contain her thoughts.

Then Johann got up to talk. His voice was soft yet commanding, and the teens hung on every word. He still had the gift of holding a youthful audience all these years later, in a different culture, a different time. He spoke from Psalms 41:9, reading the words out loud,

Yea, mine own familiar friend, in whom I trusted, which did eat of my bread, hath lifted up his heel against me.

Fear filled Heidi's heart; she hoped he wasn't referencing her. Aside from their earlier angry words, she had never done anything to intentionally hurt him.

He closed his Bible and looked at the teens. "People will let you down; your whole life, that will happen. But sometimes, it will happen so badly that you will think you cannot possibly forgive them. I'm sure everyone out here has somebody in their life who has hurt them badly, told them one thing, and done another. Maybe you thought to yourself, 'That's it, I'm never going to forgive them.'" He paused and surveyed the teens. A few were nodding, and others were looking down, but everyone was focused on his words.

"When I was much younger, I was given a beautiful gift. I like to think that God gave me the gift. Now, I'm not going to tell you what that gift was because that's not the important part; the important part is what happened with that gift. Because of it, I was happier, I felt I was serving God better, and it gave me a plan and a sense of purpose.

"Well, one day, that gift was taken away from me, and I was very confused and partially blamed myself. But years later, I found out that it wasn't my fault at all. That gift was taken away from me because somebody lied to me. And you know, it made me really, really angry with them. Why would someone who was supposed to love you do something like that to you?

"So, I got angry. And the more I thought about how I had been wronged, the angrier and more bitter I got. I got so bitter and angry that I found I couldn't talk to God properly anymore. You see, kids, the problem wasn't what someone had done to me; the problem was my response to it. I had a choice. I could be mad and angry and bitter. Or I could tell God all about it, give it to Him, and ask Him to help me forgive that person. The first solution would continue to harm me. The second solution would place it in God's hands.

"So, let's talk about forgiveness… forgiveness frees you. The minute I gave my anger and bitterness to God and asked Him to help me forgive, I was able to! It's crazy because that isn't normal for a regular old human, especially me!" A faint laugh went through the crowd of teens. "But, when God helps us, we can do things that aren't normal – like forgive someone who has wronged us."

His voice continued, calming and imploring the kids to hear him and understand. But Heidi was lost in the past, in the meaning of his words, as tears slipped down her face. He was talking about them; she was convinced, but what or who had lied to him? She would have to speak with him long enough to find out because it would make her crazy with wondering.

After Johann closed in prayer and gave directions to the campers, they dispersed quietly, as if they were still thinking about what he had said. She saw Darrin talking with a group and telling them he'd catch up with them shortly before heading to her.

"You OK, Mom?" He looked worried; he must've seen her crying again.

"I'll be fine, honey." Poor Darrin, he must be so disappointed in her visit. She could see Johann from the corner of her eye moving towards her, feel his intense gaze upon her, yet she kept looking at Darrin. She needed to reassure and let him know she needed to talk privately with Johann.

Johann reached out and gripped Darrin by the shoulder, squeezing affectionately. "You've been fabulous today, Darrin. I don't know what I would've done without you."

Darrin smiled, clearly relieved by the compliment.

"I'm so sorry for leaving you hanging all afternoon."

"No, man, it's good. Mom saw the games; she said they were fine." He stepped next to his mom and put an arm around her as if protecting her.

"Would you mind if I walked your mom back to her room

tonight?" Johann was looking at Darrin earnestly.

Darrin looked back and forth between the two of them. Heidi could see the questions written on his face as he shrugged and then leaned forward and hugged her. "Love you, Mom."

"Love you too, honey."

Darrin hesitated as if he were going to say something, then changed his mind and hugged Heidi again before moving away, walking backward. "Call me if you need me, Mom," he implored, giving Johann a pointed look.

Then they were alone, with all the new information circulating about them. Heidi had never felt more inept in all her life. Keeping her eyes averted, she sat, unsure how to start. She stared at her knotted fingers. Who had lied to him? Had this lie been the deciding factor that kept Johann from coming to her all those years ago? Or was she overreaching? Had he simply not loved her enough, and his evening message had nothing to do with her? Maybe he simply wanted to explain why he had quit writing, why he had married Amy, why he had not come to America back then after all.

"May I sit here?" The question was simple, his voice deep with emotion, the accent emphasized on 'heah,' the inflection going up with the question, the same way she remembered.

Her heart flip-flopped at the memory of what his voice could do to her, her senses alert to his signature fresh soapy smell. After all this time, she couldn't understand how his presence and the sound of his voice could affect her so dramatically. She felt betrayed by her own emotions and steeled herself, trying to remember that he had rejected her and married her best friend. She tried to nod or respond but felt frozen and incapable of movement.

He sat on the roughhewn bench seat, anyway, his elbows on his knees, his hands clasped, and turned towards her so he could see her face. "I hope my vagueness still got my message across...."

"I'm just curious...."

"There was just no way I could tell a group of teenagers about my first love."

Heidi's sharp intake of breath surprised her, and she

involuntarily glanced up. His eyes bore into hers, willing her to see his pain and regret. His image blurred as her own eyes pooled with tears, and she ducked her head to hide them.

He reached out and touched her arm. "I need to tell you about the... the lie."

She sat motionless, heart pounding in her ears, afraid of what he was about to reveal.

He continued. "When you left, I missed you with every ounce of my being. I wrote you letters, and you wrote me a few, but they... they stopped so soon?" He paused, the question in his eyes.

"A few!" Heidi was incredulous. "I wrote you dozens of letters!"

He stared at her questioningly and then took a deep breath before continuing. "Anyway, Amy was a constant friend – we were both grieving your absence. You had been so good for Amy. She was so much more full of life around you and not acting as, uh, under her dad's thumb, if you know what I mean. Ian had left to go finish University, and the plan had been for them to keep dating. But once he was away, things just cooled off between them.

"Then, one day, Karl called me into his office. I had applied for a visa and was waiting and waiting for news. So, I was hoping he had gotten word that it had come through."

"A visa?"

"You know, to come to America."

"You were trying to come visit me in America?"

"Yes – I wanted to stay awhile; I told you about it in my letters."

"Johann, I only got seven letters from you." Her voice was low and flat.

"Seven? Are you sure?"

She rolled her eyes. "I can count that high quite easily."

He rubbed his hand over his face. "Well, I sent way more than that, but you know how bad our post system was...."

"As I recall, letters got through just fine; it was parcels that went missing. Were they just plain letters?" Heidi was curious now. He had implied she had hardly sent him any. Was it possible someone had helped make the postal system worse than it actually was?

"They were plain letters, nothing but paper and pen."

He waited as if to allow Heidi to voice what they were both thinking, but she stayed quiet.

"Anyway, when Karl called me in, it was to show me a letter from your pastor at your church."

"What about?"

"He handed me the letter…. it said you were getting married."

Heidi's face turned towards him in horror. The words mobilized her yet broke her ability to speak.

"Married?! To who?" she finally managed.

"'A nice Christian young man who loves God' – those were the exact words. I'll never forget them."

"And you *believed* it?"

"I didn't want to believe it, but Amy's dad said I was experiencing denial. That facing the truth and moving on was the best thing I could do for myself and my work at the camp." He stopped and looked at her, his eyes begging her to understand, but she continued to look at him in disbelief. "You know, pretty soon everyone was coming up to me and offering their sympathy; it seemed everyone knew about you more than I did, and with your lack of letters I—"

"Lack of letters?" She could hear her voice, high pitched and loud, tinged with anger and bitterness. She stood and looked down at him, "I just told you, I wrote you so many letters I lost count." She turned her head then, looking out into the darkness as she could feel fresh tears pouring down her cheeks.

He rose slowly, "No, Heidi, I only ever got eight letters, and they were spaced quite far apart. They stopped completely about a month before I heard you were going to get married."

"Yeah, married," she mumbled sarcastically. She palmed her tears and managed bitterly, "then someone took them." She may as well now state the obvious. "I sent two or three letters every week for months. I only stopped when I realized the futility of my effort. I felt so foolish, pouring out my heart to you and getting nothing back, so I stopped." She took a shaky breath and turned back to look directly at him, "How many did *you* write because, like I said, I only ever got seven from you – seven measly letters spread out over four months."

It was his turn to be incredulous. "Heidi, I wrote you lots of letters – granted, they were short and not good like your first ones, but I wrote you." He reached out and gently touched her arm, his eyes pleading, but she stepped away.

"Well, what happened to them? What happened to *all* of them?" She rubbed the spot where his fingers had been, trying to ignore how good it felt, willing herself to keep enough distance so that she wouldn't respond to him and forget that he had married her friend.

"Someone must've taken them," he sighed, "all of them."

They both stood there, trying to face this probable fact and wondering how it could have been possible.

"Maybe it was the same person that made up the story of... of you getting married." His voice cracked on the word as if the memory of finding out she had married was still painful. He paused and looked away, his emotions obviously in shambles. Then he turned toward her and firmly gripped her shoulders, holding her captive. "That's the lie, Heidi, don't you see? Someone lied and stole our letters and kept us apart all these years."

She was frozen by his touch, her tear-blurred eyes locked on his. She wanted to believe everything he was saying, wanted to step into his embrace and cry for the years they had lost, and wanted to feel the warmth and comfort she remembered in his arms as if it were yesterday. But the specter of Amy filled that space between them.

"So, you married Amy." The statement was simple, a fact, and no matter who had lied to them, this irrefutable fact clouded everything. She shrugged away from his grip and took a step back.

He dropped his hands to his sides, defeated. "Yes, I married Amy."

Silence stretched between them, the night sounds filling the space.

"Heidi?"

She turned back to him and sat back down. "Yes?" Her voice was resigned. The ramifications of what he had just told her were sinking in. What if their letters had gotten to each other? What if someone hadn't lied and told Johann she was married? What if his visa had come through and they had been able to see each other in the US? Yet, did it really matter? "The past is the past, and there is no changing it." She heard herself speak the words and wondered what other thoughts had escaped her lips.

"Oh, Heidi," he crouched in front of her and gripped her hands, "we can't change the past, but we have the present, and right now, we are here together! Maybe we can figure out what went wrong in the past and make things right between us in the present. Maybe this accidental meeting is not such an accident after all. Maybe we can see it as a gift from God!"

His hands were sending warmth up her arms; she needed to make him let go before she made a fool of herself. How was it possible after so long? Had she not learned anything in her years of mothering and singlehood? She was supposed to be strong and logical and clearheaded. She needed to counter his argument, to get away, but she didn't want him to release the grip he had on her hands.

She dipped her head, looking at their hands, and a fresh wave of "what could've been" washed over her. "Why did you believe them?" she mumbled.

"What?" He released one of her hands and gently guided her face to look at him.

"Why did you believe them?" The question was more forceful.

"Oh, Heidi, I wish with all my heart that I hadn't, but I did. I was young and stupid and way too trusting. I loved my work and was afraid what leaving would mean. Hearing that you were married broke my heart, but it also made my path clear. I could let my love for you fade away and focus on what I had."

"Did it?"

"Did what?"

"Did it fade away?"

He released her hands and slowly stood. "No, it didn't. Do you know how guilty that made me feel? I would go days and weeks and think I was finally OK, and then your memory would surface so powerfully that I would struggle for days." He took a shaky breath. "You have to understand, I believed you were married, and I couldn't believe that I was longing for a married woman. And after I married Amy, it made me feel even worse when your memory would surface at the most random times while I myself was married. I used to pray that Amy would never find out what a terrible person I really was. I used to beg God to forgive me for my unfaithful heart."

"Did she?"

"Did she what?"

"Ever find out?"

"Yes." His voice cracked again, and he sat and put his head in his hands, the image of a broken man.

Heidi watched him in sorrow, realizing how things had been for him. Someone had lied to him; he had tried to do what was right, and had struggled because of it, struggled just like she had. She sat next to him and tentatively placed her hand on his arm.

"How?"

He wiped his hands over his face and stared into the darkness once more. "I found her diary. I knew I shouldn't read it, but we were in such a bad place that I justified reading it to try help us both. It was all in there, how she knew I still loved you, how she felt inferior because of it."

"How long had you been married?"

"Just a couple years. We hadn't been able to have children yet, and I thought she was upset because of that. After I found and read her diary, I went on a long hike. I took your letters and any other little mementos we had, and I made a fire and burned them, and I told God that He needed to burn your memory from my mind and make me the best husband I could be because I couldn't do it on my own."

"And did He?"

"Yes, He did." He turned his head and looked at her, his eyes pleading for her to understand. "I mean, I still thought about you, but your memory didn't consume me. I became a better husband, and things were better between Amy and me." He paused, looking down at his hands, measuring his words. "You must know that despite what I told you, I did love Amy." His voice deepened. "She was sweet and kind, and once I got myself straightened...." He stopped and brightened as if realizing he could move on to the happiest memory, "and then we eventually had Jacobus and that boy...."

"Where is he?" She spoke softly, letting this fresh news sink in. Johann had a son. Her anger had dissipated while he spoke, the realization of what he had been through softening her heart.

"Who? Jacobus?"

She nodded.

Johann's eyes crinkled, and he cracked a half smile as he twisted back around to sit next to her again. "He's here! I saw you talking to him!"

Realization dawned. "Jacob!"

"Yes," Johann smiled more fully. "He said if I was going to be 'John,' then he was going to be 'Jacob.' We were both so tired of you *domkop* Americans butchering our names." Johann winked at her eliciting another smile.

She laughed softly then, "Of course! He looks like Amy! I wondered what it was about him, but he doesn't have an accent at all!"

Johann grinned, "*Ja*, kids, they adjust so fast. I think it took him just a few months to sound like a regular American. Now, me on the other hand, I'll always sound like an Afrikaner. Remember how *you* used to pronounce *that* word?" He elbowed her gently.

"But what happened... with... you know... when?" Heidi couldn't bring herself to say the word.

"With Amy?"

"Yes."

251

"Ah—I..." And then he stood abruptly, running his hand through his hair, his back to her. "It happened when Jacobus was five." He turned then and angled his face slightly towards her, staring into the darkness. "You remember how unsafe it was, and I... I was stupid and let her go alone and...." His voice choked, and he shook his head. He turned away again. "I... if it's OK...." His voice caught again.

"It's OK, Johann. You don't need to talk about it."

He turned to her, a sheen over his eyes, his lips pressed together tightly, and he nodded and then sat again, his head in his hands.

Heidi waited. She knew he needed time to gain composure. His turmoil was palpable. She breathed deeply, staring at the pinpoints of stars visible above the trees, a fresh breeze blowing away the last vestiges of campfire smoke.

The verse from Isaiah 30 came to mind,

...in quietness and in confidence shall be your strength.

Heidi felt God's peace wash over her. She was so thankful the anger was gone and basked in the sudden peace that filled her soul. No matter what was in the future, all she knew was that right then, God was with her.

"Heidi?" His voice was low.

She turned to him, "Yes?"

His voice was serious once more. "Do you forgive me?"

She looked at him, the question in her eyes.

"For?" Surely he didn't want forgiveness for the lost letters?

"For believing them... believing that you were married and not trying to find out the truth for myself."

She wanted to say 'yes,' but as she thought of the ramifications, the peace she had just felt threatened to leave. Johann *had* believed them; he *had* married Amy. She knew she was being unfair, but it was too soon. She took a deep breath and finally spoke. "I do forgive you for believing them, but...." She paused; she knew forgiveness shouldn't be qualified, yet she needed to be honest. She stared towards the dying fire. "It's just... I mean, it *is* hard to realize what believing them cost us both, though." She looked back at him briefly and then away again, the pain in his eyes too much for her.

She waited, hoping he would say something, but his silence willed her to keep talking. "I... I guess I'm just going to need time to adjust to everything you've just told me." She glanced back at him, long enough to see disappointment flash in his eyes, and tried to explain. "I do understand why you would've believed them; I do! I just wish you would have... just wish you... I just need to get used to all this...." Her voice trailed off lamely, and she stood, ready to make her escape, wishing he would say something. "And... about Amy... I'm so sorry, and it's so much to... well... I just have to get used to the idea – of everything – do you understand?"

"*Ja*." His voice, tinged in anguish, was so low she could barely hear him. He stood too. "I must go and make sure Jacobus is OK. He usually goes back to Alice's house after a campfire because I often counsel people, but he is probably exhausted by now."

She turned away from him, disappointed in herself. She knew she was offering incomplete forgiveness, but in a way, it felt like he was offering an insufficient apology. He didn't seem to realize that believing them so easily meant he hadn't been willing to fight for her, for *them*. And she knew she should respect his request, but she wished he would realize the depths of how his actions had affected her. Besides, he had married Amy, and she would not overcome that barrier easily. Yet if God could so freely give her peace, shouldn't she give Johann complete forgiveness? But she needed time, time to make sure she meant it, time to make sure he realized the magnitude of the barrier between them.

As if sensing her conflict, he gently reached out and touched her arm. "May I walk you to your cabin?" His voice was a low rumble, and the accent she had loved so dearly caused her heart to hiccup.

She looked back at him and smiled slightly, the memory of that question filling the space between them. "Yes, please."

They walked in silence, his hand on her arm gently guiding her over the rocks. Before they left the shadow of the trees, he stopped and turned her towards him. "No matter what...." His voice caught as a tear slipped down his face.

Heidi looked away, unable to bear his pain as well as her own, unwilling for him to see her own tears, but he gently touched her cheek with his hand and turned her face back towards him.

"No matter what, Heidi, I... after all this time... I am so thankful to see you again." His admission was all she needed for her resolve to crumble, and, in an instant, they were in each other's arms, wrapped in an embrace that spanned the years. Their tears mingled, crying for all they had lost, clinging to each other in desperation as if to erase the years apart and forget that the past might yet keep them apart.

Heidi knew she should step back and get to her cabin before the grief overwhelmed her, but the rising tide was too great to staunch. She heard her sobs and knew she was powerless, feeling the regret and "what ifs" from the depths of her soul. "Why did you believe them?" She beat her fist on his chest. "Why, why, why, did you have to believe them?"

He caught her hand and gripped it against him, pulling her even closer. "Oh Heidi, Heidi... I'm so sorry... but I did believe them. I believed them so completely that I tried to put you out of my mind forever."

She wrenched herself free and gazed at him in anguish. "I thought what we had was the most incredible love that ever existed, and... even that was not enough." She turned, her fist against her mouth, desperate to stem her sobs and control her grief.

He pulled her against him again, "I know, I know."

She strained against the circle of his arms, but he wouldn't release her. "After you married Amy," came her muffled voice, "I just figured I wasn't able to recognize real love since both my fiancés landed up marrying my closest friends and...."

"No, Heidi," he interrupted, "Our love was real. It was so real it took me years to get over you." He paused. "Seeing you today is proof of how real it was."

She wished he would explain himself but instead, he simply held her, stroking her hair until both of their tears had stopped.

Eventually, she stepped back. She was rumpled and vaguely aware that in the morning, she would be horrified at her display of grief. For now, though, she felt numb. "I'll... I'm fine to walk the rest of the way." She turned then and stumbled away, part of her wishing he would call her back and part of her relieved that he did not. She couldn't explain herself anymore, they had both felt each other's desperation, both been consumed by memories, but she had to remember the intervening years and that crying in his arms wouldn't erase everything they had both been through.

She willed herself to not look back towards the trees for fear she would go running back. She had to remember that she was stronger now, a woman who had survived and flourished despite life's many disappointments, and she wasn't going to sacrifice all she had learned just to feel what had to be a false security in Johann's arms.

She slipped gratefully into her cabin and barred the door before falling across the bed and crying herself to sleep.

CHAPTER 28

Heidi woke the next morning to bright sunlight and the sound of running feet and happy voices. It took a while to get her bearings.

"Leaving day," she mumbled. If this camp was run by the same template as Camp Timothy, the campers would be rushing to fulfill a list of obligations before congregating in the main meeting area for a final wrap-up. She stretched, her mind flooding with Johann and everything from the evening before.

Stumbling over to the bathroom, she splashed water on her dry face. Her eyes felt like sandpaper, as if she had cried the last bit of moisture from them.

Johann had been through so much. In some ways, more so than her. But he had married and built a life with Amy and their Jacob, and she had faced parenthood almost alone, especially at the beginning and then again after her father's death. She took a long, slow breath, trying to still the warring thoughts, ever aware of the horror he must have experienced after Amy had been murdered. Now he parented alone, too. And how had Amy died? Where was he when it happened? Where was Jacob?

At the same time, guilt assailed. She had only offered Johann incomplete forgiveness. Yet, he was not to blame, and she knew it. Someone had lied to him and withheld their letters. What would her incomplete forgiveness achieve but bitterness? Perhaps she was using it as an excuse to keep him at arm's length? Was the knowledge he had married Amy so weighty that she was hiding behind a lack of forgiveness? If it were Darla or Darrin, she would tell them to forgive completely.

Truth be told, she was a hypocrite.

Heidi leaned over the sink again and splashed more water over her face, surprised again when the water turned hot. Her head pounded from crying, and her eyes were swollen. She eyed the shower, knowing how good a long hot shower would feel, when she heard a noise at the door.

Sighing, she smoothed back her hair and grabbed a towel, wiping at her wet face as she walked toward the door and then peeked out. It was Jacob, standing there, hopping from one foot to another, precariously balancing a food tray.

"Jacob?"

"Miss Alice said I was to bring you your breakfast before the campers eat." He grinned, his eyes sparkling. "I even put an extra piece of bacon on here for you."

"Why, thank you, sir!" She couldn't help but take in his exuberance as she scanned his features, noting how many similarities he shared with Amy.

"Well, here you go!" He moved the tray towards her as it tilted again, and she reached out to rescue it. "I'll be right back with your tea – Dad said I had to carry them separately." He turned to run back, looking over his shoulder anxiously as if afraid she would be gone by the time he got back.

Heidi watched him go and then turned to place the tray on a table, a warm feeling filling her soul. When had anyone ever delivered her breakfast? The apparent community effort to make her comfortable warmed her heart. And tea? Johann really remembered how she loved her rooibos? Did he ship it from South Africa?

She left the door ajar as she arranged her tray and began to make the bed, listening for Jacob's footsteps. She knew she needed to at least run a brush through her hair, but before she had the chance, she looked up at two smiling faces. It was like staring at a duplicate snapshot; everything had frozen, for those two smiles were nearly identical. Jacob had all his mom's features but his dad's smile! She simply stood there and smiled back, unable to say anything.

Jacob was the one to break the silence. "Dad thinks I can't carry a hot teapot by myself." He rolled his eyes and looked at the ceiling in a dramatic gesture that was all Amy.

Heidi knew she was staring but couldn't break out of her

reverie. She knew her smile had probably turned goofy, but she was immobilized by the two of them together, father and son. It was like staring into a photo album as someone explained the present in light of the past.

Finally, Johann moved to set the tray of tea next to her food. "That's a pot of rooibos for you and some sugar. Don't know if you still drink it, but rooibos is a camp favorite here too." He shrugged as if it were the most normal thing in the world, but his eyes bored into hers, remembering the night before.

Heidi, mesmerized by the intensity of his gaze, found her voice, "Where?" It sounded like a squeak. She cleared her throat, but before she could try again, Johann answered.

"Aunt Gillian sends it in the post. Lots of it." He shrugged again, feigning nonchalance, and elbowed Jacob.

"And she sends other stuff too." Jacob looked between them as if he could sense something between the grownups and then blurted, "aren't you going to start eating?"

Heidi saw him eyeing her bacon, and she forced herself to react. Obviously, this morning Johann was both father and camp director and would not hint at all that had transpired the evening before. Heidi would play her role as Darrin's mother and vacationing visitor. "Why yes, I'm going to eat." She pulled a chair out for each of them. "And you, young man, will have to help me eat some of this extra bacon."

"Oh boy!"

He was exuberant – over bacon. Heidi simply wanted to hug him for his cuteness, but she refrained. She gazed questioningly at Johann, willing him to know that there would be no emotional displays today, especially not in front of his son.

Johann seemed to understand her message, and his concern was replaced with noticeable relief. "I'll just leave you two to breakfast, then." He began backing up towards the door with a twinkle of mischievousness in his eyes. "Jacob, when you're done, make sure you give Heidi some privacy. I bet she'd love to brush her hair or something." And with a wink and a smile, he was gone.

Heidi reached up to touch her sleep-mussed hair, looked at Jacob, and shrugged as if she didn't care. His mouth was full of bacon, and he lifted his skinny shoulders, rolling his eyes again as if messy hair was the most unimportant thing in the world.

"So, what happens on the last day at camp?" Heidi suspected she knew most of the answer but simply wanted to listen to him talk.

Jacob grinned, kept chewing, and held up his hand while swallowing dramatically. He then grabbed her juice and took a gulp before slamming it back down in front of her and clamping his hand over his mouth, his eyes wide and horrified. "Oh no! I drank your juice, and it sloshed out!"

Heidi laughed, "I have tea. You drink the juice." She placed it back in front of him and cleaned up the spill with an already-damp napkin.

Jacob eyed the napkin warily. "Um, maybe you shouldn't use that."

"I shouldn't?" Heidi let the napkin go, giving him a sidelong glance. "And where exactly has this napkin been?"

"Um, well, you can say it dropped." He kept staring at the offensive cloth and then grabbed it and walked across the room, throwing it into a trash can. "There!" Then, he wiped his hands as if to say, 'all taken care of,' grinned his mischievous grin and sat with ceremony, sighing loudly. "Dad would like that I did that," he muttered.

Heidi was so amused by the entire scene that she simply laughed. "I'm sure your dad would be very proud of how you handled my breakfast! I'll tell him it was the best breakfast delivery ever, and I won't even mention the wet napkin." She paused and leaned forward conspiratorially. "By the way, *why* was the napkin wet?"

Jacob tilted his head, altering his voice to a loud whisper. "I can't give away classified information."

Heidi was so taken aback that she laughed even louder. "Well then, young man, the secret will have to stay with you. I will, however, just excuse myself for a minute so I can wash my hands…

you know, just in case!"

"Good idea, very good idea." He nodded vigorously. "Maybe I'll just wash my hands, too!"

Heidi knew that didn't bode well for the overall hygiene of her entire meal, but she was enjoying herself so thoroughly she didn't care. Johann was raising a well-adjusted son despite the trauma they had experienced. She wondered how long it had taken Jacob to get over his mother's death and how much he knew. He certainly didn't act like a child who had been through such an ordeal and moved countries. In addition, he also had to share his dad with busloads of teenagers every week. But here he was, a regular impish kid, bursting with the joy of living. It was a sure testimony to God's grace and Johann's parenting.

Jacob brought her out of her reverie with an announcement that he needed to go and check on the chickens. Then, in a whirlwind, he ran out, slamming the door shut and opening it to poke his head back in and thank *her* for the bacon.

She shook her head slightly, a smile playing on her lips. As the silence settled around her, she picked at part of her breakfast. She needed a clear head for the remainder of her stay, so she pulled out her Bible and tried to read. Finally, she gave up, the brain fog so thick she found she couldn't settle on one thought before another crashed in to take its place.

Help me, dear God, she kept repeating. Help me.

And then she realized. She could forgive Johann but keep her distance. He hadn't fought for them like she wished, but withholding forgiveness because he had believed them was ludicrous. She wouldn't carry a grudge; she would forgive and move on but keep her heart guarded. Amy might always be a barrier, but that was separate from forgiving Johann.

In the shower, as the trickle of water protracted rinsing the shampoo out of her hair, she made a decision. She would stay for the duration as initially planned, would enjoy her time with Darrin, and would be polite but reserved with Johann. No more crying in his arms, asking him why, talking through fifteen years of what-ifs. That was not why she had come – she was here for Darrin. Then, once she went home, she would sort through the multitude of emotions seeing Johann had dredged up and deal with them as thoroughly as she could.

So, with resolve, she exited her cabin, surprised again by the refreshing cool of the mountain air. She had changed into clean clothes, her wet hair pulled back into a clip, her skin free of makeup. They were at a camp, and she wasn't here to look good for anyone, especially Johann.

Darrin met her with a clipboard, hugged her briefly, and told her once they had gotten all the campers fed and loaded on their buses, he would have time for her. "There's a great hike you'll enjoy, so save your energy!"

She looked after his retreating figure as pride filled her heart. Darrin had come such a long way in only a few months, and she would focus on the joy of that answered prayer rather than on the insanity of seeing Johann again.

She meandered into the cafeteria, where workers were scrubbing and bustling around. Heidi located who she assumed was Alice and introduced herself.

"I'm the one you've been delivering crackers and ginger ale and tea to," Heidi smiled.

"Then you're Heidi, Darrin's mom." Without missing a beat, the woman reached forward and pulled Heidi into a hug. "It's so wonderful to meet the mother of the young man who lights this place up!" Then she looked around and started introducing the other kitchen staff.

"I heard that you knew John from South Africa," said one.

Heidi instantly recognized the challenge in her eyes. The territorial language of females was never hard to miss. "Yes, small world. Where are you from?" Replace a question with a question.

"Oh, I, well, around here." The young lady appeared deflated.

"It's just beautiful. I had no idea that cool air existed anywhere in the south during July, and it seems I've been missing out all my life." Then she looked towards Alice. "Now, put me to work so that I feel useful."

Alice quickly acquiesced, and it wasn't long before Heidi was scooping food into trays and delivering them to the serving line.

CHAPTER 29

After the campers left, Heidi, Darrin, Jacob, and Johann drove to Water Rock Knob in Johann's truck. The boys insisted she sit in the front.

"You want to help me shift, Heidi?" He cast a sidelong glance her way.

"Nope." She turned her head to hide her smile, sensing Darrin's curiosity from the back seat.

"Darrin, I tried to teach your mom how to drive a manual many years ago."

"Oh yeah?" Darrin leaned forward, apparently eager for any information about the past.

"She nearly killed my *bakkie*," he intoned.

"Dad, Americans don't say *bakkie*."

"Nope, but your dad does." Darrin poked Jacob in the ribs. "I like that word, *bakkie*, don't you, Mom?"

"Um, sure?"

And so it continued around the winding roads, onto the parkway, and then to the parking lot at Water Rock Knob. The parking lot view was stunning, and Heidi walked off towards a group of picnic tables to snap pictures while Johann unloaded two backpacks, shouldering one and handing the other to Darrin.

They set off at a good pace, with Jacob and Darrin taking the lead. Jacob, a bonafide mountain goat, hopped from trail to rock with boundless energy.

"So, when exactly did you come to America?" She was already out of breath. Sweat beaded her forehead, and she realized that despite her perceived fitness level, Florida was flat, and she was not trained for any elevation.

"Well, I have my Aunt Gillian to thank for that."

She glanced quickly at him, their eyes catching in shared memories. That Uvongo Christmas had been a highlight of her life. She snatched her head back down, determined to staunch the floodgates of those beautiful memories.

"Anyway, after Amy," he paused and took a deep breath. "After, well, you know, after...." He paused again, glancing worriedly toward Jacob. But Jacob was in an animated conversation with Darrin. He took another breath. "Well, Jacobus and I left for Uvongo to be with Aunt Gillian."

"Did the camp close?" Heidi knew it wasn't running any longer but wondered if this was what had precipitated the closing.

"*Ja.*" He stopped walking and looked back at the view their new height afforded them. "Parents would never send their children to a place where... it happened only a couple kilometers away." He rubbed his face and turned away.

"It's OK, I understand." Heidi reached out and touched his arm. Maybe she would get the whole story one day, but now she understood why he had left.

"So, Aunt Gillian became Super-Duper Aunt Gillian. She took in one broken-up man and one grieving, confused little boy. And somehow, she fixed us all up and literally sent us here."

Heidi tilted her head in question.

"Turns out Aunt Gillian is actually more financially comfortable than I realized and has friends around the world, or rather, friends who want to sell their camps to people who run camps." He spread his hands wide, apparently still in awe of this fact.

"One day, she pulls up a website and shows me this camp and tells me the property is for sale. She tells me she's going to buy it and I need to come here and run it; that South Africa has too many bad memories for Jacobus and me, and I need a fresh start. That was three years ago."

"So, Aunt Gillian owns Camp Makarios?" Heidi was incredulous.

"Well, mostly. There's a few other stakeholders and a board I answer to, but she owns the property."

"That's crazy."

"Yes, but good crazy. Coming here was the right move. Jacobus has thrived, and his nightmares slowed down after we moved. He tells me he likes the new camp, that it feels safe."

"Wow." Heidi, grateful for their exertion, would need hours to process this new information, but she also needed to revisit part of their conversation from the prior evening.

"Johann?"

"Yes?"

She took a deep breath. "I do forgive you for believing them." She felt a weight roll from her shoulders as she said the words.

He stopped and took her arm, relief evident on his face. "You do?"

"Yes. Why wouldn't you have believed them? I'm sorry for not saying so right away. My letters were missing, so you had no context." She wanted to add that she still wished he would have fought harder for them, that the barrier of Amy felt insurmountable, but, in the matter of forgiveness, she had no right to withhold it.

He put both hands on her shoulders, his eyes grateful.

"Dad!"

They both jumped apart.

"Yes?" Johann said.

"How much longer do we have to walk?"

"Not long!"

They climbed until Heidi was sore, working their way over boulders and catching glimpses of the view that was to come. Parts of the hike felt other-worldly, the rocks covered in moss, the sun muted by the dense tree canopy. And then, right where the climb intensified, they stepped into a tiny clearing and hoisted themselves up a wall of boulders that flattened at the top. Darrin went first and then pulled Heidi up next to him.

"This is incredible," she said. The view was 270 degrees, the mountains stacked one after the other, first green and then increasing shades of deepening blues until the farthest ridge touched the clouds.

She supposed this was why they called these the Blue Ridge Mountains. "What a view."

"We knew you would like it, Mom." Darrin was grinning happily as he dug into the backpacks and pulled out food and water.

***

Johann watched in satisfaction as Heidi, Darrin, and Jacob sat shoulder to shoulder, enjoying the scenery and snacks. He suspected Jacobus was enjoying the food more than the view but regardless, the scene before him was gratifying on multiple levels. He remembered vividly how much Heidi had appreciated their hikes from Camp Timothy; it was surreal to hike with her again, half the world away. He was still overwhelmed by the miracle that Heidi had stepped back into his life. Without preamble, there she was, sitting under his Counting Tree, in a different country. And Darrin was her son. Darrin, the young man who had gripped his heart from the moment he stepped off the bus back in March. Only God could orchestrate such a series of events, and he would trust that, in the same vein, God would enable him to get close to Heidi again.

He knew there were heartbreaking obstacles and complications, but he wouldn't think through each one right now. He would simply enjoy this moment in time, watching his son, Heidi's son, and Heidi herself at this incredible place.

"John, you going to eat something?"

He walked over, wanting to squeeze in next to Heidi but opting for the other side. There was no sense in pushing things, especially after her slow response to his plea for forgiveness. He understood her reticence and was relieved by her words moments before, but it still gnawed at him. He hoped she truly understood he had felt he had no other options. Circumstances had boxed him in, and being told she was married had been the death knell to his dreams regarding her. Every path he had tried had been met by a wall of resistance. First, her leaving, then the lack of letters, then the no-response on the visa, and finally, the horrifying news she had married. It had been one blow after the other, and he had finally accepted that he needed to embrace what was right in front of him and not wish for what never could be.

But now, now he wondered. If someone had fabricated the letter of her marriage, had they also stopped their letters? And what about the stalled visa? Was that government red tape or also a fabricated failure? And who? Who had done this to them? The most obvious culprit was Karl, but Karl was Amy's father; Karl had mentored and saved him from a harsh home life. Would and could Karl have done that? Could he ever even ask him? Karl and Vera were still grieving Amy. Now that he had Jacobus, he realized that losing a child must be something you never recovered from. Accusing them now would be unconscionable. And, it wasn't like it would fix the past because marrying Amy had given him many happy years and the blessing of Jacobus, the absolute joy and light of his life.

"Dad! You're in la-la land!" There was the joy and light of his daily life now, frustrated that he must have been ignoring him.

"I'll *klap* you, Jacobus, and then we'll see who is in la-la-land!"

"Johann!" Heidi sounded horrified, obviously not used to their level of banter.

Darrin and Johann laughed; Jacob grinned, then declared it was time to climb down anyway.

The return trip appeared to be harder on Heidi than she let on. Johann watched, impressed she wasn't complaining. Darrin constantly complained about the hills and the lack thereof in Florida, and Johann knew going downhill was harder on untrained muscles than uphill.

Finally, he came up next to her and offered her his arm, worried there would be a rebuff.

"Thanks." She gripped his arm gratefully.

He smiled, noting the wisps of hair escaping from her ball cap, thankful for any success – no matter how small. The hike had been an excellent ice breaker. He hoped he could think of more ways to increase her trust in him. Because now that he had found her, he would do everything in his power to make sure he never lost her again. He still grieved Amy, but with Heidi around, already the grief wasn't as sharp, and the usual recriminations already less frequent. Heidi had brought out the best in his Amy, and her presence seemed to have changed the focus of his memories. And for that, he was thankful.

CHAPTER 30

Heidi stared into her partially packed suitcase. The four days had passed swiftly; it was time to leave. She wanted to stay, but she had appointments lined up and a house to care for. Besides, she was almost out of underwear, a sure sign a trip needed to end.

Hearing a noise, she looked up and saw Johann at her door, standing awkwardly, watching her.

Her face warmed. How long had he been standing there?

"Darrin tells me you are sort of a free agent right now." Johann's eyes were wide, questioning.

She squinted at his silhouette in the open door. "You can come in and sit down, you know."

She watched him hesitate and then step into the cabin, sitting gingerly at the table. Pulling his ball cap off, he ran his fingers through his hair, then replaced it.

They were both nervous. Heidi had succeeded in not being alone with him for the remainder of her stay and felt upended by his proximity. She wished Jacob or Darrin would appear and glanced anxiously through the open door, regretting her invitation.

"You know we have plenty of openings you could fill if you wanted to work here." Johann spoke carefully.

The shirt in her hand froze in place. Taking a deep breath, she went over and sat at the other seat. "What kind of openings?" Her voice sounded high and unnatural, and she swallowed hard. She didn't think packing up her life in South Florida was necessarily the right thing, but then again, the two primary purposes of her life were no longer in Jupiter.

"Biggest one is to revamp the curriculum we use…." His eyes flicked toward her and then away. "We still use a form of the Stamp Club from South Africa, but it's all ours now, and it is clearly out of the 1980s." He scuffed his shoe against the floor, adjusting the wobbly table, "You were so good at writing back at Camp Timothy."

She sat silently, eyebrows pressed together, thinking. "I'm not exactly a Bible scholar, though." Her post-college self had been much more confident in her knowledge than now. It seemed the longer she lived, the more she realized she needed to learn.

"The doctrine is all there; it just needs to be reworked. Like before, we don't want you to change the core of the course, but if you could update the presentation like you did before and write in current examples for today's youth, that would be huge.

"Plus, if you didn't want to move here, you could do the work remotely, but it would be easier if you were here because then we could have you fill any open hours with all the other things."

"Like?"

He grinned. "You know, cleaning toilets, back-up counselor, tutoring Jacobus, peeling potatoes... all the things."

She smiled then. "Well, I probably have the most experience in the first one."

"So, maybe you'll think about it?" He adjusted the table again and stood abruptly.

"OK," she responded quietly. "Just, I don't know, email me a description and terms."

"OK." He was looking down at her.

She glanced up, and their eyes collided before looking away again. She stood and went back to her suitcase. She knew he wanted to hug her goodbye, but she didn't want to confuse herself further with any physical contact. "Um, thanks for letting me stay here. Do you mind finding Darrin for me? Need to get on the road."

"Yes, ah, sure." There was a flash of disappointment in his eyes before he turned abruptly and walked out. But then he stopped and pivoted, his frame filling the door.

She stared at him, feeling the sadness vibrating between them.

He cleared his throat. "I'm so glad to see you again, Heidi. It's, well, it's miraculous, really."

Heidi nodded, her cheeks flushing.

"Can I please just—" Then, in a moment of decision, he took two swift strides toward her and hugged her to him. Just as quickly, he stepped back, holding her at arm's length, his hands gripping her shoulders. "I want to tell you before you go that based off everything Darrin says about you…."

Heidi's heart pounded against her ribs, and she knew her face was flushed. She wanted to throw herself back into his arms and never leave, but there was way too much to sort through. She needed distance and time.

"Anyway," he continued, "I wanted to tell you."

She saw her own uncertainty reflected in his eyes.

He looked away. "I think you're amazing." His voice was low and filled with meaning. Their eyes caught at the shared memory.

"You ready, Mom?" Darrin came in, flinging the door so it hit the wall and abruptly halted. "Oh wow—"

Johann and Heidi jumped apart.

"I'm ready." Heidi's cheeks burned. "Here," she zipped up her suitcase quickly, "you can carry this." Then she squeezed past Johann and turned to face him from the doorway. "Thank you for everything, Johann. I'm glad… well, it has been good to see you again."

And with that, she stepped into the daylight.

***

Darrin waved Heidi off and watched her car drive down the gravel road and disappear around the first curve. Something big had to have happened between John and his mom, and he needed to call Darla.

As if reading his mind, his phone buzzed.

"Darrin?"

"Darla!"

"What's going on?"

"I don't know, but Mom needs to probably tell us a few things."

"With the guy, John?"

"Yes, but she calls him Yo-hahn or something like that. I mean, Darla, I just came in, and I think they had been hugging or something, and Mom looked—"

"Looked what?"

"Don't interrupt! Sheesh. I don't know, man, but upset, you know. Wait, aren't you seeing her for lunch or dinner or something today?"

"She's supposed to stop in Gainesville whenever she comes through."

"OK, well, I suggest you start asking questions."

"You bet I will. I'm dying here."

"Gotta go, but tell me anything she says." He shut his phone and pocketed it before shaking his head and heading back towards the camp buildings. He could maybe get some information out of John, too, but he would have to tread lightly.

CHAPTER 31

The miles evaporated while Heidi considered Johann's offer. Her heart screamed yes, but her mind said no. Running back to Johann without careful thought was premature.

Darla had called her twice, intensely interested about her stay at camp. Years before, Heidi had determined the twins should never find out she had chosen them over Johann. They had dealt with enough hurdles. She had worked hard to instill in their hearts that it didn't matter how they came into the world; they were unique and created for God's purpose. She had reassured them countless times that God didn't make mistakes; they weren't an accident; their family was a blessing from God; it didn't matter what others said or thought. She worried if they realized she had chosen them over Johann, feelings of guilt and inadequacy might surface. Perhaps, as they got older, she could have told them about her time in South Africa, but it hadn't seemed important nor necessary to burden them.

She arrived in Gainesville, barely registering the intervening hours, anxious to see Darla.

"So, Mom, you guys actually dated?" Darla was relentless.

"Yes, Darla, I had boyfriends before I was your mom." Heidi looked up from her taco, struck anew by Darla's beauty.

"Why didn't you ever tell us about him then?"

Heidi sighed. "You guys were four when I came home."

Darla smiled and cocked her head. "Yeah, I see your point... so, how is he now?"

"Johann?"

"Darrin calls him John." Darla was clearly enjoying the interrogation.

"Yeah, I guess I need to start as well." Heidi tried to act nonchalant. "He's fine."

"Fine or," Darla batted her eyelashes, *"fiiiine."*

"I guess it depends on your viewpoint." The restaurant was warm and dimly lit; she hoped Darla couldn't see how flustered she felt.

"Mom, come on!" Darla reached across the table and grabbed her arms. "I mean, you haven't eaten, and you won't look me in the eye." She sat back then and crossed her arms. "I think you are still in love with him." She gave a satisfied nod.

"And I think you need to give the romance novels a break and read some textbooks instead." She signaled the waitress and asked for a to-go box. How had her first trips to see her kids backfired? Instead of two happy reunions, she had worried Darrin and played defense with Darla.

***

As soon as Heidi left, Darla called Darrin back.

"I've been thinking. Remember that ring we found?"

"Nope."

"Stop crunching in my ear; it's gross – remember we were in her room, and it dumped out of her drawer?"

"Maybe… were we like seven?"

"Yes! I found that ring box, and we opened it, and right then Mom came in and—"

"—yelled at us!" Darrin finished triumphantly.

"Yes! I swear, Darrin, I think she was engaged to him!"

"Nah, she was engaged to that other guy, remember? The guy Grandpa told us about."

"Yeah, but I thought she said she gave his ring back because he," she made a strangled sound, "reused it for the new girl or something."

"So, then, no ring."

"Darrin, you have to talk to John!"

"About what?" Darrin sounded worried now.

"Ask him if they were engaged!"

"No way," Darrin finished off his chips "you can ask Mom."

Darla sighed dramatically. "How are we going to find anything else out if we can't talk to them?"

"Well, I did hear he offered her a job…."

"What?"

"Yip!"

"Like, she would just pack up and go live in the boondocks?" Darla was incredulous.

"Who knows; besides, this place is cool. I don't think she's answered him about it yet, but some of the work she could do at home, so maybe—who knows. We could ask her that."

"Trust me, next time I talk to her." Darla paused, listening, "Please tell me you didn't just lick the chip bag—"

"I'm saving the environment, and gotta go."

"Wait! So, what're we doing?" Darla felt desperate.

"Nothing, I guess, unless you ask her about the job thing."

Darla disconnected the call, frustrated. There had to be a bigger story, and that ring had to be a clue. She would find a way to get the whole story on her next free weekend home. Besides, her mom deserved a man in her life, especially after sacrificing all those years raising them. Who better could it be than this guy John, an old flame?

CHAPTER 32

It was supposed to be a routine screening, but two hours later, she was still being screened. Heidi wiped her sweaty palms along the sides of her pants and sighed. After her mom had died of breast cancer, she had started routine testing but had always been clear. Now the mammograms were an inconvenience but not something she feared. If only her mom had been routine about her screenings, but she had always touted the lack of family history and allowed too much time to lapse. Until it was too late.

Heidi wished she could text somebody but didn't want to set off unnecessary panic. This morning her biggest concern had been what she should do with the job offer from Johann. And now, here she was, everything turned upside down. They had found a "cluster of calcifications" and wanted to do an advanced screen. Of course, it would necessitate additional payment. Did she want to go ahead? It took everything in her not to be sarcastic. She assumed saying, "No, I'd rather walk around and wonder if I'm going to die young like my mom did than spend more money," might be upsetting to all the other grey-gowned women sitting with her. So, she signed the form and waited.

How's it going, Mom?

Darla.

Having smashing time.

No need to text Darla that there would be extra smashing today and that the doctor was taking forever reading the advanced screen. She sighed and shifted in her seat, wanting to appear unconcerned. When she had been trying to figure out this next phase of life, dealing with breast cancer hadn't been one of the options. Did God seriously want her to go through more trauma? Why? She was still trying to adjust to the reality of this new phase of her life.

An employee came back into the room. They all wore black scrubs and carried clipboards, giving them an official but almost ominous look. The women being tested were in light grey wrap-around gowns. The gowns had three armholes, one for one arm and two for the other, and it took at least four tries to get one on. Heidi was well practiced now; she could get hers on in two attempts. When an employee entered the room, all the grey-clad women would look up expectantly. Heidi had already tried to lighten the mood with a "love everyone's outfits today" comment but aside from slight smiles, nobody took the bait and chatted. It seemed everyone was locked in their own "will-I-be-clear" worries. At this point, though, Heidi was past the joking stage. It also wasn't lost on her how much younger she was than all the other women.

"Heidi?"

Heidi glanced up and forced a smile.

The employee smiled back, "I'm going to take you to ultrasound now."

She tried to chat with the technician, who went from friendly to distant once she started studying the image on the screen. Heidi angled her head, trying to see what the technician was measuring. And there it was. A solid mass surrounded by ubiquitous grey. Her heart sank. The technician must have measured it from five angles and then stood abruptly.

"I'm going to give you a fresh towel, but you just stay there, and I'll get the doctor."

Heidi had never seen a doctor at her screenings. The doctors were always hidden in another room, reviewing films and sending messages via the technicians. Whatever was there had made her worthy of an actual visit from the doctor, in person. And that couldn't bode well.

Panic, anger, and bitterness converged at once. She was 37 and finally starting life again. Where was the fairness in this? But, as quickly as the anger came, she forcibly halted it. Wasn't she always telling the kids that God was in control, that He loved them and wanted what was best for them? That nothing happened that He wasn't aware of? So, now was the time to give Him the panic, fear, and anger. Now. Before she spiraled into an emotional wreck.

The doctor breezed in, dressed in the same black scrubs as the other employees. "I'm Doctor Harris, and you must be Heidi," she smiled.

"And you must be from South Africa." You couldn't live in a country for over a year and not pick up on the distinct form of British-without-the-sing-song that was solely South African.

"That was quick." The doctor straddled a stool and rolled towards Heidi on the table, taking the ultrasound wand in hand. "Most people guess England or Australia, first. Have you spent time in South Africa?"

"I lived there, and yes; I know some...." she trailed off as she watched the mass materialize on the screen again.

"We need to biopsy this. It's small." The doctor was all business now. "My nurse will set something up as soon as possible."

"How long 'til I get the results?"

"24-48 hours usually. Do you take blood thinners?"

"No."

"Good, the nurse will explain everything." She replaced the wand in its holder and scooted back. "Nice to meet you, Heidi." And she was gone.

The tech helped clean off the ultrasound goop and talked her through the process and where to meet the nurse after getting dressed. Heidi listened numbly as she followed her back down the hall to the dressing room. Other women were collecting their things, their "all-clear" faces evident. Not Heidi. She felt tears gather behind her eyes but refused to cry here. No sense in ruining their relief.

It wasn't until she was in the car with the AC cranked on high that she allowed herself a good cry. This was not supposed to happen yet. She was 37. She had done all her screens. She didn't eat soy. She didn't smoke. She exercised. She ate vegetables. She drank lots of water. She rarely drank from plastic bottles. She was supposed to be starting life again, not starting the breast cancer journey. Heaven knew how it had ended for her mom.

The phone interrupted her thoughts.

Darla.

"Mom?"

"Hey, Darla." She hadn't wanted to tell her yet. Darla would worry terribly. But ignoring the call would worry Darla more.

"Are you crying?"

"Well, I was just for a bit."

"Where are you?"

"Sitting in my car. I'm heading home."

"They found something." Darla's voice was flat. "I'm coming home tonight."

"No, my darling. You are staying right there and finishing summer session."

"I can just drive home and see you and come back tomorrow." Darla was insistent.

"I tell you what," Heidi paused, thinking how she could keep Darla from making this more significant than it was. "First, I have a biopsy, and *if* that comes back with bad news and *if* I have to have surgery, I'll want you to come home... not now."

"But – well, when is the biopsy?"

"In two days – Wednesday. And I'll get results by Friday."

"But I can come tomorrow night and be with you on Wednesday."

"Now is too early. We are not going to freak out or tell people. If the biopsy is bad news, then we can deal with that, and I will want you home. But not before, OK?"

Darla finally acquiesced, and Heidi skillfully guided the conversation to Darla's summer courses.

***

Darla wasn't stupid, and she didn't sit around when an event called for action. And this was the second major event in just a few days. She still hadn't acted on the John event, but now she needed to seriously act on the biopsy event. So, she did what she always did; she called Darrin.

"One of us needs to be there, and I know you are too far away. So, you think I just go even though she told me not to?"

"When is it?"

"Wednesday."

"Two days, that fast?"

"Yeah."

"Wait a second."

Darla heard the phone move while Darrin apparently muffled the receiver and spoke to someone nearby. The side conversation went on for longer than Darla had the patience for, so she snapped her phone closed, frustrated, and tried unsuccessfully to focus back on the economics homework in front of her.

An hour later, the phone rang again.

"Why'd you hang up on me?" Darrin sounded offended but apparently not enough to wait for an answer. "John wants to come – he says he has to meet a board member in West Palm and has to go down there anyway."

"You're kidding, right?"

"Nope. I told him Mom would freak out if he just showed up at our house, and guess what he said?"

"What?" Darla was incredulous.

"He said, and I quote: 'Your mom and I have a bit more of a history than she's letting on.'"

"No. Way."

"So, guess what I said?"

"What?"

"I asked, and you're going to be proud of me for this one: I asked if they used to be engaged!"

"You didn't!"

"Yip, I did. Score one for the team!"

"Well, what'd he say?"

"Oh, he waffled around about wanting to respect Mom's privacy and then asked if I'd help Alice keep an eye on Jacob and then went to call the board member because apparently there really is a board member in West Palm Beach, and that part is not a secret."

"Mom's going to freak."

"Yip – told him that. He said he'd schedule his meeting and stop and check on Mom, and if she gave him the cold shoulder, he'd take the hint and leave. Said he was going to drop off some Stamp Club materials for her – like he couldn't email or regular-mail them?"

"Well, you'd better try change his mind because Mom is not going to like a surprise visit from her Yo-Hawn or whatever she calls him."

"Too late."

"What do you mean?"

"He already left."

"No freaking way."

"Yes, freakin' way, and Mom doesn't like us to say 'freaking.'"

"OK, Darrin, but you better be freakin' prepared for Mom to go freakin' ballistic on both of us the next time she talks to us."

"OK, Darla, but I need to go do stuff with Jacob. He's a cool kid."

Darla rolled her eyes as the call disconnected.

***

The drive was good for Johann. It allowed him time and space to think without interruption. Camp life and parenting made for continual disruption, and he hadn't had unfettered time to think since Heidi's visit. He would stop when he was too tired to drive any farther and then get up early so he'd be there by mid-morning. From what he had been able to piece together, Heidi's last fifteen years had been one of strength and sacrifice. And she had done the majority of everything alone, losing first her mother and then her father. Now was his chance to be there for her. If she sent him away, he would wait for another opportunity and try again, and then again. Hopefully, her response wouldn't be like that first night at camp when they had briefly connected before she backed off. He didn't blame her, but she had revealed enough to him on the first night that gave him hope that showing up unannounced might not be as unwelcome as Darrin thought.

Plus, now that he was alone, he could admit he was scared to death. Heidi's mom had died from breast cancer. Granted, Heidi was only 37, but he assumed that things didn't bode well for Heidi if her own mom had died of the same disease. He couldn't fathom that God would bring her back into his life only to take her away. And Darrin and his sister had already lost so much. Surely God wouldn't do that to these kids, now that they seemed to be finding their way?

He took a deep breath and stretched against his seat belt. He had a long drive. He would pray and pray—that Heidi would be OK, that the twins wouldn't have to face more heartache, and that Heidi would accept his surprise visit.

CHAPTER 33

Heidi sat at the computer and watched videos of a needle biopsy. She still needed to straighten the house and then go to the beach and paddleboard and snorkel and enjoy this day. The nurse had told her no swimming, bathing, or arm exercising for five days post-biopsy, which eliminated everything she enjoyed.

In a moment of decision, she rolled her desk chair back and started getting her beach stuff together. She loaded her paddleboard into the back of her van, securing the trunk with a bungee cord.

Heidi smiled at her board hanging out the back, proud of how she had turned her van into a carry-all for many things over the years. Paddleboards were gaining popularity in South Florida, although they had apparently been in Hawaii for years. Heidi had stumbled onto the activity thanks to Darrin's past obsession with watching surfing videos. He had seen a video of someone paddleboarding and decided they needed it. After a lot of arm twisting, Heidi allowed the twins to purchase one, despite the cost. Curiously, she had taken to it more than them; standing up afforded a better view. Now, whenever they went out, the twins kayaked, and she paddled. People would often stop and ask her about it, and she was always happy to let them try.

Throwing a small cooler bag of snacks together, she slathered sunscreen on her face and was grabbing her hat when the doorbell rang. She paused, ready to ignore it, but the garage door was up with a paddleboard hanging out of her van, so it was apparent she was home. Of course, someone would come by now, right when the tide was perfect.

Sighing, she glanced through the front door peephole and jumped back.

Taking a breath, she stepped forward and peeked again,

convinced she'd made a mistake.

Johann.

His features were distorted by the view, but it was him. He kept readjusting his ball cap and turning his head from side to side as if someone were chasing him.

She stood, debating, her heart pounding. Why Johann was standing on her doorstep was beyond her, and there was only one way to find out. Taking another deep breath and straightening her shoulders, she swung the door wide.

"Johann!" She didn't know if she sounded welcoming, shocked, or angry, but it was too sudden of a surprise to temper her welcome into something amiable.

He opened his mouth to say something but shifted from side to side instead.

"What are you doing in Jupiter?" Could she possibly sound less friendly?

He stood there and said nothing, blinking at her.

Air conditioning poured out into the open.

"You want to come in?"

"*Ja,* sure…." He took off his ball cap, leaving a mass of dirty blonde hair sticking straight up in the front and at odd angles along the top. "And, hi, I guess." He grinned halfway and stepped into the house.

They stood in the entryway observing each other until Heidi broke the silence. "Why on *earth* are you here?"

"Oh, um, a board member lives south of here." He twisted his cap and ran his hand through his hair. "He's been wanting to meet in person for a long time." He shrugged. "So, I finally came, but I am, well, you live here, so, you know—"

Heidi waited, curious, not granting him any help. This was on him.

"—I decided to visit Jupiter for myself first." He squinted at her and then looked down at his twisted cap.

The irony. For years she had dreamed of a moment like this, and now he was here, but their lifetime of regrets and uncertainty made this far from her youthful daydreams.

"You heading to the beach?" he said.

She looked down at her surf shorts and rash guard. "Paddleboarding and snorkeling – best way to see Jupiter." She regarded him quizzically. "I was just leaving."

"You want a tourist for company? Uh, if that's OK. I don't have any gear… obviously."

"Um, sure?" What else could she say?

A spark of relief flashed in his eyes.

"We have all sorts of gear," she exhaled, relieved to turn away. "Come in, and I'll find you what you need."

As she rummaged through Darrin's closet, she could hear him in the main living area, undoubtedly looking at the pictures that hung everywhere. She came out and dumped an armload of surf shorts and towels and a couple snorkel and mask sets on the couch.

She showed him how to fit the masks to his face and then pointed to the bathroom so he could change. In the kitchen, she hurriedly added more water and snacks to her cooler bag. She had no idea what he liked anymore but assumed he was still a regular guy where food was food, and it didn't really matter.

She couldn't help staring as he stepped awkwardly into the kitchen. "Not a bad fit," she smiled. Sort of like you are wearing your kid's clothes, she wanted to add but left that part off. "Do you need real lunch first, or are snacks OK?"

"Whatever you packed is fine," he indicated the cooler bag and reached to take it from her. "After driving and sitting, I'm not hungry."

Heidi's mind was riddled with questions as they moved her paddleboard to the back of his truck and added a kayak for Johann.

Johann climbed up, clipped the bungee cords over the gear, and eyed the paddleboard warily. "What even is that thing?"

Heidi set the paddles in the truck bed. "It's called a paddleboard. Still somewhat of a novelty here, but I like it." She smiled slightly, imagining Johann wobbling on the board. "You can try it, but it takes a bit of balancing, so we'll start you in the kayak."

She felt so awkward and stilted. Why was he here? Had Darla told Darrin about her biopsy and Johann overheard? Was he planning on spending the night in town? Who was taking care of camp and Jacob?

"I'll drive." It was a statement.

He regarded her evenly and dug the keys out of his pocket. "You can drive a stick shift now?" He stopped, the shared memory in his eyes.

Their gaze locked, and Heidi knew she needed to break the moment before the intensity overwhelmed her. She took the keys from him and turned away, willing the avalanche of memories back behind the wall she had built the day she'd found out Johann had married Amy.

They set off in silence as her thoughts swirled chaotically, her senses unbearably aware of his proximity. With the impending biopsy and the shock of having him in Jupiter, it was as if her mouth had lost its ability to make conversation. She hoped the tension between them would soften into an easy camaraderie because she truly needed to enjoy the day. She felt equal parts irritated and thrilled. Each side warred until her mind was a complete jumble.

Johann, apparently sensing her discomfort, started asking direct questions. Where were they going? What was that body of water? Were there drawbridges all over Jupiter? Was traffic always this congested? What was her favorite beach?

The questioning worked and got Heidi talking; she explained that they would park along the Intracoastal Waterway, where they could launch the kayak and her board.

"Are you free all day?" She glanced over at him, grateful he seemed intrigued by her beautiful town. "Guess I should've asked that first because I plan on being out for a while."

"Oh – I don't have to meet with that man until tomorrow or Thursday."

Thursday. Today was Tuesday.

"Do you have a place to stay?"

"Not yet; it was a bit of a last-minute decision."

"I guess you could stay in my dad's studio out back if you like."

"Really?" He clearly hadn't expected such an easy solution.

She maneuvered into an open spot and put his truck in park. "Well, I think it should be fine, but I'll just be gone in the morning and might need to rest tomorrow." As she spoke, she silently cursed herself for the offer. Now he would find out about the biopsy. What if she was in pain, and it was obvious? "I have to have a minor procedure." She finished lamely.

He cleared his throat and reddened. "Um, Darrin mentioned that. I can drive you there and back, you know?"

"Darrin knows?" She was incredulous. Had they all conspired behind her back and sent Johann here on a pity trip?

He cleared his throat again. "Yes, Darla called Darrin, and I overheard and decided that since I have to be down here anyway, I could help out."

"You do know I'm having a *breast* biopsy, right?" She was staring straight at him. "You want to be here for me for a *breast* biopsy?" She got out of the truck and slammed the door. What was wrong with them? They had sent Johann here to help her through *this*? She and Johann were barely comfortable around each other as it was, and Johann seriously thought he'd drive her to the appointment? Afterward, he would be at her house while she walked around in discomfort and, for all she knew, holding her tender, sore breast. What were they thinking?

She fiddled unsuccessfully with the bungee cord until Johann came beside her, releasing it easily and opening the truck's tailgate.

"Look, I know you feel ambushed." He spoke quietly. "Darla said you told her not to come, Darrin was upset, and I need to be down here anyway."

She turned away. His tenderness made her want to cry.

He put a hand on her arm. "Look, Heidi, I'm here. The way I see it is you do everything yourself. From the things Darrin tells me, you are strong for everyone. You take care of everyone. It's time for somebody to be here for you." When she didn't turn, he went on. "I can drive you. I can buy you food and cook for you. I can do whatever you need. I won't get in your way or ask you embarrassing questions. I can also leave if that will make you more comfortable."

She turned then, considering, tears pooling behind her sunglasses.

"Is that OK?"

She looked out at the water, at war with herself, vacillating between anger and relief. She wouldn't be alone, after all. She hadn't even told Sierra, who wouldn't be happy once she found out she'd been kept in the dark. She had only told Darla because Darla had asked. Once she had the biopsy results, she could update people. But not now. Not when there was so much uncertainty and potential for drama. But the flip side of keeping this to herself was that she would have been alone, but not now, not with Johann here.

"Don't you think it's weird?" She couldn't help herself. It wasn't like they were close anymore or even knew each other. The intervening years were a lifetime.

"Maybe." He smiled. "How about we first please do your snorkel adventure? Then, afterwards, if you want me to leave, I can. You're in charge."

She nodded and slid the board out to him. It was too pretty a day to waste.

They put the kayak and paddleboard into the water, loaded their snorkel gear and the cooler bag, and set off towards the bridge called "Catos" by the locals; it spanned the Intracoastal and connected Jupiter Island to the mainland. The tide moved swiftly against them, but Heidi explained the incoming tide brought in clear water directly from the Atlantic Ocean, and their effort would be rewarded.

***

Once they neared the lighthouse point, they beached the kayak and paddleboard and grabbed the snorkel gear. Heidi attached the dive flag leash to her wrist and motioned for him to follow her.

"The current will be strong," she warned, "and once we go around the corner, it will want to take us the opposite direction." She pointed and gestured, clearly in her element. "Don't brush up against the rocks; the oysters and barnacles will cut you."

He figured he'd do what she said. This was her home turf, or rather, home surf, and he had never snorkeled before.

"Stick your face in the water, Johann!"

He did and immediately started choking.

"Breathe through the snorkel!"

Now she was getting downright bossy, but he did as he was told and couldn't believe what he saw. "There's fish everywhere!" His voice came out muffled and garbled through the snorkel, but Heidi gave him a thumbs up, clearly interpreting his excitement.

When they rounded the point, the current pulled them in the opposite direction, and they had to work to stay in place. But it was astonishing. He would look above the water's surface at the buildings across the water and the boats going by and then look down again. It was incredible what was underneath them, and nobody would know unless they put on a mask and swam right in this spot.

"What are the little black and yellow striped ones? There's so many!"

"Sergeant Majors: my favorite." She dove down and came up. "And those larger silver fish with the thin stripe are snook; people love to catch them." She continued, putting her head underwater and then popping up to give a running commentary: parrot fish, angel fish, needlefish, porkfish, the yellow-and-purple-highlighter beaugregory, bar jacks with their blue outline, and sheepshead. She kept talking and pointing, and, eventually, when the density of fish thinned out, Heidi had them turn around and fight the current back to the point where, once again, it split and took them toward her board and his kayak. Here was where the fish density was at its best, and Johann found he didn't know where to look first. Once again, they had to work to stay in their spot, but it was worth all the effort.

Finally, she motioned, and they swam back to the beached kayak and got out of the water, sitting on the edge of the sand.

"It's like swimming in an aquarium!" He was in awe. All his years at the beach in Uvongo, visiting and then living with his Aunt

Gillian, he had never seen something like this. The water there was too rough and dark.

She smiled at him. "Yes, never gets old."

"Do you come here a lot?"

"Well, you need the right tide, good weather, a weekday off because boat traffic is too high on the weekends, and a good time of day. Once you line up all those things, it only turns out to be a few times each summer." She smiled and looked around contentedly. "So, you managed to arrive on a perfect snorkel day."

He glanced towards boats going by, relieved she seemed glad for his presence, and marveled at where they were. "Where does that go?" He pointed east.

"That's the Jupiter Inlet, straight out to the Atlantic Ocean!" She grinned. "The twins and I have ridden all the way out, around the inlet to the beach. Not to be done on a weekend, though, and only when the ocean is super flat, there's very little wind, and the tide is outgoing. You can then paddle to a public beach, get out and walk across the road, and land up right where we parked. But it's a huge workout and, again, a rare day when everything lines up right; plus, it requires Darla or Darrin or somebody to help me tote my board overland."

"Incredible."

They paddled to another narrow strip of sand, where she declared they could rest and get a snack before she took him to one more spot.

"You going to let me try your stand-up board?"

Heidi was digging in the cooler bag and glanced over at him. "Have at it; I need a good laugh."

He pulled the board back into the water, cautiously stepped on it, and stood on bent legs. "How's this?" He propped his hands on his hips in a clumsy pose and promptly fell in.

"Awesome." She was laughing. "Why don't you try again?"

"*Ai-ja-jai*, you'd think certain people would appreciate...." He tried to climb back on, but it slipped from under him, and he fell again.

Heidi was now doubled over. "Maybe you should start on your knees first?"

"No need to patronize me; it's not called a knee-board," he grunted. Then he stood and held and turned to her with a victory punch as the tide carried him toward the bridge.

"'Bye," she waved, laughing again.

"You could bring me the paddle," he called.

She shook her head. "I'm resting. Come get it."

It felt so good to hear her laugh. It had been the right thing to come. She was still the same Heidi who was exhilarated by the outdoors and found fun in just about any situation. He got on his belly and surf-paddled back to her, grabbing the paddle. Then, he stood up again, knees bent and feet apart, and managed to paddle in place against the current.

"It's like an ocean treadmill," he joked.

She nodded. "Impressive that you're up, especially since you're probably at the weight limit for that board, and those things are impossible to balance once you pass the limit."

"Now she tells me." He laughed. "Here I thought I just had horrible balance, but it's the board's fault." He jumped off and pulled the board onto the sand sitting next to her. "This place is amazing, you know."

"Yes," she smiled, "I absolutely love it." She indicated the cooler bag, "There's snacks in there if you want something."

He reached for it and dug around. He couldn't believe he was here, in Florida, enjoying the outdoors, Heidi by his side. It felt surreal, especially since he had wished for this so badly after she had first left South Africa.

Heidi checked her watch. "We have less than an hour before the tide turns, so we'd better keep going."

"I'm not scared to paddle against the tide, you know," he teased.

"Yes, but the water won't be as clear, *you know*," she shot back.

"OK, Madam Tour Guide," he saluted. "Lead on!"

Heidi showed him how to attach the kayak's leash to his ankle and let it drift behind him as they snorkeled towards the bridge. He couldn't believe what they could see. All up and down the pilings, fish were everywhere. They even swam through a school of a million little fish that Heidi called "chummies." After the current carried them to the other side, he asked if they could drift through one more time. This was other-worldly, and he swore he could hear classical music playing to the cadence of the fish moving before him.

CHAPTER 34

That evening they sat on the beach eating takeout. Heidi maintained that she needed to make the most of the day with her upcoming stay-at-home order.

"You know, whatever happened with Darrin over spring break, I believe Camp Makarios and its leader reset his path." She dug her toes into the beach sand, her burrito only half eaten. She waited, hoping he'd take the bait and talk about it.

He tilted his head towards her. "I still keep forgetting he's your son."

"Because of his skin color?" She was instantly defensive.

"No, not at all. You know, I'm sorry again for sounding so shocked last week at camp. I was just trying to process everything, and it came out, I mean, it sounded like—" He gazed back towards the horizon, clearly appreciating the changing colors as the sun dipped in the sky. "Like I said, I guess because of the silence, I created my own narrative, and I was completely wrong. And also, in my mind, your twins stayed four-years-old throughout the years. Maybe they aged a little, but they never grew up."

"Ah," she was relieved. Then she turned to him; she had to know. "But could you tell when Darrin came at spring break that he was super angry? Or was it not obvious to you since you were leading the whole group?"

He leaned back in the beach chair and appeared to debate the answer. "I would have had to be blind to have missed Darrin's anger."

She angled herself closer towards him, watching his face. "But what on earth did you guys say to him that brought about the change? I had tried everything and prayed and gotten counsel but then in one week...."

He stood and reached out and offered his hand. "Let's walk, and I'll tell you my side of the story. How's that?"

She wrapped her uneaten food up, and they set off at a comfortable pace towards the inlet.

"Do you remember the night of the Pop Tart incident?" Johann began.

"You mean with Mavis?" Their lives had only overlapped for 18 months, yet it seemed they had created a lifetime of memories in that short space.

"*Ja*," he paused. "Do you remember telling me that we should have a camp for black children and teach them that God, their Heavenly Father, had created them uniquely for a purpose?"

"I think so, something like that."

"Well, I remember it clearly because your voice and logic stayed in my head and convicted me."

She looked at him in surprise and then waited, looking down, watching as their feet stepped through the sand in tandem.

"Well, I went back to my room and wrote it all down, and then, over time, I developed a Bible study of sorts." He sighed deeply. "Eventually, I presented it to Karl – by then, you were already gone."

"And?"

"Karl shut me down. He told me that having Americans work at the camp was detrimental to our way of life, and I needed to get such nonsense out of my head. That the government would close the camp or the other churches would hear about it and not allow their kids to come. I was so upset. I took all my work and put it in the back of my Bible and toed Karl's line once more." He stopped walking and turned towards her, taking both of her hands in his. "But Heidi, that's basically the study I used with your son on the second night of camp."

Heidi was stunned and opened her mouth to speak but couldn't form words.

"Don't you see Heidi?" He squeezed her hands gently. "The words I used to help your son ultimately came because of you."

Tears pricked her eyes. It was miraculous.

He pulled her to him and gently wrapped his arms around her. "And all that time, I never knew that Darrin was your son. It's beautiful, Heidi; it shows that God, our Master Conductor, is at work."

They stood in silence while Heidi absorbed what he had told her. Her tears were cleansing, and the fear of tomorrow washed away in the beauty of the realization that God truly was in control.

She stepped back and wiped her eyes. "I need to read it – or hear it. We tried everything with Darrin, and nothing worked."

Johann turned his head toward the horizon. "Ironically, though, you might have said the same things that I'd said, but his heart was ready to hear it that week at camp. For whatever reason, God brought Darrin to me for that specific objective."

They started walking again, slower this time as if the depth of their thoughts had slowed their steps.

"So, besides telling him that he was created in God's image for a purpose...."

Johann smiled. "And that God knew him before he was born."

"And?" Heidi had reiterated these thoughts to Darrin and Darla since they were four.

"I told him he couldn't fix the world, but he could focus on how he could improve his own circle."

"How would that have helped in South Africa?"

"Well, that was us, Heidi, doing what we could in small ways."

"I suppose," she said. But it didn't feel like enough. She took a deep breath and plowed ahead. "I know I've probably said this before: it's too simplistic."

"Why? What's wrong with simple?"

"Well, these problems are deep-rooted and are going to require a complete overhaul; in fact, I'm not sure how they can be fixed."

"So, we do nothing?"

"No, that's not what I meant – it just seems that oversimplifying solutions seems to nullify the profound complexity and injustice of the problem."

"Why? I'm not saying it's not a huge injustice; I'm saying *because* there's a huge injustice, we need to do something, anything. And right now, the something I can do is this."

"I hear you. It's just that –"

"No, listen, Heidi. If we throw our hands up and say, 'this is wrong, and there's nothing I can do so, oh well, glad it's not me,' then we are turning our backs on people we could help. But, if we look at our sphere of influence and make a difference there, then we have started somewhere. We can then pray for opportunities to widen our sphere, and at the same time, we can be an example to others and effect change."

He stopped, picked up a small handful of shells, and threw them into the ocean.

Heidi watched as the tiny circles rippled outward and then overlapped with other circles.

"That's what I told Darrin. I told him I couldn't fix the problem that he was facing, but together, we could improve our own circles of influence. I told him he could pray for God to widen his sphere – whether as a teacher or social worker or lawyer or politician or who knows what. But we could both start somewhere. And, what if we improved our circles of influence and other Christians improved theirs?"

Heidi waited; Johann had a point.

"Look, it's the principle of a seed. A tiny seed can become a tree, and what if your kindness is that seed? Like I said, I told him that his scope to improve his circle would increase as he got older. It's a prayer that God is waiting to answer – showing us how we can serve Him and do our part to right the wrongs that go on amongst us.

"I also told him he needed to 'pray for them that despitefully use you' like Jesus commanded in Matthew and Luke. We got stuck on that one because it's hard for all of us, especially if you have been mistreated."

"Did he agree?"

"It took a while," said Johann. "But then I told him to try it with one person, and I would, too, and then we would talk about it."

"You have a person?" Heidi laughed.

"Of course; we all do."

Heidi looked out to the darkened horizon and then nudged him. "Guess that's why I pray for you."

"Ha!" He punched her playfully on the arm. "I'll take whatever I can get."

They both laughed.

"So, and that was enough?"

Johann stopped and turned her towards him. "I need to show you the whole study. But that's it in a nutshell. Probably everything you always told him. Maybe it helped because I was someone new." He picked up a flat rock and threw it, watching it skip along the surface. "There was also an incident with another kid, which I thankfully saw, and long story short, I sent that bully home."

"Ah." She wanted to ask him to elaborate but then decided against it. Clearly, the timing of Johann's words and actions had been what her son had needed. And it was all a beautifully choreographed answer to prayer. She had Darrin back and would never stop being grateful.

**

The following morning Johann was on the patio when she got up.

"Sorry you had to wait out here, but I lost the outside key to this sliding door," she tried to smile but was afraid it looked more like a grimace. Everything felt weird.

"Just out here growing gills so I can breathe in your humidity," he joked.

She tried a smile again and then turned to fill the kettle. "Rooibos or caffeine?"

"Definitely caffeine."

She found her British PG Tips, the closest tasting tea to what they had in South Africa, and stuffed bagels into the four-slice toaster. They didn't say much as they ate and then drove in Johann's truck to the facility. Feeling uncomfortable, she wondered if she should have come alone.

They sat in the nearly empty waiting room. The first ones in, it appeared. The room smelled of coffee, and HGTV played on the TV. The same black-scrubs employees were moving about behind the counter. Heidi wondered vaguely why working at a desk necessitated scrubs and why they had to be black.

"Hey, you OK?" His concern was evident.

She hesitated and then nodded slightly.

He reached over and gently took her hand, his eyes scrutinizing her face for silent acquiescence.

Her hand in his felt so good; she felt the pressure of tears building.

"I'm going to be out here, praying for you, working on my computer, and praying some more."

"It should only be an hour."

"No matter, I have lots to work on." He squeezed her hand. "Thanks for letting me be here."

She nodded but didn't attempt to answer.

Once she was in a room, they explained the procedure – an ultrasound-guided core needle biopsy. She remembered the video; it should be quick and relatively painless.

But then they started.

"Goodness, you have dense tissue." That was the radiologist.

Maybe they needed to sharpen the needle because as the doctor used her weight to push it in, Heidi watched its slow progress to the targeted lump on screen. It felt like they were in a shoving match with Heidi's tissue. Thankfully her breast had numbed up well.

"I'm so sorry," the radiologist repeated for the third time.

"It's OK," Heidi managed, "just do what you need to do to get enough." Heidi had read that if the sample wasn't large enough, the pathology would come back undetermined, and a lumpectomy might be warranted. She was hopeful the lump would be negative, so avoiding surgery was her goal.

Eventually, after multiple tries and as many profuse apologies, the doctor moved her over to mammography. Heidi hadn't watched a video of this method and was shocked at what transpired. First, they secured her breast between two plates and then, after numbing her more, bored what resembled a steel pole into the top of her breast. She watched in morbid fascination, so numb that it didn't seem part of her.

"Don't look at it," the nurse cautioned.

Heidi assumed many who watched fainted. She listened as they turned on the vacuum and heard their relief as they stated they now had plenty of tissue.

After they dressed the wounds, they went over the instructions and warned her she would be sore over the next few days. Five days of no snorkeling or swimming; between two to five days of no arm exercises. All her favorite activities on hold.

"We'll get the results to you by tomorrow afternoon," they promised.

"You're very brave," someone else said.

"Super tough," another voice added.

Back in the dressing room, she struggled to get the prescribed sports bra on while holding onto the icepack they had handed her. She wasn't walking out with an ice pack stuffed in her bra, no matter what. All the adrenaline that had kept her going over the past – she checked her watch – two hours had waned. When she walked out and saw Johann, her remaining bravado evaporated.

He stood quickly.

"Let's get out of here," she mumbled.

Once in the car, she put her head in her hands and cried. "The doctor thinks it's cancer. I can tell."

Johann cranked the AC and then reached across to hug her.

"Careful." She put her arm protectively in front of her breast and then let him pull her into a hug.

"I'm sorry, Heidi."

"It was horrible. The videos were wrong."

"I'm so sorry."

"Have to ice it," she mumbled. "Just don't look." Then she

fumbled to position the ice pack between the gauze they had provided and her sports bra. She was mortified.

But Johann seemed to take it in stride as if it was the most normal thing in the world to be there in the car with a crying woman, ice stuffed in her bra, mumbling about how the videos were inaccurate and sugar-coated, how she was going to go home and lie on the couch all day and watch movies and that maybe today was a good day for him to visit his board member.

Johann responded soothingly to her mumbling and told her he'd get her home, settled and comfy, and then head down south. "But," he promised, "I'll be back to cook dinner."

"You cook now? You know *mieliepap* doesn't exist in this country, and, plus, I still hate it."

He laughed. "You haven't heard of grits? Closest thing, I think, and much easier."

She smiled. Now she was grateful again. Much better to have him here than Darla. Shielding Darla from unnecessary fear felt right. So, she leaned back and closed her eyes. Nothing about her life had gone according to plan, so she would be grateful for the unplanned illogical presence of Johann.

CHAPTER 35

"I'm sorry I can't be here when you get the results." Johann stood in the doorway, regret written on his face.

"It's fine – if you go, I can act as miserable as I feel." The attempted joke fell flat.

He reached out and squeezed her right shoulder, well versed by now on avoiding her left side. "Promise me you'll call and tell me what they say, please?"

She glanced away. These last two days had allowed him to get closer than she had intended.

"Heidi?" His voice was imploring.

"OK," she acquiesced. She didn't have the strength to fight what was between them. It was larger than her willpower.

"You're an incredible woman, Heidi," Johann stated. "And I still think you're amazing." And then, with one last meaningful look, he turned to leave.

Amazing. Every part of their 18 months together was marked in her mind and apparently in his, too. Heidi stood there absorbing his words and tender look. It was a salve to her soul. She would savor the feeling and hold it close.

***

The day stretched endlessly. Heidi wandered the house vacillating between fear of the phone call and dissecting Johann's visit. It both appalled and astonished her how easily they had fallen back into a comfortable camaraderie. She knew they would get closer even faster if she could forget he had married Amy. But that barrier remained insurmountable.

It was a good thing he had left. She needed to protect her heart. Completely.

Heidi sighed and then sat back on the couch, careful not to jostle anything. According to what she had read, biopsy recovery shouldn't be this painful. But then, she hadn't exactly had a typical biopsy experience. She was already bruising, her breast a grotesque mix of yellow and purple and black. She carefully slid another ice pack into place and positioned her arm onto a pillow. Grabbing the remote with her free hand, she clicked through the TV Guide, hoping to find something to fill the intervening hours.

Nothing. Plus, she needed to call Sierra. Sierra would be horrified that she hadn't filled her in on any of the details; she owed her a phone call. But not today. Today she needed to wait and hope and watch the clock alone so that only her day was ruined in the waiting – nobody else's.

But then Darrin called. And Darla. And Johann, who was still driving. Obviously, their days were also ruined by the waiting. She tried her best to chat with the twins about her snorkel trip with Johann, but that appeared to be a bad idea because they asked more questions for every bit of information she shared. It was inevitable that she tell them everything. They weren't four anymore, and they needed to know the story. Wondering about unknown events could make them grow bigger in the mind than they actually were. The imagination was strange, which was why the phone needed to ring.

She needed to do something, but her mind was a jumble— complete confusion. She couldn't seem to hold a thought long enough to execute anything to completion. She walked into the kitchen, noting the half-emptied dishwasher and her uneaten lunch on the counter. The paper towel roll was empty, and the trash was too full. But lifting the bag was out of the question. Sighing, she went back to the couch. Everything would have to wait.

"Heidi? I'm coming in!" Sierra entered the living room carrying what smelled like brownies made in heaven. "Girl, you don't believe in locking your front door?"

Heidi looked up, guilty. Of course, Sierra was here. She couldn't hide anything from her dearest friend.

Sierra set the brownies in the kitchen and walked back to the couch, hands on her hips. "Anything you want to tell me?" She eyed the icepack protruding from Heidi's shirt. "That thing needs changing. Hand it here."

Meekly, Heidi acquiesced.

"Now, you drinking milk or having tea or what? We need sustenance because this is going to be a super long conversation."

"Tea."

Sierra eventually returned with a loaded tray and gave Heidi one of her fake stern looks.

And they talked and talked. Heidi told her about the trip to Camp Makarios, about seeing Johann again, about the job offer, about finding out she had a lump and needing a biopsy, about Johann's surprise visit, about her emotional bewilderment over the whole thing, over having a lump, over the family health history. She alternated between crying and talking. And Sierra simply listened, offering her tissues or brownies or more tea or whatever that part of the conversation required.

When Heidi was finished, she felt spent but relieved.

"Wow," Sierra said for probably the hundredth time. "And when is this doctor supposed to call?"

"After four... this is the slowest day of my entire life."

"Yeah, we need to go for a drive."

Heidi shook her head no. "I gave them my cell phone number too, but I bet they will use the house phone, and I don't want to miss the call."

"Well, I have two movies with me."

"Two movies? Seriously?" And this was why Heidi loved Sierra so much.

"Yip." With a flair, she pulled first one, then the other out, "*Wedding Singer...* or *Princess Bride.*"

They watched *The Princess Bride* and were laughing hysterically when the phone pierced through the reprieve.

Sierra instantly hit pause while Heidi grabbed the phone.

"It's cancer."

Two words. And everything shifted.

She looked at Sierra, anguish in her eyes. No words were needed; Sierra held her.

HEIDI SAT AT the kitchen table, staring across the still house. Her entire body pulsed with each heartbeat as if her heart had gotten stronger and louder. It just wasn't right. She had the history, but she was so much younger than her mom had been. She could feel herself sweating and knew she needed to let the kids know. But if she held onto it for a while, she could delay the inevitable.

Then she remembered her promise to Johann. She held her phone, debating, but it rang before she could text him. It was the surgeon's office. Did she have any appointments they needed to work around? No, she didn't. She needed them to get this thing out of her. As soon as possible. Maybe they hired the kindest, most soft-spoken people on the planet – it must be part of the job description – because the nurse promised they would get her in the next day for a consult.

She wanted to wait, wait until she had news from the surgeon and a plan in place. Then she would tell everyone, and they'd be saved the awful uncertainty of what lay ahead. But while she stared at the phone, justifying her delay, it rang.

Darla.

"Mom?" She sounded young and scared.

Heidi swallowed. She needed to be strong and upbeat. "Hey, sweetie."

"Did you find out?"

"Yes."

Silence.

"I'm coming home, and you aren't going to tell me not to."

"Oh, honey, just wait until daylight, at least."

"I'm coming right now. Oh, and call Darrin. I'll see you in four hours."

The phone clicked off. Heidi looked at it numbly and punched in the numbers for Darrin.

CHAPTER 36

On Friday, she awoke with anticipation and climbed carefully out of bed. Today she should see the surgeon and get a plan. Darla had arrived in good time, and they had hugged and talked and cried long into the night.

Grabbing her cordless phone in case the doctor called, she went into the bathroom and inspected her breast. The black and yellow had spread, and now red dots of varying sizes scattered across the area. She saw the disgust on her face and shook her head, wanting to dispel the image. Turning, she placed her phone carefully next to the shower, well within reach in case the doctor called.

By 10 am, she was beside herself. Why hadn't they called? She finally gave in and called them herself.

"Oh, I'm sorry, but we are waiting for the rest of your pathology," was the receptionist's reply to her query.

"But someone said they'd get me in today." She tried her best to tone down the rising panic. Where was the lady from yesterday?

"Yes, but we don't have the receptor pathology back yet, so seeing the surgeon today would be pointless."

"Can I just at least come in and ask her some questions?" Heidi hated the whininess she heard in her own voice.

"No, but as soon as we get the receptor data, we will get you in the same day," the lady promised.

"OK, can you at least tell me what the report says – the part that you have?" Her desperation for information was making her sweat.

"Um, well, I'll have to ask the nurse."

"Look, just read me what it's called. I want to come in for my appointment with some information in my head. My mom died of breast cancer, you know." Heidi hated to play that card, but for goodness' sake, these were her own records.

There was a pause and then a hurried, "invasive ductal carcinoma."

She hung up the phone slowly. Same type as her mom. It sounded so ominous but was apparently what 80% of all breast cancers were labeled. But her mom's had metastasized by the time they caught it. The radiologist had told Heidi hers was still small. Too small to have metastasized? She hoped so.

She saw movement to her side and looked up to see Darla watching from the hallway.

"Hey, sweetie," she managed.

Darla came to her then and hugged her carefully. "Did they tell you more bad news?"

Heidi absorbed the feeling of this adult child in her arms, realizing afresh how much she missed her. "No, I mean, nothing really, just have to wait and," she gave a short laugh, "you and I don't like to wait."

" 'course we don't." Darla's voice was muffled against Heidi's shoulder. She stood back. "Did you eat breakfast yet?"

Heidi tilted her head. "About three hours ago."

"Well, I'm going to eat something and then go rent us some great movies." She looked at Heidi hopefully.

Great – Darla's idea of a movie was an everything-works-out romance where everyone lands up with the perfect person in under 90 minutes. "What if you have some friends over later, or we go eat at the beach? We can just, you know, enjoy this day and while we wait, keep this topic 'taboob.'" She air quoted the words and hoped Darla would find it funny. It would do Heidi good to have the house noisy with youth.

Darla sprang into action, and Heidi smiled as she watched.

Darrin had been much quieter in his response. It upset her.

"Can you tell Johann for me?" She really didn't want to get emotional and strengthen their connection. His sympathy would make her cry.

"Is it OK if you tell him?" Darrin paused. "He's right here."

Heidi heard the phone changing hands.

"Heidi?"

"Yes." Her heart sank. She couldn't do this. She should've waited to call them.

"They told you it was positive?"

"Yes."

"I'm sorry."

"Me too." She paused, hoping he'd fill in the silence, but there was nothing. "I was supposed to see a surgeon today, but they don't have all the pathology back yet." Still quiet. "I wanted to call after I had a plan but sounds like it'll take a while."

"I'm sorry I'm not there."

"Well, it'd be kind of boring. Can't snorkel."

"Still, I'm sorry I'm not there."

She could hear someone calling him in the background.

"Look, I need to go. Can I please phone you back?"

"OK."

The door slammed; Darla had left on her mission.

Heidi glanced out at the dreary weather and began straightening the house, trying to distract herself, trying not to think of the ramifications… but then she couldn't. Nothing could stop the flood of thoughts and emotions.

Why now?

The sobs came from a deep place, a place she never knew existed. What was her life? A series of intense awful disappointments and tragedies? A sick game of "whack-a-mole" where just as she emerged from another catastrophe, whack! Down came the next disaster. Was there never to be a "normal?"

Why? Why did disappointment and tragedy have to follow disappointment and tragedy? She was 37 and had weathered more storms than most people twice her age. When would it be enough? Would the day come that she no longer had the energy or desire to poke her head out of the hole? It all felt so pointless. Maybe that day was now. Maybe she was done trying, done recovering from the Next Big Terrible Thing.

The phone rang, and she ignored its shrill pronouncement until a voice spoke through the answering machine. "Heidi, pick up." Then a pause. "I know you're there." Another pause. "Heidi, please."

She held the phone and hesitated.

"Heidi, pick up, please!"

She hit the accept button. "I'm here," was her dull response.

"Oh, Heidi, talk to me, please talk to me. Are you still alone?"

"Darla is here, but she went out."

"Talk to me; just tell me everything you are thinking." His voice was anxiety-ridden.

"Well," she took a deep breath, "I hope whoever the kids' father was, he had good genes." There. He would wish he hadn't asked her to talk.

"OK," his voice was soft, encouraging her to continue.

"Because our genes stink."

Johann was waiting for more, so she went on. He had asked her to talk, and the words couldn't come out fast enough. "My mom died of breast cancer, the twins' mom died of nobody really knows but maybe postpartum depression, my dad died of a heart attack, I don't have the emotional ability to recognize true love or keep a fiancé, who knows how my grandparents died because I don't even remember them because they died so young, so I just hope the genes from the mystery side are a heck of a lot stronger than the horror genes from my side." She sucked in a breath and went on. "But how would we know because we have no idea who the mystery side is. For all we know, that side is worse than ours. Probably alcoholism and who knows what else. So, we can't get peace of mind from that. And I have to get the twins genetically tested and maybe mental health screened and make sure they hopefully never drink, and my life is just a series of horrible, awful things and—" She held the phone away from her, covering the speaker, as the sobs came afresh.

"Don't hang up on me! Just keep talking or cry as long as you need. Just please don't hang up. Please. Promise me."

"K."

Eventually, Johann spoke again. "You still there?"

"Yes."

"Listen, you have the twins, but whether you want me or not, you have me, too. You don't have to do this by yourself. I'll come whenever I can; I'll talk to you every day. You can tell me everything the doctors say. Use me as your sounding board. Whatever you need."

"Johann, I...." how could she tell him that she couldn't handle the pressure of dating or getting past all their barriers?

"Listen, I understand." He paused, and she could tell he was choosing his words carefully. "I'm your friend, Heidi. I care about you. That's all it has to be. I just want you to know that another adult who cares for you will be there for you. Zero strings attached. Can I do that for you? Please?"

Heidi took a deep, shaky breath.

"Just a gift of friendship, just let me help you and be there for you. Please?"

"But I get the feeling, I mean I worry, you know...."

"I know, Heidi."

Even after all this time, he understood.

"I guess it's obvious," he continued, "that I would like more than friendship, but I understand that now is not the time. And, regarding all that, you can take as long as you need, OK?"

"Yes... OK."

The relief in his voice was palpable. "OK, then we are going to start with you promising to call me and rant and rave whenever you want."

"I'm sorry...."

"No! I'm your person, Heidi. Do not apologize. Let me be your safe place to say what you want."

And with that, a piece of light pierced the landscape of her mind.

CHAPTER 37

Five endless days passed before she saw the surgeon. According to her friends, her timeline was happening much faster than others, but, to Heidi, it felt painstakingly slow. In her opinion, if you found a cancerous lump, you sent a person to surgery and got it out. As soon as possible. What was the point in discussing it and waiting and protocol? It was cancer, so it didn't belong in her breast. They needed to remove it. Yesterday.

By the fourth day, she was ready to come unglued. She had called their office Monday midmorning and asked again for a copy of her records.

"Oh, Heidi Richmond, right?" The receptionist sounded quite chipper for Monday morning in a breast cancer office.

"Yes."

"I just printed off the remainder of your results!"

"OK, so does that mean I can see the surgeon today?"

"The doctor will have to look them over, and then they will try see you sometime this week."

"Sometime this *week*?" What had happened to the same-day service she'd initially been promised?

She got off the phone and started calling other surgeons' offices. Then she contacted a few friends who knew doctors. And then, she realized that she was rushing around, trying to force something and probably complicating matters further. She reminded herself of Isaiah 50:11,

Behold all ye that kindle a fire and compass yourselves about with sparks...

She was running around starting fires when something was already in the works with apparently the best surgeon in town.

With resolve, she got up from her desk and called Johann. She needed a distraction.

"Hey, you want to send me that curriculum after all?"

"Seriously?"

"Yes – going to go crazy sitting here thinking. Maybe some good old work will help me." She laughed nervously.

"In that case, I have plenty – just a minute."

She could hear muffled talking in the background, and then he was back.

"Alice is getting the files ready, and we'll send them off soon," he promised.

"Sooner the better."

"Uh, we can't pay right now, though."

"All the better. I can tell myself I'm volunteering for the greater good." She tried to force cheerfulness.

"Hey, it's OK."

"Don't be so nice."

"I'm not. I can be very, very mean... I seem to remember being called a 'meanie' once by a certain American girl...."

"Ha."

Within the hour, they had sent the first batch of files with instructions and suggestions. By the evening, she had modified and emailed back the first lesson asking for feedback. She couldn't believe how therapeutic losing herself in writing had been. With a renewed sense of purpose, she went into the kitchen to find something to eat when her phone rang.

"It's perfect." It was Johann. "I knew you were exactly what we needed!"

Heidi's heart warmed. It felt good to be needed, useful, and distracted.

"So, I can go on to the next lesson?"

Johann laughed, "You can finish the entire first section. We love it. Darrin is particularly impressed, I might add."

"Always important to keep impressing your kids. Gets harder as they get older."

CHAPTER 38

The surgeon carefully explained that Heidi's cancer was hormone positive. That meant they could do a lumpectomy and radiation afterward, and then she would start a hormone blocker called Tamoxifen. The success rate was high—apparently over 90%. The way to prevent it from ever returning was to block what had fed the tumor—her hormones. But blocking her hormones meant pregnancy, at least for the foreseeable future, was out of the question.

Not that she was planning on getting pregnant, but if she and Johann ever married—

Instantly she tried to halt the progression of her wayward thoughts. She wasn't going to marry Johann. She wasn't going to marry anyone. So, she wasn't going to get pregnant... but what if?

She called her nurse navigator, who said it was probably not safe to get pregnant while on Tamoxifen and that treatment was for five years.

42

She would be 42 before she could safely have her first child—if she married or even wanted to start that late. But her mom had died at 52. Did she want to potentially leave a child motherless at age nine or ten? The nurse also said she could stop the Tamoxifen, get pregnant, have the baby, and then go back on the Tamoxifen once more but also warned her that women on Tamoxifen sometimes took longer to get pregnant.

The solution was obvious: she needed to stop thinking of becoming pregnant. She felt embarrassed she had even brought it up. The nurse must think her crazy. Who asked about pregnancy when they were not even dating? She had Darla and Darrin. If she eventually worked at camp, she could pour her heart and soul into

309

the lives of the children that came through the camp.

Yet the feeling nagged. She didn't like feeling the option of childbirth had been taken from her. She felt boxed in, claustrophobic. Just a few short days ago, the opportunities had been limitless, and now, everything had changed.

They scheduled her surgery for the first week of August, three weeks away. That seemed way too long of a wait. Cancer was in her, growing. Surely the doctor must be wrong. Surely every extra day they waited gave it a chance to get bigger and for a rogue cell to get out, go into her bloodstream, and....

She wouldn't finish the thought, but what her conscious brain refused to acknowledge, her subconscious wreaked havoc with her in sleep. She had nightmares of sneaky cells getting out and growing massive tumors all over her body. She would wake up in a sweat, only to fall asleep and dream again. After a particularly bad night of dreams, she called the doctor's office again, begging them to move up her surgery. The receptionist and nurse navigator stayed calm, reassuring her. No, three weeks was not too long to wait. No, her danger of metastasis was not increasing every day.

Heidi did her best to stay as busy as possible. She cleaned out the house, worked on the curriculum, and took long beach walks. She spoke with Darla and Darrin whenever they were free and had almost daily chats with Johann. She and Sierra managed to get together more often than usual, and she volunteered to help with her church's Vacation Bible School. The busier she was, the better she did. But by far, the best part of the day was her chat with Johann. They would discuss the curriculum and her progress, and then they would just talk. About everything. And slowly, Heidi felt her wall of distrust diminishing. Slowly she dared to wonder if they had a future.

Together.

CHAPTER 39

Two days before surgery, she opened her door first to Darla, then to Darrin, Johann, and Jacob. Sierra had apparently known all along. Camp had ended for the summer the last week of July, Darla had two weeks off before fall term started, and everyone wanted to be there for Heidi. After three weeks of loneliness and enforcing constant busyness, their presence was a blessing. At first, she was a bit miffed to have been kept out of the loop, but she knew that the chaos would be good for her, even though she worried about how well she'd do with a houseful of people once the surgery happened. But she was fully capable of speaking up for herself, so for now, she'd simply go with the flow.

Johann and Jacob made themselves at home in her dad's studio even though Johann offered multiple times that they could get a hotel. Heidi wouldn't hear of it. She had so much space, too much space lately, so it felt good to have it used. Although indignant at their overtly cleaned-out rooms, Darla and Darrin were thrilled to be home. And within a few hours, teenagers rang the doorbell searching for both of them. The happy chaos was a welcome reprieve from the fear of the upcoming surgery. The laughter drowned out thoughts of clear margins, lymph node involvement, the fear of radiation with the possibility of chemo, and the question of ever having a baby.

The day before surgery, they all went to the beach. It was the season of scorching hot sand but flat crystal blue water. She had Darrin stop with Jacob to buy him a mask that would fit him, and then they all converged at Coral Cove beach, eventually joined by Sierra and her kids. Three beach umbrellas stood in a row, with chairs and bags placed strategically in the shade. Johann had loaded the paddleboard and kayaks into his truck and brought them down to the beach. By the time they were all set up, it looked like they had

311

moved a small country. Instantly they were all in the water, snorkeling and floating, laughing and talking.

To Heidi, it was magnificent. Here were all her favorite people at her favorite place. She swam out, pulled herself onto a recently freed kayak, and grinned from person to person. The day couldn't get any better. Darrin was teaching Jacob how to snorkel. Darla was laid out on the paddleboard, yelling at the boys whenever they splashed her. Sierra was now up on the beach, tending to the wayward umbrellas that insisted on turning inside out whenever the breeze picked up, laughing like it was the funniest thing in the world.

"Hey." Johann popped his head up next to her kayak.

"Hey yourself," she smiled back.

"You want company?" She could feel his scrutiny

"Nope, this is a one-person kayak."

"Aww, you're no fun," he joked back, splashing her.

"Dad! Put your head in the water; there's fish everywhere." Jacob was right there, ducking his head and gasping for air.

"Breathe through the snorkel," Darrin laughed.

Later, Heidi sat on the beach with Sierra.

"You doing OK, my friend?"

"Right now? Yes."

"Now you're still letting me be there tomorrow, right? Or have you changed your mind and decided maybe that a certain hunk-of-a-man would be better?"

Heidi blushed. "Actually, I've asked him not to come. You and Darla are who I want. This is breast surgery, after all. It was bad enough that he brought me to my biopsy, but the surgery is a whole 'nother level, and I just keep picturing him seeing me in my – well, you know. He was strictly relegated to the waiting room at the biopsy, but for surgery, they let one person back for the pre-op and part of post-op. That's got to be someone who can see anything and not be horrified."

"Yeah... but maybe waking up to that handsome face would be preferable to me... just saying."

"Sierra!" Heidi hit her arm playfully. "You've got to stop!

Besides, I mentally went 'round and 'round about everyone being here anyhow, but the timing worked out for the camp, and you know, the chaos is good for me – especially now. Plus," and she nudged her friend, "it's not like I got much say-so in the matter. I definitely don't need to be overthinking. And we have my dad's studio, so Johann can stay far away when I'm completely out of commission."

"Yeah, I'm sure he plans on keeping himself far, far away. Especially since he drove eleven hours to be here."

"Sierra!"

"Why're you yelling at Sierra, Mom?" Darla plopped herself on the sand next to Heidi.

"Oh, she's trying me, Darla, she's just trying me," Heidi laughed.

The women continued talking, and Heidi found herself withdrawing, simply content to sit there and enjoy this day, this moment. Watching Darrin coach Jacob along as he snorkeled, trying not to watch Johann and admit to herself how good it felt to have him here, enjoying Sierra and her kids, and relishing in the sun and salt and sand and happiness. Because today was what you had. Tomorrow would be challenging and filled with fear and uncertainty, but right now was perfect, and she would enjoy every last nuance of its perfection.

THAT NIGHT, TIRED and sunburnt, they all sat around the dining room table. The kids kept plying her with more food, saying she'd need to be super full since she couldn't eat after midnight. It was downright comical. Dinner stretched on into dessert and then coffee, and then snacks. Eventually, Jacob fell asleep on the couch, but the grownups stayed around the table.

"So...." Darla was shooting Darrin meaningful looks.

"Yeah, so...." Darrin chimed in.

Uh-oh. Heidi knew what was coming.

"You guys going to tell us the whole story now or what?" That was Darla.

Heidi looked over at Johann hurriedly. He held her eyes. "You

OK with that, Heidi?"

"Mm, maybe?" She wasn't sure. Their past had been a secret for so long that it would be difficult for her to give it all up, lay her feelings on the table, and wonder how her kids would respond. She thought carefully. "I just want you guys to promise that no matter what we say, it's a story from the past, and the past is over, so there's no sense in feeling bad or guilty about it."

"Why would we feel guilty?" That was Darrin.

Johann glanced at Heidi and then tried. "I think your mom is trying to tell you that even though she left South Africa, she came back because you were that important. We don't want either of you to feel guilty for that."

"You were four," Heidi quickly added. "You were going to be my very own children. And I couldn't let anything stand in the way of that. So," and she looked pointedly at both of them, "we will tell you the whole story if you promise me that you won't feel guilty. At all."

"Geez, Mom, we're good." That was Darrin again.

But Darla was more perceptive. "Wait, you guys broke up – and it's obvious you *were* dating – so you could come back for us?"

Johann jumped in, "Well, we didn't break up; we were going to try and make it work. That was the plan." And he reached over and squeezed Heidi's arm. "It just seems that the plan got thwarted by, uh, circumstance." He was looking at her now, his eyes boring into hers.

"OK, then, we're good," Darla looked over at Darrin, who nodded in agreement. "No misplaced guilt or whatever, just *please* tell us the story already."

So, they did, tag-teaming each other as they recounted Heidi's 18 months in South Africa. At one point, Heidi paused the story to get "visual aids," as she called it. She returned with an envelope of photographs and a painting and laid them on the table.

Johann raised his eyebrows. "You still have it?"

"Of course, I couldn't throw it away! I just couldn't have it out; the memories were too—" She shrugged.

Darla picked up the painting. "Where is this?"

"Camp Timothy. That was my favorite view, and Johann had it painted for me."

"Wow, guys." Darla set the painting down and then picked up the photographs, scooting close to Darrin so he could see them, too.

Heidi looked at Johann, a sheen of tears blurring her view. There they were in the photos, at Oribi Gorge, sitting at camp at the eating area making plans, and at God's Window, standing on the ledge, their faces filled with hope and promise.

"Wow, you guys are so young, and your hair, Mom!" That was Darrin.

"Darrin!" That was Darla. "Flat irons probably didn't exist in the eighties. Where were these photos all this time?"

"In my drawer."

Darla looked over at Darrin. Evidently, they hadn't dug around enough when they were kids.

"So, keep talking. Clearly, there's a lot to say!"

They had the twins laughing and Darla oohing and ahhing at all the appropriate moments. When they got to the part about Christmas in Uvongo, Darla was dreamy-eyed. And, when they told of their engagement, she clapped. But the end of the story was more subdued, and when they were finally finished talking, there was silence.

"Wow, guys." Darrin was the first to speak.

"What are you guys going to do now?" Darla was close to tears.

Heidi suspected that the combination of everyone's fears over the upcoming surgery was making emotions run higher than they ordinarily would have. "We're just going to get to know each other again and get on the other side of this surgery, I guess." She looked to Johann for affirmation, and he nodded thoughtfully, squeezing her shoulder.

"But who do you think made up that letter about you being married, Mom?"

Heidi looked over at Johann again, and he shook his head.

"We have no idea," he said.

"But you must have some idea?" Darla looked back at her mom. "It wouldn't have been Grandpa, would it?"

"Why Grandpa?" Heidi was shocked. She privately suspected it was Karl. He was the only person remotely capable of doing such a thing. But her dad or Vera? Not a chance. But Johann respected Karl so much that there was no point in bringing up her thoughts.

"Well, maybe since Grandma had died and he wanted to make sure you stayed here...."

"I can't imagine Grandpa doing that. But that's the thing, we really can't imagine anyone faking a letter and, it appears, hiding our letters to keep us apart."

"We'll probably never know," Johann added quietly. "But you know," he said, "I've thought a lot about it since Heidi showed up at camp last month, and I've realized that God is our ultimate Master Conductor. Regardless of how people might mess things up for us, He is ultimately in charge. And that gives me peace."

There was silence as everyone absorbed his words.

"There's just one more thing," Darrin finally said, obviously worn out from all the serious talking.

Everyone looked up quizzically.

"I think Mom needs more ice cream. She only has an hour left to eat!"

Eventually, now well after midnight, everyone headed to bed. Darla promised her alarm was set for the early morning ride to the hospital. Darrin promised his was not set because he needed to sleep in, and Johann quietly admitted his was set so he could start praying.

Heidi went into her room and stood before the mirror, examining her breasts. How different would they look afterward? Would it matter one day to Johann if – she corrected herself quickly – she ended up marrying him? Would she be two different sizes? Would she look different in her clothes? Would she have to wear a pad or mini prosthesis to balance things?

Why was she standing here agonizing over appearances? The bigger question was, had the cancer stayed contained? Were her lymph nodes involved? Her mom's cancer wasn't found until she had metastasized. Why hadn't Heidi made sure her mom was getting screened? Had she even known about mammograms when she was twenty, though? Had breast cancer even entered her thoughts or been part of any conversation related to anyone she had known?

And so it continued, question after unanswered question, as she got ready for bed and climbed wearily under the covers. Eventually, after an hour of tossing and turning, she headed out to the kitchen to pour herself some water, then remembered she was not allowed to eat or drink. She turned, noticing Johann on the chaise lounge with the studio door ajar, reading with a book light.

Quietly she slid open the patio slider and whispered, "What are you doing up?"

"Couldn't sleep."

She walked out and stood next to him. "What book is that?"

"Something of your dad's, maybe? A World War II book, but I can't follow."

Heidi nodded. The night felt endless.

Johann shifted over, "You want to sit with me?"

"Sure." She sat carefully, wanting to keep a bit of space between them, but he put his arm around her and drew her close.

"Relax, sweet lady. I'm not going to bite."

"Never said you would." Her head was against his chest, and it felt so natural.

"It's going to be OK, you know."

"Which part?" She couldn't help it. Was he talking about her surgery or them or their past or their children or the fact that her mom had died from this or the possibility of chemo or...? She couldn't finish the thought.

"All of the parts, Heidi. Just relax. Sit here with me and let your mind rest."

"OK." She would try, at least.

"Do you want to talk about tomorrow?"

"Not really." She was tired of her brain rehashing everything. She definitely didn't want to continue the thoughts out loud, not now, with the surgery only a few hours away.

317

"I'm glad you have those photos, Heidi. I burned mine; I told you that, right?"

"Yes... I understand completely. You were doing right by Amy."

"But seeing them tonight... wow... what we had was incredible, wasn't it?"

"Probably why I broke it off before I got engaged to a third guy." She gave a short laugh.

"Seriously? When was that?"

"The twins were eleven. He was a great guy. I just realized I didn't love him as much as I'd loved you. So, I figured never mind...."

"Wow."

They were both quiet then, processing. Johann set the book on the table next to him. "How about I tell you a cool bedtime story, then?"

"Sure, only if there's a happy ending."

"I'm still working on the ending...." And he proceeded to tell her all the details leading up to the camp purchase in North Carolina. How his Aunt Gillian had managed its purchase. His voice rumbled on, quiet and steady, the cadence lulling Heidi into a restful state.

Eventually, the questions stopped circling, her breathing evened, and she fell into a peaceful sleep.

***

Johann kept talking. He knew the longer he spoke, the greater the possibility he could distract her from everything that must be filling her mind. He knew she was asleep when he felt her melt against him. But he kept talking, more and more softly, hoping she would stay asleep. Once he was sure she was sleeping, he said things he didn't dare tell her yet: how he didn't need to get to know her again as she had stated earlier, how he didn't need to know the outcome of the surgery to make a decision about them. Because he loved her, with his whole heart. He loved her even more than he had in those photographs. He had always loved her, even when he shouldn't have. Now he wanted nothing more than for them to finally be together. He would be there for her, no matter what happened. And then, as fatigue swept over him, he gently kissed the top of her head and gave in to sleep himself.

CHAPTER 40

"Mom?"

Heidi stared up at Darla, disoriented. She carefully slid out from under Johann's arm and swung her legs over the edge of the chaise. "I'm awake," she whispered. "Thanks, honey." She wondered how Darla felt about finding her next to Johann, but the fear In Darla's eyes was palpable and probably had nothing to do with Johann. Heidi wanted to reach out and tell her everything would be fine, but empty words were useless.

She looked back at the sleeping Johann and sighed. He must be exhausted because he hadn't even stirred. She stood slowly and slipped into the house. Today was her D-day, and it was time to get moving.

Sierra came and picked her and Darla up promptly at 6:30. The sun was just rising, and the Florida sky already showed streaks of pink and lavender, making Heidi wish they could detour to the beach to watch it in all its splendor. Sierra had music playing softly on the radio, and the atmosphere was quiet but cozy. Heidi closed her eyes, her mind replaying the few hours before, of Johann knowing how to calm her mind and let her sleep. She felt enveloped with care and love. Here in the car was the calming presence of the best friend anyone could ever ask for and the sweetest daughter. Heidi reached behind the seat, taking Darla's hand, wanting to communicate comfort and love.

The drive was short, and soon they found themselves in a waiting room answering questions and filling out more forms.

In no time, they came to take her back.

"Can Sierra go with you?" Suddenly Darla sounded so young.

"Of course, honey. That's a perfect plan. You sit here and try not to worry, though, OK?" And she hugged her daughter, willing the tears to stay back. She pulled away and cupped Darla's face. "You don't have to be strong for me, honey, because God's got us both."

Tears slipped down Darla's cheeks as she nodded.

"I'll be right back once they got your mom in dreamland, OK?" Sierra squeezed Darla's hand and then turned towards Heidi. "We better follow our leader," she joked, casting a sidelong glance at the scrub-wearing employee waiting impatiently at the door.

After they had asked Heidi fifty more questions, inserted her IV, asked her more questions, and drawn on the correct breast, they wheeled her away from Sierra, which was the last thing she remembered.

WAKING UP WAS so hard to do. That was the overwhelming thought on her mind as she heard someone calling her name repeatedly. And now they wanted her to breathe. Well, for waking her up from the deepest sleep of her life, she would refuse to comply. That would serve them right!

"Heidi, Heidi, I said, breathe! Take a breath!"

She didn't feel like breathing for such a bossy person.

Something slipped over her face, and she felt oxygen pour into her nostrils. It felt so good. She'd breathe that. This is what she'd been missing all her life. Pure oxygen. Who knew?

"There you go," the voice sounded relieved. "Now you need to wake up."

She fluttered her eyes and tried to focus. If she complied for a moment, would they leave her alone?

"There you are," the nurse smiled. "You've been asleep for a long time."

Heidi grimaced and thought. There was a very important question she needed to ask. Then she would go back to sleep. She closed her eyes; what was that question?

"No, no, no, stay awake. Talk to me, Heidi."

Heidi opened her eyes wearily. She needed to think of that question. Something about her breast. Oh yes! Her eyes opened wider. "Did they get all of it?"

"Yes, my dear. Clear margins."

"My, uh, my lymph nodes?"

"Clear lymph nodes."

"Thank goodness." Now she could go back to sleep. She was going to be OK. She remembered that this scenario meant a high percentage of success if she did all the things, whatever they had said they were. She closed her eyes gratefully and drifted back off.

When she woke once more again, there was Sierra. "I hear you're too good of a sleeper, Heidi!"

"I got clean margins and no lymph nodes."

"You mean clear lymph nodes?"

"Sure."

"If you can stay awake long enough, they can give us instructions, and we can take you home, you know."

"What time is it?"

"It's nearly noon."

"How?"

"The beauty of sleep, my dear." That was the nurse again. "You able to listen to my instructions?"

Heidi pointed at Sierra with her eyes. "Tell her; she's smart."

Sierra laughed. "Good job, Heidi. Maybe we should sedate you more often."

The nurse smiled and put the discharge papers on the bed. "You've got to follow all of these."

Heidi barely listened, nodding at what she hoped were appropriate times so they could leave. Then she could go home and sleep.

***

Johann had spent the morning corralling the boys into cleaning. He wanted Heidi to come home to a perfectly straight house. Jacob thought it was great fun, but primarily due to his amusement at Darrin's grumbling.

"She didn't leave us here to be maids, you know," Darrin said.

Jacob, from then on, kept calling Darrin a beautiful maid, leading to impromptu wrestling matches and frustration from Johann.

He knew he was irritable and needed to stop, but he was so worried about Heidi and wanted to be there, by her side. If only she had let him come to the hospital, if only they were married, so it would be obvious he should be the one at the hospital. But he wasn't there, so he needed to whip the house and the boys into shape. Eventually, he gave up and sent Darrin and Jacob to get groceries. He would make Heidi's favorite stew, Mavis's stew, or as close to it as possible with what he still thought to be sub-par American ingredients. He missed so many basic South African foods – the breads, cheeses, the *boerewors*. He sighed.

With the boys out of the way, he made quick work of the house and the beach laundry from the day before. Then, once the boys returned, he set to work with the meal hoping it would turn out close to what Heidi had liked all those years ago. He had no idea if she would even want to eat, but he could try.

"Any news?" Darrin was at the counter, watching him work and alternately poking Jacob in the ribs.

"Nope."

Darrin sighed. "Why's it taking so long?"

"I don't know." Johann looked over at Darrin earnestly. "But you know Sierra or Darla will phone us as soon as they know something."

As if on cue, the house phone rang, and Darrin picked it up.

Johann stood by impatiently while Darrin nodded and said "uh-huh" multiple times until Johann wanted to grab the phone from him.

"Best case scenario! It wasn't in her lymph nodes, and they got good clean margins." And Darrin stepped around the counter, high-fived Johann, and hugged him and Jacob.

"So, she's better now?" Jacob obviously hadn't thought she seemed sick to start with.

"Well, she'll have to recover, but it means we all got excellent news," Johann replied. "Thank God."

It wasn't long before he heard Sierra's car pull into the drive. He rushed outside, ready to carry her if need be, but she seemed steady enough to walk herself. She was clearly loopy and embarrassed by her appearance, so he stepped back and let the ladies take care of her, hovering outside her door with Darrin and Jacob while they helped her into bed.

"You guys can go in, you know," Sierra was at the door. "I have to head on home, but Darla is here, and I'm sure in no time Heidi will be letting you all know what she needs." Then she stepped past Johann, hugged Darrin and Jacob, and was gone.

Johann wasn't so sure. He would wait and let her have time with her kids, and then he'd see her.

Later, Darla found him in the kitchen. "Mom says she smells African stew or something and wants to know if you'll bring her some."

That was precisely what he'd been waiting for. Darla showed him where the trays and napkins were, and he served up a small bowl of the stew. Then she smiled at him reassuringly as if she knew how nervous he felt.

Quietly he entered the room, setting the tray on her bedside table and sitting carefully on the edge of the bed. "Hey," he whispered softly.

She was on her right side, her eyes half open, a discarded icepack next to her, which he picked up and moved to the table.

"Hey."

"I made you Mavis's stew."

"Smells delicious." She was clearly drugged.

"You want to try some?"

"Yes."

He gingerly helped her to a sitting position, propping the pillows around her, scared to death he'd bump her surgery sites, knowing that they had also cut out eight lymph nodes from her armpit area.

"Johann?" She was looking at him earnestly.

"Yes?"

"I'm glad you're here."

He felt himself relax. He could quit feeling awkward and out of place. "You want to try eat?"

"Starving. Best question anyone's asked me all day."

He carefully set the tray on her lap and watched as she took a small bite.

"Delicious." And she closed her eyes, leaned her head back, and sighed gratefully.

His heart warmed. He was with his Heidi, and she was going to be fine. The news today couldn't have been better. He would make sure he was there for her through the recovery, and perhaps, one day soon, she would be willing to let the past go and love him again.

CHAPTER 41

The post-surgery days passed in a blur. Darla had to help her dress; she couldn't get the wrap tight enough across her breasts by herself. It mortified her, but Darla was unfazed.

"We're just girls, Mom," Darla said. "You changed my diapers, so now I change your boob wrap." This would make them laugh, every time.

It was a relief to eventually take a shower. By the third day, Heidi weaned herself from the prescription pain meds. She was tired of the fog they created and wanted to engage with everyone again.

They had created a spot for her on the couch, propped by pillows with a table of drinks and books and the TV remotes – not that there was ever enough quiet to do much reading. But she loved the activity around her, and the days passed quickly. She was the luckiest invalid around.

Darrin took Jacob to all his favorite boyhood spots – the turtle place, the parks with the best climbing trees, the beach, or over to Sierra's to hang with Tony and the boys. Darla kept mothering Heidi with all the sweet care she could offer. And Johann, well, Johann kept everything running. It amazed Heidi, but then it shouldn't. He was used to running camps with tons of kids; why wouldn't he be able to run her house?

Her surgical follow-up was the following day, and then the boys would head out, followed by Darla a week later. The thought depressed Heidi. She did not want to be alone. Unfortunately, she couldn't even start radiation until she had fully healed, which would be at least three more weeks. What would she do for three weeks alone and only partially functional? She wasn't supposed to use her left arm; they said no grocery shopping, vacuuming, or lifting. They made it sound like a vacation but to Heidi, being helpless equaled frustration, not relaxation.

"Heidi?"

"Mom?"

She glanced around. She wasn't sure when everyone had materialized, but apparently, they were waiting for her response.

"I'm sorry, I was daydreaming."

Darrin was the first to speak up. "We all think you should come back to camp with us."

"But Darla is home for another week." Heidi looked over at Darla questioningly.

"I would come, too. John says we could stay together in the guest cabin."

"I can bring your breakfast!" Jacob was bouncing excitedly.

But Heidi focused on Darla. "Is that what you want?" She knew Darla had been excited to be home and see her friends; instead, she had spent most of her time at home.

"Of course! I've got to see the place you all talk about all the time. I'll just pack for school when we leave, and then I can get back to Gainesville before classes start without having to come home again." Darla had it all figured out.

Heidi looked from one to the other, assessing their hopeful faces. "How would I get back to start radiation?"

"I would drive you to Gainesville, and Darla would bring you the rest of the way home, or we could fly you home if you are allowed to fly," said Johann.

Heidi thought for a moment and said, "Well, that settles it then. Let's start packing for Maggie Valley." And she pumped the air with her good arm while everyone cheered as relief washed through her. She wouldn't be alone after all.

***

The ride to camp was utterly therapeutic. Johann drove his truck, and Darrin and Darla alternated driving Darla's car. They kept rotating who was in which vehicle, keeping the entertainment level high. Heidi studiously avoided being alone with Johann the entire trip until they got to Asheville. With only an hour left, she let her guard down and found herself with only him as they entered the prettiest part of the drive.

He looked over and smiled at her. "If I didn't know any better, I'd say you had been avoiding me the whole drive."

"Maybe I remember another drive to camp about fifteen years ago?"

"Oh, the one where I was super friendly?"

"Definitely the friendliest drive of my life."

Johann laughed uproariously. "I was exceedingly horrible, wasn't I?" Then he reached over and took her hand. "I was remembering other drives, actually."

Heidi blushed but didn't comment. What could she say? There were too many good memories. And besides, her hand felt good in his. She rolled her shoulders carefully, wondering when the scar sites would quit hurting, and then leaned back and gazed out at the scenery flashing by. This was a good moment. Her hand in Johann's, her surgery behind them, music playing in the background, and the Smokies beckoning.

"Do you still hurt a lot?"

"Yes," she responded. "Kind of surprising. Thought it would feel better by now."

"Where does it hurt the most?" Then he reddened, as if realizing what he had asked.

"If you must know, my armpit," she laughed self-consciously.

"Did they tell you to expect that?"

"Nope." She thought a moment. "I think I was so relieved I could have the more minor surgery that I expected it to be an easy recovery. I mean, since my diagnosis, I've read blogs by people who had mastectomies, and those sound so awful. My mom had one, but my brain must not have been turned on or something. And nobody really talks much about a lumpectomy, though, and the general consensus is you dodged a major bomb, so it surely can't be that bad. All I can think is, if I hurt this much, how much worse the other must be. And, if this is the best-case breast cancer scenario and is this much pain and work and effort and endless doctor's visits, I can't even imagine what my mom went through. And I was there, you know. I was there after her surgery, and I guess I just didn't get it."

"Sometimes I think we subconsciously block ourselves from realizing the depths of someone else's pain, though. Sort of like a defense mechanism so that we can handle what's going on." He squeezed her hand, then released it so he could grip the wheel through the upcoming turns.

"But she was my mom. Shouldn't I have been more aware?"

"You were grieving, Heidi." He glanced briefly at her as if for assurance. "And you were suddenly cast in the role of mother of two four-year-olds who couldn't begin to understand what was happening around them."

She let his words settle. Johann understood.

"They didn't even know me when I got back. I had become the face in a picture, the random voice on a few phone calls, and someone they knew of but no longer knew. The first time my dad left to take my mom to chemo, they cried their hearts out. I was an imposter, a virtual stranger."

"Wow." He took the turn off the highway towards US-19. "No wonder you didn't realize the depths of your mom's pain, Heidi."

She stared unseeing at the passing scenery. "You do realize that if my mom died from it at 52 and I got it at 37 that even though this first scenario is the best case, the future is incredibly uncertain for me, right?" She watched as he gripped the wheel more tightly and cursed herself inwardly for voicing this fear out loud now, now when the day had been so full of fun and good, of camaraderie and togetherness.

"That's not a problem for me, Heidi. Besides, the percentages they gave you are very positive and, knowing you, you will do everything the doctors say." He glanced quickly in her direction. "Anyway, I want you to know that I'm here. Here for you. In whatever capacity you want me to be. As little or as much. From here on out, Heidi. That's my promise to you." He glanced over again. "Heidi?"

"OK." She wasn't sure how else to respond. She wanted to say more, to thank him, but then she would cry. And crying wasn't meant for today.

CHAPTER 42

They quickly found a routine at camp. Heidi set a slower pace but was able to work on the curriculum from the second day back. Alice started by having breakfast delivered to her room, but Heidi gently put a stop to that. Alice was busy enough with managing the kitchen and much of the office work, too. Bill, her husband, managed maintenance and took care of accounting, so Heidi did her best to pick up as much office work as possible. Even though the camp hired extra seasonal workers, the turnover was high. Someone had to keep it all rolling, and it appeared Bill was that person. Johann liked to employ both young people and retirees to give them opportunities. He said the young people needed a chance at a first job and the retirees, who were summering in the Smokies, often needed something extra to give them purpose. Many retirees would work as volunteers, which helped the budget, but Bill was the man who made it all work. Heidi told Bill she had never met a handyman accountant who could manage people so well, and he explained that the extreme variety kept him from getting bored.

Darla loved Camp Makarios and was in awe of the Counting Tree. If Heidi couldn't find her, she would invariably be at the tree.

"It's so beautiful how each of these chimes, or whatever you call them, tells its own story: of a life changed, of a kid going back home with a new purpose. What a cool place."

Heidi nodded. Darla got it.

"The meaning of the name is cool, too."

Heidi looked over, surprised. "Oh, who told you?"

Darla winked, "I know Greek."

"Since when?"

"Just kidding, Mom. I can look things up. Camp Thankful—I like it."

Heidi smiled. Johann had changed the name after the purchase was complete.

"Everything about this place makes me want to stay here and work and forget about school."

"I don't think so, young lady. Get your degree first, and then come back if you want. Come on all your breaks, too, but stick with your degree."

"Double standard, huh, Mom?" Her voice was joking.

"You have academic gifts that can't be ignored, for which you should be '*makarios*.'" Heidi winked as Darla rolled her eyes. "You'll end up more fulfilled if you grow those gifts." Heidi thought a moment. "Eventually, Darrin will have to figure out the best way to position himself, but we both know this is the right place for him for now." She reached out to hug Darla and winced at the stiffness in her left arm. It felt stuck against her side.

Darla noticed, too. "Are you allowed to start stretching that arm?"

"I don't think so. They warned me about lymphedema—you know, it getting swollen permanently—so much that I'm scared to use it at all."

"Maybe you should call them, then. I just think if you don't use it at all, it's going to make things worse."

"How'd you get so smart? Maybe we switch your major to physical therapy or something?"

"Nah, but I do know that a swimming area is calling my name. You allowed to swim yet?"

"I'll wade around. That water is way too cold for me."

***

The three weeks went by too quickly, and before Heidi knew it, it was time to head home and face radiation. She was in the office getting plenty of the curriculum materials to bring home when Johann came to the door.

"Don't take too much home, Heidi. We want you to come back."

She smiled. She hadn't told him that this was her plan.

"In fact, I was just talking with Bill, and some gift money came in, and we have enough to pay you through Christmas if you would consider coming back. I honestly wonder if Bill now finds you so indispensable that he just reallocated money from somewhere else to get you on board. If the food trucks stop half their deliveries, or the cars start running out of petrol, or the generators quit working, the truth will come out."

"Speaking of cars, we should've brought my car; I could've driven myself home. I'm doing so well." Aside from her left arm, that is. But Johann didn't need to know about that. She'd be seeing doctors non-stop for the next month. Someone would know what to do about her stuck arm. She sighed. Her complete genetic testing and thus long-term treatment plan was still on hold. They hadn't even told her for sure yet if she would need chemo. The slow decision-making made her crazy.

"Oh no." And he wagged his finger at her. "We've been so busy. This drive is the perfect opportunity to finally get you to myself for once." His eyes were questioning as if to ask if her avoidance was by design or default.

Heidi turned away so he wouldn't see the blush stealing up her neck. She was still unsure about them, but the closer she let him get, the closer she wanted him to be.

CHAPTER 43

The overwhelming and utter exhaustion from radiation was more of a surprise than the difficult surgery recovery. The women Heidi met daily in the waiting room would come in before they went to work, but she would go straight home and sleep for two hours. She barely worked on the curriculum and was so fatigued she kept forgetting basic things: like asking about her arm or remembering to take Tamoxifen.

She had waited to start Tamoxifen until after she was home from camp in case of side effects. But once she had been on it a few days, she noticed she was uncharacteristically irritable and depressed. At first, she hoped it was from being alone, but the feelings continued, and she was worried. She didn't want to be on medicine which made her want to grump or feel sad about everything. Maybe forgetting to take it was a subconscious defense mechanism.

Finally, at her first oncology care visit, she mentioned both the arm pain and the emotions to the doctor. Immediately the doctor picked her arm up and felt along the underside.

"Aha! You have cording. For some reason, it happens more often in our thinner patients. We don't know why."

"Cording?"

"See this cord-like thing here? Put your right hand right here and feel."

Heidi felt a rope-like structure deep under her skin.

"Feels like a cord, right? It's scar tissue. It will worsen if we don't get you in physical therapy." She explained that the scar tissue could prevent full range of motion. Heidi had followed the "no lymphedema" rules too religiously.

Regarding the Tamoxifen, the doctor cautioned her to stay on it. It was part of the success protocol that could prevent a recurrence.

"Could I take half a dose?"

"Half is better than none, but there is no good data on a half dose. Why don't you keep up the full dose and see if you adjust mentally?"

Heidi agreed. So now she had physical therapy three times a week and radiation five days a week. Between it all, she cried and napped. The situation was less than ideal. Sierra suggested they have nap parties, so she could come over and sleep, too. Her household was still so busy that naps were rare. Thank goodness for Sierra; she was Heidi's rock.

The radiation tanned one side of Heidi's skin at first. But then, the tan turned to irritated redness, and, despite the lotion they gave her, the irritation increased as time went on. This was all apparently "normal" and one more mark against her so-called "best case scenario breast cancer." She scoffed inwardly, thinking back to when she believed that removing a lump from her breast was just one step beyond removing a basal skin cancer.

But despite the fatigue, skin irritation, and physical therapy, she was intensely grateful for the ability to come home and sleep. And she found that as the days went on, she was adjusting emotionally to the Tamoxifen. If she felt blue, she would tell herself it was from the medication, which seemed to take the edge off.

Thankfully, there were the phone calls. Nearly every day, she spoke with at least one of the twins, and Johann was sure to call, even though it was often late at night. She would sit out on the chaise lounge and talk with him, remembering how he had calmed her and coaxed her to sleep the night before her surgery. She cherished the memory and their talks which ran from camp and family to radiation and physical therapy; they talked of everything but themselves.

On the last day of radiation, she also graduated from physical therapy by swinging her left arm fully over her head with barely any pain. The therapist handed her a daily list of exercises. That night, Heidi met Sierra for a celebratory and a goodbye dinner. Heidi had decided to return to work at camp until Christmas, and the time with Sierra was important. Of everyone in Jupiter, she would miss Sierra the most. But Sierra was selfless in her encouragement and promised she would visit with her family.

The drive back to the mountains this time was so different. Her pain was barely noticeable, and her spirit felt light. And even though her raw skin was still irritated, she was no longer hunched over and afraid of bumpy roads. She turned the radio up and sang and prayed her way to Gainesville, hardly noticing the passing time.

It was so good to hug Darla again. Phone calls couldn't replace holding her precious daughter. They talked a mile a minute over a quick lunch, and Heidi proudly swung her left arm around and showed her how she could wave her left hand from all angles without pain. And then, after more hugs and promises to talk soon, Heidi was on the road again so she could get into the mountains before dark.

When she was about two hours away, Darrin called. "Stop at the Asheville Wendy's, Mom," he said.

"I'm still an hour away from Asheville, and I wasn't going to eat 'til I got to camp."

"Stop anyway," he insisted.

So, she stopped and walked in, only to be met by Bill and Alice and, of course, Johann.

"Guys!" She hugged them all happily, hanging onto Johann for an extra moment, amazed at her overwhelming joy at seeing him again. "How'd you know I'd be here now?"

"Darla phoned as soon as you left Gainesville," Johann laughed, "and we added the hours. When Darrin called and told you to stop here, we knew we had timed it right and left right away. So now, I'm going to ride with you, and Bill and Alice are going to – wait, where did you say you were going?"

"Oh, family for the night," Bill smiled at Alice.

Heidi wondered if the couple were simply intent on playing matchmaker, but she was glad she could ride the last hour with company. Weariness had set in, and the darkening skies and winding roads made her nervous.

Johann insisted on driving and, after sliding the seat back, looked over at Heidi and grinned. "Surprised?"

"Yes, and glad. I was getting tired."

"We wondered. Even Bill and Alice were worried about you. We hatched the plan this afternoon, and I honestly don't think they have family anywhere near here but are planning on just having a night away." He winked. "They deserve a break. I told them to take tomorrow, too. We don't have campers until Friday evening, so that will also give you time to get settled before the next wave of crazy!"

He said it with such gusto that Heidi laughed. "Only someone who makes crazy sound wonderful could run a camp." She smiled wider. This was perfect. She could relax and enjoy the end of the drive without gripping the steering wheel in fear.

"You know, I was thinking this afternoon how many times I've driven you to and from a camp." His voice carried a smile. "So many times. I guess that's our thing. One day when we're old and people ask us what we liked to do, I can just say, I liked to drive Heidi to my camps."

She felt ridiculously happy and laughed again.

"How are you feeling? How's your skin?"

"Red, irritated, and angry with me, but I'm done with all that, thank goodness. And look, I can move my arm now!"

"Why don't you demonstrate how far it stretches by putting it around me?" He teased.

"Like this?" And she stretched her arm around his wide shoulders and leaned her head against his shoulder. "It's terrific to see you, you know."

The light turned red, and he quickly leaned sideways to pull her into a full hug. "You too, Heidi. I missed you so much."

A car honked behind them, and they both laughed, remembering.

The drive ended too fast, but they were met by an overjoyed Jacob and an excited Darrin. It felt like a homecoming, and she only wished Darla was there.

"Let's show her now!" Jacob looked like a jack-in-a-box.

"This way, Mom." Darrin steered her away from the guest room that had been hers the last two visits, down a path towards Alice and Bill's house. They stopped in front of a small cabin.

"Here we are!" Johann proclaimed. "Figured if you were going to live here, we would have to improve your accommodations."

Heidi stepped into the tiny cabin in awe. It appeared freshly refurbished and was private, set back from the other camp structures, yet close enough to Alice and Bill that it wasn't isolated. "Was this here all along?"

"Well, sort of," Darrin explained. "It was mostly used for storage, but it did have plumbing already, so as soon as you left, Johann, Bill, and I started renovating it. Plus, we had lots of help from two retired volunteers. Look, you have a little kitchen," and he opened a door, "and a bathroom and the water even comes out fast enough to actually shower here," and he slid open another door, "and a closet—and look, even a study area, so you don't have to sit on the bed to do your work."

Johann was looking around the space proudly. "We needed the guest cabin for visiting speakers, and it really wasn't a good long-term solution since it's right in the middle of things. The way to survive camp long term is to have your own space."

"This is—I'm just—wow." Tears filled her eyes.

"Look, Heidi, I made you pictures!" Jacob pulled her along, showing her welcome pictures he had drawn and put on the desk.

She hugged his little frame to her without reservation. This boy, this miniature of Amy's spirit, was a joy. Then she hugged Darrin, thrilled to be with one of her twins again, and turned to Johann. But her emotions were too high. She was scared if she hugged him now, she would break down and wouldn't want to let go. So, instead, she asked if they could unpack her car because she couldn't wait to get settled.

CHAPTER 44

Heidi woke each day with anticipation. Camp work gave her purpose and was the perfect transition for physical and mental healing. Her little cabin provided her the space to recharge for the chaotic camp days. It also gave her a chance to analyze her feelings towards Johann. She knew she could love him again and realized she probably already did, but reticence kept her captive.

Instead, she maintained just enough distance so that their friendship and camaraderie grew without, she hoped, any romantic undertones. Occasionally, she would catch him looking at her earnestly. Still, she steeled her heart against the feelings knowing if she gave in to them, she'd be hopelessly out of control and unable to think clearly and logically. Thankfully, he kept his promise and didn't push her, and she, in turn, gave all she had to the work at hand.

The Stamp Club curriculum was coming together, and when she found herself tired from writing, she would help Bill in the office or Alice in the kitchen. Once in a while, they needed her as a backup counselor, but mostly she stayed behind the scenes. This suited her right now. The breast cancer ordeal had left her emotionally raw, and she missed her former energy. Intellectually, she knew she was on the other side of her trial, but emotionally she still struggled. She supposed she needed time. The more distant the event, the more confident she would feel in the positive post-surgery numbers. In the meantime, she would focus on regaining physical strength. When they had no campers, she would take short hikes with Darrin or Alice and sometimes Johann if they could get away together. She needed exertion, and the physical activity boosted her well-being.

Then there was Jacob, mischievous little Jacob, whom she loved unreservedly. He would sit in the common area at night struggling with his homework, and she would invariably wind up next to him, doing the work alongside him, remembering the days of helping Darrin through his.

"I wish you were my teacher," he grumbled one evening,

erasing a hole into his math paper.

"I'm your nighttime teacher, so let's go copy this paper before it's destroyed and try again, young man." She wished she could burn the offending paper; the poor kid had had enough.

"Everything OK here?" Johann looked at Jacob as if to say he had better straighten himself up.

"Yes, we are just having a bit of a fight with a math paper. Do you mind copying this for us while Jacob and I hit the ping pong ball a bit?"

Johann took the paper from her, looking like he wanted to argue that she was being too soft on his son, but she simply smiled her thanks and hurried to catch up to Jacob, who was already bouncing the ball on the table.

"OK, every time we hit the ball, we count by fours."

"Noooo, Heidi. I thought we were playing."

"We are playing. And counting by fours. Let's see how high we can get."

"You can't argue with Mom, Jacob." Darrin laughed. "I trained her too well."

***

Frustration filled Johann's mind. He had Heidi here, and every day she did more and more to endear herself to him. She was the best thing for Jacobus, the best thing for him. But still, she held him at a distance. He copied the paper and threw away the original, hoping the teacher would accept the copy. Sighing, he studied the page – Jacobus still had so much left to do – and carried it back into the common area. Another night would end without any time alone with Heidi. Maybe he needed to quit being so patient; maybe some of the other women who had been interested in him would jolt her into making a decision. The team from Raleigh was coming soon, but he didn't think Sue would be in the group. As quickly as the thought had come, shame hit. He headed towards the table, his heart heavy.

And Jacobus was now counting by fives, chuckling with Heidi and Darrin. She was a miracle worker with kids, his Heidi. He only wished someone would work a miracle for them. He wanted to marry her, to call her his wife. But he had promised to respect her wishes, so he would. It was just getting harder and harder to do so.

CHAPTER 45

September cooled into October, and Heidi and Darrin found the change of leaves breathtaking. They decided Darla was missing out and flew her into Asheville for a long weekend.

Heidi and Darrin went to meet her, joking she was a fall-leaf tourist. It filled Heidi's heart with joy, driving through the colorful mountain roads, listening to them catch up, talking a mile a minute. They were twins, after all, and their bond remained strong despite their apparent differences. Heidi often wondered how things would change when one of them started seriously dating; she supposed time would tell.

The weekend with Darla was spent hiking, taking photos, and having a marshmallow roast around the campfire with only their skeleton crew. Darla assimilated quickly, and, in no time, Jacob was trailing her, explaining how to bait a hook, how to look for bear tracks before they disappeared for hibernation, and where Alice hid the best snacks.

On Sunday evening, Heidi and Darla headed back towards Asheville to spend the night so they could tour the Biltmore before her Monday afternoon flight. Darla wanted a spa night and, Heidi surmised, some time alone with her mom, so Heidi was happy to comply. Heidi splurged on a nice hotel; they got their nails done and sat up late, catching up wearing plush hotel robes.

"You think you'll ever marry Johann, Mom?" Darla tucked her legs under her, leaning back against the bed cushions.

Heidi regarded her thoughtfully. "Well, I was going to… once." She twisted her mouth into a half grin and tilted her head. "I could fall for him again if I let myself."

Darla was watching her closely. "Uh, Mom, you sort of already have." She scooted over and linked her arm through Heidi's.

339

Heidi reddened. "What?"

"Well, Johann's obviously crazy about you and," she sighed, "it's like watching a movie to see how he looks at you... and how you look at him."

"And you're dreaming of someone for you?" Heidi teased.

Darla elbowed her. "No deflecting, Mom, but nice try. Darrin and I need to see you safely in love before we worry about ourselves, anyhow."

"Seriously?"

"Yeah, you gave up everything for us." She turned to her quickly and hugged her. "It's such a beautiful love-and-loss-and-love-again story, really, we want it to work out. Not because it's a fairy tale, but because it's real." She pulled back. "Why don't you just relax and let yourself fall all the way?"

Tears shimmered in Heidi's eyes. "Maybe I will, sweetheart. Maybe soon."

***

Pulling into camp the following evening, Heidi realized, once again, she had scarcely noticed a drive, despite the mountain curves. Her mind kept replaying the discussion with Darla. Maybe Darla was right; maybe it was time to relax. Only 24 hours away from Johann had been too long, and she was anxious to find him and catch up. She knew he would be busy. A youth group from a nearby church was at camp for their fall break.

Heidi hated coming into a camp already in session, but the time with Darla had been more than worth it. She unloaded her car, pausing once more to gaze out at the trees before going to her cabin to leave her overnight bag. It was after 6pm, and she assumed everyone would be in the dining area. She walked in, her eyes adjusting to the crowded room, wondering where Darrin and Johann were. She had half-hoped Johann would have met her at the parking lot, but she knew the schedule and he was expecting her much later, so it was silly to feel let down. Darla's talk of love stories and movies had gotten her expectations off-kilter.

Darrin saw her and jumped up. "Hey, Mom! Over here!" She walked over to him smiling, looking for Johann, wondering again, only to see his broad back shoulder to shoulder with a petite brunette, their table crowded with teens, talking, laughing, and completely oblivious to her presence.

It was odd, this feeling of surprise, wondering who the woman was, feeling decidedly out of place and intensely jealous. She hugged Darrin, wanting to make sure if Johann turned, he wouldn't see her staring. After making small talk with her son and the kids at his table for a while, she glanced back over where Johann was, her heart sinking as she saw his head tipped towards the woman's, her playfully punching his shoulder and then his uproarious laughter. The woman raised her other hand to meet his in a high five. Stepping around the edge of the room, she slipped into the kitchen, unable to watch anymore. Maybe Alice would know something.

"Heidi!" Alice moved to hug her, and Heidi noticed the thinly veiled concern in her eyes and wondered at this sudden heightened sense of unease washing over her.

Heidi hugged her back. She needed to act natural, to pretend that it was the most normal thing in the world to come back and have Johann acting buddy-buddy with another woman. "You have some food saved back here?" Her voice sounded strange, like she was standing at the end of a long tunnel.

"Oh – uh – sure." Alice turned to grab a plate, opened the serving dishes, and, pointing in question, she filled the plate as Heidi nodded.

Heidi sighed; Alice definitely looked worried. Who was the lady? What was her history with Johann? Had he ever mentioned another woman to her? Surely, she would have picked up on it if he had. She took the plate from Alice, her stomach now turning at the thought of eating, and pulled a stool over to the counter to sit.

"So, how is everything?" She tried her best to camouflage her fear but knew she sounded stilted.

"Heidi." Alice had moved over to stand near her, her hand on her hip, her brow furrowed. "I think you need to—"

The door banged open, hitting the wall, and Jacob launched himself towards Heidi, burying his head in her waist. "Heidi!"

Gratefully she slipped off the stool and hugged his little body to her.

"You were gone soooo long." He rolled his eyes and then craned his neck, his arms still wrapped tightly about her.

"Only one night, silly," she teased.

"But I missed you, and I don't like Sue."

"Who's Sue?"

"That would be me." The voice was coming from the open door.

Heidi jerked her head up, taking in the woman's athletic figure and friendly smile. Of course, she was also pretty. Heidi's heart sank lower.

"Jacob and I had a fight with a homework paper last night, and he still isn't talking to me, are you, Jacob?" She stepped into the kitchen, walking over to Heidi. "Hi, I'm Sue."

"Hi." Heidi had her arms around Jacob, and she wasn't going to let go to shake the woman's hand.

"You must be Heidi."

"That's me."

"Darrin's mom?"

"Yup." Heidi knew she needed to inject some friendliness into her voice.

"Am I missing a – Heidi?" Johann filled the space in the doorway, twin spots of color filling his cheeks.

"Hey." She could feel the woman looking between them and Alice, standing awkwardly to the side.

"When'd you get in?"

"She's gonna help with math stuff, right Heidi?" Jacob's little arms were still clamped around her. He leaned his head back, "please?"

She ducked her head down, even with his, so their foreheads were touching. "Of course, silly boy. I rushed back, especially for math."

He jumped away and swung his arm in victory. "Yes!"

Heidi stood and dumped the contents of her plate into the trash. "You come to my cabin in ten minutes and bring some of Alice's cookies, and we'll get started, OK?" she spoke in the general direction of Jacob, keenly aware of the other adults in the room staring at her. Then, she tilted her head towards the interloper. "Nice to meet you, Sue." And then slipped past Johann, avoiding eye contact, and out into the open air, grateful for the fresh coolness; she took full breaths, trying to calm her racing heart.

The beautifully crisp night contrasted with the roiling thoughts clambering through her mind. Her chest hurt, and she wanted to throw up. She felt stupid. She had never thought to calculate another woman into her decision about Johann; it was thoroughly unsettling. Of course, someone like Johann would be a magnet for other women, and she couldn't expect him to sit around indefinitely waiting for her, even if he had said he would.

Had Sue been at camp before, perhaps before he had found Heidi again? That would make sense. Maybe they had dated, and maybe she was here expecting things to pick up from whatever mystery place they had left off. And, of course, she was friendly and pretty, obviously cared about kids, and looked in excellent shape. She probably didn't have a bucket list of issues either, like breast cancer and dead parents and adopted kids and broken engagements and relationship insecurities.

Heidi knew she had gotten soft physically since breast cancer, but between the enforced rest and the fatigue of radiation and her arm giving her fits, exercise had fallen by the wayside, and she felt sluggish and out of shape.

She kicked at a rock, listening until it came to rest. She walked on, pausing on the bridge, the water rushing towards the swimming area, as a thought exploded in her mind: why should Johann wait for a broken Heidi to make up her mind when somebody whole stood right in front of him? The thought morphed and bounced around as she watched kids spill out of the dining hall towards the outdoor meeting area. Apparently, tonight was bonfire night. An image rose of Johann huddled next to Sue in front of the fire, and she shuddered.

She wished she hadn't told Jacob to come for help because then she could climb up to the observation point and watch the stars and pray God would halt the cacophony in her head.

She reached her cabin and sat on the outside bench, deciding it was better to wait for Jacob than go inside. Surely, she was overreacting and being unnecessarily paranoid. Inhaling deeply, she determined to stem the tide of thoughts and focus on the little boy running up the path towards her.

Jacob dove headfirst into her midsection. "Don't leave again, Heidi."

She leaned over him, ruffling his hair. "I'm not planning on it," she forced a laugh, wondering at his obvious insecurity.

"Where's your math?" She set him away from her, scanning his little body.

"Right here." He pulled the creased paper out of his coat pocket.

Oh dear, another crumpled mess for his poor teacher. Heidi led him inside and found a fresh sheet. "We'll copy everything onto here. We don't want to hand in something all wrinkled up, do we?"

He shrugged, staring at her earnestly.

"Let's get started now, OK?" She sat at the desk and pulled out the other chair for him, but still, he stood there.

"I don't want Sue to be my mom."

So much for paranoia; now she felt full-blown panic. She spoke carefully, trying to keep her voice even. "I don't think your dad's about to marry Sue, Jacob."

"But I saw him kiss her." He had stepped closer to Heidi, his eyes wide.

"When?" Heidi tried to temper the shock in her voice.

"The other time she was here."

So, they *had* dated. Seriously enough to kiss, even. The paranoia was warranted. All of it. And now she needed to put all that aside and do a math paper with a scared little boy. She and Jacob made quite a pair, but she was the adult, so she needed to play her role well and ease his fears. It felt good to focus on something concrete....

CHAPTER 46

Morning couldn't come soon enough. Heidi barely slept, her mind at war with her exhausted body. Part of her blamed herself for her indecisiveness, the other part felt anger towards Johann, and yet another part realized she could be overreacting. There was only one way to fix this: to face it head-on.

So, with resolve, she got up early, washed the grit from her eyes, and tried to make herself look presentable. Slipping into the kitchen even before Alice, she started the coffee and stood in the open door, inhaling the scents of a fall morning in Maggie Valley. She took in the fiery leaves tinted with fuchsia, golden yellows mixed with dark red, and the lingering green. It was magical, and her heart lifted. Today held promise. Surely whatever had transpired the night before could be explained in the light of day.

Balancing her bagel and coffee, she stepped into the office, cracking the window to expel the staleness. She turned on the computer. Her heart jumped in anticipation; last night, in the middle of her worry and fear, she had scribbled a few thoughts down for the next section. Smiling wryly, she dug the crumpled paper from her pocket and smoothed it on the desk, waiting for the computer to boot up. She leaned back in the chair and closed her eyes. No matter what, today would be a good day. She was on the other side of breast cancer, she had a job with purpose, and she was strong.

Taking a sip of the coffee, the bagel forgotten, she started to type quickly, trying to get the rush of thoughts onto the screen before they left her. The sounds of camp stirring to life came through the open window, and she smiled despite herself, letting the words flow from her mind to the screen, her anxiety over Johann on a temporary reprieve.

Without warning, the door flung open. "Heidi?"

She inhaled sharply, jerking back.

There stood Johann, his hand on the door, his hair still wet from the shower, his presence filling the small office. "Didn't mean to scare you."

"I was… um… deep in thought."

"Kind of early."

"Yeah," she shrugged, "woke up early." She looked down, unwilling to meet the intensity in his gaze, hoping her make-up had successfully camouflaged the dark circles under her eyes.

"You disappeared last night."

She could feel his scrutiny and the corresponding heat building in her cheeks.

"Did you have a good time with Darla?" he asked.

"Yup." She looked out the open window, determined to slow her heart rate and keep the interaction placid.

He came into the room then, shutting the door behind him, rolled the other office chair over next to her, and sat, his knees practically touching her. "You going to tell me what all this," he waved his hand back and forth in the space between them, "strangeness is about?" His eyes were scanning her face.

All of Heidi's resolve evaporated. How *dare* he? "I'm not the one flirting with a girl named Sue." A girl named Sue? Kind of like the song but different. She had to push her lips together to keep an absurd giggle from escaping.

"What?"

She shrugged. "I guess you have every right to flirt with whoever you want, though, so it's no big deal." She hated how she sounded.

"What on earth, Heidi?" He raised his eyebrows, the twin spots of color already evident on his cheeks.

"I mean, I had convinced myself I was imagining things, but then Jacob came to do math and told me how he doesn't want Sue to be his new mom, so obviously…." She shrugged again, turning away, angry with herself for the tears she could feel threatening to spill over.

Johann let out a deep breath and leaned back. "Oh boy." He ran his hand through his hair and looked away.

She whipped back around, settling her voice to hide her turmoil, "Just don't; I mean, I know I'm dragging things along, but just don't, can you not…."

He leaned forward again. "Say it, Heidi."

"Don't play with my heart, OK?" Hot tears tracked down her cheeks, splashing onto the computer keys.

He snatched his head up, his eyebrows drawn together. "What… how do you mean?"

"I thought you said I had time to… you know… um… figure us out?"

He reached out and wiped her cheek with his thumb. "But you do, Heidi. Why do you think—"

"I didn't realize there would be," and she grimaced, "competition."

He leaned back again, clarity dawning across his features. "Man, I'm an idiot."

Heidi ducked her head, wiping at her eyes, regretting her own display of insecurity, vaguely recognizing the gong sounding in the background and Johann's phone ringing simultaneously. This wouldn't be resolved now, and she had made a fool of herself.

He silenced his phone and leaned forward, regarding her intently. "I hear you, Heidi. I promise. But I need to go." He drummed his fingers on the desk. "Listen, meet me at the lookout point during morning games, OK? Please?" He stood, rolling the chair back to its spot, keeping his eyes on her. "Heidi?"

"OK."

***

Johann was angry – with himself. The more he thought through the brief events from the night before, the more he could see why Heidi had been upset, especially considering what Jacob had told her. He and Sue had briefly dated over a year ago, and he hadn't expected to see her back at camp after they had broken things off.

But yesterday, she had arrived with her church, full of life and zest for all things camp, with her refreshing friendliness and humor, and he had enjoyed catching up with her again. But maybe too much, maybe enough to make others wonder, especially when he hadn't even noticed Heidi's return or realized the depths of his son's fears. He only hoped he hadn't led Sue on. She was a great lady, but not for him; that's why he had ended things. Now he needed to run around and ensure he was clear with everyone. It broke his heart that he had made Heidi afraid, but at the same time, it did show him how much she cared about him. Maybe it would all ultimately work out for the best.

Then he felt terrible. Had he subversively meant to make Heidi jealous? What was wrong with him? How could he not have been more careful? But the adoring attention *had* felt good. He was tired of worrying about where he stood with Heidi, tired of hiding his feelings.

But that wasn't an excuse to act like the teenagers he tried to lead.

He walked into the dining hall, met by the noise of campers, the clang of plates and cups, and the cafeteria chairs squeaking. Sue was already waving him over, pointing to a spot she had saved, but he simply waved back and walked over to Darrin.

Darrin looked worried. "I have a camper who refuses to get out of bed," he said.

"You told his youth leader yet?"

"Nope, can't find him."

"OK, I'll go see what I can do. Listen, can you run games this morning, though?"

"Yeah, sure, if you can get my camper out of bed," Darrin joked back.

Johann walked over to Sue to ask where their youth leader had gone and then headed to Darrin's cabin. This was camp life, putting out fires all day long, hoping you made a difference. But no matter what, he needed to make sure he met Heidi at the point on time. "Don't play with my heart, Johann." He could hear her words echoing in his head, and the last thing he wanted to do was bring her more heartache.

***

Heidi climbed to the observation point early, her camera in hand. The bright blue sky and colors spread before her, framed perfectly through her viewfinder. She tested wide angles and then close-ups, trying to focus on a single leaf while blurring the view beyond. She stopped short of using an entire roll of film, cradling the worn camera in her lap.

She sensed him before she heard him and turned, holding her hand up to make him pause, wanting to take his picture framed against the cobalt sky. She zoomed in, and her breath caught at the look in his eyes. She snapped the photo and then lowered the camera, her hands shaking.

He sat next to her, taking the camera from her. "This still the same one?"

"Yes, everyone says I need to go digital, but I can't part with it."

"Wow." He turned it slowly in his hands. Then, setting it down, he spoke. "You and I, Heidi, we have so many beautiful memories." He took a deep breath and took her hands in his. "I want to make many, many more." He squeezed her hands gently. "With you. Nobody else."

"But Jacob, and I know I shouldn't listen to a kid, but kids sense things and…."

He rubbed his thumbs over her hands and sucked in a breath. "Sue and I dated during my second year here. I eventually ended it because things felt wrong after Amy and moving, and to be honest, you were always the face of what love meant, and I couldn't get that image out of my head." He paused, his eyes searching hers.

Heidi twisted her hands in her lap, her face warm under his scrutiny, his words echoing in her head.

Johann took a deep breath and continued. "I didn't expect to see her again, frankly, and when she arrived yesterday she was friendly and fun, and I just didn't think about the message I was sending by responding in kind. I can only imagine how it looked to you, and I feel terrible." He paused. "I'm sorry, OK?"

"OK." She still couldn't look at him.

He shifted back towards her and placed his hands on her shoulders. "Like I said before, you can have as long as you need. There is no competition. None."

She leaned into him and let him hug her tightly, squeezing her eyes to stop the tears, her tension ebbing. "I'm so sorry I've been so fickle. I feel like I'm being unfair to you and high maintenance and just…." She trailed off. "I feel immature and terrible."

"That makes two of us." He laughed ruefully. "Maybe we get too much practice from the teens we try help."

She squeezed him back, wanting to signal her agreement.

"We're going to be OK, Heidi. Don't worry." His voice was muffled against her hair.

"OK." She closed her eyes in relief, absorbing the feel of his arms, the comfort of his presence. But she still felt bad for her reaction. So, taking a deep breath, she stepped back.

"I want you to know, Johann, this insecure person isn't who I am. I want you to know I am embarrassed by my actions."

"It's OK, Heidi."

"But is it?" She sighed. Where had her independent, overcomer attitude gone? Was this a Tamoxifen issue, or had her heart truly never healed from loving and losing Johann all those years ago?

"I'm sure my actions didn't help." He took her back in his arms. "How about we meet here periodically and do more of this?" He angled his head back to look at her, a grin on his face.

"Good plan," she said. And she smiled as she rested her head against his shoulder, grateful for the moment. The barriers in her mind seemed to be evaporating; maybe it was time to tell him she was ready to commit.

CHAPTER 47

It was a rare Saturday morning without campers, and as Heidi sat on her tiny porch drinking coffee, she thought back over the prior week. Despite Johann's assurances, she had been glad to see the exhaust of Sue's car and hoped it would be a while before she had to share the same space with Sue again. Heidi had done her best to keep things casual but detached and figured any heart to hearts or explanations needed to happen between Sue and Johann. She trusted Johann, so she stepped back and let the week play out, grateful every time he sat with her or casually put his arm around her, all the little things that told another woman what she needed to know.

Heidi took another sip of coffee, redirecting her thoughts, determined to regain her emotional strength, fortitude, and confidence. And, if she couldn't, she would find a counselor to talk with, someone who could help her get back on track. She owed it to herself and her children. In the meantime, she would stay aware of her thoughts and actions and would continue to spend time in God's Word, praying for direction.

As the morning mist lifted, she saw Jacob fishing on her side of the stream. Grabbing her mug, she walked out to him, surprised at how cold it was in the mountains. It was barely November; soon she would have to give in and buy herself a coat.

Jacob sat on a rock, fishing pole in hand, swinging his legs. Heidi didn't expect he'd get much more than a little brook trout, but something was better than nothing. She crouched down next to him.

"You like to fish?" he asked.

"Not really, but I like to sit with people who are fishing," she replied, adjusting to a sitting position.

"Cool, well, you can stay here with me, then," he tilted his head towards her and then added, "and if I hook one, I'll let you reel it in.

351

That might help."

"Help what?"

"You to start liking fishing. If you catch one, then fishing catches you."

"Wow, Jacob, that's a perfect phrase. Did you make it up?"

"Yup." He waited, then let more line out and watched his bobber. "You know, my mom was killed by some bad people, right?"

That was the last thing Heidi thought he'd say; she was expecting a fishing lesson. She murmured a quick prayer for wisdom and then responded as calmly as she could, "Yes, your dad told me."

"It's cool you knew my mom."

"Your mom was my best friend in South Africa. I thought of her as my South African twin because we were the same in so many ways."

"Oh." He thought for a moment. "Maybe that's why I like you." He grinned, embarrassed now.

"Well, you remind me of your mom," Heidi smiled back.

"Really? How? I'm a boy!"

"Well, you have the same eyes, and you have the same expressions when you are thinking, and you have the same kindness towards people that your mom had."

His bobber bobbed, and he set the hook. "Man, I missed it." He reeled in to check his bait and then stopped. "I always think if my mom was so kind, why did mean people have to hurt her?"

Heidi opened her mouth, trying to formulate a response.

"I mean, she was probably just standing there looking at her flat tire and was so glad to see someone had come to help her. She probably smiled at them and said hello. She always had snacks and little Bibles that she gave to everyone. They could have helped her, and then she could have handed those things to them. So why did they have to be so mean to her?"

Heidi was way out of her depth here, but she would try. He was talking, and she would listen. She hadn't realized that Amy had been murdered on the side of the road. She knew that South Africa was unsafe, even when she was there, but after she had left, things must have escalated. She wondered why Amy had been out driving by herself. Even when she had been at camp, everyone had always gone out in pairs.

"Angry people do terrible things, Jacob." She felt so inadequate.

Jacob nodded and rebaited his hook. "That's why my dad said he made that kid leave camp – the kid who was mean to Darrin."

"You remember that?"

"Oh yes, it was so cool because my dad was like, you're so angry that you're mean, and I know what mean people can do, so you can't stay here."

"Your dad is a very wise person."

Jacob nodded, distracted. "One time, I accidentally stuck myself with the hook, you know."

"Ouch," Heidi was having trouble keeping up, so she kept praying.

"It hurt really bad, and I wondered if a small hook could hurt so bad how bad my mom hurt when they stabbed her with their knife." Big tears were rolling down his cheeks as if a switch had flipped.

Heidi scooted over and took his small frame into her arms wishing Johann would appear. "Oh, Jacob, I'm so very sorry."

"Do you think it hurt badly?"

She rubbed his back and considered how best to answer him. "Maybe it did, Jacob, but your mom was so close to God that she probably was praying and felt God right there with her."

"You think?"

"When you're scared, and you pray, do you feel God near you?"

"Sometimes, or I call my dad." His voice was muffled, and Heidi worried she was failing him. "But why didn't God just send a snake or something to bite those guys and then save my mom? There's snakes all over there."

"We won't know the answer to that, Jacob. But one day, when we are in heaven, we can ask God."

"Do you think that would make God mad at me if I asked Him

that when I pray?"

"Never. God is our Father; He understands everything."

***

That night, while Johann tucked Jacob into bed, he said, "I don't think I'll have bad dreams anymore, Dad."

"That's great, Jacobus." Johann was surprised. Jacob's dreams had diminished markedly after they had moved to the US.

"Jacob, Dad. You must call me Jacob." He looked at Johann sternly. "Anyway, Heidi says she thinks when those mean men were, you know, hurting mom that mom was praying, and she would have felt God with her. If you feel God with you, stuff isn't as bad, so I think maybe it didn't hurt as bad as I thought before."

Johann was stunned. Tears were filling his eyes. He hugged his son close to him and let them flow. Hiding his tears wouldn't help anyone.

"Well, I think you are a very wise boy, Jacobus."

"Jacob, Dad. You have to practice at home, too, you know."

"Jacob, I think you are a wise boy."

"Heidi is very nice and pretty, you know. Maybe you should marry her."

"Oh really?"

"Yeah, you want me to ask her for you?"

"No, son, if I ever ask her, I need to do it myself!" Johann was laughing through his tears.

"Well, I can help because I'm not afraid to talk to her like sometimes you are."

"I'm not afraid to talk to her!"

"Yes, you are," he exclaimed. "The other day, I saw you looking at her, and I thought, 'Dad must be afraid to talk to her.'" He leaned back and put his small hands on Johann's cheeks, so they were eye to eye. "So, when you're afraid, you just take a deep breath and tell yourself it's no big deal, and you just start talking, OK?"

"OK, son," there was nothing to do but go along with this, despite his emotional whiplash, "I'll try that."

"Tomorrow?"

"Sure, tomorrow."

Johann shut the door carefully and stepped out onto the porch. He wished he could find Heidi now, but he wouldn't leave Jacob alone sleeping. He flipped open his phone and sent her a text.

U still up?

Come sit outside at my house?

He held his breath, waiting for the response. The word was 'verandah,' but he wasn't going to text that. 'Porch' was the American word he'd forgotten.

K

After a few minutes, he saw her walking along the pathway, and his heart picked up its pace. He was anxious to hear about her talk with Jacob, to thank her.

"Hey," her voice was soft and uncertain.

"Here, I have a spot for you. He had moved his Adirondack chairs closer together, wishing for a bench swing instead.

"Jacobus talked to me tonight." He may as well get straight to the point.

"I wondered if he would." She looked anxiously over at him. "I wanted to let you know, but the day happened, and I hope—"

He reached over and took her hand. "Shhh, you were wonderful. I had him meet with a counselor some after we got here, but I think you just made more progress than all those sessions."

"I never knew it happened like that." Her voice was soft, hoping he would give her his version of the story.

"*Ja*, to this day, I can't believe I let her go alone. But she was insistent. It was just a quick run, there and back, the middle of the day, just to grab some more bread." He sighed deeply. "When she didn't come back after too long, I got Karl's truck, and we went looking." His voice deepened in the memory.

"Karl was very angry that I had let her go alone, but Karl had always held her back and never let her do anything, so I decided from the beginning to not be that way. Turns out I was horribly wrong." He shook his head and looked over at Heidi. "We found the truck – and her – only about 3 kilometers from camp. That's all. They killed her for her handbag and a few measly *rands*. I just —" He swallowed hard and tried to stop the flood of tears.

Heidi knelt beside his bowed head, cradling it to her. "I'm so sorry, Johann. So sorry."

"I think about it," he gulped, trying to grab a breath between sobs, "over and over. All I had to say was 'don't go alone' or 'wait until I can go with you,' and we would've never even had a clue what a terrible thing we avoided. I think about it and wonder why – how – and Jacobus only five years old." He shook his head against her.

***

Heidi had no words; what could she say to help? There were no words. So, she simply held him and let him cry.

Eventually, he was spent and pulled back. "Here," he whispered as he held out his hands to pull her up from kneeling.

She stood slowly, her hands still in his. "It's OK, Johann, I'm—" She stopped. How could she say she was honored he would share this with her? It sounded cliché.

"You know what Jacobus told me tonight?" He looked up at her and attempted a smile and then stood too, rubbing his thumbs over her hands, "He told me that he thinks I'm afraid to talk to you."

"Really?"

"Yes, he told me sometimes you just have to be brave and say something when you need to."

"OK?"

"So, I'm going to say that I'm beyond thankful for you, Heidi. Your presence here is, well, it's just—" and in a swift movement, he stood and pulled her to him and hugged her fiercely.

She stood in the circle of his arms, grateful and thankful that, for this moment, they were together. The past was a confusing jumble, and the future uncertain, but she would allow this moment. And, he had trusted her enough to tell her his story, a story that only a handful of people knew. And for that, she was honored. She didn't know what would or could become of them given their history, but she knew their deepening friendship was repairing the distrust she felt between them.

In a moment of decision, she stepped back. "You guys should come and spend Christmas in Florida with us. We could have a real Florida Christmas, and it will be warm weather, so it will be almost like you're back in the Southern Hemisphere again."

"Seriously?" He looked pleased.

"Yes, we can go to the beach on Christmas day if you like. And Jacob can help us set up the tree, and Darla will be home, and it will be wonderful."

His face was serious now. "Like a family."

She flushed. "Yes, like a family."

***

The next morning at breakfast, she filled Darrin in on her plans, and then Jacob ran in and hugged her.

"Dad says we're going to your house for Christmas! And Darrin can take me snorkeling! And Dad says it's hot there! It was going to be so lonely and boring and cold here with everyone gone."

She squeezed him back happily. "You know your dad saved me from spending Christmas alone at the camp one year. He took me to the beach by your Aunt Gillian's house, and we—" Out of the corner of her eye, she saw Johann, and he was listening.

"That was a fun night." His eyes were intense.

Heidi looked up, caught Darrin's interested stare, and scraped her chair back. "I have to go call Darla," she mumbled.

CHAPTER 48

The computers hummed as Heidi waited for them to boot up. Fresh cold air wafted through the barely opened window carrying sounds of campers heading into the cafeteria. The room smelled of coffee, and Christmas lights twinkled on a makeshift tree. This last week of camp had been easy. The church had brought so many volunteers that camp was practically running itself, and Heidi was grateful to be back in the office. Her heart hummed with anticipation, and she smiled as Johann walked in.

"Three more days!" She couldn't contain her excitement. She felt ready to take the leap and let Johann know… she should tell him this Christmas. There had to be a fun way to essentially ask him out. After keeping him at arm's length for so long, she needed to make her intentions crystal clear. She could see their future, here at camp, building a life together and doing the work they were both meant to do. It was freeing.

"Um, Heidi." His voice was serious.

She stopped getting things out and stared at him warily. "Are you OK?"

"I, uh, just got a phone call from Karl and Vera."

"Oh?" A shadow fell across her heart.

"They told me they are planning to come here for Christmas. They wanted to make it a surprise, but they didn't know how to get to camp without letting me know. Plus, they wanted to make sure we'd be here before they finalized their tickets."

Instantly she felt the joy drain out of her. "Oh." Her voice was flat. She couldn't breathe.

"Jacobus is their grandson, you know."

Of course, she knew. The truth closed in. Karl and Vera were probably the reason things hadn't worked out all those years ago, and now Karl was making one of his decrees, and Johann would bow to it.

"We will have to cancel our visit. I'm very sorry."

"But Johann, we had plans."

"What do you want me to do, Heidi? Tell them not to come?"

"Tell them you won't be here! Tell them to come later. I mean, tell them to come to Florida instead, even. They're retired, aren't they? They can come any time." She barely recognized the hard edge in her voice.

"I can't do that to them." His voice was resigned.

"But you can do that to us?" She was incredulous. She beat her palm against the desk. "We. Had. Plans."

"Come on, Heidi. What am I supposed to tell them?"

"Tell them no! Tell them you are coming to see me! Wait!" She stood as realization dawned. "Do they even know about me?"

"Well, I mean…."

"You're kidding me! Not even a casual mention? Why not?" She was shaking.

"What was I supposed to say? You've been dragging your feet." He held up his hands to stop her from responding, "which I can understand and can wait like I said. But, sending their minds down a path that might never reach its destination makes no sense." His voice was ragged. "They lost Amy, and they blame me. And if I told them… I just couldn't do that to them yet, until I know what we are."

"Let me get this straight: they don't know about me or my foot dragging?" She rolled her eyes. "Jacob hasn't mentioned me to them even?"

"Jacobus barely talks to them on the phone. The calls are expensive."

"Unbelievable." She stepped back. "*Herr Karl* will always come between us." Her voice was low and somehow controlled, but her body trembled with disbelief.

"Heidi, listen to me; try to understand." He stepped forward to grip her arms, but she pulled back.

"No, Johann, you listen to me. I had excused the past, knowing how young we were, how poor communication was back then, how trapped we both were by our circumstances, how I could totally understand why you believed them. And I was *finally* able to get past the ramifications that I lost another fiancé to a close friend. Finally! But this…" and she waved her hand between them, "this shows me I am not first; I might never be, which is a huge problem if we ever…."

"Heidi, no, that's not how it is. You have to believe me."

"Actions speak louder than your meaningless words, Johann." She pushed past him and rushed to her cabin, nearly tripping over Jacob as she stepped out of the office door.

She called Darrin and left a voicemail, asking him to come to her cabin when he was free. She would buy him a plane ticket home so he could stay and finish the camp week. Tears flowed as she haphazardly packed her suitcase with her most important things. They could give away the remaining stuff she'd accumulated to whomever; she wasn't coming back. Disbelief, anger, frustration, and hurt roiled together until she could barely think.

She left the laptop she'd been using on the table along with a note with her password. Someone else could finish the curriculum. And then she left Darrin another message, apologizing and explaining that she had to go but would send him his flight information once she had it and would see him in a few days. It was probably best he hadn't responded; Darrin couldn't see her like this. She would also call Alice later and explain.

In less than an hour, she was on the road. She could see the bright dots of campers in the distance returning from the morning hike. It contrasted sharply with her despair as if mocking her. Johann hadn't even tried to come after her, completing the death knell on what she had hoped would be their future.

CHAPTER 49

Heidi knew she was taking the curves too quickly, so she forced herself to slow down. But then her thoughts would race, and she'd drive faster. Once more, she decelerated. Killing herself on a sharp mountain curve wouldn't solve anything. Not that there was anything to solve regarding her and Johann. They were done.

And this must have been why she had taken so long regarding Johann. Her delay, or *foot-dragging*, had been wise after all. He wouldn't or couldn't put her first when given a choice. Why hadn't he even tried to find a solution? Johann could have asked them to add a connecting flight to Florida. Not that she wanted to include Karl in her Christmas plans, but she would have helped find them a hotel and included them. Yet Johann hadn't even told Karl and Vera about her. How was that possible? What had he said about his trips to Florida and her working at camp? Did he call her by another name, or did he simply lump her into all the other workers? Never mind that she loved Jacob like a son. Didn't that rank somewhere in things to tell Jacob's grandparents?

And if she let this go and said she understood and excused it, he might never put her first. Today he had made that clear, crystal clear. She needed to—

Suddenly she heard a loud retching sound from the back of her car. She stomped on the brakes and pulled over onto the narrow gravel edge. Jumping out of the car, she ran to the back, opening the hatch, her heart pounding.

And there, curled in a ball, lay Jacob, crying and holding his stomach and saying he was sorry. There was evidence of his car sickness all over her luggage.

"Jacob!" Her horror and shock couldn't be quantified. She could've killed him the way she'd been driving.

How had she not seen him? Johann must be out of his mind wondering where he was. She'd been gone for nearly an hour.

"Jacob." She tried to speak calmly. He was terrified. She put her hands on his little arms and helped him sit up, ignoring the stench and mess everywhere. "Listen to me. It's OK. I'm here. I'm not mad at you. Can you climb out?"

She helped him as he lowered his skinny legs to the ground below and then gripped his shoulders as he turned and retched again onto the ground. "It's OK, it's OK," she rubbed his back and held him the best she could. She had to get it into his head that she wasn't angry with him, that nobody was angry with him. And she needed to call the camp and let them know she had him. Which meant she'd have to face them. All of them.

Heidi heard the police cruiser before she saw it, the radio voices and the crunch on gravel. Thank goodness help had come.

The officer approached cautiously while she gripped Jacob, still crying incoherently.

She tried to explain that Jacob had stowed in the back of her car without her knowing. But when the officer asked about his parents, he answered that his mom had been murdered, and things spiraled out of control.

"Let me just call his dad! Let me get my phone!" She could sense their distrust and knew that one misstep and she'd be handcuffed and in the back of their cruiser. Thankfully Jacob clung to her, refusing to let go, sobbing and mixing up his Afrikaans and English.

"He was hiding in the back of my car. I heard him throwing up!" They had to believe her. The alternative was horrifying. She turned to the other officer. "Can I get my phone? It's in the passenger seat." She moved towards her car, and officer number 1 stepped in front of her, saying something to his partner. More radio sounds, more talking, and it sounded like maybe they were talking to Johann. Please, God, let them be talking to Johann.

She was trapped in this spot, Jacob attached to her legs. She knelt before him. "Jacob, honey, can you tell these men what happened so they can call your dad?"

He hiccupped; his tear-streaked face contorted into anguish. "I... my dad is going to be mad... I wanted... Florida for Christmas." And then he flung himself against her again, nearly knocking her over.

What could she say to calm him down? She couldn't lie to him, couldn't tell him it would all be OK, but surely if she—

Just then, officer number 2 approached. "Ma'am?"

She jerked her head up, noting a change in his demeanor.

"We have the boy's father on the phone. He's on his way. We can't wait here; we'll take you to wait for him at the precinct."

"Oh," she swiveled her head anxiously, "can, can I drive us there myself?" The last thing she wanted was to get into a police car.

He nodded. "We'd like the boy to ride with us, though." The officer was already kneeling in front of Jacob. "How would you like to ride in the police car with me?"

Jacob stared uncertainly, his grip on Heidi even tighter. "Am... am I going to jail?"

"No," the officer's voice was gentle. "We are going to meet your father at the station, and your friend will follow us there."

"You're coming, too, Heidi?"

"Yes, sweetie, I'll be right behind you."

Somehow, the little boy desire to ride in a real police car outweighed his fear, and he nodded.

The drive seemed interminable. With Heidi following behind the cruiser and her hands shaking, she felt like they'd never arrive.

Eventually, they pulled into the precinct parking lot, where Johann was pacing and running his hands through his hair. Bill hovered nearby, the driver-side door to his car open, the engine still running. As soon as the cruiser stopped, Johann opened the door, grabbed his son, pulled him against him, set him back to look at him, and then pulled him against him again.

Heidi watched, immobile. She couldn't head to Florida with her car in its current state, but the last thing she wanted was to face everyone at camp. Eventually, there was a tap on her window. It was

Bill. They were all going back to camp. Johann could drive her car if she preferred. She was too shell-shocked to argue, and besides, the last thing she needed was to make a scene in front of a police station.

She stepped out of the car to move to the passenger seat, and Johann was one pace in front of her, Jacob's legs wrapped tightly around him. She couldn't look at Johann. Not here. Everyone was watching. But he wouldn't move.

"Are you OK, Heidi?" His voice was gentle, his hand on the open door.

She ducked down under his arm. They would have to talk, but she felt raw. There would be no more irrational moves. Shame blanketed her; her outrage could have resulted in tragedy.

Heidi didn't remember much of the drive. She only remembered getting into the passenger seat of her car with Johann taking the wheel and Jacob sitting in the back. And she remembered the smell.

"I threw up, Dad."

"We'll clean it up, don't worry."

Heidi said nothing. What could she say? She had left in a blur of self-righteous anger. She rolled down her window and let the cold December air wash over her, feeling the sting as it hit her tears. What a hideous mess today had become, and despite the fact they were all together, the underlying mood was one of despair. Johann didn't love her enough. He had proved it again. She felt numb. She hadn't been careful enough, and now her heart was broken. All over again. Could a broken heart heal three times, or was there a limitation to these things? Maybe it would stay broken, and she'd turn into a sad, bitter woman. She couldn't imagine picking herself up and recovering. Again.

They pulled into the camp, and Darrin and Alice came running, not asking questions, apparently prewarned by Bill. Alice went straight to Heidi, helping her out and instructing Darrin to grab her bags from the back. Bill must have prepped them well because nobody commented on the smell or the state of Heidi's bags. Jacob was asleep, and Johann scooped him into his arms. He turned to Heidi.

"I'm going to take care of Jacobus; will you please stay at camp until we talk?" His voice was soft, imploring.

Heidi nodded dumbly. She wanted to tell him no, that she would leave as soon as she could get everything cleaned up, but everyone was watching.

At her cabin, Alice instructed Darrin to leave the bags outside.

Darrin turned to hug Heidi, but she put up her hand. "I'm covered in everything... please come back in a little while, and I'll hug you and tell you everything, I promise."

"You'll be here?" He looked scared and worried.

"Yes, honey, I'll be here." Her poor son. She could imagine how frightening the morning must have been for him. Why had she allowed herself to be so stupidly irrational? "I promise. I'm so sorry for making you worry. We'll talk then, OK?"

Alice instructed her to go in and shower and to throw her clothes out on the porch so she could launder them.

"Oh Alice, you have dinner to get ready now, don't you? I'll get it all."

"No, my dear, everyone else can help fix the next meal with Bill's help. Plus, there's so many workers they can all pitch in. I'm helping you; no arguments."

Gratefully Heidi walked into her cabin. She saw the computer and note from what felt like days ago. She stepped into the shower, let the hot water stream run over her, and cried until her head throbbed. Throwing on sweats and an old T-shirt, she scrounged through her toiletry bag, searching for ibuprofen.

As if on cue, Alice knocked on the door and came in with a tray of food. Taking in Heidi's swollen red eyes, she set the tray down and held out her arms. "Oh, you poor dear, come here."

Heidi let her hug her, grateful for the comfort and for the food. Now she could safely take a pill without her stomach revolting.

"Johann and I had a terrible fight, you know." Heidi felt she owed her that much of an explanation.

"I wondered."

"He told me today he was canceling Christmas with us because his in-laws were coming – you know Karl and Vera? Did you ever hear of them?"

"Briefly, he doesn't talk much about them, and Jacob never mentions them, so I figured they weren't close."

"They don't like me. Well, Vera did, but Karl never did." Heidi took a small spoonful of the soup and then swallowed the ibuprofen.

"But this is the crazy part." She took a shaky breath. "Johann never told them that I was back in his life." She needed to tell someone to see if they also found it strange, to ensure she wasn't overreacting. When Heidi saw Alice's look of shock, she felt free to continue. "I mean, they know me. I was Amy—their daughter and Jacob's mom—I was her friend. Clearly, I wasn't part of Karl's master plan, but the fact that Johann never even told them I was back in his life, after all we have done together, after Darrin working here, and now me, and them coming to my house for my surgery and him caring for me. It just makes no sense and makes me feel like I don't matter; that he's embarrassed by me.

"So, I was so upset, I just left. Which was stupid. I'm not an irrational person, but this, this hit a nerve, I guess because I was always wondering." She paused. How to explain herself? "You see, I've wished and wondered and then dismissed and wished again... if maybe Johann could have fought for us more, back when we were young. Then I tell myself I'm being unreasonable—that both of us were operating under incorrect assumptions from blocked information and that I also stopped trying to get in touch with him. But now, sixteen years later, he for sure had the chance to fight for me—for us—yet he clearly chose not to. I was so careful not to get close to him, but I did, and now look.

"And then Jacob got in my car, and I never knew. I guess he really wanted to come for Christmas, and he heard us fighting. And then he got sick, and the police stopped, and Jacob was in a state, and when they asked him if I was his mom, he said his mom had been murdered...." Heidi put her head in her hands. The rest of the story was obvious.

Alice reached out and gripped her arm. "I'm so sorry, Heidi. I would've been upset, too."

Heidi looked up. "It's just that ever since breast cancer, I'm more emotional, and I've been working on it—you know, trying not to overreact, trying to regain my equilibrium and be the person my kids need me to be. But Johann and I have such a history that I thought I'd finally come to terms with, and now… now I just don't know.

"I shouldn't have driven off like that. I should have taken a hike and calmed down and then told him we were through when we could talk like rational adults. What must poor Darrin think? And to think Jacob was in the car that whole time…."

Alice took both of Heidi's hands in hers. "We are human, Heidi; we get upset. And you have a valid reason for being upset."

"But I shouldn't have driven off."

Alice sighed. "Yes, you shouldn't have driven off. But you did. We make mistakes, and we learn from them and move on."

"And I thought Johann loved me again."

"It's pretty obvious he does. But you are right to take a step back and see how this plays out. You are right to want him to put you first, especially if you eventually plan to marry."

"You know, I think I need counseling which is something I never imagined I'd need. I miss who I used to be. I keep praying and reading my Bible, but I still can't get back to my before-cancer-self. Maybe it's the medicine or the fear of recurrence, or maybe it's just worrying about Johann and me. Who knows? And how on earth will I ever get over Johann for a second time?" Fresh sobs came in gulps.

Alice skirted around the table and hugged her. "Oh, Heidi. We will pray for a miracle. In the meantime, just don't be too hard on yourself."

Heidi nodded, relief at unburdening herself permeating her mind. "I think I'm going to try take a nap. Can you tell the others? Can you make sure you tell poor Darrin I'm OK, too? I promise I'm not going to leave or do anything crazy. Today was enough crazy for the rest of my life."

Alice hugged her and took the food. "I'm praying, dear Heidi. Our God is big and can sort all of this out, you know."

Heidi stood and shut the door after her. She needed to sleep off her headache and figure out what to do next.

   ***

Johann felt conflicted. He wanted to dunk Jacobus in the hottest bath and scrub him and then feed him, but the poor kid had passed out as if his misadventure had been too much for him. So, he put a towel on the bed and laid him on that, removing the offensive shirt and throwing it away.

He then called Darrin to ensure the camp was on track for the remainder of the afternoon and took a deep breath before calling Amy's parents again. It would be late in South Africa, but he needed to talk to them.

He had been wrong, exceedingly wrong, and he knew that. Keeping Heidi a secret from them had not only harmed Heidi but nearly harmed his son. Jacob clearly loved her dearly, and it was time that he stood up to Karl. Praying for strength, he dialed the number and got Vera.

She sounded so happy and excited to come and visit them that he almost backed out, but he needed to be honest – with everyone. He asked Vera to get Karl so he wouldn't have to repeat himself and then told them the whole story. How Darrin had come to camp and been Heidi's son. How she now worked at the camp and that he had fallen in love with her again. How Jacob loved Heidi and her children and couldn't wait for Christmas – that the plan was to leave for Florida in two days and stay through Christmas.

He asked them if they would consider coming a few days later so they could celebrate a delayed Christmas together at camp. He would split his time with Heidi and them, gladly, but he couldn't back out on the plan to be in Florida for Christmas. And then they could stay as long as they wanted.

"Vera?" The line was so silent he wondered if they had been

disconnected.

"I'm here, Johann," her voice quivered. "Let me talk to Karl, and we can get back to you, OK?"

But before Johann could reply, Karl let out a string of accusations, the likes of which Johann hadn't heard since his own childhood. He could hear Vera crying in the background, telling him to stop, but nothing stopped Karl. Johann was ungrateful and a lying idiot who had gotten their daughter murdered and then stolen their grandchild and was now refusing to let them see him.

"After everything I did to make sure this wouldn't happen!" He screamed so loudly Johann had to pull the phone from his ear.

"You mean hide letters? Or make up a story about Heidi being married? Is that what you mean?"

Silence. Johann had hit his mark.

"Karl? You did it, didn't you? You made sure that Heidi and I would never be together. That's why you are so angry now." There was more silence and then a click. "Karl?"

Johann paced like a caged animal. Karl had all but admitted it.

Karl was the culprit.

The phone rang, its shrill pierce halting his step. He grabbed it before it woke up Jacobus.

It was Vera. And she was weeping. "Karl told me everything, Johann. I never knew. I never, never knew." There was a long pause; he could hear her taking deep gulps of breath. "I'm so sorry, Johann. I love you. I will phone you tomorrow, but I know we won't come this Christmas. I just can't. Not after...." Her crying increased. "I love you, Johann. You were... you were a good husband to my Amy, and you are a good Dad to little Jacobus."

And then she hung up. She had confirmed it and yet done her best to comfort him despite her own shock and heartache. And that was Vera. His heart ached for both her and him now. They had both been deceived, and they had all suffered.

And now he needed to go to Heidi. He needed to tell her everything. But he wasn't sure she would see him, and there was no way he would leave his Jacobus alone, even for a little while.

369

***

After her nap, Heidi tried to eat a snack bar and then bundled herself up. She peeked through her window, noting it must have rained earlier. She needed peace. Peace only that sitting at the Tree could provide, even if the temperature hovered at 40^0F. She also needed to find Darrin and reassure him, but she knew he would be with campers at dinner, so now wasn't a good time for that, but the perfect time for escape.

She slipped out of her cabin, stepping carefully along the wet stones. Darkness had already blanketed Camp Makarios in stillness. Glancing towards the main buildings, she could barely make out the shapes and mingled teenage voices and then what appeared to be Alice knocking at Johann's door. She ducked down, hoping she wouldn't be visible to whoever opened his door, and then moved quickly into the trees. The crisp cold air cleared her foggy mind, and she breathed deeply. She walked over the bridge, holding onto the railing, and then stepped under the Tree, inhaling the mildly sweet scent. She turned slowly, allowing the peace to soothe her weary mind, taking in the chimes silhouetted against the large branches. Beyond those symbols of thankfulness, stars covered the night sky, twinkling joyfully, heedless of her sorrow.

"He made the stars also." She whispered the words from Genesis 1, reveling in the beauty above her as she walked to the bench and sat, the smell of the earlier rain permeating the air. She could feel the peeling bark through her new coat. She snuggled into its warmth, wiggling her toes in her new fleece-lined boots. She would leave the coat and her boots behind, exactly as she had in South Africa all those years ago. A tidal wave of sorrow washed over her.

She couldn't imagine staying and working alongside Johann anymore. It would be too painful. Her life had simply become a series of mishaps and deaths and broken relationships and disappointments, including the recently added specter of breast cancer. But here, under the Tree, she could look at all the chimes and what they represented and allow God's peace to soothe her soul. Because that was the only thing she could count on. Ever. And that would have to be enough. She leaned her head back and thanked God for His presence and realized it was, indeed, enough. But still, she knew from experience the deep sadness that saturated her being would require months of recovery. She doubted she'd ever allow another man in her life, but that was immaterial right now. God had promised never to leave nor forsake her.

She heard Johann before she saw him, coming along the path, hands in his pockets, his gait unmistakable. In a moment, he was standing before her.

"Can I sit here?"

His voice and inflection and the moment were so like another moment nearly sixteen years ago that she had trouble responding.

She nodded imperceptibly.

He sat on the edge of the bench as if afraid to scare her away. She watched as he started to talk and then stopped, twisting and untwisting his hands, leaning forward on his elbows, angled towards her.

She waited. Whatever he wanted to say, he needed to say it. Then she could say her piece and go to her room and pack her loaner suitcase and be on her way. She needed to shut the door to this part of her life for good.

"I want to tell you how sorry I am for everything that happened today." He stopped, looking at her as if assessing her. "The police, everything, it must have been awful."

She nodded. The mortification of defending herself to the police with Jacob hysterical had been beyond anything she had ever experienced. For many reasons, it had been a top ten worst day of her life.

"Are you OK?"

"I shouldn't have driven off like that. I was wrong; I'm very sorry. To think Jacob…."

"You had the right to be upset, and Jacob snuck into your car without you knowing."

She looked at him quickly and then looked down. "How is he?"

"He's still asleep. I never even got to bath him or feed him or anything."

Heidi leaned her head back against the Tree and closed her eyes. Poor little Jacob. She hoped the experience didn't bring back his nightmares.

"Heidi," he waited until she opened his eyes and looked at him. "I want you to know I just talked with Karl and Vera again." He rubbed his face in his hands, his voice monotone, wracked with grief. "It was him all along, Heidi. Karl. He lied to keep us apart."

She turned to him, her eyes wide.

"Now, it seems sixteen years later, he wants to do the same thing all over again." Johann paused. "You should have heard the things he said to me – especially when I told him we had promised to spend Christmas with you – it was the ugliest string of accusations and insults I could have ever imagined coming from anyone, much less him."

Heidi put her fist to her mouth. Hearing the words of what she had secretly suspected was still shocking.

"He was the only real dad I ever had; I thought he loved me like a son. Seems like I had three chances at a dad, and they all ultimately failed me. I pray all the time I never fail Jacob, that I never repeat the mistakes of the father figures that were in my life, but today I did. Today I failed Jacob. I failed Amy. And I failed you, Heidi. And I'm so, so, sorry." He knelt before her then and gripped her hands. "Please, dear Heidi. If I had known it was Karl, I would have never—I'm so, so sorry. You have to hear me and believe me."

Tears flooded Heidi's eyes as she felt his grief. She pulled him toward her, cradling his head, pressing her cheek against his, gripping his back, trying without words to let him know how much she hurt for him. They had already been through the realization of betrayal after the bonfire on her first night last July, but for Johann, this was a fresh wave of betrayal. The betrayer had a name and a face, and it was the last person on earth he had ever expected.

Johann pulled slightly away from Heidi, enough so he could

talk. "How could he have been my father-in-law all those years and known it was all because of his lie? How could he have counseled me when I was so torn up about your supposed marriage? How...?" His voice broke once more as he pressed his face against her.

"Maybe," she paused, searching in her mind for something that might comfort Johann, "maybe, he truly believed he was doing what was best for everyone – for Amy, his family, the camp, for you... maybe that's how he justified it."

"No." Johann's voice was emphatic. "We will not make excuses for him! Look what he did to us, to poor Amy. She knew... she knew all along that I still loved you – for years – I could see the disappointment in her eyes. And me? I was so consumed with guilt for not being the man I should've been, for knowing I shouldn't have taken the easy path and married her. Oh, Heidi," and he paused and put his hands on either side of her face, "can you ever forgive me?"

Heidi wasn't sure how to respond. What was he asking forgiveness for? He had asked her to forgive him at the bonfire, and she still felt guilty about her slow response. She had been disappointed in his actions, how he had so seemingly easily turned to Amy, and now for how he had so quickly wanted to change their Christmas plans. But disappointment was one thing; him asking her forgiveness again was different. Maybe she should have him clarify. This was important and pivotal for them if they were to ever have a future, and she did not want to gloss over it.

"Why?" she managed, looking away.

"For not fighting for us – not then and not even this morning." He tilted her head, willing her to look back at him. "Heidi," his voice was soft and pleading, "I never fought for us – that's what I want you to forgive me for. I simply did what Karl and Amy and everyone else wanted, and I ignored the person who meant everything to me because there were too many roadblocks. I believed their lies, that what we had was a camp romance, not made to last. I believed Karl when he said that all the roadblocks were a sign from God—never mind, he was the actual roadblock." He paused, struggling to find words, wiping her tears with his thumbs. "You, Heidi, are worth every obstacle, and from today onward, I am going to fight for you with every ounce of my being... if you'll have me... if you'll forgive me... if you'll give me one more chance... even though I don't deserve it." His voice tapered off the words hanging between them.

"You know," he spoke over the chimes in the breeze, "you can take as long as you need to answer me. I'll just spend that time proving that I mean what I say, that from now on, I'm going to fight for you with every ounce of my strength, that I love you with all my heart, and that this Christmas at your place I'll...."

Heidi had placed her fingers over his lips. "Oh Johann, *of course, I forgive you."* She was in his arms then, crying and repeating the words over and over. She realized the barrier that Amy posed was gone. He had melted her last reserve when he had told her he loved her, but she wanted to make sure she had heard him correctly. She backed away slightly, a shy look on her tear-filled face, "just so you clarify what you just said."

"That...?" Then realization dawned across his features. "That I love you?" He smiled and grabbed her against him, "that I love you, love you, love you?"

"Yes, that," she breathed, her back against the Tree and his face inches from hers.

"I love you." And he leaned and kissed her cheeks, forehead, and eyes, punctuating each kiss with a declaration of his love.

Then he stopped and simply looked at her, running his free hand through her hair. Heidi caught it and kissed it and took a breath. "I'm sorry for being so irrational today and confused and fickle before this. Please forgive me... you've been so patient with me and... and... I love you, Johann." Her voice trembled with sincerity, and he caught her to him, vowing he would never let her go again.

CHAPTER 50

All four of them crammed into her car for the drive to Gainesville, where they would meet Darla and then caravan home for Christmas. Johann drove, Heidi played Christmas music, and Darrin and Jacob alternated between punching and poking each other to sleeping.

Heidi had finally managed to talk with Darrin after the campers left. "I put you through enough, Mom; I figured you could give me a bit of payback. Just so that's it, though, because I have had it up to here." And he indicated a level well above his head and then drew her into a hug. "I am *so* relieved that you and John have figured yourselves out because the two of you were making Darla and me crazy." Heidi had laughed. Her relief was incomparable.

The reunion with the Barnes family was joyous, and with all hands on deck, they got the house into Christmas order. It quickly lost its closed-up-mustiness and twinkled with the hope and promise of Christmas and togetherness.

Christmas Eve came quickly; after many introductions, they all crammed into a pew together at church. The music started, the congregation stilled, and Heidi closed her eyes and let the music wash over her soul. Last year, sitting in this exact spot, flanked by Darla and Darrin, Gladys nearby, she had known that she could very well be alone the following year. After shouldering family responsibility at such a young age, she had privately vowed that she would never hold them back from what they wanted – even if it meant leaving her alone. And now, instead of sitting at the service alone, she was surrounded by more love than she could have ever imagined. Jacob was tucked against her side, and Johann sat next to Jacob with his arm along the back of the pew, his hand gently gripping her shoulder. Darla was on her other side with Darrin next to her – two young people who swelled her heart with pride. Down the row, she could see Gladys, and up front were the McManns, ready to be part of the service. The Barnes family filled the row behind them, and Heidi felt blanketed with happiness.

Darrin caught her eye and winked – she knew he felt proud of his role in bringing her and Johann back together. His decision to forgo starting college had paid off for all of them.

There was a break in the music as a young man came to the podium to speak. Darrin nudged Darla playfully, raising his eyebrows and causing her face to redden. She turned toward Heidi with widened eyes as if to say, "Can't you get him to stop!"

Heidi smiled back. Darrin obviously assumed he needed to expand his talents. It amused her because she knew Darla would find endless ways to get him back.

After the service, plenty of people came by to talk and catch up. Plenty more were curious about Johann and Jacob, but Heidi merely introduced them as an old friend from South Africa and his son. Out of the corner of her eye, she caught Darrin, Darla, and the young man from the program speaking to each other, Darrin gesturing widely and then conveniently walking off, leaving Darla alone with the young man. She then watched as Darrin sidled up to a group of teen girls clustered around a girl who looked more Darrin's age. She saw him say something, and the girls giggled as they turned to introduce him to their friend. Yes, Darrin was in top form tonight. She turned back to the people around her and caught Johann's eyes watching her. Her cheeks reddened. It was hard to stand and make small talk when she wanted to shout to the world that she loved the man she had introduced as a friend. Yet, it was marvelous to stand and watch the pockets of happiness around her, knowing she had her own private happiness.

She was about to say they should leave when Darla and Darrin appeared, telling her they wanted to take Jacob to look at Christmas lights.

"I'm sure we all can go together, don't you think?" Heidi looked from one to the other in surprise. Shouldn't they all stay together? She looked at Johann, expecting him to agree, but instead, he seemed happy to let them take Jacob.

"Jacobus will have fun," Johann said. His voice sounded rehearsed, and Heidi looked over at Darla for help.

"Let's go!" Darla said, ignoring her mom.

"Great!" Darrin high-fived Jacob as he grinned with delight. "We'll have this young man back to the house in no time and...."

"But Darrin," Heidi broke in. They really should stay together on Christmas Eve.

"Oh, Mom," Darla chimed in. "We won't be gone long; we just want to start a kids-only tradition with Jacob."

Kids only? Darla hadn't wanted to be a kid since she turned six and declared she needed her own bedroom. And Darla sounded rehearsed, too. They were all up to something, and she was about to protest again when Johann tilted towards her and whispered something about saying yes. She turned and looked into his eyes and saw something different—was it nervousness? Pleading? She looked at Darrin, and his eyes were full of mischief; Darla's were avoiding her, and Jacob had Darrin by the arm, ready to leave *now.*

"Well, I guess I'm outnumbered then." She would play along, despite her disappointment, if only to ease that worried look in Johann's eyes.

Jacob stopped, "Oh, you can come too, Heidi."

"No!" Everyone chorused at once. Jacob looked startled, and Darrin swooped him up like a sack of potatoes.

"Love ya, Mom—we'll see you in an hour!" And Darrin carried Jacob out into the parking lot, with Darla scurrying behind, looking back and smiling knowingly.

"Don't forget to come back in time for hot choc—" but they were gone.

Heidi looked at Johann, and he refused to meet her eyes, simply shrugging. "How about you and I take this unexpected alone time to run by and see that moon path on the ocean you like so much?"

"Well, OK." She did her best to sound game but wished they hadn't split up. Christmas Eve meant surrounding yourself with as many people you loved as possible.

"Come on," he said as he put his arm around her and led her to the parking lot.

Wordlessly, they walked to his car, where Johann struggled to find the keys and then fumbled and hit the wrong button. The pulsing shriek pierced the air and caused everyone to stop and look at them. Johann pushed every button on the key fob to no avail, so Heidi grabbed the keys and hit "panic."

Silence.

"Ai-ja-jai." Johann shook his head, dismay evident. Without another word, he took the keys back from her and got into the car.

Heidi could hear him muttering to himself in Afrikaans. She caught words like *"domkop"* and *"befok,"* and the rest didn't make sense to her.

They drove to the beach in silence, and Heidi wondered at the sudden turn of events. Something was up, and Johann was obviously nervous, so she reached out and took his hand. She loved this man; whatever had gotten him off-kilter, she wanted to communicate her love and put him at ease.

They pulled up to the beach, and Johann hit the curb, trying to park.

He cleared his throat, "Are you ready to find that path?"

She smiled encouragingly. She would do her best to be part of the script everyone else seemed to be following.

It was a crystal clear evening, the moon sending the reflection of a perfect path across the water. Johann took her hand as they walked down the steps, and her heart swelled with joy. They took in the scenery together and then, in silent agreement, began walking slowly along the shore. The low tide had left behind perfectly packed sand, the breeze December-cool and refreshing.

Johann kept stopping and looking around and then walking. Heidi went along with him. She would enjoy this moment for all its glory—walking on a moonlit beach with the man she loved on Christmas Eve.

Abruptly Johann stopped and took her other hand, turning her towards him. He cleared his throat and opened his mouth, "Heidi?"

His voice was low and gravelly.

"Yes?"

"I… well… before…. um, you see, when before I asked you to…." He cleared his throat again and looked away, taking a deep breath.

"Yes?" Her voice was softer now, wondering.

"You know when we were young, at God's Window, and I asked you to marry me?" The words came in a rush.

"Yes." She whispered, squeezing his hands.

"I loved you then, you know." His voice was soft, his eyes remembering.

"Yes." She had known and had loved him dearly.

"And all those years in between… I tried not to love you."

"Yes." She had done the same thing. Wrapping up his memory and her love and giving it to God, asking Him to take it from her because loving him while he was married was wrong.

"And then, we found each other this summer."

"Yes."

"And the love I had tried to get rid of came flooding back. And I love you more now than I knew was possible. And you love me, right?"

"Yes." There were tears in her eyes.

"So, Heidi," he fumbled in his pocket with shaking hands, went down on one knee, and opened a little box. "This is the stone from the same ring I first gave you."

"But how…?"

"Darla helped me." He paused, pointing with a shaky finger. "This stone is a symbol of our past, but this one of our present and this one, our future."

"It's beautiful," she breathed, taking in the three stones catching the moonlight.

"Will you marry me, Heidi, and I mean, as soon as possible?"

She laughed. "Yes, Johann, as soon as possible!"

And then he slipped the ring on her finger and stood and kissed her and swung her around with joy.

Epilogue

They were married beneath the Counting Tree the second week of January. The day held significance for them both since it was the very day she arrived in South Africa all those years before. Sixteen years to the day that she had landed at Jan Smuts airport and been greeted by a disgruntled camp worker named Johann, she became his wife.

Darla was her maid of honor, and Darrin gave her away. Jacob was the ring bearer; Sierra's Big Tony officiated. The entire Barnes family was there, along with Alice and Bill. They kept the ceremony brief because of the cold and then celebrated and ate cake in the cafeteria, which had been transformed by Alice and Darla.

At sunset, the photographer grabbed the wedding party for a few more shots at the Counting Tree, but everyone scattered quickly to escape the cold, everyone but Johann and Heidi. The moment was too poignant to rush; the view, the chimes, and their Tree wrapped them in beauty and promise.

She stood in the circle of his arms, taking it all in, her heart full. "I love you, Johann." She turned her face up to him.

"And I love you, Heidi-my-Heidi," he whispered, lowering his lips to hers. A breeze blew through the Tree, the chimes responding, echoing past and present blessings, providing promise for what lay ahead.

And then they turned, hand in hand, headed back to their family and their future, hearts lifted with love and thanksgiving to God, the Orchestrator of it all.

15993584R00215